ST. HELENA LIBRARY
DISCARD
St. Helena Library

SEP 1 7 2003

ST. HELENA PUBLIC LIBRARY
1492 LIBRARY LANE
ST. HELENA, CA 94574-1143
(707) 963-5244

# THE EXCALIBUR ALTERNATIVE

**BAEN BOOKS by DAVID WEBER**

*Honor Harrington:*
On Basilisk Station
The Honor of the Queen
The Short Victorious War
Field of Dishonor
Flag in Exile
Honor Among Enemies
In Enemy Hands
Echoes of Honor
Ashes of Victory

*edited by David Weber:*
More than Honor
Worlds of Honor
Changer of Worlds

Mutineers' Moon
The Armageddon Inheritance
Heirs of Empire

Path of the Fury

The Apocalypse Troll

The Excalibur Alternative

Oath of Swords
The War God's Own

*with Steve White:*
Insurrection
Crusade
In Death Ground
The Shiva Option *(forthcoming)*

*with John Ringo:*
March Upcountry
March to the Sea

# THE EXCALIBUR ALTERNATIVE

## DAVID WEBER

THE EXCALIBUR ALTERNATIVE

This is a work of fiction. All the characters and events portrayed in this book are fictional, and any resemblance to real people or incidents is purely coincidental.

Copyright © 2002 by David Weber. A shorter version of this novel was published as "Sir George and the Dragon" in *Foreign Legions*, edited by David Drake, © 2001.

All rights reserved, including the right to reproduce this book or portions thereof in any form.

A Baen Books Original

Baen Publishing Enterprises
P.O. Box 1403
Riverdale, NY 10471
www.baen.com

ISBN: 0-671-31860-8

Cover art by Patrick Turner

First printing, January 2002

Library of Congress Cataloging-in-Publication Data

Weber, David, 1952–
The Excalibur alternative / by David Weber.
p. cm.
"A Baen Books original"—T.p. verso.
ISBN 0-671-31860-8
1. Life on other planets—Fiction. 2. Great Britain—History, Military—1066–1485—Fiction. 3. Roman—History, Military—Fiction. 4. Time travel—Fiction. I. Title.

PS3573.E217 E93 2002
813'.43—dc21 2001043636

Distributed by Simon & Schuster
1230 Avenue of the Americas
New York, NY 10020

Production by Windhaven Press, Auburn, NH
Printed in the United States of America

10 9 8 7 6 5 4 3 2 1

*For Bobbie and Sharon, my two favorite ladies.*

# 1

Demon wind greeted pallid daylight with hell howl fury. It was no true daylight, although somewhere above the clouds of seething black the sun had heaved itself once more into the heavens. It was only the devil's own twilight, slashed with body-smashing sheets of rain and spray, the rolling concussion of thunder, the bellow of wind, and the endless keen of rigging, all punctuated by the sodden percussion of torn canvas flailing to destruction.

Sir George Wincaster, Third Baron of Wickworth, clung to a stay, feeling it quiver and groan with strain while he kept to his feet by raw, hopeless force of will alone. The lifeline the vessel's captain had lashed about him when the hideous gale first burst upon them yesterday morning had ringed his chest in bruises, salt sores stung his lips, and rain and spray had soaked into his very marrow. He felt as if heavy horse had charged over him and back again, and despair was a leaden fist about his heart. He had been too ignorant to understand the captain's terror when first the weather broke, for he was a soldier, not a sailor. Now he understood only too well, and he watched almost numbly as the battered cog, creaking and groaning in every frame and stringer, corkscrewed down yet another mountainous, slate-gray wave, streaked with seething bands of spray and foam, and buried its round-cheeked prow deep. Water roared the length of the hull, poison-green and icy as death, plucking and jerking at his limbs and groping after every man on the staggering ship's deck. The hungry sheet of destruction smashed over Sir George, battering the breath from him in yet another agonized grunt, and then it was past and he threw his head up, gasping and hacking on the water which had forced itself into his nostrils and eyes.

The cog fought her way once more up out of the abyss, wallowing as the water cascaded off her deck through buckled rails. Broken cordage blew out, bar-straight and deadly as flails on the howling torrent of wind, and he heard the hull crying out in torment. Sir George was a landsman, yet even he felt the ship's heavier motion, knew the men—and women—laboring frantically at the pumps and bailing with buckets, bowls, even bare hands, were losing ground steadily.

The vessel was doomed. *All* the ships of his expedition were doomed . . . and there was nothing he could do about it. The unexpected summer gale had caught them at the worst possible moment, just as they were rounding the Scilly Isles on their way from Lancaster to Normandy. There had been no warning, no time to seek shelter, only the desperate hope that they might somehow ride out the storm's violence on the open sea.

And that hope had failed.

Sir George had seen only one ship actually die. He was uncertain which, but he thought it had been Earl Cathwall's flagship. He hoped he was wrong. It was unlikely any of them would survive, but Lord Cathwall was more than the commander of the expedition. He was also Sir George's father-in-law, and they held one another in deep and affectionate respect. And perhaps Sir George *was* wrong. The dying ship had been almost close enough to hear the shrieks of its doomed company even through the storm's demented howl as it was pounded into the depths, but the darkness and storm fury, broken only by the glare of forked lighting, had made exact identification impossible.

Yet even though it was the only ship he had seen destroyed, he was grimly certain there had been others. Indeed, he could see only one other vessel still fighting its hopeless battle, and he ground his teeth as yet another heavy sea crashed over his own cog. The impact staggered the ship, and a fresh chorus of screams and prayers came faintly from the men and women and children packed below its streaming deck. His wife Matilda and their son Edward were in that dark, noisome hellhole of crowded terror and vomit, of gear come adrift and washing seawater, and terror choked him as he thought of them once again. He tried to find the words of prayer, the way to plead with God to save his wife and his son. He did not beg for himself. It wasn't his way, and his was the responsibility for bringing them to this in the first place. If God wanted his life in exchange for those so much dearer to him, it was a price he would pay without a whimper.

Yet he knew it was a bargain he would not be permitted. He and Matilda and Edward would meet their ends together, crushed by the soulless malice and uncaring brutality of sea and wind, and deep within him bitter protest reproached the God who had decreed that they should.

The cog shuddered and twitched, heaving in the torment of over-strained timbers and rigging, and Sir George looked up as the ship's mate shouted something. He couldn't make out the words, but he knew it was a question, and he shook himself like a sodden dog, struggling to make his mind function. For all his ignorance of the sea, he had found himself doomed to command of the ship when a falling spar killed the captain. In fact, he'd done little more than agree with the mate's suggestions, lending his authority to the support of a man who might—*might!*—know enough to keep them alive a few hours more. But the mate had needed that support, needed someone else to assume the ultimate responsibility, and that was Sir George's job. To assume responsibility. No, to *acknowledge* the responsibility which was already his. And so he made himself look as if he were carefully considering whatever it was the mate wanted to do this time, then nodded vigorously.

The mate nodded back, then bellowed orders at his exhausted, battered handful of surviving sailors. Wind howl and sea thunder thrashed the words into meaningless fragments so far as Sir George could tell, but two or three men began clawing their way across the deck to perform whatever task the mate had decreed, and Sir George turned his face back to the sea's tortured millrace. It didn't really matter what the mate did, he thought. At worst, a mistake would cost them a few hours of life they might otherwise have clung to; at best, a brilliant maneuver might buy them an hour or two they might not otherwise have had. In the end, the result would be the same.

He'd had such hopes, made so many plans. A hard man, Sir George Wincaster, and a determined one. A peer of the realm, a young man who had caught his monarch's favor at Dupplin and the siege of Berwick at the age of twenty-two, who'd been made a knight by Edward III's own hand the next year on the field of Halidon Hill. A man who'd served with distinction at the Battle of Sluys eight years later—*although*, he thought with an edge of mordant humor even now, *if I'd learned a bit more then of ships, I might have been wise enough to stay home* this *time!*—and slogged through the bitterly disappointing French campaign of 1340. And a man who had returned with a fortune from Henry of Denby's campaign in Gascony five years later.

*And a bloody lot of good it's done me in the end,* he thought bitterly, remembering his gleaming plans. At thirty-five, he was at the height of his prowess, a hard bitten, professional master of the soldier's trade. A knight, yes, but the grandson of a commoner who had won both knighthood and barony the hard way and himself a man who knew the reality of war, not the minstrels' tales of romance and chivalry. A man who fought to *win* . . . and understood the enormous changes England and her lethal longbows were about to introduce into the continental princes' understanding of the art of war.

And one who knew there were fortunes to be made, lands and power to be won, in the service of his King against Philip of France. Despite the disappointments of 1340, last year had proved Edward III his grandfather's grandson, a welcome relief after the weakness and self indulgence of his father. *Longshanks would have approved of the King,* Sir George thought now. *He started slow, but now that Denby's shown the way and he's chosen to beard Philip alone, the lions of England will make the French howl!*

Perhaps they would, and certainly Edward's claim to the throne of France was better than Philip VI's, but Sir George Wincaster would not win the additional renown, or the added wealth and power he had planned to pass to his son, at his King's side. Not now. For he and all the troops under his command would find another fate, and no one would ever know where and when they actually perished.

The corpse light of storm-wracked afternoon slid towards evening, and Sir George realized dully that they had somehow survived another day.

He was too exhausted even to feel surprised . . . and though he tried to feel grateful, at least, a part of him was anything but. Another night of horror and fear, exhaustion and desperate struggle, loomed, and even as he gathered himself to face it, that traitor part wanted only for it to end. For it to be over.

To rest.

But there would be rest enough soon enough, he reminded himself. An eternity of it, if he was fortunate enough to avoid Hell. He hoped he would be, but he was also a realist—and a soldier. And Heaven knew that even the best of soldiers would face an arduous stay in Purgatory, while the worst . . .

He brushed the thought aside, not without the wistful wish that he and Father Timothy might have argued it out one more time, and made himself peer about. The second ship was still with them, farther away as darkness gathered, but still fighting its way across the heaving gray waste, and he could actually see a third vessel beyond it. There might even be one or two more beyond the range of his sight, but—

Sir George's stumbling, exhaustion-sodden thoughts jerked to a stop, and his hand tightened like a claw on the stay. A cracked voice screamed something, barely audible over the roar of wind and sea yet touched with a fresh and different terror, and Sir George clamped his jaws against a bellow of matching fear as the *shape* burst abruptly and impossibly through the savage backdrop of cloud and rain.

He couldn't grasp it, at first. Couldn't wrap his mind about it or find any point of reference by which to measure or evaluate it. It was too huge, too alien . . . too impossible. It could not exist, not in a world of mortals, yet it loomed above them, motionless, shrugging aside the fury of the gale as if it were but the gentlest of zephyrs. Gleaming like polished bronze, flickering with the reflected glare of lightning, a mile and more in length, a thing of subtle curves and gleaming flanks caparisoned in jewel-like lights of red and white and amber.

He stared at it, too amazed and astonished to think, the terror of the storm, even his fear for his wife and son, banished by sheer, disbelieving shock as that vast *shape* hung against the seething cloud and rain.

And then it began to move. Not quickly, but with contemptuous ease, laughing at the gale's baffled wrath. It drifted over the more distant of the cogs he'd seen earlier, and more light appeared as portions of its skin shifted and changed.

*No, they're not "changing,"* Sir George thought numbly. *They're* opening. *And those lights are coming from inside whatever it is. Those are* doors, *doors to chambers filled with light and—*

His thoughts stuttered and halted yet again as more shapes appeared, far smaller this time, but with that same unnatural stillness as the storm howled about them. Some were cross shaped, with the grace of a gliding gull or albatross, while others were squat cones or even spheres, but all were of the same bronze hue as the huger shape which had spawned them.

They spread out, surrounding the half-foundered cog, and then—

"Sweet Jesu!"

Sir George turned his head, too shocked by the lies of his own eyes to wonder how Father Timothy had suddenly appeared there. The snowy-haired Dominican was a big man, with the powerful shoulders of the archer he'd been before he heard God's call decades before, and Sir George released his death grip on the stay to fasten fingers of iron on his confessor's arm.

"In the name of God, Timothy! *What* is *that thing?!*"

"I don't know," the priest replied honestly. "But—"

His voice chopped off abruptly, and he released his own clutch on the cog's rail to cross himself urgently. Nor did Sir George blame him.

"Holy Mary, Mother of God," the baron whispered, releasing Father Timothy and crossing himself more slowly, almost absently, as an unearthly glare of light leapt out from the shapes which had encircled the other ship. Leapt out, touched the heaving vessel, embraced it . . .

. . . and lifted it bodily from the boiling sea.

Someone aboard Sir George's own vessel was gibbering, gobbling out fragments of prayer punctuated by curses of horrified denial, but the baron himself stood silent, unable to tear his eyes from the impossible sight. He saw streams of water gushing from the ship, draining straight down from its half-flooded hold as if in a dead calm, only to be whipped to flying spray by the fury of the wind as they neared the sea below. Yet the shapes enfolded the cog in their brilliance, raising it effortlessly towards the far vaster shape which had birthed them, and he winced as someone aboard that rising vessel, no doubt maddened by terror, hurled himself bodily over the rail. Another body followed, and a third.

"Fools!" Father Timothy bellowed. "Dolts! *Imbeciles!* God Himself has offered them life, and they—!"

The priest broke off, pounding the rail with a huge, gnarly fist.

The first plunging body struck the water and vanished without a trace, but not the second or third. Additional shafts of light speared out, touched each falling form, and arrested its deadly fall. The light lifted them once more, along with the cog, bearing them towards those brilliantly lit portals, and Sir George swallowed again. A mile, he had estimated that shape's length, but he'd been wrong. It was longer than that. *Much* longer, for the cog's hull finally gave him something against which to measure it, and the cog was less than a child's toy beside the vast, gleaming immensity that rode like a mountain peak of bronze amidst the black-bellied clouds of the gale's fury.

"*Were* they fools?" He didn't realize he'd spoken—certainly not that he'd spoken loudly enough for Father Timothy to hear through the crash of the sea and the wind-shriek, but the priest turned to him once more and raised an eyebrow. Even here and now, the expression brought back memories of the days when Father Timothy had been Sir George's tutor as he was now Edward's, but this was no time to be thinking of that.

"*Were* they fools?" Sir George repeated, shouting against the storm's noise. "Are you so certain that that . . . that *thing*—" he pointed a hand he was vaguely surprised to note did not tremble at the shape "—was sent by God and not the Devil?"

"I don't *care* who sent it! What matters is that it offers the chance of life, and while life endures, there is always the hope of God's mercy!"

"Life?" Sir George repeated, and Father Timothy shook his head, as if reproaching his patron and old student's slowness.

"Whatever its ultimate purpose, it clearly means for now to rescue that ship, and possibly all of us who remain alive."

"But . . . *why*?"

"That I don't know," Father Timothy admitted. "I've known enough of God's love to hope it is of His mercy, and seen enough of man's evil to fear that it isn't. Whatever its purpose, and whoever sent it, we will find out soon enough, My Lord."

Sir George's cog was the last to be lifted from the sea.

He had regained at least the outward semblance of his habitual self-control and hammered a shaky calm over the others aboard the vessel by the time the lesser shapes surrounded the ship. Now he stood at the rail in the armor he had not cared to don while the only threat was the sea, gazing at the greater shape with his wife and son beside him. It might strike some as less than heroic to cling to his wife, and he tried to look as if the armored arm wrapped so tightly about her sought only to comfort *her*, but the two of them knew better. As always, Matilda supported him, pressing her cheek proudly against his shoulder even as he felt her tremble with terror, and he turned his head to press a kiss into her sodden, wind-straggled hair. For fourteen years she had stood beside him, one way or another, always supporting him, and a vast, familiar tenderness swelled within him as he drew strength from her yet again.

He kissed her hair once more, then returned his eyes to the vastness hovering above them. His people knew that he knew no more about what they faced than they did, but the habit of obedience ran deep, especially among the men of his own household and their families, and the need to find some fragment of calm in pretending their liege knew what he was doing ran still deeper. He felt their eyes, locked upon him as the light flooded down and the scream of the wind and the thunder of the sea were abruptly shut away. There was no sense of movement, and he kept his own gaze fastened on the huge shape awaiting them rather than let himself look over the rail and watch the sea dropping away in the sudden, unnatural silence. He dared not look, lest the sight unman him at the moment when his people most needed him.

Their uncanny flight was rapid, yet their passage sent no breeze across the deck. It was as if the air about the ship had been frozen, locked into a stillness and quiet which had no place in the natural world. Sheets of rain continued to lash at them, yet those sheets burst upon the edges of that tranquil stillness and vanished in explosions of spray.

For all its swiftness, the journey seemed to take forever, and Sir George heard the rapid mutter of Father Timothy's Latin as they soared above the tumbling waves. But then, abruptly, it was their turn to pass through the opened portal, and Sir George swallowed as he saw the other cogs sitting like abandoned toys in the vastness of the cavern inside the huge shape.

There were a total of nine ships, including his own. That was more than he'd dared hope might have survived, yet little more than half the number which had set out for France, and he clenched his jaw. Whether or not it had been Earl Cathwall's ship he had seen die, the earl's vessel was not among those in the cavern.

The cog settled on the cavern floor, and Sir George tightened his grip on the rail, expecting the ship to list over on its rounded side when the light released it. But the vessel did nothing of the sort. It sat there upright, still quietly gushing water from its sodden interior, and he made himself release the rail.

"Let's get a ladder over the side," he told the mate.

"I don't—" the man began, then stopped himself. "Of course, My Lord. I'll have to rig something, but—"

He broke off again, this time with an undignified squeak, and Sir George had to lock his jaws to withhold an equally humiliating bellow as some unseen hand lifted him from his feet. His arm tightened about Matilda, and he heard Edward's gasp of sudden terror, but neither shamed him by crying out, and his heart swelled with pride in them both.

The invisible hand was as gentle as it was irresistible, and he drew a deep, shuddering breath of relief as it set them on their feet once more. Everyone else from the ship followed, floating through the air like ungainly birds, all too often flapping arms or legs in panic as they floated, until all stood beside the beached cog, bewildered and afraid and trying not to show it while they stared at Sir George in search of guidance.

"You will walk to the green lights on the inboard bulkhead," a voice said, and, despite himself, he twitched in astonishment.

"Witchcraft!" someone gasped, and Sir George fought the urge to cross himself in agreement, for the voice had spoken in his very ear, as if its owner stood close beside him, yet there was no one to be seen! And there was something very strange about the voice itself. A resonance and timbre such as he had never heard . . . and one which, he realized from the expressions about him, had spoken in *every* ear, and not his own alone.

"Witchcraft or angelic powers, we seem to have little choice but to obey, for now at least," he made himself say as calmly as possible. He offered Matilda his arm, glanced at their son, and then turned to survey the others from the ship. "And since that seems to be the case, let us remember that we are Christians and Englishmen."

"Well said, My Lord!" Father Timothy rumbled, and then bestowed a fierce smile much better suited to the archer he once had been than the pacific man of God he had since become upon his companions. "If it be witchcraft, then God and His Mother will surely protect our souls against it. And if we face some force of the mortal world, why, what mortal force has there ever been that *Englishmen* couldn't overcome?"

Several voices muttered agreement—no doubt as much in

search of self-reassurance as Sir George himself at that moment—and the baron led the way towards the green lights blinking ahead of them.

It was a lengthy walk. Almost despite himself, he felt his pulse slow and some of his own undeniable terror ease. In part, he knew, that stemmed from the distraction of his inveterate curiosity. He couldn't stop himself from looking about, marveling and wondering at all he saw.

The gleaming floor was some strange sort of alloy, he decided, although he doubted any smith had ever even dreamed of such a huge expanse of metal. It wasn't the bronze it resembled, he felt certain, yet it rang gently under his spurs and had the smooth, polished sheen found only on metal. Which was preposterous, of course. He was only too well aware of the expense of a chain hauberk or a cuirass. It was absurd to even suggest that something as vast as the shape within which they found themselves could truly be made of metal, and yet that was the only conclusion he could reach.

The lights were equally strange, burning with a bright steadiness which was profoundly unnatural. Whatever provided their illumination, it wasn't burning oil or tallow. Indeed, there was no sign of *any* flame, as if the builders of the shape had somehow captured the light of the sun itself to release when they required it.

He blinked, wondering why he was so certain that the shape had been "built." Surely witchcraft—or, perhaps, the hand of God—was a more reasonable explanation than that any mortal being could have constructed such a wonder. Yet for all his confusion and remaining fear, Sir George discovered that he had become somehow convinced that all of this was, indeed, the work of hands neither demonic nor divine.

It was a conviction which found itself abruptly challenged when they reached their destination.

The passengers from the other cogs were already gathered there. Like Sir George, all of the knights and most of the men-at-arms clearly had snatched up their personal weapons before they left their ships. Many of the archers carried their bow staves, as well, but none had strung them. Hardly surprising, given the state their bowstrings must be in. Yet even without the bows, there were weapons in plenty in evidence among the crowd of men which had coalesced between the "bulkhead" and the expedition's women and children. That should have been a source of some comfort to Sir George, he supposed.

It wasn't.

His hand tightened on the hilt of his own sword, and his nostrils flared as he came close enough to see what held all the rest of the English frozen.

*So much for "mortal hands,"* he told himself with a queer sort of calm, and made himself release his hilt and straighten his shoulders.

The . . . beings lined up along the bulkhead were not human. Far from it, in fact. The shortest of them must have stood at least a foot taller than Sir George's own five feet and ten inches, and Sir George was one of the tallest men in the expedition. Yet that was the smallest, least significant difference between them and any man Sir George had ever seen.

All of them went on two legs and possessed but two arms each, but that was the end of their similarity to men. Or to one another, really. Indeed, the creatures were so utterly alien that their very strangeness had prevented him from immediately realizing that there were two different sorts of them.

The first were clad in cunningly articulated plate armor which certainly looked like steel, rather than the combination plate and mail Sir George was accustomed to, and armed with huge, double-bitted axes. Despite their height, they were almost squat for their size, and the opened visors of their helmets showed huge, bulging eyes and a depressed slot. The slot was set far too high in their faces to be called a nose, although there was nothing else it *could* be, and fringed on either side with hairlike fronds which stirred and crawled uncannily with their breathing. The wide, froglike slit of a mouth below the nose-slot and eyes was almost reassuringly homey compared to the rest of the ugly, orange-skinned and warty face in which it was set.

The second sort wore seamless, one-piece garments, predominately deep red in color, but with blue sleeves and legs. Those garments covered them from throat to toe and shoulder to fingertip but could not hide the fact that they had too many joints in the arms and legs they covered. It was as if God (or the Devil) had grafted extra elbows and knees into the creatures' limbs, and their hands and feet were larger in proportion to their bodies than those of any human. But there was worse, for the garments stopped at their throats. They offered no covering or concealment for the gray-green hide—the glistening, *scale-covered* gray-green hide—of the creatures' faces, or the vertical, slit-pupilled eyes which gleamed like liquid silver, or the lizardlike crests which crowned their snouted, reptilian heads. Yet for all their grotesqueness, they lacked the somehow malevolent air of menace which clung to their wart-faced companions.

"Demons!" someone behind Sir George gasped, and the baron swallowed hard. His hand clamped tighter on his hilt, and it took all his self-control to keep the blade sheathed, but—

"Dragons!" someone else exclaimed, and Sir George drew a deep breath and nodded hard.

"Aye, dragons they are, like enough!" he said loudly enough to be sure all of those about him heard it . . . and choosing not to look too closely at the wart-faces. The label was probably wrong even for the scale-hides, of course. At the very least, dragons were born of Earth, and he felt a deep, sudden and instinctive assurance that wherever or whatever these creatures sprang from, it was *not* Earth. Yet, however inaccurate, the label was also correct.

*And the men may be less prone to panic over "dragons" than "demons,"* he thought with something like detachment. *Of course, they may* not *be, too.*

He drew another breath, sensing the fragile balance between terror, discipline, caution, and ignorance which held the armed men about him precariously still. In many ways, he was astounded such a balance could have held even for a moment, for these were trained fighting men. Trained, *English* fighting men, soldiers every one of them.

But this threat was so far outside their experience that even Englishmen might be excused for uncertainty and hesitation, he told himself . . . and thank God for it! Whatever else those wart-faces and dragon-men might be, they were obviously part and parcel of whatever power had created the ship in which they all stood. Assuming they truly were mortal, Sir George never doubted that his men could swarm them under, despite the wart-faces' armor, but he had no illusions about the efficacy of edged steel against the other defenses such a power could erect to guard itself.

*For that matter, we have no reason—as yet—to think our rescuers might be hostile in any way. After all, they were under no obligation to pluck us from the sea. If they wished us ill, they had only to leave us there. We would all have been dead soon enough.*

He felt the silence stretch out as those from his own cog joined the rear ranks of the crowd. He gave Matilda a final hug, then stepped forward.

Men who had stared fixedly at the grotesque creatures started and looked over their shoulders as they sensed his approach, and he heard more than a few muttered prayers (and curses) of relief as he was recognized. He was as stained and ragged as any of them, but his dark spade beard and the scar down his right cheek were well known, almost famous, even among those who had followed Earl Cathwall or Sir Michael rather than Sir George. More to the point, perhaps, Earl Cathwall was dead, and Sir Michael was awaiting them in Normandy . . . where even the slowest must realize they were unlikely to arrive. Which meant every one of those men looked to Sir George Wincaster for leadership and guidance.

Now they drew apart, opening a path for him. One or two, bolder than the others, actually reached out to touch him as he passed, whether to lend him reassurance or to draw confidence of their own from him he didn't know.

Sir Richard Maynton stood at the very front of the crowd, and his head turned sharply as Sir George stepped up beside him. With the losses their command structure had taken, Sir Richard had almost certainly become Sir George's second in command, which was unfortunate, in a way, for Sir George knew him less well than he might have liked. On the other hand, he couldn't misread the relief in Sir Richard's eyes.

"Thank God!" the other knight said quickly. "I feared you, too, had perished, My Lord!"

"Aye?" Sir George managed a chuckle. "I can understand that well enough. *I* thought I had perished a time or two, myself!" Several others chuckled at his feeble joke, and he clapped the other knight on the shoulder.

"Indeed," Sir Richard agreed. "In fact, My Lord, I—"

The knight closed his mouth with an almost audible click, and a chorus of muffled exclamations rippled through the crowd facing the dragon-men and wart-faces as a brighter light flashed. An opening appeared in the bulkhead, snapping into existence so abruptly that the eye almost missed the way the panel which formed it *flicked* aside, and another being stood within the sudden doorway or hatch.

If the wart-faces and dragon-men were alien, this being was even more bizarre, although, in many ways, it seemed more comical than menacing. Its garment was the same deep red as the dragon-men's, but its garb was *solely* red, without the blue sleeves and legs, and a gleaming pendant hung about its neck to dangle on its chest. It was also short, its head rising little higher than Sir George's own chest, and the exposed portion of its face and throat was covered in plushy purple fur. Like the others, it went on two legs and had two arms. Its hands had only three fingers, but each had been given an extra thumb where a man would have had his little finger.

All of that was odd enough, but the creature's face was more grotesque than a mummer's mask. It was broad and flat, with two wide, lipless mouths, one above the other, and no trace of a nose. Worse, it had three black eyes: a single, large one, its pupil invisible against its obsidian darkness, centered in the upper part of its face, and two smaller ones set lower, flanking it to either side. And, as if to crown the absurdity of its appearance, its broad, squat head was topped by two enormous, foxlike ears covered in the same purple fur.

Sir George stared at it, shocked as even the wart-faces and dragon-men hadn't left him. They, at least, radiated a sense of watchfulness, even threat, he felt he understood, but *this* creature—! It might as easily have been a demon or a court jester, and he wondered whether he ought to smile or cross himself.

"Who leads this group?"

The voice was light, even delicate, with the piping clarity of a young child's. It spoke perfect English, and it appeared to emerge from the upper of the demon-jester's two mouths, although the lipless opening didn't move precisely in time with the words. Hearing it, Sir George was tempted to smile, despite all that had happened, for it seemed far more suited to the jester than to a demon. But the temptation was faint and brief. There was no expression in that voice at all, nor, so far as he could tell, did any hint of an expression cross that alien face. Yet that was the point—it was an *alien* face, and that was driven brutally home to Sir George as he realized that, for the first time in his life, he could not discern the smallest hint of the thoughts or wishes or emotions of the being speaking to him.

"I do," he replied after a long still moment.

"And you are?" the piping voice inquired.

"I am Sir George Wincaster, Baron of Wickworth in the service of His Majesty Edward III, King of England, Scotland, Wales, and France." There was a hint of iron pride in that reply, and Sir George felt other spines straighten about him, but—

"You are in error, Sir George Wincaster," the piping voice told him, still with no hint of expression. "You are no longer in the service of any human. You are now in the service of my guild."

Sir George stared at the small being, and a rumbling rustle went through the men at his back. He opened his mouth to respond, but the demon-jester went on without so much as a pause.

"But for the intervention of my vessel and crew, you all would have perished," it said. "We rescued you. As a result, you are now our property, to do with as we choose." An inarticulate half-snarl, fueled as much by fear as by anger, rose behind Sir George, but the demon-jester continued unperturbed. "No doubt it will take primitives such as you some time to fully accept this change in status," its expressionless voice continued. "You would be wise, however, to accustom yourselves to it as quickly as your crude understanding permits."

"*Accustom* ourselves—!" someone began furiously, but Sir George's raised hand cut the rising tide of outrage short.

"We are Englishmen . . . Sir," he said quietly, "and Englishmen are *no one's* 'property.' "

"It is unwise to disagree with me, Sir George Wincaster," the demon-jester said, still with that calm, total lack of expression. "As a group, you and your fellows are, or may become, at any rate, a valuable asset of my guild. None of you, however, is irreplaceable as an individual."

Sir George's jaw clenched. He was unaccustomed to being threatened to his face, and certainly to being threatened by a half-sized creature he could have snapped in two over one bent leg. Yet he made himself swallow it. The wart-faces and dragon-men behind the demon-jester were ominous evidence of the power which backed him. Even worse, Sir George was achingly aware of the presence of his wife and son.

"Unwise or not," he said after a long, still moment, "it is

I who command these men. As such, it is my duty to speak for them. We are all grateful for our rescue, but—"

"I do not want your gratitude. My guild and I desire only your obedience," the demon-jester interrupted. "We require certain services of you—services you should find neither difficult nor distasteful, since they are the only ones you are truly trained or qualified to provide."

Sir George's hand clenched once more on the hilt of his sword, but the demon-jester ignored the movement, as if the very notion that something as childish as a sword might threaten *it* was ludicrous.

"We require only that you fight for us," it went on. "If you do, you will be well treated and rewarded. Your lives will be extended beyond any span you can presently imagine, your health will be provided for, your—" The three eyes looked past Sir George, and the creature seemed to pause for a moment, as if searching for a word. Then it continued without inflection. "Your mates and young will be cared for, and you will be granted access to them."

"And if we choose *not* to fight for you?" Sir George asked flatly.

"Then you will be compelled to change your minds," the demon-jester replied. "Analysis indicates that such compulsion should not prove difficult. You are, of course, primitives from a primitive and barbaric culture, so simple and direct methods would undoubtedly serve best. We might, perhaps, begin by selecting five or six of your mates and young at random and executing them."

A ball of ice closed upon Sir George's stomach. The threat was scarcely unexpected, yet he hadn't counted on how the emotionlessness, the total lack of interest or anger, in the demon-jester's piping voice would hone the jagged edges of his fear. He forced himself not to look over his shoulder at Matilda and Edward.

"If such measures should prove insufficient, there are, of course, others," the demon-jester continued. "Should all else fail, we could attempt complete personality erasure and simply reprogram you, but that would probably prove excessively time consuming. Nor would there be any real point in it. It would be much more cost effective simply to dispose of all of you and collect a fresh force of fighters. One group of barbarians is very like another, after all."

"But *these* barbarians are under arms, sirrah!" another voice barked.

Sir George's head snapped around, and he felt a stab of dreadful certainty at what he would see. Sir John Denmore was barely twenty years old, young and hot-blooded, with more than his fair share of arrogance, and he punctuated his fierce statement with the steely slither of a drawn blade. His sword gleamed under the unnaturally brilliant lights, and he leapt forward with a vicious stroke.

"God and Saint G—!"

He never completed the war cry. His sword swept towards the demon-jester, but the creature never even moved. It simply stood there, watching with its alien lack of expression, and the young knight's shout died in shock when his sword struck some invisible barrier, like a wall of air. It flew out of his hands, and he gaped in disbelief as it spun end over end away from him. Then he shook himself, snarled, and snatched at his dagger.

"Hold!" Sir George shouted. "Put up your—"

But he was too late. This time the demon-jester made a small gesture, and Sir John gurgled and stopped dead. His eyes bulged wildly, his expression one of raw terror as rage turned into panic, but he couldn't even open his mouth. He was held as though in a giant, unseen spider's web, dagger half-drawn, utterly helpless, and the demon-jester gazed at Sir George.

"It is well for you that you attempted to stop him rather than joining in his stupidity," it informed the baron. "But I see you truly are primitives, and so require proof of your status. Very well. I will give it to you."

"There is no need—" Sir George began.

"There is whatever need I say there is," the demon-jester piped, and held out a two-thumbed hand to the nearest dragon-man. The dragon-man's alien, silver eyes met Sir George's for just a moment, but then it reached to its belt and drew a strange device from a scabbard. It extended the thing to the demon-jester, and the shorter creature adjusted a small knob on the device's side.

"You only think you are armed, Sir George Wincaster. Your swords and arrows do not threaten me or any member of my crew. Our own weapons, on the other hand—"

It raised the device in Sir John's direction almost negligently, and then Sir George cried out in horror. He couldn't help himself, and neither then nor later did he feel the shame he perhaps ought to have. Not when the terrible ray of light, like lightning chained to the demon-jester's will, crackled from the device and smote full upon Sir John's breast.

Its touch was death . . . but not simply death. The young man's chest cavity blew apart as if from the inside, and heart and lungs exploded with it. A grisly storm front of blood and shredded tissue flew over those about him, a stink of burning meat filled the air, and men who had seen the most hideous sights war could offer recoiled with cries of horror. But worst of all, Sir George realized later, was the dead man's silence. The fact that even as the hell weapon was raised, even as his expression twisted—first with terror, and then in agony—the young knight never made a sound. Was unable even to writhe or open his mouth. He could only stand there, frozen, more helpless than any lamb before the butcher, while the demon-jester calmly blew his body open.

Even after death, Sir John was not allowed to fall. His corpse stood upright, face contorted with the rictus of death, blood flooding down from his ruptured chest to puddle about his feet.

Had it not been for the proof that no one could touch the creature, Sir George would have attacked the thing himself, with his bare hands, if necessary. But he had that proof . . . and he had his responsibilities, and his duty, and his wife and son stood behind him. And so he did something much harder than launch a hopeless attack.

He made himself stand there, with the blood of a man under his command dripping down his face, and did nothing.

His motionless example stilled the handful of others who would have attacked, and the demon-jester regarded them all for a long, deadly silent time. Then it reached out and, without taking its triple-eyed gaze from Sir George, handed the lightning weapon back to the dragon-man.

"I trust this lesson is not lost upon your warriors, Sir George Wincaster," it piped then. "Or upon you, either. You may speak for these men, and you may lead them in combat, but you are no longer their commander. I am. Unless, of course, someone wishes to challenge that point."

It made a gesture, and the mutilated corpse that once had been an arrogant young knight thudded to the metal floor like so much dead meat.

# II

Sir George held himself under iron command as Denmore's butchered body struck the deck. Behind him, he felt a fury which matched his own, but all the white-hot anger of his men was chilled by the terror of the demon-jester's demonstration of power. He understood that terror, for he shared it . . . and not simply for himself. But he couldn't permit himself to dwell upon the danger to Matilda and Edward, lest it unman him when he could not afford to be unmanned. And so he simply stood there, gazing at the demon-jester.

"Now," the demon-jester's piping voice was as emotionless as ever, as if Denmore's murder meant no more to him than swatting a fly, "we may proceed with your processing. I advise each of you to remember that none of you are irreplaceable."

He stood for one more moment, considering the motionless humans with all three eyes, then turned his back upon them. The door by which he had entered opened as swiftly and unexpectedly as before, and he stepped through it without another word.

Sir George watched him disappear, wondering what was to happen next and doing his best to appear confident and uncowed. He doubted that his pose could truly fool anyone into believing he was either of those things, but the same rules which required him to pretend he was required his officers and men to pretend they believed him. The thought brought a small, unexpected smile of genuine amusement to him, but that smile vanished as another voice spoke from thin air.

"You will follow the guide lights," it said. It was the same voice which had first greeted them, and it was quite unlike the demon-jester's. In some ways, it sounded closer to human, for its even tenor tone held none of the high, piping note his had, and although it was equally emotionless it was also less . . . dead-sounding. "Males will follow the red light. Females will follow the green light."

Sir George's shoulders stiffened, and his hand slid once more to the sword hilt at his side. He drew a sharp breath and opened his mouth, but before he could speak, another hand fell upon his elbow.

He turned his head, and found Matilda at his side. Her dark blue eyes were haunted by the same fear of separation he knew was in his own, and he felt a sudden burn of shame as he saw the grief for her father's death under that fear. She had lost even more than he, yet she held her head up proudly, and despite their fear and sorrow, her eyes held his steadily. She said nothing, yet nothing was required, and he drew another breath, deeper and slower than the first, and made himself nod.

She was right. The reek of seared flesh and ruptured organs and blood from what had been Sir John Denmore reminded him only too clearly what price resistance might carry. Yet it was hard, hard to submit.

"Males will follow the red light. Females will follow the green light," the invisible voice repeated. It paused for a few seconds, then spoke yet again. "Males will follow the red light. Females will follow the green light. Failure to comply with instructions will be severely punished."

There was no more emotion in the final sentence than there

had been in any of the earlier ones, yet the threat woke Sir George from his momentary immobility, and he shook himself, patted the slender hand in the crook of his elbow, and turned to face the men and women behind him.

"It would appear we have no choice but to obey," he said flatly. "I like it no better than any of you do, yet we have all seen how readily these . . . creatures will kill. We have no option, for now, at least, but to do as we are bid."

Something like a sigh seemed to ripple through the ranks of exhausted, saltwater-soaked humans, and he felt the urge to rebellion run out of them. He waited a moment longer, to be certain, then gave Matilda's hand a final squeeze, removed it from his arm, and raised it to his lips. He kissed it, then released it, and watched her turn, her head high, and walk towards the green light. Lady Margaret Stanhope, wife of Sir Bryan Stanhope, stepped from the crowd to follow her, and then other women did the same. Sir George watched his wife with burning eyes, torn between pride in her, fear for her, and shame at his inability to protect her, then turned to where his son stood among the other men and boys.

"Edward," he said quietly, holding out his hand, and his heart swelled with pride as the boy came to him. Edward's face was white and strained, and his eyes carefully avoided the mutilated body bleeding on the deck, but he held up his head with all the courage of his lady mother, and if his hand trembled as he put it into his father's, it gripped firmly.

Sir George squeezed back, trying to communicate even a little of the pride he felt in him, then turned resolutely to the red light, bobbing gently in midair, and walked toward it.

The other men fell in behind him, first by ones and twos, and then in clumps, and two of the wart-faces came behind them all with a strange, hopping gait fully in keeping with their froglike appearance.

The light led them across the bronze floor of the huge compartment for what seemed miles. It wasn't, of course, but that didn't change the way it felt. Perhaps it was because none of them had ever imagined a room the size of the one in which they found themselves. The greatest cathedral in the world was as nothing beside it. Indeed, Sir George suspected that any building he had ever seen—and most entire villages, for that matter—could actually have been placed *inside* this one, vast, metal-floored chamber. The abandoned cogs were no more than discarded toys behind them when they finally reached a clifflike wall of the same bronze-colored alloy.

The red light never paused, and another of those sudden doors appeared before them as the light passed through it. Sir George followed it, not without a fresh sense of trepidation. After the vast expanse of the cavern about them, the passage beyond the door felt small and cramped, even though it was at least ten feet across and equally high. He looked down to give Edward an encouraging smile but didn't even glance over his shoulder at the other men.

He heard the louder echoes of their feet on the metallic floor as they followed him into the passage's closer confines. He also heard the mutter of their uneasy comments, but they were careful to keep those mutters quiet enough that he could pretend he hadn't.

Their journey down the new passage was much shorter than the hike across the original compartment had been, and then another door opened and the lead ranks of their corridor-narrowed column stepped into a fresh chamber. This one was far smaller than the first one had been, and additional doorways opened off of it. There were ten of the arched openings, and red lights flashed above nine of them while another red light burned steadily above the tenth.

"You will pass through the door with the steady light," the disembodied voice informed them, and Sir George and Edward stepped towards the unblinking light. Other men followed them, but still others split off and headed for different doors, and Sir George stopped.

Most of the others paused, as did the much greater number still passing down the corridor towards the antechamber.

"He said the steady light," Sir George said.

"I know, My Lord," someone said. It was Walter Skinnet, the sergeant of Sir George's mounted men-at-arms, and he raised his hand and pointed at an arch three doors to the left of the one surmounted by the unblinking light. "That one," he added.

Sir George stared at him, then looked back at the door towards which he and Edward had been headed. The light burned a steady blood red while the one above Skinnet's chosen door flashed jaggedly.

"I see the steady light here," Sir George told him, gesturing at his own door.

"So do I, Sir," an archer said.

"Me, too," someone else offered.

"I see it over there," a seaman from one of the cogs said, pointing at still a third door.

"No," yet another man said, his voice edged with fear. "It's over there!"

He pointed at a completely different door, and Sir George's nostrils flared as he inhaled deeply.

"All right, lads!" He made his voice come out firm and crisp. "After all we've already seen, let's not let a thing as small as this unman us!"

The incipient panic eased, and he gave a sharp, barking laugh.

"I don't know how it's done," he went on, "but clearly they've some clever trick to make each of us see our own steady light where they want us to. No doubt it's their way to split us into smaller groups, and if none of us care much for that, it's hardly unexpected, either, now is it?"

One or two men shook their heads, and he shrugged.

"Very well. You men there in the passageway pass the word back up the hall so the lads behind you will know what to expect. The rest of you." he shrugged again, "follow whichever light looks steady to you."

He paused long enough to see his orders obeyed, then gave Edward another smile and stepped through their own door.

The chamber beyond was larger than the antechamber, though still enormously smaller than the one in which they had met the demon-jester. More men followed him and Edward into it, until there must have been almost a hundred of them. The crowd filled the compartment but without undue crowding, and Sir George looked about him curiously.

The chamber was oval, with walls of the same ubiquitous bronze metal. The ceiling was much lower here, but it wasn't really visible. Not clearly, at any rate. Looking up, all he could see was an opalescent glow of light. It was odd, like everything else that had happened to them from the moment the bronze shape appeared among the clouds, but the light seemed to fall not from any single source but as if from some deep well or shaft. He had the distinct impression that there was a definite roof or ceiling above him, but he couldn't seem to *see* it.

He lowered his eyes from the light and they narrowed as he realized that despite the seeming brightness of the illumination which filled the chamber, his vision wasn't dazzled in the least. He had just filed that observation away beside all of the other strange things which had enveloped them all when the tenor voice spoke again.

"You will remove all clothing and place it in the storage compartments," it announced, and the featureless bronze walls shifted suddenly as scores of narrow doorways flicked open. Sir George stepped over to the nearest one and examined the shelf-lined space beyond it.

"You will remove all clothing and place it in the storage compartments," the voice repeated with inhuman patience, and Sir George grimaced. He cared no more for this order than any of the others they had been given, but as with the others, he saw no option but to obey.

"Help me with my armor, Edward," he said calmly.

The "storage compartments" disappeared the instant the last garment had been placed in them. Sir George was hardly surprised, but that made him no happier to see his arms and armor disappear. He looked around and saw the same unhappiness in each of the now-naked men sharing the compartment with him and his son, yet despite his own dislike for being separated from his sword, he also felt a slight but undeniable sense of relief. The demon-jester had amply demonstrated the futility of attempting to attack him, but as long as the men possessed weapons, the temptation to use them would exist. He felt not only vulnerable but demeaned at being deprived of the sword and spurs which were the emblems of his knightly status, but the knowledge that no more of his men would be slaughtered as young Denmore had been—or not, at least, for the same reason—was partial compensation.

"You will now be cleaned," the voice told them, and someone cried out as a thick vapor began to fill the chamber. It arose from the floor, climbing quickly up past knees and thighs, and Sir George felt Edward's hand clutch his once more as it enveloped them.

The baron squeezed back reassuringly and smiled at his son with a sudden quirk of genuine amusement as he realized how the need to reassure Edward distracted him from panic of his own.

The thought was a fleeting one, and he looked back down as the vapor rose above his hips. It was warm, almost sensually comforting once the immediate surprise had passed, and he felt himself relaxing as it wrapped itself about him. He had never felt anything quite like it. It was almost like plunging into a hot bath, but there was a tingle to it, almost like kneading fingers massaging skin and muscles, which felt undeniably pleasant.

He looked around as the vapor rose to chest height and saw echoes of his own relaxation in the faces of the others in the compartment. Then the vapor rose over his head, and he inhaled deeply, drawing the freshness and the sense of cleanliness deep into his lungs.

He was never certain afterward how long he and his companions stood enveloped in the clinging vapor. He doubted that it could have been as long as it seemed, yet he was confident that many minutes passed before the vapor withdrew as silently and swiftly as it had appeared. He felt like a man awakening from a deep sleep, and when he looked down he realized that the salt sores on his face and the dark rings of chest bruises left by the brutal hammering his lifeline had administered aboard the foundering cog had disappeared.

His exhaustion and weariness had gone with the bruises, he realized. Indeed, he felt fresh and renewed, filled with energy, and he saw shoulders straightening and backs stiffening throughout the chamber as the others reacted to the same sensations.

"Well, lads," he said with a chuckle, "I'm not about to kiss our new 'commander's' arse, but that turned out better than I feared it might!" Several of the others laughed, and if there was a tinge of hysterical relief in their laughter, he ignored it as he inhaled hugely, expanding his chest. "I'd not say no to a week's rest or so, but we've made a fair start on recovering."

"So we have, Sir," one of his men-at-arms replied, and Sir George clapped him on the back.

"Best to remember that not everything that happens to us will be . . . unpleasant," the baron pointed out, and pretended not to hear the slightly dubious edge of the mutters of agreement. "I—"

"You will follow the red light out of the compartment," the emotionless voice interrupted him, and he grimaced.

"Our master's voice," he observed ironically, and this time the answering laughter sounded much closer to normal.

"You will follow the red light out of the compartment," the voice repeated, patient as the very stones, and Sir George shrugged and led the way through the suddenly appearing door with Edward at his side.

"As you yourself said before we were 'processed,' My Lord, I see no alternative but to accept that . . . that . . . creature's demands." Father Timothy's tone was heavy. "For the moment, at least."

"I mislike such advice," Sir Richard Maynton sounded like a man drinking soured wine, "yet I have no better to offer in its place, I fear."

"Nor do I." Sir George kept his own voice calm and measured, though he doubted that it fooled anyone. Or perhaps it did. After all, at the moment most of the men in this compartment undoubtedly *wanted* to be fooled.

The baron leaned back in the obscurely uncomfortable chair the bodiless voice—"Computer," if he'd understood the outlandish name aright—had provided at the demon-jester's orders. None of the humans had the slightest idea of how that chair and the others like it had been made to appear. They had sprung up out of the metal deck like fairy toadstools, and they appeared to be made of the same alloy as that deck. How anyone could make bronze or steel "grow," or make it soft and yielding beneath the weight of their bodies, was yet another of the unending mysteries which had enveloped them, but at least this one gave them someplace to park their arses.

It would have been nice if the chairs had been properly proportioned for the people sitting in them, but it was obvious that the otherwise luxuriously enfolding furniture had been designed for something with longer legs and shorter torsos than any human would ever have. It was yet one more reminder of how completely outside their previous existences they had been thrown.

Nor was it the only reminder.

Sir George looked down at the odd garment he wore. It was like and yet unlike the garments worn by the demon-jester and his dragon-man guards. It was a different color, to begin with—a dark green, with black trim along the sleeves and legs—and it didn't cover his hands as theirs did. It did include incredibly comfortable "boots" that were extensions of its legs, and it was also a looser fit than any of the alien creatures aboard this ship seemed to prefer. For all of that, its fit was far snugger than anything he had ever worn before. And more comfortable, he admitted almost against his will.

He and the men who had been "processed" with him had found the peculiar, one-piece garments waiting when they emerged. All had appeared to be of one size, and none of them had known how to open the strange seals which served in place of buttons or laces. The baron hadn't been alone in his dismay at the sight of the strange clothing, but the tenor voice had insisted that this was what they must wear, and then it had patiently instructed them in how to unseal the garments' closures and get into them.

Once donned, each garment had shifted size as required until each man was more comfortably fitted than any of them, including Sir George, had ever before been, and more than one hardened soldier's face had creased in a huge, childlike smile of delight at the comfort of the integral boots' thick, cushioned soles. Men who spent so much of their lives marching towards and away from battle appreciated well-fitted boots, and surely no king had ever boasted more comfortable ones than these!

Sir George had to admit that he shared their happiness over the boots, but he was less than completely delighted by the garments. He wasn't the only one wearing one of them at the moment, for everyone in the chamber, including Matilda and Father Timothy, wore precisely the same thing, and he felt a fresh stir of resentment as he glanced at his wife. The clothing that was simply "snug" for him clung to every supple curve of Matilda's body, and he would have been more than human not to note how the eyes of the other men in the compartment were very carefully not noticing that.

Matilda, on the other hand, appeared completely oblivious to how revealing her clothing was. He doubted very much that she could be as calm as she chose to appear, but he would not embarrass or shame her by showing his own anger at seeing her so displayed. Besides, she was undoubtedly correct. Irritating and infuriating as their captors' insistence on clothing all of them in these same, revealing garments might be, it was minor beside all of the other things which had already happened to them. And which might, as she had quietly reminded him on the way to this compartment, happen yet.

And if he had required any additional reminding, there were the two wart-faces and the pair of the dragon-men standing against the compartment wall. Sir George suspected that the watchful guards were there precisely to remind them of their helplessness. Certainly, if the demon-jester's words and those of the other voice which had guided them through their "processing" could be made to sound in their very ears, then their captors could also listen to anything they said without being physically present. The guards were simply the demon-jester's way of reminding them of his presence . . . and demands. No doubt the baron would have called exactly such a meeting if left to his own devices, but he had not been given that option, and the demon-jester's *order* to call it had stung. Sir George was a soldier, accustomed to obeying commands, as well as giving them, but he had never chosen to serve the demon-jester, and the ridiculous looking creature's uncaring arrogance was infuriating. He gave his orders as if Sir George and all of the other humans with him were of less importance than the same number of hunting hounds.

But however infuriating their "Commander" might be, Sir George had no intention of allowing his fury to show. He might not be able to read the demon-jester's emotions or expression, but that didn't necessarily mean the reverse was true, and the demon-jester had made his readiness to kill to make a point only too clear. So when he had ordered Sir George to "inventory" his guild's new "assets," the baron hadn't even been tempted to argue. Nor had he been blind to the need to establish and maintain an unshaken internal human chain of authority, and now he considered the six men and one woman in the compartment with him. He and Matilda had taken the two chairs at the very front of the chamber with a calm assurance of their right to precedence. The baron had allowed no sign of hesitation or doubt to cross his face or color his manner, and he'd been just as careful to conceal his undeniable sense of relief when none of the other men challenged his authority.

The fact that Father Timothy and Sir Richard had settled down to his and Matilda's left and right respectively had helped knock any temptation to challenge him on the head. Father Timothy would have supported him under any circumstances, but Sir Richard was another matter. Given how the death of Earl Cathwall and the uncanny fashion in which they had been rescued—or captured, depending on how one cared to look at things—had turned the planned expedition to France into chaos, Sir Richard might very well have seen an opportunity to seize power for himself. After all, less than a third of the total surviving men-at-arms and archers had been under Sir George's personal command. Almost half had been recruited by Earl Cathwall, and he supposed it might technically be argued that their oaths passed to Matilda and so, indirectly, to himself upon her father's death. The point, however, might have been argued, and the remaining soldiers and *all* of the surviving mariners could legitimately claim never to have been under his own orders.

On the other hand, all of them knew by now that none of them would ever see France or their own homes again, and all of them were desperate for someone to tell them what to do.

"What are our numbers, Father?" the baron asked after a lingering moment of silence.

"Better than I had feared, My Lord," the Dominican replied. As Sir George's confessor, Father Timothy had assumed the duties of chief clerk for the baron's portion of the expedition from the very beginning, and Earl Cathwall's clerk had perished with him. That had elevated Timothy to the role of record keeper and quartermaster for the entire expedition. It was one he was well suited to, for he had always had a gift for numbers, and his priestly calling had also made him a reassuring presence as he circulated among the survivors. Now he pursed his lips as he cast his mind back over the numbers he had collected. Sir George knew the priest well enough to guess how badly he longed for something to have jotted his notes and counts upon, but they had neither parchment nor paper nor ink, only Father Timothy's memory.

"Of the seventeen vessels with which we set out for France, nine survived," he began. "I haven't been able yet to make a completely accurate count, but God has been even kinder to us than I had first thought, and, through His mercy, far more of our people have survived than I had believed possible. My current, rough calculations are that our present company includes one hundred and eighty-two seamen, four hundred and seventy-three archers, two hundred and fourteen men-at-arms, four knights, nine squires, and, including myself, six clerks. In addition, we have another fifty-seven able-bodied men, including drovers, cooks, horse farriers, fletchers, laborers, and two blacksmiths. In total, we can thus count nine hundred and forty-five fit men in all, most of whom are trained and under arms."

Sir George nodded. Father Timothy was right; the numbers were much higher than any one in the compartment could have expected, although they were still small enough, given his suspicion that the members of their small company were all the Englishmen—indeed, all the human beings—that they would ever see again.

"And the women and children?" he asked.

"Including your own lady wife," the priest said, "we have thirty-two wives, not all of whom have . . . ah, enjoyed the sanction of Mother Church upon their unions, and twenty-seven more women who are no one's wives. We also have a total of twenty-six children under the age of ten, and six babes in arms. Finally, there are in addition fourteen apprentices of differing ages bound to various of our craftsmen and drovers."

"I see." Sir George nodded, his face carefully expressionless, as he digested the numbers. Fifty-nine women was more than he had anticipated, but it was only one woman for every sixteen men, and God only knew where that sort of imbalance would lead in the end. From Father Timothy's tone, the priest was already considering the same sorts of questions, and Sir George was devoutly grateful to have Timothy and not some other, narrow-minded cleric along. The Dominican's experience as a soldier had left him with more pragmatic and less condemning attitudes than many of his fellow priests, and they were going to need all of the pragmatism and understanding they could find.

"Very well," the baron went on after a brief pause. "Thanks to Father Timothy, we know what strength we possess."

"At least what strength in men, My Lord," Sir Richard put in, and leaned forward to look across Sir George at Father Timothy. "Have we any good idea of what livestock survived, Father?"

"Not yet," the priest admitted. "I don't expect to discover that very many of our animals lived, particularly given that both horse transports were among the missing vessels, but so far I've seen at least a few chickens, and Mistress Nan's swine seem to have survived."

"I suspect that we may rely upon our captors to feed us, at least," Matilda Wincaster said.

If any of the men in the compartment were surprised to hear Lady Wincaster speak up, they were wise enough to keep their tongues between their teeth. Sir Richard and Sir Anthony Fitzhugh, the expedition's two senior knights after Sir George himself, were too courteous to comment, and Father Timothy knew Matilda and Sir George too well to feel the least surprise. The other three men present—Rolf Grayhame, Walter Skinnet, and Dafydd Howice—were as familiar with Matilda's outspokenness as the priest. Grayhame had commanded Sir George's bowmen for over six years, while Skinnet had served as the master of his horse for almost ten. Howice had never been part of Sir George's household, but the gray-haired, oak-thewed Welshman had been the second in command of Earl Cathwall's guard since Matilda was eleven. Sir Adrian du Col, Howice's superior, had died with the earl, and the Welshman had succeeded to his spot. Sir George regretted du Col's death, but Howice was a welcome addition to his own officers, both as an immensely experienced soldier and as someone whose loyalty to Matilda was absolute.

"Even such as he must realize that people must eat," Matilda went on now, "and he scarcely gave us the opportunity to bring any great store of food with us." She grimaced wryly, and one or two of the men chuckled. "It follows that we may assume he intends to feed us from his own stores, I would say."

"Assuming that whatever they eat is anything but poison for human folk, My Lady," Fitzhugh agreed, jerking his head at the wart-faces and dragon-men standing silently against the wall.

"I doubt that our 'Commander' would have stolen us away without first determining that he could keep us fed, Sir Anthony," Matilda replied. "I don't say that I look forward to discovering what he might consider food, but there would be no more point in taking us to poison than in taking us only to see us starve."

The knight looked at her for a moment, then nodded, and she shrugged.

"However that may be, though, I suspect that you were thinking of more than eggs and bacon, Sir Richard," she said.

"Indeed I was, My Lady. As Father Timothy says, we lost both of our horse transports, and that was a most serious blow."

Sir George nodded gravely. The same point had already occurred to him. Indeed, there was no way it could not have occurred. Even without the loss of the two transports, they would have had all too few horses for their needs, because they had intended to rely upon the mounts Sir Michael had spent the last two months and more procuring for the expedition in France. Of their total strength of men-at-arms, almost two hundred were trained to fight mounted. That would have been a small enough cavalry force at the best of times, even given their relatively high percentage of archers to offset their weakness, but without horses, those mounted men-at-arms became only so many more infantry.

"From what the . . . 'Commander' has said," the baron said, picking his words carefully, "I believe that one of his purposes in demanding an accounting of our resources may well be so that he might procure at least some of the items and supplies we require. Certainly," he snorted with bitter humor, "he can have little doubt that we have lost many of the things we need, given the manner in which his guild 'recruited' us!"

"With a commander of our own kind, I would be certain you're correct, My Lord," Sir Richard said with a small nod. "On the other hand, these . . . folk are so different from us, with such different ways and powers, that they may not realize what our true needs are."

"An excellent point," Sir George agreed, and it was. It was also one which had already occurred to him, but he was glad to see that Sir Richard had considered the same possibility. "However," the baron continued, "if that's the case, it will be one of my tasks to explain those needs to the . . . 'Commander.' "

"I trust you'll forgive me, My Lord," Sir Anthony said, "but I'm just as happy to leave that task to you!"

"As anyone with wit would be," Matilda said dryly. "At the

same time, my lords, I think we would be both wise and prudent not to ascribe too great a power to our new 'Commander.' "

Most of the men in the compartment looked very much as if they wanted to stare at their liege's lady in disbelief, but Father Timothy nodded firmly.

"Well said, My Lady!" he agreed. "Well said, indeed. Whatever powers these creatures possess, they are far less than the power of God, and the Lord will be with us wherever we may fare."

"Of course He will, Father," Matilda said. "Yet that wasn't precisely what I meant." She glanced at Sir George, and her husband nodded for her to continue. "What I meant, my lords," she went on, letting her gaze circle the compartment very much as her father might have, "is that I think it would be wise of us not to mistake these creatures for demons or devils. That they are strange to us, and possess arts and abilities we don't yet even know of, far less comprehend, is undeniable. Yet I think the 'Commander' would have been less ready to demonstrate his weapons' power or to post such guards over us while we speak—" she nodded at the wart-faces and dragon-men against the compartment wall "—if he were not himself mortal. There would be no need for him to teach us to fear him or to watch over us so carefully if he were truly more than mortal."

"No doubt you are correct, My Lady," Father Timothy said after a moment. "Yet whether they be mortal or not doesn't change the fact that their powers and abilities are far greater than our own."

"Indeed it does not," Matilda replied firmly. "Nor do I mean to suggest for one instant that the fact of their mortality should tempt us to follow in Sir John's footsteps. Wherever these folk spring from, and whatever it is that they desire of us in the end, they have already demonstrated, as I'm sure they intended to, that our weapons cannot harm them. No, my lords, I meant only that I believe that their abilities spring not from the powers of Hell but from mortal skills and knowledge which we simply do not possess. We must remember in our dealings with them, and most especially in any dealings with the 'Commander,' that for all their power and all the wonders of this vessel, they are no doubt fallible and so may fail to fully understand our essential needs unless we explain them carefully."

She did not, Sir George noted, suggest that the fact that their captors were mortal implied that they could be killed even if merely human weapons couldn't harm them. It was a point worth putting away for future consideration, but also a dangerous one, and not simply because discussing it might prompt the "Commander" to take additional precautions. No, it was dangerous because dwelling upon it might tempt someone to attempt to act upon it, despite the grisly object lesson of young Denmore's fate.

"I will certainly bear that in mind in describing our needs and capabilities to him, my love," he said, with a careful emphasis on "capabilities," and she smiled slightly as she nodded back.

"Very well," the baron said more briskly, returning his attention to the men in the compartment. "We know roughly what our numbers are, and that we don't have the mounts we require. I believe my lady is correct in her belief that the 'Commander' intends to feed us and has the means to do so. Since these folk have said they will require us to fight for them, however, reason suggests that we must next consider what our needs of arms and other equipment may be. Given our numbers, I would be most surprised to discover that the 'Commander' intends for us to undertake siege operations without additional support, or to storm a city or fortress. If he does, then he clearly overestimates our capabilities . . . which," he added dryly, "seems unlikely."

The others surprised themselves by chuckling, and the baron's white teeth flashed in a bearded smile.

"I think we must assume that this guild the 'Commander' has spoken of intends to employ us as a field force. Why anyone with the powers and abilities they possess should need such as we to do their fighting I don't pretend to understand at this time, but I cannot believe they would go to such trouble to force us to serve them unless their need was both real and great. If that's true, then I think we must also assume that whatever battles they set us to fight will be hard ones, and also that it will be in their interest to see us as well equipped to give them victory as possible."

Several of the others nodded slowly, and all looked thoughtful as Sir George continued.

"This vessel of theirs, and all of the wondrous tools and powers they possess, suggest to me that they ought to be able to meet any reasonable request we might make of them. Surely, not even King Edward's exchequer could provide even a tiny fraction of what their ship alone represents! Bearing that in mind, I would have you all consider not simply what we may have lost of weapons and equipment, but also what we might wish to have had but never did." He smiled thinly. "Let us make the best of our situation, my friends. If we must fight for demon-jesters, then let us do it as the best equipped army England has ever sent afield . . . even if England never knows she has."

"I have considered your needs and the supplies you wish to request." The demon-jester's voice was as childlike and emotionless as ever, and Sir George wished yet again that the strange little creature had something a human could recognize as an expression. He stood facing the "Commander" across a beautiful, delicately wrought table of what appeared to be finest crystal. The demon-jester was seated in a comfortable, thickly upholstered chair which fit him perfectly and would have been far too small for any human, but no chair had been offered to Sir George. Nor was the baron unaware of the two dragon-men who stood protectively behind the demon-jester, watching him with their strange slit-pupilled, silver eyes.

The "Commander" paused, his own eyes fixed upon the baron and his foxlike ears half-cocked. No doubt the position of his ears was an expression—of sorts, at least—the baron reflected. If so, it wasn't one he recognized, yet he had the distinct impression that the demon-jester was waiting for him to react to his bald pronouncement.

"But I haven't yet told you what it is that we require," the baron said carefully after a moment.

"It is not necessary for you to do so," the demon-jester told him. "I have heard all that passed between you and your subordinates, and the computer has generated a complete list of all of the items you discussed."

Sir George remained far from certain what or who "Computer" was. Although the demon-jester spoke of him as dismissively as he might have referred to some minor clerk, the baron had already deduced that he was much more than that. Indeed, from what Sir George had already seen—or heard, rather—it was clear that Computer was a combination of the demon-jester's bailiff, military commander, and chief minister, and the English had already become accustomed to hearing Computer's tenor voice instructing them in the rules and regulations to which they were now subject. He had also initiated them into some, at least, of the mysteries which surrounded them and was busy instructing them in how to activate and deactivate some of the wondrous devices in the shipboard quarters to which they had been assigned. How any one being could discharge all of those duties simultaneously was more than Sir George could imagine . . . and so was the reason which could make someone that capable so obviously subservient to someone like the demon-jester.

Not that any of that mattered very much at a moment. What mattered was that the "Commander" already had (or thought he did, at any rate) the details of all that the baron was about to request . . . and that he (or Computer) had, indeed, been able to eavesdrop on all that was said. Sir George took careful note both of that confirmation and of the need to remind everyone to watch their words most carefully at all times.

"Most of what you think you need will not pose any great difficulties," the demon-jester continued in that unearthly voice. "The personal armor, the weapons, the harness and saddles—all of those can be readily produced by this ship's machine shops and synthesizers. Indeed, the only possible difficulty may be that the equipment you have described is so primitive. The industrial modules are configured to produce spares and other components for the ship and its support systems, and it will take us some time to properly program them to manufacture such crude items."

Once again, Sir George felt himself afloat upon a sea of half-understood and completely foreign concepts and ideas. Whatever device or magical power translated the demon-jester's own language into English obviously found itself required to create completely new words to label some of those concepts. That was undoubtedly a marvel. Unfortunately, simply attaching a label to something did nothing to explain what that something was. Not that the demon-jester seemed particularly concerned about explaining anything to someone he manifestly considered so far beneath himself.

"The one need you have identified which may pose some small challenge," the half-sized creature said, "is the matter of the horses. For technical reasons which need not concern you, the transport of such large animals is sometimes difficult. In the case of some similar species, the phase drive survival rate is low. We do not yet know whether this would be the case for your 'horses,' but the possibility exists."

He paused, looking—expressionlessly, of course—at Sir George, and the baron frowned.

"Are you saying . . . Commander, that there is no point in acquiring them in the first place?"

"I am saying that it may turn out in the end that there is no point," the demon-jester corrected. "That, however, is something we do not yet know for certain. Nor do I know how essential such beasts truly are for your military efficiency. While you and your subordinates discussed your need for horses at some length, you clearly felt no need to analyze precisely why you require them."

"Why we require them?" Despite himself, Sir George couldn't quite keep all of his incredulity at such ignorance out of his tone.

"You are primitives," the demon-jester told him in that infuriatingly dispassionate voice. "Your weapons and your tactics are so crude that no civilized species is remotely familiar with them. While the fact that you are such primitive barbarians is the very thing which gives you value to my guild, it also means that we do not possess the background data to fully evaluate ideas and practices which you obviously take completely for granted. It would be like expecting a civilized being to understand the techniques involved in skinning an animal for its pelt with nothing but one's teeth."

Sir George was very careful about his expression, but his jaw muscles bunched. It was hard to decide which was the more infuriating—the demon-jester's dismissal of the English as little more than dumb brutes, or the casual completely, matter-of-fact fashion in which he did it.

Nonetheless, the baron decided, there actually was some reason to what the creature had just said, for it was clear that Matilda had been correct. The demon-jester and his guild *were* limited in their understanding of things the English took completely for granted, if only because it had been so long since they had been required to understand them.

The demon-jester had paused once more, and Sir George gave himself a mental shake.

"We use horses for many things, Commander," he said then. "On the other hand, although we as yet understand very little about your . . . guild's abilities, it seems likely to me that we will no longer need to do some of the things for which we use horses, or oxen, for that matter. I speak here of draft animals for carts or wagons, or beasts to plow the fields, and such matters as that."

He paused, and the demon-jester's ears moved slightly once again.

"You will not require draft animals or farm beasts," his piping voice confirmed.

"I thought that might be the case," Sir George said with a nod. "But while we may not require them for those purposes, we will continue to need them for warfare, if we are to fight most effectively. At need, any of our men-at-arms can fight dismounted, but it isn't what some of them are best trained to do, and it would require us to sacrifice much of our mobility. None of the men with us are trained as heavy horse, but their ability to move rapidly about the field of battle and the . . . shock or impact when their charge strikes home make them far more effective than they would be afoot."

"I see." The demon-jester sat back in his chair and was silent for several seconds, then turned his attention back to Sir George.

"You say that your men will be 'more effective' on horses. Can you quantify the degree by which their effectiveness will be increased?" The creature paused, and Sir George looked at him, uncertain just what he was asking.

"You are even more primitive than I had thought possible," the demon-jester said after perhaps three heartbeats. "It is, I think, a sufficiently simple question that even you ought to be able to answer it, however. What I wish you to tell me is whether your 'men-at-arms' will be twice as effective mounted as on foot, or three times, or four."

"I would say that they would be at least twice as effective," Sir George replied after only the briefest pause of his own. He spent another few seconds ensuring that he had a firm grip upon his temper, then continued as reasonably as possible. "At the same time, Commander, it would be a mistake to consider only their effectiveness in the direct exchange of blows as the single factor in deciding whether or not to provide them with mounts."

"Explain," the demon-jester commanded.

"They are only one portion of my—your—total force. Each portion has its own strengths, its own weaknesses, its own part to play upon the field, however. If one portion of the total is weakened, then all are weakened, and what the force as a whole might accomplish is lessened. If I have no horse, then my mobility, my ability to react quickly to events or to recognize and exploit opportunities, will be greatly reduced."

He paused again, thinking hard, then shrugged.

"I suppose, Commander, that much depends upon what enemies you expect us to face, and why. In a purely defensive fight, the loss of my horsed element would pose less of a difficulty. I would still miss them, and their absence would be a handicap, but it would be a smaller handicap. In an attack upon a fortified position, again, horse is of less importance and wouldn't be missed as greatly. But if we're to fight open field battles, where maneuver is necessary and the features of the ground to be fought over may vary greatly from battle to battle, then the loss of my mounted force would create a serious weakness."

"I see," the demon-jester said. "I had not considered that something as antiquated as an actual riding beast could possess such significance for military operations. But as I have said, my guild is not accustomed to thinking in such primitive terms. For most of our history that has not mattered greatly, but of late things have been . . . different. So perhaps it behooves me to pay even greater attention to you and your warriors' requirements and capabilities than I had thought."

He paused once more, and for a moment Sir George assumed that the pause was for silent thought. Then he realized that the creature's speaking mouth was still moving, although he could hear nothing. For that matter, he realized now, he had *never* heard the demon-jester's actual voice, only the voice of whoever or whatever translated the "Commander's" language into human speech. Was that because the guild's arts kept him from hearing the other? Or was it because of something else? Was it possible that human ears simply couldn't hear the demon-jester, and if so, why not?

He gave himself another mental shake as he realized that the demon-jester's speaking mouth had stopped moving. The alien, purple-furred face gave no hint of what the creature might have been saying, or who or what he might have been saying it to, and the baron found himself longing passionately for some way to make an expression—any expression—cross it.

"I have given orders to return to your world," the demon-jester told him, and, despite himself, Sir George swallowed hard. It wasn't truly a surprise. He'd known from the very beginning that the stupendous, bronze vessel had never been born of any world peopled by humans, and the inevitable implication of that had been that he, his wife and son, and all of their people were bound for *other* worlds. He had no idea where those other worlds might lie, but he had thought he was as prepared as a man could be for the knowledge that he and his had been exiled to them, yet to hear it confirmed so casually hit like a fist.

"We will obtain the necessary genetic material and clone sufficient horses to meet your needs," the demon-jester continued. "There are drawbacks to this approach, but it offers advantages which more than outweigh the disadvantages. Among others, it will provide us with an ongoing supply if, as I fear is likely, these animals prove poorly suited to phase drive stasis. With the proper timing and techniques of forced growth, we can produce fresh mounts for your men for each battle."

Sir George drew a deep breath and asked God for patience. Not that God seemed to be paying a great deal of attention to his prayers of late.

"Commander, I don't understand a great deal of what you just said. In particular, I don't understand the word 'clone' at all. But if I've grasped the core of what you propose, I fear you are underestimating the 'disadvantages' of what you intend."

"Explain," the demon-jester said again.

"If you are proposing to somehow magically 'grow' fresh horses for us before each battle, then you are overlooking the need for us to train those horses and to accustom them to us even as we accustom ourselves to them. It takes a great deal of time—years—to properly train a horse for war, Commander. It isn't something which we could do in a day or two before taking them into battle. Moreover, each horse and each man are different, yet for a mounted man to perform at his best in battle, he and his mount must thoroughly understand one another. They fight not as individuals, but as one . . . as a *team*, and so we must also allow sufficient time for them to learn one another's ways."

"This is most unfortunate," the alien said. "Are you, then, saying that we must somehow provide you with trained mounts?"

"That would certainly be best," Sir George replied honestly. "If that proves impossible, however, we have the knowledge and skills to train them ourselves, assuming that we can be provided with sufficient space and time in which to do so."

"That would be better than nothing, I suppose," the demon-jester said, "but it would still be less than ideal. It would not be possible for us to operate our phase drive at higher than fifty percent power while you performed that training. Given the efficiency and translation curves, that power reduction would have serious consequences for our mobility."

"Commander, you are speaking now of things so far beyond my knowledge that I would have no idea at all of how to advise you," Sir George told him.

"Obviously," the demon-jester told him in what was probably a condescending tone, although there was no way for Sir

George to be certain. The alien gazed him for several seconds, then continued.

"On the other hand, there are other things upon which you can advise me. For reasons which need not concern you, it is desirable for us to limit contacts—which will be remembered, at least—with your kind on your planet. To be honest, it was for that reason that we selected your force to meet our needs in the first place. You would have perished without us, and your fellow humans will simply assume that that is precisely what you did do. If, however, we return to secure these horses for you, we risk being seen and leaving witnesses behind. This could create . . . undesirable complications for my guild. It will therefore be necessary for us to find a location in which the beasts you require, preferably already trained, can be obtained with the least risk that we will be observed obtaining them."

"I assume," Sir George said very carefully, "that you wouldn't wish to consider the possibility of sending me or one of my senior knights to purchase them for you?"

"You assume correctly," the demon-jester said.

"In that case, and given that you don't wish for anyone to see you, or any of your other servants, then undoubtedly the best opportunity would be a raid on some great noble's stud farm, preferably by night, when no one could see you or your servants clearly."

"And these 'stud farms' are isolated? There would be few humans about?"

"Depending upon the manor in question, yes," Sir George replied. "Much depends upon which manor you choose, of course. In even the best case, however, there will be some people about. Grooms, horse trainers, farriers. . . . There are always at least some peasants and their families who might well see you, even on the darkest night."

"You need not be concerned about that aspect. It would be as well to choose a manor where the numbers of humans present are relatively low, but those humans who might see us will never have the opportunity to report our presence to anyone else."

The calm announcement sent an icy chill through Sir George. It was impossible to mistake the demon-jester's meaning, and the baron felt a stab of bitter guilt. He was tempted to tell the alien that he had changed his mind, that the horses were unimportant—certainly not vital enough for the demon-jester to risk a return to Earth! But it would have been pointless. The half-sized creature wouldn't have believed him anyway, not after the way in which Sir George had just finished explaining exactly why he *did* need them. And even if the demon-jester had been likely to believe his sudden change of heart, he owed the men under his command the truth. Those horses wouldn't simply make them more effective in combat; the mounts would also make it far more likely that his men-at-arms would survive battle.

None of which made him feel any better about the realization that he had just unintentionally sentenced the entire population of some remote manor to death.

"The question, of course," the demon-jester went on, as if completely unaware that anything he might have said could have distressed Sir George in any way, "is which manor we should choose?"

The speaking mouth moved soundlessly once again, and the tabletop changed suddenly from diamond-clear crystal to an exquisitely detailed image. The alien waved Sir George closer, and the baron frowned. There was something about that image. . . . He couldn't put his finger on what that something was, for he had never seen anything quite like it. Or had he?

His frown deepened, and then he inhaled sharply. No wonder it looked so odd! Surely no human had ever dreamed of gazing down from such a height upon the earth below! Could even the highest-flying bird ever reach such a dizzying altitude? Before the huge bronze shape had appeared in a storm-sick sky to rip him away from all he had ever known, the baron would have said positively that nothing could have attained such a height. Now, however, he had learned that "impossible" meant far less than he had ever believed it did.

His wondering eyes moved slowly across the incredible image. He had never seen its like, not in the most beautifully detailed map, but surely that island was England. There was Ireland, as well, and the Irish Sea, and the Channel! And there—

His sense of wonder deflated suddenly as he recalled why he was looking at this dizzying picture of the world from which he and his people had been stolen. Somewhere upon it was a manor which was doomed to utter destruction . . . and the demon-jester would make Sir George Wincaster choose the slain.

He gazed longingly at the island he would never see again, but then he looked away. If someone must die, they would not be Englishmen. Nor would they be Welsh—or even Scots! No. If he must condemn innocents to death, he would at least choose them from among someone whose destruction might weaken the enemies of the monarch who had made him a knight.

He looked up at the demon-jester, then back at the map, and reached out a finger to the magically detailed folds and valleys and trees of France.

"I would recommend one from this area," Sir George Wincaster, Third Baron of Wickworth, told the small, bizarre creature which had made itself his master.

# III

"He's a devil, that one."

"No doubt," Sir George agreed as he stood beside Walter Skinnet and watched Seamus McNeely with the tall, coal-black stallion.

They stood in yet another cavern of gleaming bronze-colored alloy. In some ways, the English had begun to become accustomed to their new "home." In other ways, such as the compartment in which he and Skinnet stood, the vast ship became only more uncanny.

There was no way Sir George could be certain, but he had come to suspect that the interior of the demon-jester's huge vessel was not fixed. It seemed preposterous, yet they had seen ample evidence of the fashion in which their captors could change and modify *portions* of the interior. The chairs which had "grown" out of the deck for that first meeting with what had become the baron's council had seemed an impossible marvel, but since that day subsequent levels of marvel had begun to dull some of the English's awe. They had become no less marvelous, but familiarity applied even here.

Like the "stables." Sir George knew the ship had contained

no area configured to house horses before the demon-jester agreed to provide the English with mounts. There would have been no need for one. Besides, the demon-jester and Computer's tenor voice had spent almost three hours drawing a complete description of a proper stable from him. There would have been no need for that if they'd already had that information.

Yet when the horses were finally brought aboard (once again, Sir George's mind flinched away from the thought of what their acquisition had cost the manor from whence they had come), the stables had been ready and waiting. Vast stables, larger than any the baron had ever imagined, and with an attached exercise area at least three acres in extent, all at the heart of the huge ship. He saw no sign, looking about the stable cavern, that this space had ever had any other shape or purpose.

Of course, the stables weren't the only part of the ship which had been reshaped for its current use. For all of the casual contempt with which the demon-jester obviously regarded his human captives, he had bestowed upon them wondrous comforts without apparently even realizing how wonderful they were. One was "Computer." Sir George still had no idea just what Computer was, but he suspected that Computer was even more capable and responsible for even more duties than he had first assumed. The baron was tempted to think of him as the demon-jester's familiar, although he made a conscientious effort not to. Despite all of the "magical" aspects of their ship-prison, the attitude of the demon-jester and his constant references to "advanced species" and "technology" had convinced Sir George that what he actually saw was not magic but simply developments of the mechanical arts far beyond the capability of any human. Which wasn't to say that those developments would *always* be beyond human reach, although the "Commander" seemed oblivious to that possibility . . . or its potential consequences. However advanced the demon-jester's arts might be, he was as arrogant and foolish as any Frenchman Sir George had ever met. No doubt he felt secure in the invincibility of his devices and his dragon-man guards, but only a fool would show his contempt for soldiers in his service, however they came to be there, as plainly as he.

Nowhere did that arrogance show more clearly than in the combination of threats and bribery with which he attempted to enforce his will. The threats had been made manifest enough with the murder of Sir John Denmore; the bribes had taken longer to emerge, but in their own way, they were as impressive as the threats, and Computer was part of them.

It was Computer who had directed them through their "processing," and just as the demon-jester's own voice reached to every ear, wherever they might be within the ship, so did Computer's. But unlike the demon-jester—or, for that matter, the wart-faces or the dragon-men, none of whom had so far uttered a single word in any human's hearing—Computer also *listened.* One had only to speak his name for him to hear and respond, no matter where or when. Nor did it appear to matter to Computer who it was who called upon him, for he responded as promptly to the youngest apprentice as to Sir George himself. And whoever or whatever he was, Computer displayed a curious mixture of the demon-jester's own contempt for the English combined with a readiness to inform and teach which appeared infinitely patient.

It was Computer who had taught the English how to summon forth the many marvelous aspects of their quarters which were so much a part of the demon-jester's bribes. And, despite himself, Sir George had to admit that those bribes were seductive. King Edward himself could not have commanded many of the luxuries which the demon-jester, Computer, and the vessel in which they were imprisoned made available to even the lowliest of Sir George's men. True, their quarters were cramped, but each of Sir George's officers, even those with neither wife nor mistress, had at least one small compartment to himself. The common soldiers and the relatively small handful of civilians had to make do with a common barracks, but even the barracks boasted such incredible amenities as hot and cold running water, beds and tables and chairs which emerged from the deck or disappeared back into it upon command, and the restorative white vapor—all available from Computer upon request.

There were limits, however, to what Computer was prepared to explain. He always responded when he heard his name, but all too often his only response to a question was,"That information is not available at this level of clearance." He was obviously under orders to prevent the English from learning anything which might have allowed them to discover the nature of the demon-jester's mysterious guild, whither they were bound, or what might become of them in the end. It was an order he obeyed assiduously, yet he had allowed at least a few bits of knowledge to escape him.

In some ways, it was becoming difficult for the English to remember that there had ever been a time when they hadn't been aboard the demon-jester's stupendous ship. If Computer was to be believed—and Sir George saw no reason why he should bother to lie, when, as he had amply demonstrated, he could always simply refuse to answer—then the ship was voyaging between the very stars even as he and Skinnet stood speaking. The idea of such travel verged too perilously close to heresy, or at least blasphemy, for Sir George's comfort, yet his concept of reality was acquiring a certain elasticity. He had little choice in that regard; it was a matter of adjust or succumb to madness, and he had too many responsibilities for that. Nor would Matilda have forgiven him, he thought with an inner grin.

That grin faded slowly as he watched McNeely and the stallion. It was impossible to say precisely how long they had been aboard the demon-jester's ship, for when there was no sun or moon, there were no days or nights. It never became entirely dark in the corridors and passages of the portion of the stupendous vessel which had been set aside for the use of Sir George and his people, but the lighting dimmed on a regular basis which seemed to correspond more or less to the length of a normal day. There was no way to be certain that it did, however, and thereby hung yet another of the endless chain of things for the baron to worry about. Computer apparently saw no reason to keep track of time for them, and with neither calendars nor any means to know how their "days" corresponded to those of the world they had always known, there was no way to keep track accurately of saints' days, Christmas or Easter, or even whether or not it was truly Sunday!

Father Timothy, as the only ordained priest aboard, had brought that concern to Sir George's attention. Fortunately, he had been wise enough to do so privately, and Sir George, Matilda, and he had been able to discuss the difficulty between themselves before anyone else appeared to have thought of it on his own. In the end, Timothy had found himself with yet another responsibility as their official timekeeper.

"All we may do is the best that mortals can," Sir George had declared finally. "God surely understands the difficulties we face, and no doubt He'll make allowances for us. With neither dawn nor sunset, we can only count the days as best we may and set aside Sundays and feast days when our count says they fall."

"I can't say I like it, My Lord," Father Timothy said heavily, "yet neither can I see any other avenue open to us. And, as you say, surely God, in His infinite mercy, will forgive us if we err."

"No doubt He will," Matilda agreed, "but I fear that some of our folk may react . . . poorly once the implications strike home fully. Some of them already find it difficult to believe that the wart-faces and dragon-men are truly mortal and not demons, whatever we may tell them."

"Which is why it is particularly important that we present a united front on this matter," her husband said with a nod. "We must be certain Sir Richard and Sir Anthony and all the other senior officers are forewarned and prepared to take the same position when we make our announcement."

"And the same for those who aren't soldiers," Matilda said thoughtfully. "I should discuss this first with Lady Margaret, I think. Sir Bryan isn't our most senior knight, but his lady is levelheaded, and the other women already look to her almost as much as to me for advice and counsel."

"A good choice, My Lady," Father Timothy approved. "And I will take Tom Westman aside."

Sir George nodded. Westman was their master smith, a skilled craftsman who was highly respected among the common folk.

"It might be as well," Matilda suggested after a moment, "to point out that the dates set by Mother Church for religious days have been changed from time to time to reflect our best understanding of when they ought to fall. We have no councils of bishops to aid us, but surely God will guide us, armed by our Faith, now that we find ourselves forced to set dates of our own."

"So long as no one suspects me of attempting to usurp the authority of Rome!" Father Timothy said with a slightly uneasy chuckle.

"No one will accuse you of usurping anything, Timothy," Sir George replied. "Yet I think you must accept that you stand the closest to bishop or archbishop we have or are ever like to have."

"I cannot claim such authority, My Lord!"

"I didn't say you must," Sir George said calmly. "Yet whether you claim it or not, you come closer to it than anyone else among us, and all our folk, gentle and common alike, will look to you for guidance." He smiled almost compassionately at his old tutor and reached out to rest a hand on one broad shoulder as the priest looked at him uneasily. "Come, Timothy!

Wasn't it you who taught a young boy that no man may turn his back upon the task God calls him to? And at least you have this—God is always present, always with us, and you can always ask Him for guidance. My own position is less comfortable, for I fear it would take more time than we have for me to consult with the King or his Council!"

"As you say, My Lord," Father Timothy had acknowledged, and if he continued to cherish doubts about the authority thrust upon him, no sign of that had colored his manner when the question of holy days finally arose. Despite the united front of their leaders, some of their people remained uneasy, and Sir George knew it. But it was only one of many sources of uneasiness, and by far the greater part felt only relief in resigning that particular worry into the capable hands of Father Timothy, particularly once he was able to establish a regular cycle of "Sunday" masses. Whether it was the "right" Sunday or not mattered far less to them than that it was *a* Sunday, and they embraced the comforting tradition of their faith eagerly.

Fortunately, explaining to the demon-jester why they needed a compartment to sanctify and set aside as God's holy church had been less difficult than Sir George had anticipated. The alien had granted the request with thinly veiled contempt for such "primitive superstition," but that attitude was only to be expected. It was certainly part and parcel of every other attitude he had demonstrated, at any rate, and Sir George wondered occasionally if such bizarre creatures as he or his wart-face or dragon-man servitors had souls to concern themselves over in the first place.

That was yet another problem for Father Timothy, however, and not one the baron worried himself unduly over. Particularly not when he had so many others to solve, including the one which brought him here today with Skinnet.

"I know you've a taste for spirit in your horses, My Lord," the grizzled veteran said now, "and I've not seen a better horseman. Mind," he added, a faint smile gleaming in his eyes,

"I've seen some as good. Aye, and some of them came to grief looking for 'spirit' in a horse, now that I think on it!"

"I'm sure you have," Sir George acknowledged.

"And so has Seamus," Skinnet pointed out, jutting his chin at the bald-pated trainer trying the stallion's paces.

Seamus McNeely, the Irishman Sir George had made the master of his stables years before, was working cautiously with the horse, and the baron hid a smile as he watched. Seamus had begun his career as a stableboy at the age of six. That had been over forty years ago, and there were few equine idiosyncrasies he hadn't encountered in that time. From the way in which he was working this particular horse, it was obvious that experience-honed warning signals were sounding in his brain.

"If you'll pardon my saying it, My Lord," Skinnet went on with the diffident obstinacy a long time henchman was permitted, "you'd be wiser to stay away from him. Or to have him cut."

"No," Sir George said firmly.

"If you'll not cut him, then best to put him to stud. It's not always true what some say, that only a fool would ride an uncut stallion, but that one . . ." The experienced cavalryman shook his head. "He'll kill someone for certain someday," Skinnet predicted gloomily. "You see if I'm not right!"

"As long as it's the right someone, I've no objection," Sir George said mildly. "And I'd rather have a beast with spirit under me when my own life is on the table."

"I'll not argue with you there," Skinnet conceded, "but there's spirit and there's pure, poison meanness, and that's what this devil has in plenty."

"Perhaps, and perhaps not. We'll see what Seamus thinks after a day or two."

"With all respect, My Lord, Seamus McNeely would say the sun rises in the west if you ordered him to," the compactly built veteran said with a short chuckle, but then he shook his head. "No, that's not fair to old Seamus. He'd not *say* the sun rises in the west, but he'd do his damnedest to make it rise there!"

"And so he should, if I told him to," Sir George shot back with a grin, and Skinnet laughed. But the laugh was brief, and his expression was serious as he shook his head once more.

"All very well, My Lord, all very well. But we'll none of us think it funny if that devil breaks your neck! Bad enough if something like that had happened in France, but now—?"

"I'm mindful of what you're saying, Walter," Sir George replied after a long moment. "But if I'm to lead and command, then lead and command I must, and on the field, I want Satan himself under me!"

"Aye? Well, if it's Satan you want, My Lord, I think you've found him, right enough."

"What progress have you made with training your beasts?"

Sir George stood facing the demon-jester across the same crystal table. The chamber in which the table sat had changed since his last visit here. The walls were a dark, soothing green, and the space directly behind the demon-jester had assumed the breathtakingly real appearance of a shady forest glade. The trees and lush, low-growing bushes with their brilliant crimson and gold blossoms resembled nothing Sir George had ever seen before. The tree leaves were long fingered, delicate, and seven pointed, and the tree trunks were covered in a bark which looked almost like the soft fur of a cat. The bushes had knifelike leaves that were almost black, veined in red, and even as he watched some small, careless creature came too close to one of them. The entire bush flexed and quivered as if struck by a sudden, high wind, and then its limbs pounced.

That was the only word Sir George could think of for it. The limbs *pounced*, striking downwards, their leaves turning inward like the knives they so resembled, and the bush's prey squealed a high, piercing note of agony as hooklike briars seized and tore at it. The bush thrashed and jerked for a few more moments, then all was still once more.

"What progress have you made with training your beasts?" the demon-jester repeated, and Sir George pulled his eyes away from the forest glade.

"Good progress, Commander," he replied. "Some of them aren't really suited to the field, but we have enough good mounts to put under two hundred men. I would prefer to continue training with them, but for the most part, I feel satisfied with what we've accomplished."

"I am glad to hear it," the demon-jester told him. "We have spent too long at half power as it is. We shall be forced to operate at almost ninety-five percent power levels for the remainder of the voyage to make up the lost time. This will entail a certain degree of risk to the vessel and all aboard it, and we must begin immediately. If we wait any longer, the power levels and risk factor will become entirely unacceptable."

"I'm sorry if we've delayed you," the baron said with great insincerity, "but the training time we took was necessary. Without it, we couldn't have fought with full efficiency for you."

"I am aware of that. And if I were not convinced that it was true, then you would be dead," the demon-jester piped.

Sir George made no reply to that. There was nothing he could have said even if he'd wanted to, and he didn't want to.

The demon-jester watched him with all three eyes for a few more seconds, then twitched his ears ever so slightly.

"You and your people and your horses will be placed in phase drive stasis," he said. "The first time you experience this, it may cause some panic, especially among primitives such as yourselves. It will be your task, and that of your officers, to maintain order during the process and after recovery."

"You and Computer have mentioned this . . . stasis, before,"

Sir George said in his most reasonable voice. "Neither I nor any of my officers are clear about just what may be involved in it, or even what it is. If we're to 'maintain order during the process,' it would be very helpful if we knew what was to happen."

There was a long moment of silence, as if the demon-jester were considering what Sir George had said. Then he spoke once more in the fluting, uninflected voice of whatever accomplished the translating.

"Living creatures cannot survive the physical stress exerted upon their systems by a phase drive field operating at power levels in excess of fifty percent. This is an unavoidable consequence of attaining supralight velocities. To protect the crews and passengers of our vessels from the dangers involved, we place them in stasis. Your crude language and primitive worldview do not contain the referents which would permit me to truly explain this process to you. However, you may think of it as being placed in a deep sleep, from which you will not awaken until the completion of the voyage."

"Sleep?" Sir George regarded the demon-jester with carefully hidden skepticism, then glanced at the forever silent, forever expressionless dragon-men standing watchfully at the demon-jester's back.

Despite himself, the baron found himself fascinated by the dragon-men. Over the long weeks he and his people had now been aboard their ship-prison, the wart-faces had begun to emerge as an at least partially known quantity. They had a language of their own—of sorts, at any rate—but it seemed to be a poor and clumsy tongue, composed primarily of grunts and growls, interspersed with an occasional whistle. Unlike the humans or dragon-men, they were not garbed in one-piece suits, either. Instead, they wore heavy tunics dotted with metallic studs, almost like leather jacks . . . and, also unlike the humans, at least a few of them were allowed to retain weapons. Since the activation of the "phase drive" the demon-jester kept going on about, no one had seen them in proper armor or armed with the axes which appeared to be their accustomed weapons, except in the presence of the demon-jester personally or another of the ship's crew. But several of them carried heavy truncheons, almost maces, wherever they went. They had turned up along the walls of the exercise chamber the first time Sir George's longbowmen had been permitted to practice their archery. Despite the disgusted protests of his archers, their shafts had been headless, which had made the presence of what were so obviously guards more than a little superfluous in Sir George's opinion, but the demon-jester obviously wasn't interested in the baron's opinion.

The wart-faces had put in more frequent appearances in the humans' portion of the ship after that, especially whenever the troops drilled with the blunted practice weapons Computer issued to them for that purpose. Their function, obviously, was to police and intimidate the English, but they were only partly successful. No one was foolish enough to think that the obviously physically strong and tough creatures would be easy opponents, but neither were English soldiers easily intimidated. Like Sir George himself, his troops appeared to be quite confident that they could have swarmed the wart-faces under if they'd had to.

Of course, the attempt would undoubtedly prove fatal in the long run, because the wart-faces who were allowed into the humans' area were no more than expendable bludgeons as far as the demon-jester was concerned. The wart-faces couldn't even open one of the abruptly appearing and disappearing doors unless the demon-jester or one of the other crew members opened it for them. And whatever else the wart-faces might have been, clearly no one, themselves included, thought of them as members of the ship's actual crew.

Sir George certainly didn't. There was an obvious hierarchy of status among the denizens of the demon-jester's ship, and the wart-faces had almost as much status as trained mastiffs . . . which was to say, considerably more than the humans enjoyed. The baron had seen only a very few true crew members, although he was unsure whether that meant he had seen only a small fraction of the total crew or that the crew was impossibly small for a ship of such vast size. He would have inclined toward the former explanation, if not for Computer's and the demon-jester's casual demonstrations of how much their "technology" allowed one being to accomplish.

Most of the crew members he had actually seen were neither wart-faces nor dragon-men, but rather members of yet a fourth species, very tall and spindly looking. They had very long legs for their height, and Sir George felt certain that the chairs which had been provided for himself and his Council's first meeting had actually been designed to fit their sort of body.

The only other member of the demon-jester's own species any of the humans had yet seen was the Physician, who was clearly the second ranking member of the crew. Computer occasionally referred to the Physician as the "Ship's Doctor," or "Surgeon," but he was unlike any human surgeon. He used none of the instruments with which Sir George's military experience had made him only too familiar. Instead, he relied upon still more of the mysterious devices, with their flickering lights and occasional humming sounds or musical tones, that sometimes seemed to pack even this enormous ship to the bursting point. Precisely what any of those devices did was, of course, yet another mystery their captors had no intention of sharing with them, nor had Dickon Yardley, Sir George's senior surgeon, been able to suggest any answers. Despite their ignorance as to precisely what the Physician did, and how, every single human—men, women, and children alike—had been required to visit him in the chamber Computer called "Sick Bay" and submit to his poking, prodding, and peering.

In some odd way the fact that the Physician wasn't human

had actually made that easier to endure, but the examinations had remained arduous trials for most of the English. Sir George had found his own experience sufficiently daunting to make him wish passionately that he had been permitted to accompany Matilda, or at least Edward, when it was their turn. That had not been allowed, however, and perhaps it was just as well. Matilda had been uncharacteristically reluctant to discuss her visit to Sick Bay, but she had said enough to make Sir George doubt he could have made himself stand by, threats or no threats, and watch the Physician maul and prod her.

Despite that, he had to admit that the Physician's ministrations, coupled with the draconian hygiene regulations which the Physician and Computer had hammered home, had produced a something very like a miracle. For the first time in Sir George's experience as a soldier, there was not a single case of illness of any sort in his entire company. Not one. Not a flux, not a fever, not even a common cold. Nothing.

That made even putting up with the Physician endurable.

Yet the opportunity to see other members of the crew had only served to strengthen Sir George's conviction that the dragon-men held a special position, somewhere between full members of the crew and the wart-faces. Unlike the wart-faces, the dragon-men had yet to utter a single sound anywhere any human might have heard it. Of course, the English saw much less of the dragon-men than of the wart-faces, for unlike the wart-faces, the dragon-men had never again entered the human-occupied portion of the ship once the original processing procedures and initial meetings of the baron's Council had been completed. Perhaps that was part of the reason for Sir George's fascination with them—the fact that familiarity had been given no chance to wear off the corners of their strangeness.

Still, if he'd seen less of them than he had of the wart-faces, he'd seen far more of them than any of his followers had. At least one was always present, like a silent, gray-green-scaled shadow, whenever he was admitted to the crew's portion of the ship to report to the demon-jester or receive orders from him, and he had long since realized that the dragon-men were as unlike the wart-faces as it was possible for any creature to be.

The wart-faces moved with an odd, toadlike gait that was well-suited to their powerful, hulking bodies. There was nothing even remotely graceful about them, and they seemed to radiate a sullen, dangerous violence, as if they were in fact the half-trained brutes they appeared to human eyes. They were . . . enforcers of the demon-jester's will, an extension of the same terror tactics he had introduced when he murdered young Denmore on that very first day.

But the dragon-men, for all their alien appearance, moved with a sort of lean grace. Sir George suspected that they were even stronger physically than they appeared, probably more powerful than the wart-faces themselves, yet they did not carry themselves with the same ponderous air of threat. And unlike the wart-faces, who appeared to be limited to their truncheons under normal circumstances, the dragon-men always bore the fire weapons like the one which had killed Denmore.

Yet for all of that, it was obvious to Sir George that the silent dragon-men were no more members of the ship's crew than he himself was. More trusted and perhaps somewhat better treated than the English, yes, but still inferiors. Still . . . slaves.

Now the guard standing behind the demon-jester returned the baron's half-questioning gaze with those oddly beautiful, completely inhuman silver eyes and his customary alien inscrutability.

"How can we 'sleep' for so long a period?" Sir George asked finally, returning his eyes from the dragon-man to the demon-jester.

"I did not say it would be sleep; I said that you could think of it as sleeping," the demon-jester replied.

As always, it was impossible to tell from his translated voice whether he felt impatience or irritation at being asked questions. On the other hand, Sir George had discovered that for all his other character flaws—and God knew they were legion!—the demon-jester wouldn't punish him for asking questions. If he grew tired of answering them, he would simply ignore them, but that was all he would do . . . unlike his reaction to anything he might perceive as defiance. Sir George was a brave and hardy man, yet the mere memory of the one time he had argued with the demon-jester for a sentence too long was enough to break him out in a cold sweat. The term "punish" took on a whole new meaning when a three-eyed, alien creature touched the crystalline pendant around his neck and a man's very bones became white-hot irons buried in his flesh.

"I used the term sleep because there is no point in trying to explain the actual process to you," the demon-jester went on now. "I might have used a great many other words and terms in an effort to communicate the techniques of stasis and the reasons for it, but your primitive language and brain would be unable to grasp their meaning. What matters is that so far as you and the rest of your people will be able to tell, you will simply go to sleep and awaken, well rested and fresh, when we reach our destination."

"I see." The demon-jester might not punish questions, Sir George reflected, but he was quite capable of answering them in a way which made his utter contempt for the person who had asked them clear. Not that he'd been any more contemptuous this time than he always was. Indeed, Sir George had come to question whether or not the demon-jester even realized he was showing his contempt. Or that humans might be intelligent enough to recognize it when he did. Or if there were any difference between those two possibilities.

"When we do arrive at your destination," the baron went on after a moment, "what will happen?"

"That is not your concern," the demon-jester's piping voice told him. "When the time comes, you will be told what it is necessary for you to know in order to discharge your function."

"With all due respect, Commander," Sir George replied, "if our 'function' is to engage your enemies in battle, then the more you can tell me about the sort of enemy we may face, the better. I need that information in order to plan my tactics and train and rehearse the men in them."

"You will fight who we tell you to fight, when we tell you to fight them, and where we tell you to fight them," the demon-jester informed him.

"I haven't suggested that we wouldn't," Sir George said very carefully. "But if you will recall the matter of the horses, and why we needed them, I think that the conversation we had then should suggest to you why I need as much knowledge as you can give me. And why you should permit me to formulate my own battle plan."

"And why should we do such a thing? How can primitives such as you grasp the reasons we require you to fight or plan the battle as well as we can?"

"We might surprise you with our understanding of the reasons you send us into battle." Sir George's voice was level, and he held the demon-jester's three-eyed gaze with his own. "As a rule, it's usually wise to tell your field commander what it is you hope to accomplish, so that he can adjust and respond most advantageously to the fleeting opportunities which can present themselves in the midst of battle. But that decision is up to you, of course.

"Whatever the goal you seek, however," he went on, "the nature of your enemy, his numbers, his weapons, how he normally fights—if we're to achieve victory for you, these are things which must be taken into account by someone who understands my own troops' capabilities. And as you yourself have said, your people are too advanced to fully comprehend what my primitively armed and equipped soldiers can and cannot accomplish. I, on the other hand, am fully aware of both their strengths and their limitations.

"I won't pretend that we are eager or happy to fight for you, Commander. You wouldn't believe me if I did, for you know as well as I that we never chose to serve you or your guild. But you may believe me when I say that we are even less eager to die, and in that much at least our desires run together. You wish us to fight for you and achieve victory; we wish to stay alive, and staying alive requires us to win the battle for you as quickly and efficiently as we may. It seems to me, then, that the more complete my knowledge of your enemies is, and the greater my freedom to plan the tactics which we will employ, the better we may each achieve our goals."

He started to say something more, then closed his mouth firmly. He might very well already have said more than enough, and he felt his jaw clenching in anticipation of the agonizing punishment the demon-jester had inflicted once before. Yet even as he awaited punishment, his eyes never wavered from the demon-jester's, for what he had just said was neither more nor less than the simple truth. The very thought of allowing the demon-jester to plan the actual tactics for a battle was enough to make a grown man's knees weak. Sir George's mixed force of archers and cavalry was a potent and flexible tool of war, but only in the hands of someone who understood its strengths and weaknesses and who knew better than to place too great a strain upon it.

And whatever he might think of the demon-jester, his guild, or its objectives, Sir George was determined to lose no more of his men than he must.

"It may be that there is something in what you say," the demon-jester told him after a long, nerve-twisting pause. "As you have been honest with me, I have always been honest with you. If you fight well for my guild, we will reward you with long life, good health, and good care. If you do not fight well for us, we will destroy you and seek out another force of primitives who can and will achieve our goals for us. And, as you have pointed out, we are much less conversant than you are with all of the capabilities and weaknesses of your force. But if we permit you to plan your own tactics, then be warned that we will expect complete victory from you. And if we do not receive it, then it is entirely possible that you will be discarded and replaced with one of your officers."

"I understand," Sir George replied levelly.

"See that you do," the demon-jester said in his fluting, uninflected voice. "Because if we discard and replace you, we will have no reason to preserve your mate, either."

Sir George Wincaster's eyes popped open.

He lay still for several slow, deep heart beats, staring up at the opalescent ceiling from the large, coffinlike device in which he had gone into "stasis."

The heavy gray mist which had filled it when first he had lain down in it had dissipated, replaced by the normal air of the ship with its slight, omnipresent tang of lightning. He was naked, as he'd been when sleep overtook him, and he felt a remembered rush of anger. All the humans had gone into "stasis" naked, men and women alike. The Physician had seemed completely oblivious to any reason this might have evoked resentment, and only the memory of the punishment the demon-jesters could inflict, and the knowledge that it would be inflicted upon Matilda and Edward, as well, had prevented Sir George from rebelling against this fresh humiliation.

But he *had* remembered that punishment, and the courage which would have accepted it for himself was unequal to accepting it for his wife and child. And because that was so, and because he couldn't allow his example to lead others into the same rebellion and the same punishment, he'd managed—somehow; he doubted he would ever truly know how—to keep his tongue behind his teeth and still.

Even through his fury and resentment, he'd felt a yet fiercer stir of pride at how regally Matilda had held her head as she disrobed in the presence of dozens of men. She had somehow transformed the humiliation into a badge of courage and composure, and he had felt a different sense of pride as his officers averted their eyes from her nakedness. Some of the other women had objected. Some had wept, and at least one had become hysterical until the Physician sprayed something into her face, but the others—the vast majority of them all—had taken their example from Matilda, just as the rest of his men had taken theirs from his officers.

Now, as awareness flowed back into him, he knew that they would face the reverse of the same ordeal, but he didn't have to do that yet, and so he lay there a moment longer, allowing his newly awakened senses to report back to him. The air about him was chill, much closer to the cool, almost cold temperatures the demon-jester preferred than to the temperature at which the humans' quarters were normally kept. He shivered slightly, but the nip of the chill was insufficient to pierce the sensation of well-being and rest which suffused him. It was as if the sense of vigor and health the cleansing vapor always left in its wake had been doubled and redoubled while he slept. As if he could leap tall fortress walls in full armor or fly like the storm winds of Heaven itself.

He inhaled deeply, savoring the sensation of pressure and strength in his chest, then sat up smoothly in his "coffin" (the Physician had called it a "stasis bed," but it still looked like a coffin to Sir George) and looked around.

Other men were sitting up in their own stasis beds. Sir Richard, Sir Anthony, Sir Bryan, and Rolf Grayhame were all within ten yards of him, but even as his eyes swept over them, his sense of euphoria vanished.

The stasis beds on either side of his own were still closed, still filled with the gray mist . . . and with Matilda and Edward.

# IV

"There was no reason to awaken them at this time," the demon-jester said. There was no more expression in his voice than ever, nor did his body language give any hint of his feelings, and Sir George wondered if the small creature was properly grateful for the two dragon-men who towered behind him, one at each shoulder. Despite all that had happened, despite the example of young Denmore, despite the punishment Sir George himself had endured, he wasn't at all certain he could have kept his hands from the demon-jester's throat had those guards not been present.

"We do not require their services; we require those of yourself and your warriors," the demon-jester continued. "Their presence would only have distracted you when you ought to be preparing for and concentrating upon the battle you are here to fight. All of your attention should be upon that task."

"Our ability to concentrate will be hampered by our concern over the safety of our . . . mates," Sir George got out through gritted teeth.

"Your mates and young are completely safe . . . so long as

you fight well and achieve victory," the demon-jester told him. "Nothing can harm them in their stasis beds, and if you bring us the victory we require, they will be awakened and restored to you as your justly earned reward. If you do not fight well, of course, there will be no reason for us to awaken them."

Sir George stared at the purple-furred face with a hatred more bottomless than he had ever imagined he could feel, yet there was nothing at all that he could do . . . except for the thing his commander—his *master*—demanded of him as the price for the return of his love.

"Very well, Commander," he managed to say in a voice he scarcely recognized. "In that case, let us prepare to do just that."

Sir George looked down as if from a great height, floating disembodied above the plain of deep purple grass, as the huge, six-limbed creatures lumbered forward. Each of them stood at least nine feet tall, with two legs and four massive arms, all covered in long, coarse hair. The hair's base color ranged from a dull ocher through rust to an almost painfully bright red, but each creature's pelt was also marked with a mottled black or brown pattern of spots and rings.

There were two armies of the creatures, moving towards one another in an awkward-looking, hunched lope that managed to cover ground with surprising speed. None wore any armor, although the patches of leathery skin he could see here and there, peeping through the coarse hair, looked tough enough to stand for armor if it had to. For weapons, most of them carried a pair of two-handed axes which dwarfed even those of the wart-faces. Others carried maces, flails, or long pikelike spears, and a very few, perhaps five percent of the total, carried quivers of long darts, like javelins.

As the two armies neared one another, the warriors with the darts began to hurl them, and the disembodied baron tried to purse nonexistent lips in a whistle of astonishment. The dart-throwers carried some sort of sticks, and as he watched, he saw them fit the butt ends of their darts into the ends of the sticks. Then they snapped their arms up in graceful arcs, and the sticks were like extensions of those arms. The alien creatures were already far longer-limbed than any human, and the sticks gave them a reach and allowed them to exert a leverage which sent their darts whistling out to unbelievable ranges.

Sir George had never seen anything quite like it, but it reminded him a little of the staff sling he had once seen a shepherd use. He'd never known where the shepherd, a Scot, had gotten the sling, and the lad hadn't been very accurate with it, but he'd been able to throw stones to an extraordinary distance. These four-armed monstrosities, on the other hand, were *extremely* accurate, and he judged that their range was very close to that of a Genoese crossbowman. His longbowmen could outmatch that by at least a little, and their rate of fire would be higher, but not as much higher as it would have been compared to crossbows. In fact, with four arms and two throwing sticks each of these creatures could come very close to equaling a single longbow's rate of fire.

Fortunately, neither army seemed to have very many of them, and he wondered why that was. If *he* had commanded either of those forces, he would have mustered every dart-thrower he could find!

But the reason, whatever it was, became immaterial as the two armies continued to close through the deadly hail of darts. Their blood, he noted, was a bright orange, quite unlike human blood, except for the way it spurted and ran as darts drove into bellies and chests and four-armed corpses thudded to the ground like so much slaughtered meat or shrieked and writhed in agony that was all too humanlike.

Even with their high rate of fire, none of the dart-throwers on either side had emptied their quivers when the two charging battlelines slammed into one another, and Sir George's immaterial eyes narrowed. The demon-jester had called the English "primitive"; Sir George wondered what he would have called *these* creatures. The baron was no stranger to the terror and howling chaos of hand-to-hand combat and the way every soldier's world narrowed to the tiny space within the reach of his own weapons, yet never in all of his battles had he ever seen anything like *this*—not even from an army of Scots! Indeed, he doubted that anyone had ever seen its like since the days when men finally stopped painting themselves blue before going out to hack and hew at their neighbors.

There was no formation, no effort to maintain line or interval. There were simply two mobs of nine-foot monsters, each armed with two axes or spears, or here and there one spear and an axe, or a pair of massive flails, all slashing and stabbing away at anything that came into range. It was sheer, howling bedlam, without rhyme or reason, and it went on far longer than he would have believed it could.

While it lasted, casualties were brutal. However thick the hide under their coats of coarse hair might be, in the end it was only hide over flesh and bone, and not one of those warriors carried a shield. Nor, so far as he could tell, had any of these hulking warriors ever even heard of the notion of blocking or parrying blows when it might have been attacking, instead. It was all offense and no defense, and blood soaked the grass and turned dry soil into gory mud. Either the fighters were in the grip of battle madness, or else they were too stupid to realize how dreadful the carnage was . . . or so unlike any human Sir George had ever known that the death toll truly didn't matter to them at all. Those were the only explanations he could think of for how long those two armed mobs stood toe-to-toe, smashing away at one another in an orgy of mutual destruction.

But finally one side had had enough. Its surviving warriors turned to flee, and, as always happened, their foes howled and lunged forward as they turned their backs, cutting down still more of them.

In the end, the routed side managed to outrun the victors—partly because they had thrown away their encumbering weapons, and partly because those who are fleeing from death always tend to be just a little faster than those who are simply pursuing to kill.

Sir George floated above the field of battle, watching the victors tend crudely to their own fallen and slit the throats of their wounded enemies, and then, slowly, his vision faded away.

Sir George sat upright on the comfortably padded bench and, as Computer had instructed him to do when the "briefing" ended, removed the "neural interface" headset.

His hand trembled ever so slightly as he set the headset aside. Computer had told him what he would see, but he'd lacked the experience to fully understand what the unseen voice was telling him. He hadn't realized that it would be *real*—that he would be able to hear the shrieks of the wounded, smell the subtly alien copper scent of the blood or the all too familiar sewer stench of ruptured organs and death. This was one piece of the demon-jester's magical arts that the baron felt no desire to understand. Not just now. Not until the familiar shudders and belly tightening echoes of combat had worked their way through him and subsided.

He heard a small sound behind him, and turned to see Sir Richard, Rolf Grayhame, Walter Skinnet, and Dafydd Howice sitting up on their own benches. Their individual responses to what they'd just seen were interesting. Grayhame and Howice looked almost completely normal, more thoughtful than anything else. Skinnet looked much unhappier than either of the two archers did, but that was obviously because he was considering the size and reach of the opponents he and his men-at-arms would be required to meet weapon-to-weapon. But Sir Richard looked very much like Sir George felt, and the baron found himself smiling sympathetically at the slightly older knight.

"Tough bastards, if you don't mind me saying so, Sir," Grayhame said after a moment. "Don't care much for how far they can throw them spears of theirs, either."

"I'm not so very happy about that my own self," Howice agreed. "Still, Rolf, I'm thinking our lads have the range on them, by a bit, at least."

"Not by much," Grayhame grumbled. "Not by near so much as I'd like, any road!"

"Aye," Skinnet grunted, "but at least your lot can stand off and shoot the bastards. *My* lads won't have that luxury."

"No," Sir George agreed, "they won't. On the other hand, I've no intention of sending you off to face them until they've been softened up a bit, Walter. Not when I'm riding along with them, at any rate!"

"With all due respect, Sir George," Maynton put in, "I'm of the opinion that you *shouldn't* be riding along with them even then. You're the one man we can least afford to lose."

"We can't afford to lose anyone at all, if we can help it," Sir George replied. "And if I'm going to send men off on a charge, then it's a charge I'll be making, too."

"You might as well give over, Sir Richard," Skinnet said sourly. "I've been trying for years to convince him that there might be just a mite of sense in putting the commander someplace besides dead center in the front line of a charge. You'd almost think he was French."

"There's no need to go insulting me, Walter," Sir George said mildly.

"All my life I've called a spade a spade, My Lord. I'm not about to change now."

"Well, whether you've a mind to change or not," Sir George told him, "I'm of the mind that with a little forethought and a little planning this might not be so very bad after all."

"And just how did you come to that conclusion, if you don't mind my asking, My Lord?" Skinnet responded with the skepticism of a retainer who knows his liege's trust in him is complete.

"Why, you said it yourself, when you were abusing me just a few moments ago," Sir George said. "They may be nine feet tall and covered with hair, but the way they just come right at you reminds me mightily of French noblemen or the Scots, and Computer says that what we've just seen is typical. So I'm thinking, the way to see them off is the same way His Majesty welcomed the Scots at Halidon Hill."

"I do not like this plan," the demon-jester piped.

"I can't say that I'm entirely pleased with it myself, Commander," Sir George replied levelly across the crystal table. "Unfortunately, the estimates of the enemy's strength which Computer has provided, added to the distance to which they can throw their spears, leaves little other choice. By Computer's most favorable estimation, we'll be outnumbered by at least six to one, and our bows give us much less of a range advantage than I could like. Moreover, despite their lack of armor, these creatures will be very dangerous opponents when it comes to hand blows . . . not to mention the fact that each of them has twice as many arms as any of my lads do."

"If the ratio of forces is so unfavorable," the demon-jester said, "then you should use all of your manpower."

"My plan does use all of my *trained* manpower." Sir George emphasized the adjective heavily in hopes that whatever translated for him and the demon-jester would pick up the stress.

"It does not use over ten percent of your total force of males," the demon-jester stated, and Sir George nodded.

"You're correct, of course, Commander," he acknowledged. "But you yourself have told me time and again that my men represent a valuable asset for your guild. The men whom you wish me to use aren't trained for this sort of task. We've begun training them, but making a master bowman is a lifetime's work, and the mariners and drovers you 'rescued' with us were never soldiers. If we attempted to use them as archers, they would only get in the way of our men who already know what they're doing. Nor are any of them trained cavalryman, and I doubt that they could even stay on their horses if we attempted to use them as such. And if we attempted to use them as dismounted men-at-arms, especially against such foes as these, they would be slaughtered for very little return."

"If they are so useless," the demon-jester suggested, "then there seems little point in retaining them."

An icy shiver went through Sir George, for he had no doubt what the demon-jester meant.

"I didn't say they were 'useless,'" the baron replied, choosing his words very carefully. "What I said, Commander, is that *at the moment* they're untrained. That's a weakness which we can correct, given time. I doubt many of them will make archers by the standards of Rolf Grayhame or Dafydd Howice, although I could be wrong even there. In any case, however, I feel confident that they can be trained as men-at-arms, in which case they would represent a significant and welcome reinforcement to my existing trained soldiers. But whatever we can teach them to be in the future, at the present moment committing them to battle would be simply to throw away their lives to little point. It would be . . . wasting your guild's resources."

"I see." The demon-jester sat in thought for several moments, his two smaller eyes half-closed while he considered what Sir George had just said. Then all three opened wide once more and fastened upon the baron.

"Very well. I understand your reasoning, and while I dislike the conclusion you have reached, I am forced to concede that preservation of guild resources should take precedence in this instance. Nonetheless, I do not like the way in which you plan to employ the men you are willing to use in combat. You should attack the enemy, not stand on the defensive."

"Against such numbers, we have no option but to adopt a defensive position," Sir George explained with much more patience than he felt. The demon-jester opened his speaking mouth, but the baron went on before the creature could say anything.

"Commander, you've informed me that the objective of your guild is to compel these creatures to enter into an agreement to trade only with you." *Although*, Sir George thought, *I cannot begin to imagine what such creatures could possibly have to trade of sufficient value to bring your "guild" here in the first place!* "From what you and Computer have told me, the key to achieving that objective is to force this Thoolaas tribe to submit to your will, because its power and the awe in which the surrounding tribes hold it will lead all of them to follow its example. To accomplish that, it will be necessary to decisively defeat the Thoolaas in battle, yet the Thoolaas' warriors alone outnumber us almost sevenfold. If we attack them and give them the advantage of the defensive position, our losses will be severe, even if we triumph at all. Heavy losses will weaken our value to your guild in any future campaign, and they would also mean that if any tribe declines to follow the Thoolaas' example, my men would probably be too few to compel additional tribes to submit.

"This means we must find a way to convince the Thoolaas to attack *us* in a place and at a time of our choosing. After studying the manner in which they fight with Computer's aid, I feel confident that we can not only defeat them but inflict very heavy losses upon them if we can convince them to do what we wish. And once they've been weakened by losses upon the field of battle—and had some of the heart taken out of them by the knowledge that we've already crushed them once—we can take the battle to them with much greater safety and effectiveness if that is still required."

"And if they choose not to attack?"

"I think that very unlikely," Sir George replied. "With Computer's aid," he stressed the disembodied voice's role in his planning, "my senior officers and I have watched over a score of their battles. These tribes have only a poor concept of defensive tactics in the field, but their villages are well fortified, with earthen walls and wooden palisades, and they would appear to have a much sounder notion of how to defend such works than they have of how to fight defensively in the open field. In addition, their dart-throwers are undoubtedly even more effective and dangerous from behind the cover of walls and palisades than in the open, where my archers can get at them readily.

"Fortunately, they appear to dislike that style of fighting and will adopt it only when their villages are actually threatened by forces larger than they themselves can muster. If the numbers are even near to equal on both sides, however, they almost always choose to attack rather than to be attacked. Since their numbers will be so much greater than ours, and since they can have no concept of what our weapons can do to them, I feel confident that they would rush eagerly to the attack under any circumstances. In this instance, however, I have labored with Computer's advice to devise a strategy which will *assure* that they do so, and it's for that reason that I've selected the specific field I've chosen."

He gestured at the imagery hovering just above the crystal tabletop. Or what he still thought of as a "tabletop," at least. In fact, he was beginning to have his doubts that whatever it was actually had anything a good Englishman would consider a "top" at all, for there was something very peculiar about it. He'd had no opportunity to examine it closely himself, yet nothing the demon-jester had ever set upon it in his presence had made the slightest sound, and objects seemed to slide over it even more easily than they might have slid over slick, winter-polished ice. At the moment, however, the nature of the demon-jester's furnishings was of considerably less importance than the image hovering above it, and Sir George had to admit that that image represented one aspect of the demon-jester's arcane arts of which he wholeheartedly approved.

Since the first time the demon-jester had shown him England and her neighbors through the eyes of God's own eagles, the baron had spent much time studying the marvelous "electronic" maps and "satellite and overhead imagery"

Computer could produce upon request. It had been difficult for him, at first, to visualize the reality accurately from the "satellite imagery," in particular, because the pictures were so unlike any human map with which he had ever worked. Familiarity and practice, however, had overcome those difficulties, and he was awed by the unbelievable detail Computer could produce. No map he'd ever seen on Earth could match the precision and accuracy of this imagery . . . especially when Computer imposed a "three-dimensional, holographic topography" upon it and allowed him to see every rise and fall, every swell and hollow and stream, down to the tiniest rivulet, in true dimensions rather than as a flat representation. The baron had always had a tactician's eye for terrain, but no human commander had ever possessed the ability to visualize a field of battle with such devastating accuracy. Despite his servitude to the demon-jester, the soldier within Sir George rejoiced at the advantage he had been given. "Maps" such as these trebled his effective strength . . . at the very least.

The imagery currently displayed above the demon-jester's tabletop was one of Computer's "holograms" which showed a large hill, thickly grown in the dark purple grass of this murky-skied place. It rose perhaps fifty or sixty feet above the surrounding plain at its highest point, and its perfect roundness proclaimed that, despite its size, it was artificial, and not the work of nature. The hill was large enough that he could place his entire force upon it with some room to spare, if he arranged his formation carefully, and its stone-faced slopes angled sharply up from the level of the plain before the gradient eased off into something much more gentle as it continued upward to the summit.

"Computer has told me that this hill is sacred to the Thoolaas tribe," Sir George told the demon-jester. "It is the tomb in which they bury their heathen kings and priests, as sacred to them as Jerusalem itself to us. If we place our force upon it, they *will* attack us."

The baron did not add that the site he'd chosen for the

battle offered no means by which the English could retreat if things went against them. He disliked that far more than the demon-jester possibly could have, even if it had occurred to the small creature, yet he saw no real alternative. It was obvious that his value to the guild, and that of his men, as well, depended solely upon their ability to win victories. If they lost that value, there would be no reason for the guild to retain their services, and he had no doubt whatsoever that the demon-jester would slaughter all of them as the cheapest and simplest way to rid himself of his poor investment. Almost worse, it had also become equally obvious that the demon-jester, for all of his arrogant self-confidence and contempt for the English, was less competent than some drooling village idiot when it came to planning and organizing a single battle, far less an entire campaign.

Computer had been much more forthcoming than Sir George had expected when the baron pressed him for information about the Thoolaas and the other local tribes, and Sir George had rapidly come to the conclusion that the demon-jester's analysis of the local situation was both overconfident and wrong. True, the Thoolaas were the largest and most powerful single tribe in the vicinity, and their king claimed the title of hereditary overlord, along with tribute, from all of his neighbors. But from what Computer had said, his authority was far more a matter of tradition than of fact. His "vassal" war chiefs were an unruly, independent-minded lot who were constantly at war with one another and who never bothered themselves with the formality of seeking his authority before marching out to slaughter one another. Only the other tribes' longstanding, traditional rivalries and the Thoolaas' chieftain's ability to keep their jealous leaders divided by playing one off against another had so far prevented two or three of them from banding together to overthrow him and bring an end even to his nominal authority.

From Sir George's perspective, that meant that defeating the Thoolaas could be no more than a first step in achieving the demon-jester's full purpose. These creatures clearly were at least as stubborn as Scots and as divisive as the Irish, which meant the defeat of one tribe, be that defeat ever so sound, was very unlikely to terrify its neighboring rivals into prompt submission. At least one or two of the other tribes—probably an alliance of several of them—would also have to be defeated before all of the local chiefs and subchiefs were prepared to submit. He had put that suggestion forward as diffidently as possible in his first strategy meeting with the demon-jester, but the idea had been waved aside. The "Commander" was positive that the elimination of the Thoolaas alone would solve all of his problems, and Sir George had decided not to argue the point. He'd made his own view a part of the record, and perhaps even the demon-jester would be able to recognize that he had been right after the fact.

And perhaps not. Sir George had seen altogether too many nobly born humans who were so sublimely confident of their own judgment and wit that they were fully capable of ignoring even the most painful lessons of reality. *Particularly*, he thought bleakly, *when someone other than they has to pay the cost for their stupidity in blood and pain and death.* That could very well be the case here, as well, but at least the demon-jester claimed to set a high value upon them as an "asset" of his precious guild. If his claims were honest, then perhaps he would at least be bright enough to learn from experience that it was valuable to listen to Sir George's advice.

But whatever the future might hold, the unpalatable present truth was that the demon-jester expected Sir George to deliver a quick, decisive victory. The baron might have managed to dissuade him from ordering an all-out frontal assault on the principal village of the Thoolaas, but that was the only concession he'd been able to win. And he felt confident that if, having obtained it, he failed to achieve the speedy triumph the demon-jester sought, he himself would be discarded at the very least. It was virtually certain that he would also be turned into an example of the price of failure for whatever of his subordinates survived to be elevated in his place, and Matilda and Edward would almost certainly die with him, probably—hopefully—without ever even being awakened.

His mind tried to shy away from that thought like a frightened horse, but he'd forced himself to consider it and face it fully. That, too, was one of the responsibilities of his rank, for if the demon-jester was willing to remove *him*, the hopelessly incompetent creature would undoubtedly insist upon exercising direct and total command over whoever replaced him.

And that would spell disaster and the ultimate death of all of those under his command and protection.

That was the reason Sir George had chosen a position from which there could be no retreat. In the long run, there was no option but to attain total victory or to perish anyway, and the position he'd selected gave him the best opportunity for victory. *Not to mention,* he thought mordantly, *the fact that men who know they* cannot *run away have no option but to fight to the death.*

"As long as I'm allowed to entice them into coming to me when and where I choose," he told the demon-jester with an absolute confidence he was very far from feeling, "I will promise you the victory you seek, Commander."

The demon-jester regarded him in silence for several endless heartbeats.

"Very well," the creature said at last. "I would still prefer a swift, decisive attack that would take the Thoolaas by surprise and crush them in a single blow, but as you have said, you have far more direct experience than I in the employment of such crude and primitive weapons. I will allow you to fight this battle as you wish . . . but I strongly recommend that you honor that promise and produce the victory my guild requires."

It was remarkable, Sir George thought, how much chill threat could be packed into a completely expressionless and uninflected sentence.

~ ~ ~

"Can't say I much care for this position, M'lord." Rolf Grayhame hawked and spat a thick glob of spittle into the unnatural, purple-colored grass as he turned his head, sweeping his eyes over the featureless plain which surrounded the hill. Thanks to Computer's demonstrations, he was as familiar as Sir George with how quickly the natives' loping gait devoured distance . . . and knew that no human footman could hope to outrun them even if he got the chance to retreat. "Nor for this whole damned place," he added with a grimace.

"I'm not exactly overjoyed by either of them myself," Sir George told the powerfully built archer calmly. "Unfortunately, they're the ones we have, so I suppose we'll just have to make the best of them."

Grayhame chuckled sourly, then nodded and touched his forelock with a bob of his head.

"With your permission, M'lord, I'd best go make one more check."

"Go on, Rolf," Sir George said with a smile. "And remind the lads that whatever *he* might have to say," the baron jerked his head at the strange device Computer called an "air car" where it hovered unnaturally in midair above them, "this little brawl really is important."

He saw a trace of surprise on the archer's face and barked a laugh. Grayhame's reaction didn't surprise him in the least. The demon-jester had spent the better part of an hour exhorting "his" troops to do battle in the name of his guild. If it hadn't been for the life-or-death power he held over all of them, his ludicrous, bombastic harangue would have had every man of them in stitches of laughter. The very thought of "honoring the guild we serve with the offering of your courage and blood" was enough to make any one of Sir George's hardened veterans laugh—or puke—and the thought that the demon-jester could think them stupid enough to be taken in by such bilge was even worse.

"Oh, I don't give a rat's arse for him and his precious guild!" the baron grunted to the bowman. "They could all take the pox and rot, for all of me, and the sooner the better! But whatever we may think of them, our lives depend on convincing them that they need us, and that means winning."

"Not to mention the little matter that if we lose, the four-arms will slit all our throats, M'lord," Walter Skinnet put in dourly, and Sir George chuckled.

"Aye, not to mention that," he agreed, then waved at Grayhame. "So be off, Rolf, and pass the word."

"Have no doubt of that, M'lord," Grayhame assured him with a crooked grin, and trotted off while Sir George turned back to survey the field around their hilltop position.

There were enough subtle and not so subtle differences between this place and Earth to make the entire scene seem just slightly unreal, like a fever dream or a hallucination. The sun was a cooler, dimmer thing. The "trees" which dotted the plain about the burial hill were too tall, too spindly, and completely the wrong color. Even Sir George's own weight felt wrong, for he was too light on his feet and felt too charged with energy. He was accustomed enough to the surge of energy which the threat of battle always seemed to bring forth, but this was different. He'd mentioned it to Computer when the "tenders" from the demon-jester's main vessel had deposited the English and all of their equipment and horses here, and Computer had replied that the local "gravity" was lower and that the local air contained more "oxygen" than that to which the English were accustomed.

The baron had no idea what "gravity" or "oxygen" were, but if they could make him feel this way, then he wanted all of them he could get!

His mouth quirked in a grin at the thought, but it was fleeting, and his eyes narrowed as he continued his survey.

The oddly colored grasslands stretched to the limit of his vision, broken up only by an occasional, small clump of trees and the steeply cut banks of the small but deep river that wound around the western edge of the hill upon which the English stood. The lands were flat enough that the Thoolaas' main village was clearly visible on the far side of that stream, perhaps five miles from the hill, and even as he watched he could see the surging tide of the tribe's warriors shoving and jostling for position as they loped through the grass, waist-high on a human and reaching almost to mid-thigh on them, towards the ford that carried the trail from their village to their burial hill. Even at their pace, it would take them some time yet to reach the hill, and he could make out very few details from here, but the deep, rhythmic booming of their war drums already came faintly to his ears.

"How many dart-throwers do they have, Computer?" he asked quietly.

"Approximately nine hundred and seventeen out of a total force of approximately six thousand two hundred and nine," Computer's voice replied in his ear.

Despite the fact that Sir George knew Computer reported everything he heard to the demon-jester and the rest of the crew, hearing the other's voice at this particular moment was a great comfort. The numbers Computer had just reported, on the other hand, were not. Without the mariners and other untrained men Sir George had convinced the demon-jester not to commit, he had barely eight hundred men in total. True, sixty percent of them were archers, but the enemy had him outnumbered by two-to-one even in missile weapons, and his bowmen were much more lightly armed for close combat than his men-at-arms, with only daggers, short swords, and an occasional maul or hammer to supplement their bows. If the rest of that horde ever got to grips with them, the longbowmen would be at a deadly disadvantage.

Which meant that somehow Sir George had to prevent the Thoolaas from getting to grips. That was where the hedge of sharply pointed wooden stakes set into the slope of the hill came in. Not to mention the caltrops hidden in the river and seeded thickly through the tall grass all the way from the edge of the stream to the foot of the hill. And also not to mention the double line of dismounted men-at-arms between the stakes and the front ranks of the archers. It was ironic that after arguing so strongly with the demon-jester about the necessity of horses, he had dismounted all but fifty of his men-at-arms for the very first battle.

Of course, he reminded himself, turning to look at the ranks of horses being held at the rear of his formation, once the Thoolaas had been broken—*if* they were broken—he would need all of those mounts for the pursuit he intended to put in. In the meantime, Skinnet and the fifty mounted men under his and Sir Richard's direct command represented Sir George's only true reserve.

At least his men were by far the best armed and armored troops he had ever led into battle, he reminded himself. For all of the demon-jester's contempt for the crudity and primitive nature of their equipment, the "industrial modules" of the guild's huge ship had met and surpassed all of the requests Sir George and his advisors had submitted.

Like every commander of his day, Sir George was only too intimately familiar with the cost of properly equipping men for war. Knights and mounted men-at-arms usually had priority, because they were the decisive element in hand-to-hand combat, where protection against hostile blows was paramount . . . and because knights were usually wealthy enough to afford better quality armor. No liege lord or captain could possibly have afforded to provide his entire force with such armor, however, and the archer and the footman-at-arms usually had to make do with less effective but far cheaper forms of armor. An archer was fortunate if he could afford brigandine rather than simple leather jack, and a footman was fortunate if he could afford a proper haubergeon instead of brigandine. Even knights and mounted men-at-arms were frequently forced to substitute boiled leather for the bits of plate armor used to reinforce their mail.

But not Sir George's men. Their armor might not be made of the same marvelous alloys as the ship or even the armor of the wart-faces, but it was made of a better steel than any smith born of Earth had ever forged. There was far more of it, too, and, unheard of though it was, every mounted man's armor was identical to every other mounted man's . . . and all of them were as well armored as any knight Sir George had ever seen. Indeed, the entire company's equipment had attained a uniformity and quality Sir George had never dreamed of when he first set out for France.

Men being men—and, especially, Englishmen being Englishmen—there had been some grumbling when the equipment that had been taken from them during their "processing" wasn't returned. That grumbling had faded quickly once the veterans began to recognize how much that equipment had been improved upon, and Sir George had never even been tempted to complain. Oh, he missed the familiar armor that had once been his father's, but that was no more than a nostalgic wistfulness, the loss of something which had connected him to people and places forever lost to him. His new armor was both lighter and far more efficient at protecting him from enemy weapons, and he was much too practical to regret *that*.

Even their horses were better protected. The destriers the demon-jester and his mechanical servitors had stolen one bloody night in France were not the massive chargers of true heavy horse, nor were they as heavily armored as those chargers would have been, but that was fine with Sir George, who preferred mobility and endurance to ponderous weight, anyway. Yet even though he had never been as enamored of heavy horse as most of his contemporaries, or perhaps *because* he never had, he was delighted with the barding and horse armor the demon-jester's modules had created. Like his own, it was lighter and tougher than anything he'd ever seen on Earth, and it afforded a high degree of protection without overburdening the mounts. Which was just as well, since the demon-jester's fear that horses might prove ill suited to phase drive stasis appeared to have been well founded. Computer told Sir George that they had lost no fewer than ten of their mounts during the voyage here (wherever "here" might be), and Sir George disliked thinking about what that promised for the long-term future.

But for any long-term problems to require his attention, he reminded himself, watching the Thoolaas horde loping closer and closer, he had to survive the present.

He raised one hand and beckoned for Sir Richard and Skinnet. The knight and the sergeant handed their reins to Sir Richard's squire and crossed to him.

"It looks to me," he said quickly, eyes never leaving the four-armed warriors, "as if these . . . creatures intend to do exactly what we'd hoped they would and come straight at us. If they don't, it will be up to you two and your lads to keep them off our backs until I can change front. I want you to withdraw the reserve another hundred and fifty paces and keep a close eye to the rear and flanks."

"Aye, My Lord," Sir Richard replied. Skinnet simply nodded, and the two of them moved quickly back to their men and began issuing orders.

Sir George left them to it, and returned his attention to the enemy.

*The odds are little worse than I faced with the King at Dupplin*, he thought. He'd pointed that out to his men in his own less bombastic, and more professional, prebattle speech, and it was close enough to true to satisfy them. Sir George had based his present deployment upon the one that had been used that day, and he truly expected it to give him victory, yet there were significant differences between Dupplin and this field, and he knew it. For one thing, although Edward III's army had counted no more than five hundred knights and fifteen hundred archers against almost ten thousand Scots at Dupplin, the odds against him had been only five-to-one, not eight-to-one. For another, the Scots at

Dupplin had boasted no archers, whereas the Thoolaas had more dart-throwers than he had longbowmen. And, for yet another, Scots weren't nine feet tall and equipped with four arms each.

*Still, it's not as if we haven't done it before*, he told himself firmly as the oncoming warriors reached the far side of the stream and began splashing into it, bellowing their deep, strange war cries while the drums thundered and boomed behind them.

*They should be discovering the first caltrops about . . . now*, he thought.

As if his thought had been a cue, a huge shudder seemed to run through the front ranks of the charging Thoolaas. War cries turned abruptly into bellows of anguish as huge, broad, six-toed feet came down on the wickedly sharp caltrops. They were an ancient, simple device, no more than four-pronged pieces of wire, arranged so that however they lay, one prong was always uppermost. Designed as an anticavalry weapon, they were equally effective against the feet of infantry . . . especially when their presence was unsuspected. And it had certainly been "unsuspected" this time. The barefooted Thoolaas had never encountered such a weapon, and they shrieked in agony as the deadly sharp steel transfixed their feet. Hundreds of them fell, thrashing in torment, screaming even more loudly as they fell on still more caltrops, and many of them drowned in no more than three feet of water.

The entire leading edge of the aliens' formation—if such a mob could have been called a formation in the first place—came apart. But it didn't stop. Battle fever, contempt for the puny, half-sized runts on the far side of the river, resentment of the demands of the demon-jester's guild, and fury at the desecration of their burial hill, carried them onward, and Sir George's eyes narrowed in satisfaction as he watched their formation shift. At his request, the demon-jester's servitors had spent the previous night silently and stealthily sowing the river with caltrops for well over a mile, both upstream and down. But the ford directly opposite the burial hill had deliberately been left clear, and now the Thoolaas funneled towards the center of that ford, packing closer and closer together as they realized that none of the vicious, invisible, foot-destroying caltrops blocked their charge directly towards the hill.

Sir George grunted in fresh satisfaction as the four-armed warriors crowded more and more tightly into a single mass. The sheer press of bodies should greatly reduce, if not completely eliminate, the effectiveness of the Thoolaas' dart-throwers by denying them the clearance they required to launch their deadly missiles, and he waited another five heartbeats, then drew a deep breath and nodded sharply to Rolf Grayhame, who stood watching him steadily.

"Nock arrows and draw!" Grayhame shouted.

Sir George had split his archers, putting half of them on each flank of his line and slightly forward, though still behind their rows of wooden stakes, so that their fire converged on the tightly-packed column of Thoolaas warriors charging through fountains and rainbows of spray towards their position. His longbowmen were veterans all, each capable of putting twelve shafts into the air in one minute and hitting a man-sized target at two hundred paces with aimed fire. But this day the range was considerably less than two hundred paces; their targets were far larger than any human; and almost five hundred bows bent at Grayhame's shout.

"*Loose!*" he bellowed, and half a thousand bowstrings sang as one.

No one who had never seen English bowmen in action could have imagined the fierce, deadly hiss as that storm of arrows slashed upward with a great slithering scrape of wooden shaft against bowstave. The very air seemed to buzz as their fletching cut through it like some vast, sun-obscuring shadow of death, and then they came slicing downward like unleashed demons.

The Thoolaas shrieked in fresh agony, far worse than that inflicted by the caltrops, as the lethal rain blasted into them. Each shaft was a yard long, with a broad, razor-sharp head that drove effortlessly through the archers' unarmored targets, and for one eerie second before the howls of pain drowned them out, the solid, meaty thuds as they struck home were clearly audible from where the baron stood. Hundreds of the natives went down, but Sir George blinked in astonishment, for the deadly shafts had fallen much deeper into the Thoolaas' formation than he had expected. He snapped his head around in surprise as the front ranks of the enemy charged onward even while those fifty yards behind them shrieked and died, but Grayhame was already bellowing furiously at his archers. Some of the bowmen looked confused, but they were given no time for confusion to become uncertainty or panic before Grayhame barked fresh orders, and then a second flight arced upward.

This one fell closer to its intended targets, and the archers dropped into the familiar rhythm as they sent a third lethal storm hissing upward. And a fourth. *A fifth!*

The longbows had adjusted their trajectories fully by the fourth volley, and Sir George watched in a deep amazement that not even his experience at Dupplin or Halidon Hill could have prepared him for. Computer had said there were six thousand warriors in that force; in the next ninety seconds, his bowmen put *nine* thousand shafts into the air. When the last of them came down, the battle was effectively over. Oh, the arrows continued to fly for at least another two or three minutes, but the sheer, hammer blow carnage of that first minute and a half had shattered the Thoolaas. Despite the range and accuracy of their own dart-throwers, they had never experienced the horrific killing power of such massed, rapid, deadly fire. Probably as much as half their total army was killed or wounded in that initial, shrieking ninety seconds of slaughter. Another quarter was killed or wounded as the survivors turned and fled in howling terror, and Sir George straightened his spine as he watched them go.

For just a moment he allowed his eyes to linger on the windrows of Thoolaas strewn across both banks of the river and mounded across the stream itself like some hideous, arrow-pierced dam of flesh that turned the water downstream into a sludge of orange blood. All throughout those piles and hillocks of bodies motion twisted and writhed while the inhuman—in every sense of the word—moans of the wounded and dying rose like some horrible hymn of Hell.

He gazed upon that ghastly sight, a hardened warrior shocked despite himself by the carnage he had unleashed, and then he turned his back upon it and nodded to young Thomas Snellgrave, his squire and standard bearer.

Thomas was white-faced, and his hands trembled ever so slightly, but he returned his liege's nod and waved Sir George's standard in the prearranged signal. All through the English formation, movement and stir began as the dismounted cavalry who had thickened the protective line of footmen began moving towards the waiting lines of horses. Sir Richard and Walter Skinnet came trotting up from behind to join them, and Sir George walked across to the nervous groom holding the tall, midnight-black stallion.

The baron nodded to the groom, took the reins, and heaved himself into the saddle. It was a maneuver he'd learned to execute, despite his armor, when he was little older than his son now was, but it seemed much easier here. Because of that "gravity" and "oxygen" Computer had babbled about? He didn't know, and he wondered briefly if one of those factors also explained the extra range which had taken his archers by surprise. Perhaps Computer would explain it to him later if he asked, he thought, then brushed the question aside.

The horse he'd named Satan moved uneasily under him, fighting the bit and showing tooth while he rolled a wicked eye at anyone or anything, human or equine, that dared to encroach upon his space. Sir George heard the stallion's whistling challenge, but he had no time to worry over so minor a matter. He leaned forward in the saddle and rapped the horse smartly between the ears with one gauntleted fist. It wasn't a hard blow, but it did its job, for he and Satan had come to terms long since, and strength wasn't required to remind the stallion that the insignificant creature upon his back was his master. There was a symbolism there, an analogy, which Sir George chose not to examine too closely. He glanced over as young Snellgrave tucked the base of the standard's staff into his right stirrup and urged his own gelding up beside Satan.

Sir Richard moved into position to Sir George's right, with Skinnet on his left, and the baron nodded one last time in satisfaction. It was a small enough cavalry force, particularly given that at least a thousand Thoolaas had escaped the slaughter at the ford. But small or not, it was all he had, and so it would have to do. At least every man of it was well-mounted, well-armed, and well-trained.

As he looked upon his mounted men, Sir George made himself accept that some of them were about to die. The one-sided massacre the archers had inflicted would not be repeated this day. Perhaps he could have left the Thoolaas fugitives alone. After such savage losses, surely their surviving chieftains and shamans would submit to the demon-jester without further bloodshed! But he couldn't be certain of that, and he had been ordered to *crush* them beyond doubt or question. He dared not leave this task half-done, not when the survival of all of his people depended upon his ability to demonstrate their value conclusively to the demon-jester and his guild. And so he would insure the Thoolaas were broken beyond hope of future resistance, even if he must kill another thousand of them, or lose a dozen of his precious, irreplaceable men, to do it.

"All right, lads," Sir George Wincaster said calmly. "We've a way to go to clear the caltrops in the river, and no time to waste. Let's be on our way."

~ ~ ~

The trumpet call sent the small force of English cavalry swinging to its left, and the column deployed into a line on the move. The maneuver was as swift and well drilled as any commander could have asked, and it was as well that it was, Sir George thought grimly. The river lay two miles behind, the village lay three miles ahead, and the knot of Thoolaas warriors between his men and their homes numbered perhaps four hundred—twice his cavalry's strength. Worse, at least a score of dart-throwers stood behind them, and the spearmen and axemen sent up a howling scream of rage as they spied the cavalry.

The baron was unhappy at coming face-to-face with so many warriors, but at least they represented a third or more of the total force Computer estimated had escaped the slaughter at the ford. If they could be broken decisively, it was unlikely any other sizable force would coalesce.

The problem was ensuring that the aliens were the ones who were broken.

He took one more moment to glance to his left and right along the front of his line and grunted in satisfaction. Then he nodded to his trumpeter and slammed down the visor of his bascinet.

"Ready!" he called through its slots, and the trumpet sang.

He could have used Computer to carry his verbal orders to each of his men even here, but he'd chosen against it. His troopers were accustomed to the trumpet commands, and he had decided not to throw any more new, confusing experiences at them in this first battle than he must. There would be time enough for improvement and adaptation later, assuming that they won this fight.

All along the English line, lances swung down, Sir George's among them, at the trumpet's command, and he settled himself more firmly into the saddle while Satan stamped impatiently beneath him.

"At a walk!" he commanded, and the trumpet sang again.

The cavalry stirred back into motion, walking their mounts towards the weapons-waving mob of Thoolaas. He waited two or three more heartbeats, then shouted again.

"At a trot!"

The line of horsemen spurred to a trot, hooves thudding on firm earth as they gathered speed and momentum, and the Thoolaas warriors screamed their war cries and flooded to meet them.

"*At a charge!*"

The trumpet sang a final time, and a deep, hoarse bellow went up in answer from his troopers as the trot became a gallop. Sir George's vision was narrowed by the slots of his visor, but he saw the dart-throwers' arms come forward, saw the slender, javelinlike spears leaping from the throwing sticks. He smelled the dust, horse sweat and his own, and felt the sun which had seemed so dim in the murky sky beating down upon his armor while the equine thunder of the charge enveloped him. The spears came slicing wickedly downward, one of them impacting with a force and weight that struck his shield like a hammer. Somewhere he heard a horse screaming, and there were human screams mingled with the sound, but there was no time to think about that now. No time for anything which could distract him from the task at hand.

A huge Thoolaas came at him—a veritable giant, even for its own kind—with an enormous battle ax clasped in each pair of hands. The creature was as tall as Sir George mounted on Satan, and it shrieked its hatred and its war cry as it lunged towards him. But big as it was, and long as its arms were, they were shorter than a ten-foot lance, and it shrieked again as the bitter steel lance head slammed squarely into its chest.

The Thoolaas went down, but the impact ripped the lance from Sir George's grip. He was too experienced to try to maintain his grasp upon it at the expense of losing speed or balance, and his sword swept from its sheath in a reflex as automatic as breathing.

Satan thundered forward, screaming his own battle rage yet swerving, obedient to the pressure of Sir George's knees, and then the baron rose in his stirrups as another warrior confronted him. An ax and a huge, clumsy flail swung at him in a scissorslike attack, and the unbelievable shock as his shield took the weight of the flail nearly knocked him from the saddle. In an odd sort of way, the ax that struck home almost simultaneously actually helped him keep his seat. It slammed into the new, solid steel backplate which covered his hauberk, driving him forward and to the side, almost diametrically against the impact of the flail. It was like being trapped between two sledgehammers, but the baron maintained his balance, and his sword swept out and around with deadly precision.

The second Thoolaas tumbled backwards, his throat a blood-streaming gash while Satan trampled him underfoot, and suddenly Sir George was through their line, and he grinned savagely as Satan thundered towards the dart-throwers.

The alien missile troops carried no hand-to-hand weapons at all. Two last-ditch darts slammed into him—one turned by his breastplate, and the other skipping off of the plate cuisse protecting his left thigh—while a third bounced from Satan's barding, and then Sir George was upon them. He rose in the stirrups as he passed between two of them, and his sword severed one's arm on the downstroke, then split the other's skull on the backhand recovery. A third alien reached up for him with one pair of hands, trying to drag him from the saddle while two more hands stabbed furiously at him with bronze-headed javelins. But his armor defeated the javelins, and he slammed his shield into the alien's forehead. The creature staggered backwards, and one of his troopers who had somehow retained his lance came past the baron at a gallop. The lance's steel head punched deep into the stunned Thoolaas' belly, and then Sir George and his companion were reining in hard as their speed carried them beyond the last of the aliens.

Satan turned like an antelope under him, all trace of rebellion or resistance vanished, and Sir George's eyes swept the field.

The Thoolaas formation, such as it had been, had shattered like crystal under the impact of his charging troopers. Individually huge and powerful though they might have been, the aliens had discovered that even the ability to use weapons with all four hands was insufficient to overcome the discipline and armor of their far smaller opponents. At least half the aliens were down, and even as Snellgrave arrived beside Sir George with his standard, the handful of warriors who hadn't fled were being cut down by the surviving English. Other troopers were thundering in pursuit of those who *had* fled, hacking them down from behind in the ancient penalty cavalry had always exacted from infantry who broke and ran. This infantry, however, was very nearly as fast as the cavalry pursuing it, and Sir George turned to his trumpeter.

"Sound the recall!"

The trumpet notes blared out, cutting through the clangor and clamor of the battle, and the troopers responded quickly. Here and there someone took a moment longer to finish off one of the aliens, but these were experienced veterans, many of them personally trained by Sir George and Walter Skinnet over the course of years, not French knights. They were professionals who weren't about to allow enthusiasm or some half-baked concept of honor to overcome good sense, and they broke off and rallied quickly about his standard.

Sir George made a quick estimate of their numbers. He could see at least a dozen of his men scattered among the Thoolaas' wounded and dead, and several more humans were on foot. Horses were down, as well, but his initial impression was that more men had been unhorsed than had had their mounts killed under them. He didn't know how many of those armored figures sprawled in the trampled, bloody purple grass were dead, and how many were only wounded, but he had a very good notion of what would happen to any unprotected wounded the Thoolaas came upon. Under other circumstances, he might have relied on the dismounted troopers to protect their fallen comrades, but the Thoolaas were simply too big for him to count upon men on foot, however well equipped or led, to hold them off, and he raised his visor and turned to Skinnet.

"Walter! Tell off twenty men to secure our wounded!"

"Aye, Sir!"

"Sir Richard!"

"Here, My Lord!"

"We'll continue to the village. When we reach it, take your half of the force and swing around to secure the gate on the east side."

"Yes, My Lord!"

"Very well." Sir George gave the field another glance, then grunted in gratitude when one of the dismounted troopers reached up to hand him a replacement lance.

"My thanks," he told the dismounted man, and turned his head as Skinnet urged his horse up beside Satan. The stallion darted his head around as if intent on taking a chunk out of Skinnet's gelding, but Sir George checked him automatically, and the grizzled veteran chuckled grimly.

"Told you that one had the devil in him," the master of horse said.

"So you did—and a damned good thing on a day like this!"

"No argument from me on that, My Lord. Not now."

"Good!" Sir George flashed a smile, teeth white against his spade beard in the shadow of his bascinet. "And are we ready now?"

"Aye, Sir." Skinnet gestured at the twenty-man troop he'd chosen to detach, and Sir George nodded in satisfaction. He recognized the senior man, a dour, unflappable Yorkshireman named Dickon who had been with Skinnet even before Skinnet joined Sir George. He was the sort who would keep his head and hold his men together, rather than allow them to scatter or straggle, and the baron knew he could count on Dickon to hold off any reasonably small group of Thoolaas who might threaten the wounded. And, Sir George thought grimly, Dickon was also experienced enough to fall back with everyone he could save if a *large* group of the aliens turned up, rather than sacrifice his entire command in a hopeless defense of the wounded.

"Very well," Sir George said again. "Let's be on our way."

"It's a pity they can't use those things to fight, My Lord," Sir Anthony grumbled. "If we can't hurt them, then neither could the four-arms, and a score of archers shooting from that sort of cover could have decided this whole thing in an hour!"

The other knight sounded thoroughly disgusted, and Sir George had to nod in agreement.

The pallid sun of this dimly lit world was settling into the west, and the crackle and smoke of the Thoolaas village's burning palisades rose into the darkening sky. Most of his men, Sir George knew, would have preferred to torch the entire village, not just its defensive works, but his orders had been firm. The senior surviving Thoolaas war chief had surrendered what remained of his warriors on the condition that their village be spared, and the object was to compel the locals to accept the terms of the demon-jester's guild. That would be far easier to do if the natives had reason to believe acceptance could buy mercy or at least leniency . . . and that promises of leniency would be honored. Besides, he thought cynically, the rest of the village would undoubtedly be destroyed soon enough. He and his men had killed or wounded at least ninety percent of the tribe's warriors. It wouldn't take long for one or another of their rivals to finish off anything the English left intact.

But that reflection floated below the surface of his thoughts as he and Sir Anthony watched the demon-jester's mechanical servitors sweeping over the plain around the village. Some of them were much like the demon-jester's own "air car," only much larger, and even as Sir George watched, one of those descended briefly to a landing, then rose once more.

"A horse, that time, I think," Father Timothy said quietly.

The priest had come forward to join Sir George as soon as it was safe. Indeed, he had arrived rather too quickly for Sir George's peace of mind. The baron knew Timothy's faith had made him as close to fearless as any mere mortal was ever likely to be, just as he knew that the priest's many years as a soldier had imbued him with both an appreciation of the dangers of any battlefield and the prudence to avoid them. Despite that, the thought of what losing his old friend, confessor, and irreplaceable spiritual guide for his people would cost had brought a sharp rebuke to his lips when the Dominican arrived.

"There were no wounded among the archers," the priest had replied reasonably, "but there were hurt and dying men here, in need of shriving."

That had silenced Sir George's objections, even if it hadn't done much about the emotions which had sparked them in the first place. He could scarcely complain about Timothy's determination to discharge his priestly duties, but he made a quiet mental note to set Matilda to work upon the old man. If anyone could convince him of his irreplaceability, it would be she . . . and Sir George knew from intimate personal experience just how unscrupulous she could be in framing her arguments when she knew she was right.

His mouth had twitched in a smile at the thought, but that smile had vanished instantly as he recalled that Matilda and Edward remained in stasis, sleeping hostages for the satisfactory discharge of his master's commands.

Now he watched the rising vehicle with the priest at his shoulder and frowned.

"What do you think they want with them?" he asked, and Father Timothy shrugged.

"I have no idea, My Lord," he admitted, his eyes troubled.

"Those same . . . vehicles collected all of our wounded immediately after the battle. Why they should also collect the dead, and especially dead animals, rather than leave them for us to provide decent burial to is beyond me. I'm more than half afraid I would dislike the reason if I knew it, though."

"You and I both, Father," Sir Anthony grunted with a nod, and Sir Richard added his own agreement as he walked up to the baron.

"Why we should like anything about this cursed 'guild' is a mystery to me," Maynton observed. The other knight had been supervising the burning of the palisades, and from the look of his armor and the singed spots on his surcoat, he'd gotten a bit too close to his work. Indeed, he was still slapping at a smoldering ember on the chest of his surcoat as he reached the baron.

"Aside from the fact that so far most of us are still alive, I would be inclined to agree with you," Sir George told him, reaching out a gauntleted hand to help slap out the ember. "On the other hand, I suppose it might be argued that the fact that we *are* alive is your question's best answer."

"Aye," Sir Richard admitted. The last stubborn trace of smoke died, and he nodded his thanks to his liege. "There is that, My Lord," he went on. "Although it seems plain enough to me that it's *you* we owe the most of our survival to."

"There's truth in that, My Lord," Sir Anthony rumbled in his deep voice. "I've seen a fight or two in my time, and I'll not say these . . . Thoolaas—" he pronounced the alien word carefully (and poorly) "—were the best organized army I've ever seen. But they're not so bad as all of that. Aye, I've seen Scots and even French who were more poorly led, and these have to be the toughest bastards I've ever faced! However it may seem *now*, beating their arses like this was nowhere near so easy as you made it look."

"I suppose that's true enough," Sir George agreed, "but it was you and Sir Richard and the other lads, and especially Rolf's bowmen, who made any plans of mine work. And however 'easy' it may have looked, the fact remains that we've lost at least fifteen men, and that's assuming none of the wounded die."

"Fifteen men for a victory like this is a miraculously low price, My Lord," Sir Richard pointed out, while the four of them watched one of the oxen-sized mobile water fountains land beside a clump of dismounted cavalry. The horses pulled uneasily at their picket pins as the vehicle landed, but the troopers crowded around it eagerly, and the fountain of cold, crystal-clear water leaping and bubbling from its top sang musically as it spilled into the wide catcher basin below. The men took turns, drinking deeply and burying their sweaty faces in the cleansing water, and then three of them began hauling water to the waiting horses in their helmets.

"Fifteen men *is* a low price," Sir George conceded. "Or it would be in Scotland, or even France. But here, where there will never be any replacement of our losses, even one man is a high price to pay."

"There's more than a little truth in that, I'm afraid," Father Timothy agreed, and all three of the knights knew it was the old soldier in him as much as the man of God who spoke. "On the other hand, there's no saying that every foe you face will be as formidable as these Thoolaas were."

He did a much better job of pronouncing the alien word than Sir Anthony had managed, and Sir George smiled tiredly.

"Of course there isn't, Timothy. But there's no saying the opposite is true, either, now is there? Suppose these Thoolaas had had proper steel instead of bronze. Or that they'd been armored as well as our lads are. Or that they'd had a proper mix of dart-throwers to axemen. Who's to say that the next enemy we face *won't* have those things?"

"We can only put our faith in God and pray that they won't," the priest replied after a moment, and this time Sir George surprised himself with a laugh.

"Oh, I'll certainly add my prayers to that one, Timothy!" he chuckled. "Still and all, though, I expect God probably listens a little more closely to you than to me, so I'll ask you to see to that part of it. *My* job will be to balance the problems of sustaining the 'Commander's' faith in us as the 'resource' his guild needs most in all the world while keeping him from assuming that we can do *this*—" the baron swung an arm at the burning palisades behind them and then out across the darkening field of battle "—no matter who he sends us up against."

"It would appear you were correct," the demon-jester said, and paused as if to invite a response.

He and Sir George faced one another once more across the table which might or might not have had a top of crystal. The chamber in which that table sat, however, bore no resemblance at all to the one in which they had last met. This time, the table seemed to sit at the bottom of a deep lake, surrounded by clear water and gently waving strands of some kelplike weed while vaguely fishlike creatures swam in and out of the weed's shadows. If Sir George hadn't amassed so much first-hand experience with Computer's ability to generate "holograms," the realism of the illusion would have terrified him. Even as it was, he felt distinctly uneasy watching something the size of a shark "swim" past fifteen feet above his head.

If the demon-jester felt even the faintest twinge of discomfort, he hid it extraordinarily well. Given that he was the one who'd selected this particular . . . decoration, it seemed unlikely that it could bother him deeply. Still, Sir George wasn't quite prepared to rule out the possibility that the demon-jester had made his selection not because it was one with which he himself was completely comfortable, but because it was one he expected to make Sir George *un*comfortable. There had been times enough in Sir George's own life when he had deliberately managed meetings in ways intended to keep his subordinates off-balance.

Because it was possible that the demon-jester was attempting to do just that, Sir George chose not to respond to the possible opening. Instead, he simply clasped his hands together behind him and waited patiently for the small alien to continue.

If his silence discomfited the demon-jester in any way, his "Commander's" expressionless, piping voice gave no hint of it when he spoke again.

"What remains of the Thoolaas have accepted my guild's terms," he went on after a moment. "None of the other neighboring tribes have done so, however. Indeed, two of them—the Laahstaar and Mouthai—actually attempted to 'kill' the remote communication units I dispatched to them to demand their submission. They were, of course, unable actually to damage the units, but their response appears . . . unpromising.

"In light of these developments, I have been compelled to reconsider the analysis of the local social dynamic which you put forward originally. I suppose that it was in some ways inevitable that someone so much closer to the primitivism and barbarism of these creatures should be better able to understand them than a civilized being. However that may be, the fact remains that the other tribes have so far declined to recognize the inevitability of submitting to my requirements. It therefore seems probable that, as you had also suggested might be the case, additional battles will be necessary to drive that inevitability home. The current computer analysis supports your initial conclusions, and further suggests that it would be advisable to allow some time to elapse before administering these primitives' next lesson. This will allow the opportunity for combinations of the local tribes to form and reform, which should present the chance to both identify the most likely sources of effective leadership among those who would oppose us and to play the various factions off against one another."

The demon-jester paused once more, his unblinking eyes focused upon Sir George. The baron gazed back for several seconds, and then the demon-jester made a small gesture with one hand.

"You will please respond to what I have just said," he commanded.

"If you wish," Sir George agreed, then pursed his lips in brief thought before he began.

"I'm not surprised that Computer agrees with my original suspicions, now that you and he have had the opportunity for additional thought, particularly in light of the reactions of the Laahstaar and Mouthai. I suppose it might be argued that it would be wiser to act immediately to crush the tribes which are presently loudest in their refusal to submit to the guild's demands. A sharp additional lesson, delivered directly to those who have made themselves the leaders in opposing you, could well dissuade other tribes from following in their footsteps.

"It would seem to me, however, that the course Computer is advising you to follow offers advantages of its own, although there are aspects to his plan which somewhat concern me."

"Describe the advantages," the demon-jester said.

"The most obvious ones are that by giving the tribes which are likely to refuse to submit to the guild time to come together in open opposition to you and to your demands, you will not only draw them into identifying themselves for you, but gather them together in a single faction. If all of those likely to oppose you are united in one group, then the defeat of that single group should lop off the heads of all of the probable sources of opposition in one stroke. And, as Computer has already suggested, it would also give you the opportunity to identify those who will see an advantage in joining their fortunes to yours. This could not only provide us with allies for any additional campaign we must undertake, but also tell you which of the native leaders are most likely to continue to protect your interests, which they will see as their own, following our departure."

"A cogent summation of the computer analysis," the

demon-jester remarked, and yet again Sir George wished passionately for some guide by which to assess the other's emotions. Was the demon-jester's statement the expression of approval the toneless words might have suggested? Or was it an ironic dismissal of Sir George's arguments?

"You stated that you had some concerns, however," the demon-jester continued. "Describe those concerns."

"One serious concern is that the more time the locals are given to consider the fate of the Thoolaas, the more likely they are to recognize the many ways in which the Thoolaas contributed to their own defeat. It's difficult for anyone to change the fundamental nature of the way in which they've always fought, Commander. Certainly, my own people have seen sufficient proof of that in our campaigns in Wales and Scotland, not to mention France. Yet difficult isn't the same thing as impossible. If the Laahstaar and Mouthai ponder what happened to the Thoolaas carefully, they may well attempt to make a greater and more effective use of their dart-throwers in future engagements. Now that I've had the opportunity to face those darts directly, I have discovered that my archers hold a greater advantage over them than I had initially expected to be the case. Indeed, my bowmen can fire to extraordinary ranges here—due, Computer tells me, to the lower 'gravity' of this place."

He paused, and there was a moment of silence. Then the demon-jester spoke.

"That is undoubtedly correct," he said. "It is not surprising that the effect came as a surprise to one as primitive as yourself, as you possessed no prior experience with changes in planetary environments. It should, perhaps, have occurred to me to consider such things and to point them out to you, but my inexperience with such crude, muscle-powered weapons prevented me from thinking about such matters."

He sat back, obviously done speaking, and Sir George shrugged.

"Whatever the cause," he said, "our weapons outrange

theirs by a considerable margin. Nonetheless, if they can bring sufficient dart-throwers together and mass their fire against us, our losses will be far heavier.

"And that brings me to my gravest concern: our casualties. The Physician has already restored most of our wounded to duty. In fact, he has assured Father Timothy that *all* of the rest of our wounded will be likewise restored within the next day or two."

The baron chose not to mention his astonishment, even now, after all of the marvels he had already seen aboard this ship, that that could be true. Not even the belly and chest wounds that would have spelled certain death on Earth appeared to worry the Physician in the least.

"Even when all of the wounded are returned to us, however," he went on, "we will still have lost fifteen men and eleven horses which cannot be replaced, and—"

"Four men and six horses," the demon-jester interrupted, and Sir George frowned in confusion.

"I beg your pardon?" he said.

"I said, that your actual losses are four men and six horses," the demon-jester said. "The remaining eleven men and five horses were sufficiently intact for resuscitation to be cost effective."

"'Resuscitation'?" Sir George repeated cautiously.

"It is a relatively simple procedure for any civilized race," the demon-jester told him. "So long as the brain itself is not seriously damaged, and barring catastrophic damage to vital organs, biorepair and resuscitation are not difficult, although it can be costly enough in terms of resources to make the process too expensive to be worthwhile. I realize that these concepts may well be beyond your primitive, superstitious comprehension. Nonetheless, the fact remains that the ship's medical systems will be able to 'bring back to life' all but four of your warriors and six of your horses."

Sir George stared at the demon-jester, stunned as he had not been since the very first day of his captivity. He'd believed his daily exposure to the wonders of the demon-jester's "technology" must have prepared him for the ready acceptance of any miracle it might produce, but he'd been wrong. If he understood the demon-jester correctly, then eleven men who had been dead—not simply wounded, but *dead*, with neither heartbeat nor breath—would be restored to life like so many present-day Lazaruses.

The simile sent a cold shiver down his spine. He'd come to truly believe what he had insisted upon in front of his followers from the beginning, that the demon-jester, for all of his marvels and tricks, was no more than mortal. That his kind had simply mastered arts which humans hadn't yet learned to duplicate. But *this*—! If the demon-jester's guild could raise the very dead, like the Savior Himself, then *were* they truly mortal? For that matter, did the very concept of mortality even exist for such as they?

No. He shook himself mentally. Whatever else the demon-jester might be, he was no god. If the Physician could use the "technology" of sickbay to save men whose bowels had been opened or whose lungs had been pierced so that blood bubbled at their nostrils and air whistled through the holes in their chests, then was it really so very great a step to breathe life back into the dead?

A part of him insisted that it certainly *was*, but another, greater part recognized that it was only a difference in degree, not in kind. And, he reminded himself, whatever seeming miracles this "technology" of the demon-jester's could create, he remained sufficiently fallible that he'd failed to recognize the blind spots in his own analysis of the situation he faced on this world. By his own admission, the "primitive" whom he had stolen from Earth had demonstrated a far better grasp of the locals' probable reactions and responses than he had.

"Very well," the baron said after a moment. "Four men and six horses. Although those numbers are lower than the ones I had believed applied, those who are actually lost remain impossible for us to replace. If we face additional combat against an alliance of the locals who can put more warriors than the Thoolaas into the field against us, it's likely that our losses will be higher, even under the best circumstances. If the faction opposed to you not only musters a larger army against us but also considers what happened to the Thoolaas and adjusts its tactics, losses on our part will increase. Moreover, the caltrops which we employed to such good effect against the Thoolaas are unlikely to come as a surprise in any future battle—certainly not to the extent to which they surprised the Thoolaas, at any rate. Even if they make no changes in their manner of fighting other than to avoid rushing into the sort of trap we were able to set at the river ford against the Thoolaas, they will substantially increase the effectiveness of their warriors, which will increase the cost to us of defeating them."

"Does a warrior like you fear death?" the demon-jester asked.

"Of course I do," Sir George replied. "Any man must fear death, especially if he's unshriven when it comes upon him. In this case, however, I speak less as a mortal who fears death for himself than as a soldier who recognizes that every man he loses decreases his military strength. And as our strength declines, so our ability to gain the victories your guild expects of us will decline."

"You do not believe you will be able to overcome an alliance of the local tribes, then?"

"I didn't say that," Sir George replied. "If it is indeed possible to identify the tribes who will support you against the Laahstaar and Mouthai, then it ought to be possible to recruit warriors from those tribes to take the field with us. If my own forces serve as the core of a larger, combined force, then our effectiveness will be multiplied and our losses should be reduced. My fear is less for what can be accomplished here, than for our long-term ability to sustain ourselves in your service."

"I see. It is good that you think in terms of sustaining a

guild resource, but you need not concern yourself with such matters. Those decisions are properly made by myself, both as your Commander and as the senior representative of my guild present. Your only concern is to facilitate the execution of my commands as efficiently as possible. To that end, I may solicit your advice, but the decision on how we will proceed is mine, not yours, and I will make it."

Sir George clasped his hands more tightly behind himself and forced himself to remain silent, and the demon-jester considered him for several moments in matching silence.

"In the meantime, however," the small alien went on eventually, "I am pleased with how well you and your warriors have fought for my guild. I will address them shortly to express my pleasure personally to them. In addition, as a reward for your hardiness and bravery, I will have your mates and your young removed from stasis and reunited with you while we await further developments among the locals. I trust that you will be properly grateful for this reward."

"Oh, yes," Sir George said, showing his teeth in something even the demon-jester should have been hard pressed to call a smile. "Oh, yes, 'Commander.' I feel certain that all of my men will be properly grateful and recognize the reason we've received this . . . reward."

## -V-

The sentry outside the striped pavilion came to attention as Sir George approached. The baron nodded an acknowledgment of the man-at-arms' salute, then stepped through the open tent fly, unbuckled his sword belt, and placed the sheathed weapon on a wooden rack. A foot fell softly on the luxurious rug behind him, and he turned with a smile as Matilda stepped out of the huge tent's inner chamber. She crossed to him and rose on tiptoe, offering her lips, and he kissed her soundly.

"How went your meeting?" she asked, settling back on her heels as she broke the kiss.

"As well as any of the others," he replied with a shrug. "Which is to say it could have gone better, but it might have gone much worse."

"Timothy taught you to be much too philosophical as a boy, my love," Matilda said with a hint of severity.

"Strange that you should say so," her husband replied with a crooked grin, and reached out as one of the mechanical servitors provided by the demon-jester floated up with a goblet of fine wine. "My father said much the same, from time to time. Usually, as I recall, just before my arse made the acquaintance of his belt for some infraction or another."

"That," Matilda said, "doesn't surprise me in the least."

"I thought it might not." He took a second goblet from the tray atop the hovering metallic sphere and pointed with his chin at the pair of camp chairs flanking the chessboard on the table beside the pavilion's central pole. Matilda accepted the wordless invitation and sank into the chair facing the white pieces. An interrupted game was arrested in mid-progress, awaiting their attention, and Sir George hid a smile as even now Matilda took a moment to consider the board and—no doubt—her next move.

He paused long enough to plant another brief kiss on the part of her hair, then handed her one of the goblets, and took the facing chair. He stretched out his long legs before him, and leaned back, letting his eyes roam around the richly appointed tent.

The pavilion's fabric looked like the finest silk, but it wasn't. In fact, its fabric was even lighter and tougher than silk, yet far more efficient as an insulator. It billowed gently on the breeze blowing across the encampment, and he heard the strange, wailing songs of what passed for birds on this world through the thin walls. The scents which floated on that breeze had become familiar during the weeks the English had camped here, yet whenever he concentrated upon them, the subtle differences between them and what he would have smelled on Earth were only too apparent. He would have found it difficult to define precisely what those differences were, but their existence was undeniable, yet another reminder that men had not been born in this place.

He glanced back out of the open fly, past the sentry who stood with his back to the tent. A half-dozen youngsters went racing past, equipped with fishing poles and obviously headed for the deep stream on the west side of the camp. Edward was among them, and the baron nodded in approval as two of the younger men-at-arms jogged after them in full armor to keep an eye on them. He had no doubt that Edward would regale him and Matilda over supper with tales of the monster fish which had miraculously evaded him at the very last moment, or that the men-at-arms would solemnly attest to the escapees' enormous size. It was a pity that Computer had been forced to warn them that this world's fish were deadly poison for humans, but that had done nothing to diminish the ages old fascination water, fins, and scales had always exercised upon boys of Edward's age.

He watched the children out of sight, then returned his attention to the camp itself. From where he sat, he could see three more pavilions, each almost as luxurious as his own, set aside for the other knights of his company. Beyond those were still more tents, even larger although less luxurious, where his officers and sergeants shared their own quarters. And beyond those, stretching outward in concentric rings towards the palisade and earthen walls that rimmed the encampment, were yet more tents, each housing twenty men. At Sir George's forceful request, the demon-jester had provided separate, smaller tents for any man accompanied by his wife, and the unattached women and their children shared two large common tents which were carefully watched over by their own sentries every hour of the night and day.

Fires burned before several of the tents, although there was no real need for them, given the efficiency of the "space heaters" with which each tent was equipped. No doubt some might have thought that was silly, Sir George reflected. But it was also one more aspect of the way in which the English tried to pretend that they were not entirely adrift in time and space, and there was nothing at all "silly" about that.

Despite his lack of any readable expression, it had been obvious from the demon-jester's comments that he had been . . . perplexed by Sir George's request to establish an encampment outside the ship. In many ways, Sir George could understand his "Commander's" confusion, because comfortable though their tents were, they were still a considerable step down from the many marvels and casual comforts which had been available to them aboard ship. Yet even so, they contained marvels of their own which made even the lowliest trooper's quarters as luxurious as anything a crowned king might have enjoyed on Earth. And they also offered one absolutely priceless thing the ship couldn't: the illusion, however brief and fragile, that they were still free men.

His gaze flicked to the racked sword, and even as his right hand raised the goblet to his lips, his left hand fell to his side and touched the reassuring hardness of his dagger hilt. Aboard the demon-jester's ship, he and all of his men were prohibited from bearing arms at any time, aside from the blunted weapons used in training, and even those poor counterfeits had to be surrendered at the end of each training session. Nor was any human outside one of the training chambers permitted armor—or, for that matter, any object made of iron or steel—aboard the ship.

Here, it was different. To some extent, it had to be. Computer had selected the site for the camp with Sir George's assistance, and it was placed far enough from any of the native tribes here on the world Computer had finally gotten around to telling Sir George was called Shaakun to make an attack upon it extremely unlikely. Unlikely wasn't the same thing as impossible, however, and so, much as would have been the case in France, had the company ever reached it, weapons and armor must be kept ever close at hand. It was probably foolish, given the demon-jester's demonstration of their weapons' inefficacy against him, but having a good, honest sword or lance or bow to hand made men who had begun to feel like chattels walk once more like *men.*

It was unlikely the demon-jester understood them well enough to recognize that. Certainly the small, ridiculous-looking creature had demonstrated an unerring ability to say precisely the wrong thing at the wrong time. Sir George sometimes wondered if his "Commander" had once read a treatise which explained what an officer was supposed to say and do to inspire his troops. He certainly acted like some clerk who had stuffed his head with book knowledge unfettered by any polluting contact with reality or experience! Yet if he had perused a treatise, it had obviously been a very bad one . . . or else one which had been written for some sort of creatures very unlike any man Sir George had ever commanded.

His mouth twitched, on the very verge of a chuckle, as he recalled the ludicrous speech with which the demon-jester had announced to the company that, as a reward for its defeat of the Thoolaas, it would be permitted to camp outside the ship and all of the other humans, including their women and children, would be awakened from stasis to share their tents with them. If the "Commander" had had an ounce of common sense, he would have confined himself to that bare announcement and let Sir George worry about exhorting the troops to perform equally well the next time. But he'd been unable to do anything so sensible, and so the company had stood in ordered ranks for almost a full hour while the demon-jester's piping voice blathered on about their "heroic bravery" and "matchless puissance" and "selfless devotion to our guild." Only the ferocious glares of their officers and one or two bloodthirsty threats muttered from the corners of Rolf Grayhame's or Dafydd Howice's mouths had prevented outright laughter from sweeping the ranks. Sir George hadn't blamed the men at all, but he'd been vastly relieved when the demon-jester finally finished and his air car carried him back to the ship. Their "Commander" would not have reacted well if he'd realized how his "loyal and courageous warriors" actually regarded his bombastic speech.

But perhaps the baron wronged him. It was entirely possible that the demon-jester wouldn't have been concerned in the least. After all, what did a superior being such as himself care for the crude and ignorant amusement of such primitive barbarians?

"You have that thinking-about-other-things look again,"

Matilda told him, and he gave his head a brief shake and returned his attention to her.

"Forgive me, my love. I was merely recalling the 'Commander's' inspiring speech following the battle. I wish you hadn't missed it."

"I, also," she said, but she shot him a sharp-eyed glance as she spoke, and he shrugged. No doubt she was right to worry, for he had allowed a bit too much of his true opinion of that "inspiring speech" to color his tone. Computer seemed able to hear them at almost any point in the encampment; certainly he had demonstrated that he could hear them at any point within their tents and pavilions, and that suggested he was monitoring all of their conversations just as Sir George was certain he did aboard ship. The baron, Father Timothy, and Sir Richard between them had discovered four or five places within the confines of the encampment where Computer didn't respond when called upon, and Sir George had made careful note of where those places were, but he wasn't prepared to risk any injudicious conversations even there. The fact that Computer seemed not to hear them when they called for his attention was no guarantee that he truly couldn't.

On the other hand, Sir George was coming to the conclusion that whatever translated the demon-jester's language into English and his own words into whatever it was the demon-jester spoke did as poor a job of translating *his* emotions from his tone as it did of communicating the demon-jester's to him. Again, that was not a conclusion he intended to put to the test, but he was honest enough to admit that his control had slipped more than once in conversation with his "Commander," and the demon-jester seemed not to have noticed a thing on any of those occasions.

"But to return to my original question," Matilda went on, "how did your meeting with the 'Commander' go?"

"Things are proceeding much as I predicted they would," he told her with another shrug. "The Laahstaar and Mouthai continue to rant and rave and demand the rejection of the 'Commander's' terms, not to mention our own bloodthirsty extermination. Computer has done a remarkable job of eavesdropping upon even their inner councils," he went on, arching one eyebrow, and she nodded vigorously to show she'd understood his hint, "and it seems certain that the senior chief of the Laahstaar sees our defeat as the means whereby he will be able to replace the Thoolaas as the royal tribe. From what he's been saying to his subchiefs, the senior Mouthai chieftain will undoubtedly suffer a fatal accident at the height of their battle against us, because the Laahstaar have no desire to see their authority weakened and diluted as that of the Thoolaas was."

"How very homelike," Matilda murmured with a slight smile, and Sir George nodded.

"It does rather remind me of Scottish lairds or Irish 'kings,' " he agreed. "Especially since the Mouthai appear to be planning something similar for the Laahstaar."

"Oh dear." Matilda shook her head. "It seems dreadfully unfair for such innocents to find themselves in your toils, my love."

"Not my toils," Sir George corrected. "The 'Commander's.' I'm merely an advisor, much as Computer. The final decisions, of course, are entirely his."

"Of course," she said quickly, and her expression was contrite. Indeed, it might have been a little frightened, and Sir George reached across the chessboard to touch her cheek lightly. Matilda, he knew, was concerned that the demon-jester might regard a subordinate who was too competent as a threat. Given the strange-looking little alien's ruthlessness and contempt for his unwilling human troops, there was little doubt in her mind—or Sir George's, for that matter—that if any one of them did become a threat in the demon-jester's eyes, that person would die quickly.

Sir George understood his wife's fears, and he wasn't about to discount or ignore them, yet he had become more and more convinced that it was virtually impossible for the demon-jester to conceive of any circumstances under which Sir George or any other human could pose a genuine threat to such a superior and civilized being as himself.

Oh, he took endless precautions to assure his own security and that of the ship. No human could open any of the hatches or doors which would have permitted them to move beyond the portion of the ship to which they were confined. None of them were permitted weapons aboard ship, and the armed wart-faces who watched over them there (and who, Computer had finally informed Sir George, were properly called Hathori) were a constant reminder that disobedience or rebellion meant death. Even here, in their isolated encampment, a full score of heavily armored, ax-armed Hathori wandered about, or stood glowering from the small hill above the camp upon which a "landing shuttle" from the ship rested. The English weren't unarmed now, and after what they'd done to the Thoolaas, even creatures as stupid as the Hathori obviously were must have realized that they could be killed any time Sir George or his men took it into their heads to kill them. But that was fine with the demon-jester. The Hathori weren't truly there as jailers; they were there as an alarm or a forward picket. If any of the humans were so foolish as to attack them, the demon-jester's vengeance would be sudden and complete, and they knew it as well as he did.

Yet for all those precautions, or perhaps because of them, the demon-jester never truly believed that any of his barbaric, unwilling mercenaries could truly threaten him. Even if they'd tried to, his precautions would surely thwart any rebellion, and because of that he was far more casual and careless about what those humans might be thinking or doing than Sir George would ever have allowed himself to be in the other's place.

Not that it was likely to make a great deal of difference in the end, of course, because however routine they might have been, the demon-jester's security measures *were* effective.

Dangerous as it was even to let himself dream about it, Sir George had been unable to keep himself from searching daily for any means by which he might escape or overthrow the demon-jester, and so far he'd found absolutely nothing to suggest either might be possible. It was the more galling because it was only the demon-jester's "technology" and the unswerving loyalty of Computer which made that true. Without those advantages, the demon-jester, his ship's crew, his Hathori, and probably even the perpetually silent dragon-men would have stood precious little chance against Sir George's veterans. But he had those advantages, and the baron was not about to let himself forget that.

"Meanwhile," he went on in a tone of determined cheer, "the tribes which favor accepting our—or, rather, the 'Commander's'—terms seem to be falling into line. Two of them have made their minds up already and sworn everlasting fealty and perpetual loyalty to the 'Commander' and the guild." He rolled his eyes, and Matilda covered her mouth with a hand to stifle a giggle. "At least four others appear to be strongly inclined to the same direction, and Computer and the 'Commander's' mechanical envoys are negotiating with still more."

"And the other side?" Matilda asked.

"It seems likely that the Laahstaar and Mouthai will be able to attract more of the local tribes than we will," Sir George admitted with a shrug. "Computer and I are still attempting to make some sort of estimate of what that will probably mean in terms of numbers when we finally bring them to battle, but the situation is still too unresolved. At the moment, I would estimate that we and our allies will be outnumbered by something like three to two. It might be somewhat higher than that, but not, I think, by too much."

"That seems quite a large enough advantage for them," Matilda said tartly, and he smiled.

"I would prefer for the advantage to be on the other side myself," he acknowledged. "Especially since the Laahstaar, at least, seem to have taken what happened to the Thoolaas to heart. They'll be much more cautious than the Thoolaas were, I think . . . or they'll *attempt* to be, at any rate. It's always easier for a commander to decide to be prudent and cautious than it is for him to convince his troops to be the same, though. Once battle is actually joined, it's the troops who matter, and these creatures are so accustomed to charging to the attack that I think it will be next to impossible for any chieftain to convince them to adopt a defensive stance.

"But whatever the size of the force they manage to put together in the end, they'll definitely need some weeks to hammer out questions of command, organization, and precedence. It will be worse than putting together an *English* army, love, though I never thought I would hear myself say anything could be worse than that! And while they're busy getting themselves sorted out, Rolf, Walter, and I will be busy sorting out our 'allies.' By the time we have their dart-throwers properly trained and massed to support our archers, I feel confident that we'll be able to handle whatever the Laahstaar and Mouthai can put into the field against us."

"But with what losses among our own folk?" Matilda asked softly, and her glorious blue eyes were dark. Sir George smiled at her as reassuringly as he might. He knew she was genuinely concerned about the possible loss of *any* of their men, but he also knew who her greatest fear was reserved for.

"Men die in battle, Matilda," he said quietly. "Even with allies among the natives, it seems likely that some of our men will die in this one. But not many, I think." Her eyes burned into his, and he met her gaze steadily. "I am speaking the truth, love," he told her. "Before we faced the Thoolaas I hadn't fully realized just how good the new armor and weapons provided by the 'Commander' truly are. The most poorly armored of our footmen are as well armored as any knight serving under King Edward in France, and all of our horse are better armored than any one I ever saw on a field of battle on Earth. Our weapons are superior to those of the natives, and so is our training, and I'm confident that our losses will be low, unless some evil chance leads to our complete defeat, and that seems most unlikely."

"I know that here," she said, touching her forehead. "But here—" she touched her breast "—confidence comes harder. You're a good husband and a good man, George, and I love you. Yet I think sometimes you don't really understand how hard it is to watch the one you love ride into battle and know you cannot ride with him."

"Probably not," he agreed, reaching out to cup her cheek once more. "I understand enough to know how little I envy you that burden, though," he went on, "and I would do anything I could to ease it for you. Yet the choice of whether or not to ride off to war is even less mine here than it was in England, and at least we know that our 'Commander' regards us as a 'valuable asset' to be expended as sparingly as possible." He smiled and reached for a lighter note. "And you won't be shut of me so easily as all that, My Lady! Even if I were to fall, the Physician and his arts would be like to restore me to you, anyway."

"That isn't the funniest jest you ever made, George," she told him, and his smile faded before the look in her eyes.

"You're right," he said. "It wasn't. Forgive me."

"Oh, of course I do, foolish man!" she said, reaching up to capture his hand and squeeze it firmly. "And it was foolish of me to take it wrongly, when I know you meant it only to reassure. Yet . . ."

Her voice trailed off with something very like a shudder, and Sir George's hand squeezed hers back while he nodded in understanding. The demon-jester had been correct; eleven dead men had been returned to them from the Physician, and the company's reaction to that uncanny fact might have been disastrous. The baron suspected that only the warning the demon-jester had so casually given him had prevented the troops' reaction from being even worse than it was, yet it had been bad enough.

The resurrected men themselves had no memory of what

had happened to them from the moment they were struck down. Not any clear ones, at any rate. They'd been slow, almost stupid, for the first day or so after their return—in some ways like men who had drunk too much wine, and in others like some shambling parody of one of the demon-jester's mechanical devices. It had been difficult for them to recognize their own names when they heard them, and their efforts to reply to questions had been clumsy and wandering, like those of someone whose wits were wanting.

All of the wounded who had been treated by the Physician had recovered from their injuries with miraculous speed. Few of them had any truly clear memories of how their wounds had been healed, but the one or two who did spoke of being shut into a close-fitting crystal cabinet which enveloped all but their heads and which had filled rapidly with something very like the cleansing vapor of the ship's communal baths. But this vapor had been different—stronger, denser, almost like a liquid rather than a gas—and it had burned and tingled as it flowed over them. It hadn't been *pain*, they'd all agreed, with varying degrees of certainty. It had only been . . . different. A sensation they couldn't truly describe, and which Sir George hoped he could avoid discovering from personal experience.

Yet whatever it was, and however it worked, it had left its mark upon the wounded men, for the portions of their bodies which had borne the wounds had emerged a deep red in color. Not the color of blood, but rather the deep, lobster-like shade of Englishmen foolish enough to expose their skins to the blazing sun of Spain or the Mediterranean. Yet for all of its darkness, there'd been no pain, no sensitivity to the touch, and the red shade itself had faded quickly over the next day or two.

Their eleven Lazaruses had been the same shade of red, but they had been red all over, and the color had faded much less rapidly. Logically, Sir George supposed, that should have been reassuring, especially to men who'd carried the same tint upon their own skins as a result of wounds which they had survived, but it hadn't been. Instead, it had only added to the sense of supernatural dread which seeing dead men walking had evoked in almost all of his troopers.

No, he thought. Be honest. That dread had been evoked not just in his troopers, but in himself, as well, despite the demon-jester's forewarning. Things might have turned ugly indeed, he conceded, if not for Father Timothy. Thank God he'd been wise enough to take the priest aside and warn him the instant he could! Timothy had been no less shocked than he was. In fact, his shock was probably worse, for he had always been taught—and taught others—that miraculous cures and healing were gifts from the power of God, and no one could ever have mistaken the demon-jester for one of the Lord's saints!

Fortunately, Timothy had been given the better part of two days to prepare himself. He'd spent the vast majority of that time in prayer and fasting, seeking divine guidance, and when he emerged from his vigil, his eyes had been calm and confident. When all of the troopers had shrunk back from the returned men, some making signs against evil or even, in one or two cases, reaching for weapons, Timothy had rounded upon them like some broad shouldered, white-bearded bear of God. The power of his voice when he denounced their fears and exhorted them to accept God's miraculous acts, however bizarre the circumstances under which those acts had been accomplished, would have done any true bear proud, and the frightened soldiers who'd cringed before the inexplicable had looked unmistakably like small boys who had incurred the wrath of an irate tutor as the priest's familiar, homey thunder broke upon them.

Yet for all that, there was still that lingering sense of the uncanny. The unspoken question—fear—of whether or not the men who had returned to them were truly the ones who'd been taken from them in the first place. *Were* they the same men? Or were they changelings? The same flesh but animated by . . . something else?

Sir George truly believed Timothy was right. Of course he did! After all, God could act through whomever He chose, even a demon-jester who was a parody of anything upon His Earth. But still . . .

"I trust Timothy," he told Matilda firmly. "If he says these resurrections are miracles of God, to be accepted as such, who am I to argue with him? Yet even though I trust him and believe he's correct, my emotions have yet to catch up with my faith and my intellect, I fear." He smiled at her. "You aren't the only one who continues to find the entire affair uncanny, My Lady! If I didn't find it that way, no doubt I wouldn't be so clumsy as to try to turn aside my own concerns with an ill chosen jest."

"I fear we will have a great many other equally 'uncanny' things to which to adjust before we're finished," she told him, giving his hand a final squeeze. Then she released it, and leaned back in her camp chair, sipping from her goblet.

"You've always had a gift for understatement, my love," he told her wryly, and she snorted.

"Say rather than I've always had a gift for blurting out the first thought to come into my head, and you'd be closer to the mark!"

"Hardly that, although it has occurred to me upon occasion that your father probably had no idea what he was about to unleash upon an unwary world when he encouraged you to learn to read."

"Oh, I think he had a very clear idea what would happen," she told him with a chuckle whose sadness had dimmed as passing time dulled the knifelike edges of her loss. "I think he was more than pleased to have a daughter to spoil as his youngest child, and I don't think he worried himself too much over the handful he was about to bestow upon whatever unfortunate husband he finally found me!" She snorted again. "In fact, he probably thought it was only fair that whoever wed me wind up with a wife as hardheaded as his own!"

"Now there you're probably absolutely correct," Sir George

agreed, and it was his turn to chuckle. But then his chuckle faded into something softer and warmer as he let his eyes rest upon his wife.

He knew how unhappy she was to have been able to bear only one child. She'd miscarried twice before Edward's birth, and lost two more children after that, and the thought that she was barren, unable to provide him with the additional heirs needed to safeguard the succession of his hard-won lands and titles, had been both her greatest regret and the cause of her greatest sense of failure. Well, Sir George shared her sadness, just as he had shared her grief with each child they'd lost. And, yes, he too had spent sleepless nights, especially when some childish ailment had left Edward feverish and restless, worrying over how many hopes and plans, how much of the future, resided in one fragile child. There were so very many ways a child could die before attaining his majority, and every one of them had gone through the baron's mind at one time or another.

Yet for all of that, he had never once seriously considered taking another woman to his bed to bear the additional sons and heirs many another noble would have considered absolutely essential. He was only human, and here and there, especially when he was in the field, far from home and feeling his loneliness and mortality, there had been moments of temptation. Strong moments, some of them, for he was a vigorous man, and one women had always found attractive. But they'd been only moments, never more than that. Some of his peers had made jokes about his chastity and fidelity, but only his closest friends had dared to do so to his face, for Sir George Wincaster had a temper, and very few men had ever desired to meet him with a weapon in hand.

For the most part, though, there had been an edge of begrudging admiration in the humorous comments that had come his way—the admiration of men who saw someone doing something they themselves could never accomplish . . . and which, despite a nagging suspicion that they *ought* to want to accomplish it, they had no true desire to emulate. Yet the truth was that it had never been that difficult for him. Partly that was because he was a man who took his sworn word seriously, and what oaths had he ever sworn more solemnly than the ones he'd taken upon his wedding day? But much as he would have liked to believe that it was his iron sense of honor which had kept him true to his wedding vows, he knew there were two other reasons which had at least as much to do with it. One was the fact that, in all his travels, he had never met a woman he found more beautiful than the one who had consented to become his wife. But the second, and by far the more important, was that however unmanly some might think it, he loved his wife more than he loved life itself, or even his honor. He could be as clumsy and as maladroit as the next man. He could hurt her with thoughtlessness, or carelessness. He could even, however fleetingly, be angry with her, and lash out with hurtful words when he was. But the one thing he simply could not do was to knowingly and deliberately betray or hurt her. That he would die before doing.

Something of his thoughts must have showed in his expression, for Matilda's eyes softened, and he inhaled deeply as her beauty smote him once again. Not everyone, he knew, would have called her beautiful. She was tall for a woman, taller than many men, with a strong nose and chin which spoke all too accurately of a strong-willed, stubborn character. Just as many would have considered her overly tall, she had broad shoulders for a woman and long, strong fingers, not the dainty, white hands of a "proper" noblewoman, and she moved with the athletic stride of a lifelong horsewoman. Her gowns had always seemed too confining for someone with her energy, and the magnificent golden spill of her hair was too often confined in a tight bun which kept it out of her way as she lost herself in one of her precious books, or her daily journal, or the endless sketchbooks she had filled since her father imported an Italian drawing master when she was thirteen. She had an oval face, and a figure so slender that at twenty-nine she might well have been taken for someone ten years younger . . . and any denizen of Castle Wickworth could have added that she had the Devil's own temper. Yet they would also have told anyone who asked that it was a temper which was roused by injustice or falsehood or acts of unthinking stupidity, not one born of vindictiveness.

Not a wife for everyone, Lady Matilda Wincaster . . . but the only imaginable wife for him, and a brief, icy chill went through him as he realized yet again what a deadly weapon the demon-jester had to use against him, if ever the creature realized it.

"You have that look again," she told him.

"Do I, indeed?"

"Yes, you do. And in the very middle of the day, too," she said primly.

Sir George glanced out the tent fly. The dim sun of Shaakun was sliding towards the west, already half entrapped in the uppermost branches of the spindly trees on that side of the encampment, and he looked back at his wife.

"It's well past midday," he disagreed calmly.

"Not by more than an hour, at the most," she replied. "And what about Edward?"

"He and his cronies won't be back from their current fishing hole for hours," he said confidently.

"Perhaps not. But he's not the only one likely to come searching for you, now is he?"

"No, but he *is* the one most likely to manage to come bursting in unannounced."

"Oh, and so you can be confident Father Timothy won't drop by to discuss Elisabeth Goodthorne's latest indiscretion? Or that Sir Richard and Walter won't decide that this is the very evening you need to decide how to reorganize the mounted men-at-arms? Or Rolf and Dafydd won't—"

"No, but I *can* be confident that if I tell the sentry to inform any or all of them that I am . . . otherwise occupied they'll leave us in peace," he told her with a slow smile.

"Shocking! I am *shocked* that such thoughts could divert you from the requirements of your duty, My Lord!"

"Blame it on those garments our 'Commander' has provided you, and not on any weakness on my part," he suggested, and she laughed like a flurry of silver harp notes. He supposed a proper husband should still find the tight-fitting, one-piece garment horrifyingly immodest and forbid his lady wife to display herself in public so revealingly clad. But the truth was that that shockingly immodest garment suited her tall, slender shapeliness amazingly well. Not all the women attached to the company were equally fortunate, although by now all of them had been forced to more or less adjust to it, since they had no option. But Sir George had decided, after a deplorably easy tussle with his conscience, that this was one innovation of the demon-jester's with which he wholeheartedly agreed.

"And what, My Lord, did you have in mind to occupy yourself with, if I might ask?" she demanded.

"Of course you may ask, My Lady," he told her with a grave courtesy only slightly undermined by the twinkle in his eyes. "However, I believe, all things being considered, that it would probably be simpler for me to demonstrate rather than attempt to explain."

"Would it indeed?" she purred.

"Oh, yes," he told her softly, rising and walking around the chessboard towards her. "Indeed it would."

"It seems a bit different today, M'lord."

"A masterful understatement, Walter," Sir George said dryly.

The two of them stood side-by-side beneath Sir George's banner and gazed outward at the moblike "formation" of the combined tribes led by the Laahstaar and Mouthai.

It was a large, sprawling formation. Computer had provided Sir George with regularly updated estimates of the maximum size of the force the native alliance could put into the field, but as the baron gazed out over that surging sea of hostile, four-armed warriors, he wondered if Computer had gotten his sums straight this time. According to Computer's current tabulation, the eight tribes which had come together, after a fashion, under the leadership of the senior war chief of the Laahstaar counted a total of approximately forty-one thousand warriors, of whom perhaps three-fourths could actually be brought to any field of battle. That should have meant that the maximum Sir George, his men, and their own native allies, led by the Sherhai, Naamaal, and Tairnanto tribes, could face would be some thirty-one thousand.

At the moment, it looked to Sir George as if at least twice that number of broad-footed natives were busy trampling the purple-bladed grass into dust as they headed for his own position. No doubt anxiety was making him count at least some of them more than once, but it still looked like an enormous force.

*Well, of course it does!* he told himself. *The bastards are twice our size, after all. No wonder it looks as if there are twice as many of them!*

"Well, M'lord, I'd best be getting over to Sir Richard." The master of horse looked at his commander for a moment, and his smile was crooked. "Do us all a favor, and try not to get yourself killed," he suggested.

"I was planning not to," Sir George replied. "My wife would never forgive me if I let that happen."

"With all due respect to your lady wife, M'lord, it wasn't her I was thinking about just now," Skinnet replied. "I was thinking what a right mess this would be if someone else—" he jerked a surreptitious thumb in the direction of the air car hovering overhead "—was trying to hold this carnival together."

Sir George glanced upward at the air car, and grunted something between a laugh and an exasperated sigh.

"I take your point," he told his henchman. "Now take

yourself over to Sir Richard and see to it that he doesn't let his enthusiasm get the better of him!"

"Don't you be worrying over that, Sir," Skinnet assured him. "Sir Richard and I, we've come to understand each other. And if we hadn't, his squire and I certainly have." The tough old veteran chuckled nastily. "If I thought we'd need it, I'd have had someone take a wee knife to his saddle girth last night."

"You're an evil man, Walter Skinnet!" Sir George scolded with a grin.

"Aye?" Skinnet seemed to consider for a moment, and then tossed his head in an armored man's equivalent of a shrug. "No doubt you're right, M'lord. Still and all, they say as Purgatory isn't all that bad a place. And think of all the dukes and earls I'll have to keep me company!"

He laughed again, and then he and his gelding trotted off towards the mounted human force clustered about Sir Richard's personal standard. Sir George would have preferred to be over there in Satan's saddle himself, but he couldn't. Officially, the army of natives about him had been assembled by the demon-jester. It was even possible that the demon-jester himself actually believed that, but Sir George and all of his troops knew better. It was the baron, working through the translating offices of Computer, who'd truly put that army together. And it was also the baron to whom everyone in that army, natives as well as humans, looked for command.

Some of the friendly tribes shared generations of mutual enmity, with blood feuds as tangled as any Scottish clan might have boasted. Common need and the scent of advantage to be gained might have brought them together temporarily, but the mere thought of finding themselves under the command of one of their cherished enemies would have been intolerable. Sir George, on the other hand, was the chosen field commander of the "godlike" demon-jester, the strange, alien champion whose vastly outnumbered troops had completely destroyed the Thoolaas' power and killed almost five thousand of their warriors for the loss of only four of his own.

He knew they considered him almost as uncanny as the demon-jester himself, and that sense of awe, coupled with the fact that he came from outside their customary quarrels and struggles, made him an acceptable leader when none of their own could have been. All of which meant he had to be right here, in the center of his line, where the most senior chieftains could see him and where he could see *them*—and the unfolding battle—clearly.

Personally, he could have done without the role of champion or the responsibilities which came with it, but he'd had no choice but to accept them both. And so he'd spent the last month (as nearly as Father Timothy could calculate it) combining the warriors of the three principal tribes allied with the demon-jester and the smaller bands of their vassal tribes into an army that, as of this morning, counted nineteen thousand natives and his own English. It hadn't been a simple task, yet in some ways it had been far easier than he had anticipated. The native leaders were as treacherous, scheming, and unscrupulous as the leaders of any feudal army Earth had ever boasted, but they had nowhere near the experience at translating their treacherous schemes into success. Sir George hadn't spent the last fifteen years of his life rising to command in the feudal armies of England without learning to deal with much more capable plotters. The graduate of a far more sophisticated school, he'd played the various combinations skillfully off against one another.

The hardest part had been keeping the demon-jester at arm's length while he did it. The baron still was far from clear about why the demon-jester and his guild were bothering with this world in the first place. So far as he could tell, the locals had absolutely nothing that should have attracted merchants who commanded the demon-jester's marvels and "technology," and even if they did possess some unsuspected treasure, the demon-jester's roundabout way of going after it seemed particularly stupid. There had to be some reason for the mysterious guild to be involved here, even if Sir George couldn't imagine what that reason was, but if the guild was determined to control trade with the natives here, why not simply move in with their superior weapons? A small force armed with the fire weapons the dragon-man guards carried could easily have defeated an army far larger than the one currently headed in Sir George's direction . . . even under the demon-jester's inept command. Well, perhaps not with the demon-jester in command, he amended. After all, the demon-jester had raised military incompetence to a level of art not even a Frenchman could have rivaled.

That incompetence had become glaringly apparent the instant the demon-jester began attempting to assemble the coalition of native leaders Sir George had warned him would be required. In fairness to the demon-jester, at least some of his maladroitness probably stemmed from the fact that he'd never anticipated that such an alliance would be necessary, but that was part of the problem. Obviously, he had expected Sir George and his company to deliver a quick, salutary drubbing to the local potentate, following which he would dictate terms and speedily depart. Unfortunately, there had *been* no local potentate—not in any meaningful sense, at any rate—and even if there had, the severity of the "drubbing" the Thoolaas had received had completely broken their power. Apparently, it had never occurred to the demon-jester that, as a long-term policy, shattering the military capabilities of the people who were supposed to enforce one's terms upon their fellows was a self-defeating proposition.

The more Sir George had watched the demon-jester in action here on Shaakun, the more puzzled he'd become. Even leaving aside the matter of why someone with the weapons and capabilities the demon-jester possessed should require the services of swordsmen and archers, there was the question of how the demon-jester could be so incompetent at using them now that he had them. It was as if he'd begun this entire effort, from the moment he first stole the English from their own world, with only a vague, theoretical notion of just what he intended to do. For all his invincible assumption of superiority, he seemed to be learning as he went . . . and it was painfully evident that he was not an outstanding student.

In some ways that was good. As long as he was willing to allow someone who did know what he was doing (like one Sir George Wincaster) to get on with the practical management of the campaign, the consequences of his incompetence could be minimized. And the discovery that he required Sir George's insights and political skills as badly as he required the baron's military talents might well work in the English's favor. It certainly was working that way at the moment, at any rate, although it was also possible that it could turn into an additional danger for Sir George personally in the future. No wise general wanted to find himself completely dependent upon someone else to whom his troops looked as their true commander, and more than one such "indispensable" man had been put aside or quietly murdered when his personal stature became a threat to his superiors. On the other hand, from the beginning, the demon-jester had been completely contemptuous of the possibility that his army of stolen Englishmen could ever be a threat to him. It followed from that towering confidence that he could never visualize any way in which that army's devotion to its original commander could ever threaten him, either, and Sir George devoutly hoped that nothing would change the demon-jester's mind in that regard.

Whatever might happen in the future, though, it had been up to Sir George and Computer to identify the factions and ambitions swirling amongst their "allies" and to manipulate them to the demon-jester's advantage. And so they had, the baron thought, standing atop the ridge line at the center of his position and looking up and down the front of his combined army.

His line stretched for the best part of three quarters of a mile in either direction from where he himself stood, much further than he could have liked, despite the fact that he'd held out almost five thousand warriors as a reserve and that his main formation was as much as twelve ranks deep at what he expected to be the critical points. That was one reason Skinnet and Sir Richard were operating as a detached command on his right. Sir Bryan Stanhope, with Dafydd Howice looking over his shoulder to keep him out of mischief, had another small force of cavalry on the left, while Rolf Grayhame and Sir Anthony Fitzhugh commanded the archers in the center. Splitting his cavalry that way reduced its effectiveness, but it also let him use the detachments to stiffen the resolve and discipline of his more questionable native contingents.

Yet the dispersal of his horse was the least of his worries at the moment, for he was about to do something no human commander in history had ever done: exercise direct, personal command over an army of twenty thousand . . . men. Even attempting to control such a huge force would have been futile on Earth, but Sir George enjoyed certain advantages no Earth commander ever had. Computer's "overhead imagery" could watch over the entire battle with an eagle's eye, and Computer's reports would keep him updated on its course with an accuracy no scouts' reports could hope to equal. Even better, Computer could speak to him or to any of his subordinate human commanders here on the field just as easily as he could in their encampment, and he could relay orders and questions faultlessly.

Sir George wished he had thought more closely about all of the implications of that before his first battle against the Thoolaas, but he'd considered them at length since then. And he'd also come to the conclusion that he'd probably been right not to unsettle his men by adopting too much of the demon-jester's "technology" in that battle. But he'd worked with it in training exercises with them since until they were completely comfortable with it, and the fact that he no longer required trumpet signals or couriers to control his troops completely changed the nature of war. There would still be any number of things which might go wrong, but watching an entire army disintegrate from the confusion of orders gone astray wouldn't be one of them. Better yet, his ability to communicate orders instantly to any one of his subordinates turned his entire company into an extension of his own brain. He was in a position to enjoy a flexibility and sureness in execution such as no human field commander had ever known.

The inclusion of so many natives tended to dilute that flexibility to some extent, but the demon-jester's "communication relays" helped even there. There weren't as many of them as Sir George could have desired, but they had been distributed to all of the principal chiefs and most of the subchiefs, and Computer could use them to relay Sir George's translated orders to his native levies. For some reason he couldn't quite unravel, Computer had seemed a bit uneasy over that when he first proposed the idea. It wasn't anything Computer had said, but Sir George had come to recognize the reticence Computer fell back upon when one of his own questions obviously touched upon information the demon-jester had decided he was not to have. At first, he'd thought it would simply be rejected out of hand, but then Computer had changed his mind (or the demon-jester had overridden his reluctance), and Sir George wondered what could conceivably have caused Computer to hesitate even briefly. That ability to communicate quickly and surely was an absolutely priceless tactical advantage, and as one of the "god devices" the "Commander" could provide, it had also helped to cement the locals' acceptance of the demon-jester as at least semidivine.

Sir George, a good Christian for all of his faults, was just a bit uneasy at passing off the demon-jester, of all creatures, as "divine." The fact that he himself enjoyed something of the status of an archangel in their eyes bothered him even more, but not nearly enough for him to consider foregoing the advantages it offered. After all, he consoled himself, none of the natives had ever heard of Christ, so either they were all doomed to Hell anyway, or else a merciful God must have made other arrangements. And if He had, then it was most unlikely that anything Sir George could do would upset them.

He chuckled, eyes still on the steadily approaching enemy force, at the thought . . . and even more of Father Timothy's expression when he'd shared it with the priest. Oh well. No doubt Timothy would come up with a suitable penance eventually.

Then he shook the thought aside. The enemy was coming on much more slowly and deliberately than the Thoolaas had, but they were still drawing close enough that it was time to leave off his woolgathering and focus his attention on the matter at hand.

The opposing force was less of a mob than he'd first thought. It still boasted nothing he would have called discipline, but now that it was approaching, he could at least see what its commanders had had in mind. Two massive columns, each over a hundred warriors across, were headed roughly for the center of his own line. There must have been eight or nine thousand natives in each of those columns, and another four or five thousand had been detailed to cover the columns' flanks. The rest of the force, a solid mass of dart-throwers, was positioned between the columns, and he grimaced at the sight. There were at least seven or eight thousand of them, and this time the natives had been careful to adopt a formation which would not inhibit their fire.

Their intention was clear enough. They planned to deluge the center of his own force with javelins as they closed, then slam those twin columns through his shaken and decimated ranks like a pair of battering rams. As tactics went, it both had the virtue of simplicity and made the maximum use of their superiority in numbers. True, there was very little subtlety to it, but in Sir George's experience, subtlety was a poor substitute for overwhelming strength, anyway.

On the other hand . . .

"The Tairnanto are becoming restless." Computer's tenor voice was as emotionless as ever as he spoke in Sir George's ear. "Some of their subchiefs are pressing for permission to attack."

"Tell Chief Staramhan to remind them of the plan!" Sir George said sharply.

"Acknowledged," Computer replied calmly, and Sir George reached into the front of his bascinet to rub his nose irritably. All he needed was for his "allies" to revert to their normal tactics at the last moment!

There was no doubt in his mind that they would have done precisely that if left to their own devices, even though they must have known that the disparity in numbers would have led to inevitable defeat. They were even more like the French than he'd thought, in that respect, and only his "archangel" status had permitted him to break them, even imperfectly, of that gallic impulsiveness. Unfortunately, he couldn't be certain that they would *remain* broken of it.

He swung himself into the saddle and took his reins from Snellgrave. For a moment, he considered riding down the line to Staramhan's position to make his point in person, but he banished the temptation. It would take him several minutes, even on Satan, to get there, and those were minutes he could not afford to waste. He had a much better view of the approaching enemy from here than he would from Staramhan's location on his left. Besides, riding over to quell one trouble spot would only ensure that he was out of position to deal with any others as they arose. Better to rely upon Computer's ability to relay his commands and stay where he was.

This relying on superior communications took some getting used to, he thought with a snort. He must remember not to let old habits betray him into casting away the advantages they bestowed.

The enemy force's pace was increasing. They were still too far away for him to make out individual voices, and even if he'd been able to do that, he would have been unable to understand what they were saying. But he didn't need to be able to hear individuals or to understand the natives' language to know what they were shouting. The deep, guttural rhythm of a chanted war cry rolled back along the lengths of the columns, the war drums thudded harder, louder, faster, and the entire mass of the opposing army accelerated quickly.

There was a new note to their war cries, one of what he rather thought was contempt. They were jeering at his own troops, taunting them for standing their ground rather than charging to meet them as proper warriors would. A small stir went through the ranks of his own army, but the chiefs and subchiefs stilled it quickly, and Sir George permitted himself a nasty smile as his formation settled back. His allies were holding their ranks after all, and that meant the oncoming natives were about to discover how much more dangerous than warriors *soldiers* were.

The enemy moved from the long, steady lope with which the natives normally covered ground into a full run, hurling themselves forward, and Sir George felt himself tighten internally as a cloud of javelins went up from their dart-throwers.

"Shields now, Computer!" he shouted, and all along his formation, the large, rectangular pavises he had introduced went up like protective roofs.

The baron's native allies had protested vociferously when he first introduced the concept of shields. None of them had liked the idea of giving up half of their hand-to-hand weapons for what was basically a useless piece of wood. But he'd insisted, and when he demonstrated the reason for his insistence, much of the protest had faded into silence. There were still reservations, but they were prepared to give the concept a try . . . especially when Computer reported to them the number of dart-throwers the enemy had managed to amass.

Now the slender javelins came sleeting down like lethal rain, and Sir George heard the rattle and thud as their bronze heads slammed into the interposed shields. Screams went up as some of the javelins found a home in flesh and bone, but the vast majority of them were intercepted and bounced harmlessly aside or embedded themselves in the shields.

The rain of fire from the enemy dart-throwers seemed to hesitate for a moment as the unprecedented shields blunted their attack, and Sir George smiled again. Pavises were more common at Earthly sieges, where they were used to protect archers against return fire, than in the field. But that was because *human* archers required both hands to use their bows, and so each pavise had to be held by someone else or else mounted permanently in place on a supporting framework. The natives of Shaakun, on the other hand, had four arms each, and so they could shield themselves and still have two hands free for weapons. They might have felt under-armed compared to someone with weapons in all four hands, but they seemed to be getting over that, Sir George thought. They were shouting just as loudly as their foes, now, and most of what they were bellowing sounded like insults directed at the enemy dart-throwers.

The rest of the enemy army howled furious war cries and lunged forward, but Sir George had expected that. As the twin columns came on, he barked another order, and his own dart-throwers sprang into action. Because they, too, carried pavises, their rate of fire was lower than that of their opponents, but despite the smaller total size of his army, Sir George actually had more missile troops than the other side did, for he'd recruited them ruthlessly from every tribe. It hadn't been easy, because the locals were as prejudiced in favor of hand-to-hand combat as French knights were, which explained the low proportion of dart-throwers he had initially observed. The combination of javelins and throwing sticks was the customary hunting weapon of Shaakun, and most of any tribe's warriors had at least some skill with it, yet they stubbornly insisted on meeting their enemies one to one.

Sir George had solved that problem by being even more stubborn than they were, and in the end, over half his total native force consisted of dart-throwers. Many of them had insisted upon bringing along axes or flails as backup weapons, but each of them also had at least one full quiver of javelins, and now they sent a lethal cloud of darts back at their enemies.

Despite the fact that the other side's dart-throwers could use all four arms, and thus could maintain a considerably higher rate of fire, the contest was brutally uneven. Sir George's missile troops swung their pavises aside and exposed themselves only when they actually launched one of their own javelins. Their targets, on the other hand, were totally unprotected, and the oncoming columns began to slow as the warriors in the lead ranks stumbled over the javelin-sprouting bodies of their fellows.

Half of Sir George's dart-throwers concentrated on the heads of the columns. The other half sent their javelins directly back at the opposing dart-throwers, and the enemy's fire faltered as the lethal shafts showered down upon them. The air was clotted with javelins, war cries, dust, and the shrieks of wounded and dying natives, and Sir George strained his eyes to see through the dust of thousands of charging feet.

"Computer! Tell Rolf to concentrate on the right-hand column!"

"Acknowledged," the passionless voice responded, and a moment later something twanged like half a thousand discordant harps. There were far fewer human archers than native dart-throwers, but their rate of fire was higher, their range was longer, they were more accurate, and the heavier armor the demon-jester's "industrial modules" had provided them with was almost completely proof against the incoming javelins.

Their arrows slashed into the right-hand enemy column, the one which had been least disordered by the fire of Sir George's dart-throwers, and the consequences were immediate.

What had been a steady tide of casualties became a flood, and the entire column stumbled to a halt in a tangle of dead and wounded bodies. It hung there for a moment, the decimated survivors of its lead ranks standing shocked and confused, knee-deep in shoals of writhing bodies, and in that moment it was lost. Sir George had seen it on a dozen other fields—the instant when the belief that victory was within one's grasp suddenly transformed itself into the conviction of defeat—and he recognized it now.

The column hung on for a few more moments, wilting as the terrible waves of arrows and javelins slashed through it, and then, suddenly, it disintegrated. It didn't fall back, didn't retreat. It simply . . . came apart. One moment it was a solid mass of warriors; the next, it was a fleeing mob of individual refugees, each seeking his own safety in flight.

"Tell Rolf to shift to the dart-throwers!" Sir George barked. "And instruct Walter and Sir Richard to advance their wing and take the Mouthai flank guard from the right. If they can, I want them to circle completely around to the enemy's rear and come at them from the back!"

"Acknowledged."

Sir George heard Computer's acknowledgment, but he hardly noticed. The right column had been shattered and driven into flight, but the left one was still coming on. He would have preferred to rake it with arrows as he had the other, but the attackers hadn't hit the exact center of his line. He'd placed his archers there to receive the assault, but the way the enemy had slipped to Sir George's left meant his bowmen were concentrated too far to his right, and a slight rise would have shielded the oncoming natives from much of Grayhame's fire. Better to throw the longbows' weight into completing the destruction of the enemy's missile capability and let his allies, stiffened by Sir Bryan and his armored foot and horse, deal with the column.

Javelins continued to slam into the oncoming natives up to the very last moment, and the dreadful weight of fire tore huge holes in their formation, but they came on anyway, carried by their battle frenzy and howling their war cries. The rows of pointed wooden stakes and the thickly-seeded caltrops which had been strewn among them slowed the attackers, but still they came on. The warriors in their lead ranks absorbed stakes and caltrops alike with their own bodies, as their predecessors had absorbed the javelins, and at last the survivors were able to close with their foes.

But Sir George's waiting allies were more than ready for them. Unlike the charging column, they were unshaken, and they scented victory in the blood. They'd taken their own losses from the javelin exchange, but those losses, however painful, were a pittance compared to what they might have been. What they *would* have been without the pavises their human commander had insisted they use. Even the most stubborn among them realized that, and they also knew their enemies were already more than half broken.

Many of them discarded their shields, now that it had come down to the melee. The dart-throwers dropped their throwing sticks and snatched up axes, and Sir George heard a gleeful howl go up from his allies as they hurled themselves to meet what was left of the left-hand column. The enemy's dart-throwers might have taken advantage of the sudden disappearance of the shields which had so blunted their own attacks, but they were no longer capable of taking advantage of anything. Those of Sir George's native troops who weren't part of the melee continued to hammer them with javelins of their own, but it was the steady, pounding rain of clothyard shafts which truly broke them. It wasn't even that the arrows were more accurate or more destructive than the javelins flaying their ranks. They *were* more accurate and destructive, but that was almost beside the point. What truly mattered was that they were the emblem, the symbol, of the strange, two-armed demons who had completely changed the way war was supposed to be.

The right-hand column had already disintegrated. Now the

dart-throwers began to follow suit, shedding individual warriors, first in trickles, and then in floods. For all their courage, the tribesmen lacked the discipline to stand under the vicious pounding, and the entire dart-thrower force came apart in turn.

The left-hand column was still in action, but its front was splintered and broken. Almost half of the total attacking army had already been driven from the field, and the flattened, blood-slick grass was heaped and mounded with the bodies of warriors who would never again be driven from any field. The conviction of defeat was upon the column, and as more and more of Sir George's allies swarmed forward to meet it, it found itself enveloped and outnumbered. The column formation which had given it so much weight as it charged forward now hamstrung its ability to defend itself, for those at the center of the formation could only stand there, unable to advance or retreat, while their more numerous enemies cut their way inward from both its flanks.

And then Sir Richard Maynton and Walter Skinnet completed their enemies' ruin. The handful of human cavalry were an armored spearhead of steel, the wicked tip of a sweeping charge of over three thousand of their native allies, almost as fast on foot as the humans were mounted. The charge had swept out to Sir George's right and then, at his relayed orders, hooked back and in, sweeping around the troops the enemy had put out to cover his left flank to take what was left of the dart-throwers in the rear and then thunder onward into the rear of the one remaining enemy column.

Sir George watched that column fly apart, like a bag of meal thrown into the air on a heavy wind. It shattered into thousands of individual, fleeing warriors, and he knew the battle was won. It was not yet *over*, for there were still thousands of enemies upon the field, and some of them would stand and fight to the death. His allies would lose many more warriors before they swept up all the pieces, and his own men would take casualties, as well. But the outcome was no longer in doubt, and he allowed himself the luxury of a brief, fervent prayer of thanks.

Then he opened his eyes once more, straightened his shoulders, and nodded to young Snellgrave.

"Let's be going," he said, and sent Satan trotting forward to join the slaughter.

# -VI-

"You have done well. My guild will be pleased," the demon-jester's voice piped in Sir George's ear.

The small alien sat in his air car, hovering no more than six feet above the ground so that Sir George could look almost straight across at him through the open vehicle window as the baron sat in Satan's saddle. The light, expressionless voice seemed even more grotesque than usual as Sir George turned his head away to gaze out over the heaped and mounded bodies of the slain. Never in all his days, not even at Dupplin or at Halidon Hill, had he seen such slaughter. Not even the devastating defeat of the Thoolaas had littered the field with so many corpses, and human or not, the groans and whimpering moans of the wounded and dying sounded much the same. The aftermath of battle, the smells and sights and—especially—the sounds, was what had always truly haunted the baron, and as the aftermath of *this* battle washed over him, a sudden wave of fury filled him.

His armor was splashed and spattered with blood. His sword had been gummy with more of the same and clotted with hide and hair before he cleaned it, and his body ached in every muscle and sinew. A final, despairing charge of warriors who had known they were defeated, whose only remaining purpose in life had been to reach and kill the author of the destruction of their tribes, had very nearly succeeded. The howling tide of ax-wielding barbarians had slammed into his personal bodyguard, and if they hadn't—quite—managed to kill Sir George, they *had* hacked down his squire. Thomas Snellgrave would never be knighted now, the baron thought grimly. The young man had flung himself between three shrieking Laahstaar warriors and his liege while Sir George was fully engaged against two others, and not even the Physician could restore life to someone whose head had been entirely severed and whose body had been hewn limb from limb by the vengeful axes of warriors who had known they were doomed.

Nor had young Snellgrave been the only human fatality. Seven more of Sir George's men were "dead," and from the reports he'd received, it seemed likely that at least two of them would remain that way despite even the Physician's healing magic. Three lives might not weigh for much against the thousands upon thousands of other lives which had been taken away this bloody day, but in an odd sort of way, it was the very smallness of the number which made it hit so hard. It was one a human mind could envision and feel, not a vastness impossible to truly comprehend. And unlike the anonymous natives whose bodies covered the plain as far as the baron could see, the men those lives had belonged to had been part of his own life. They had been *his* men, faces he'd known, individuals—people—for whom *he* had been responsible. They'd gone into battle under his orders, and they had died there, and one of them left behind a wife and three children.

The filth and suffering, the horror and the loss, weighed down upon the baron. A hard man, Sir George Wincaster, and a tough one. A soldier who'd seen massacre and casual cruelty enough before this day even when both sides had been human, and one who was no more immune to the fierce pride of victory against overwhelming numbers than any other man. Oh, yes, he was all of those things. But he was also the man who had wrought the savagery which had covered this purple-colored grass on this alien world with agony and blood. His was the mind which had created the alliance which had made it all possible, and his was the voice which had launched his men and their allies into the vortex. He knew that, and the guilt for what stretched as far as he could see weighed down upon him like the very millstones of God.

And now the demon-jester hovered beside him, floating like some evil sorcerer of legend above the Hell-spawned landscape, untouched and clean despite the unspeakable carnage. Congratulating him. Telling him how well he'd served in that voice which was never touched by emotion. No doubt that emotionlessness was largely the product of whatever translated the demon-jester's language into English, but not all of it was. Sir George had spent too much time with the demon-jester, heard too many of his dismissals of his "inferiors'" right to be considered even remotely his equal, to doubt that for a moment. His "Commander's" satisfaction was genuine, however little feeling there might be in his voice, and that satisfaction was unshadowed by even a trace of the horror which haunted Sir George. The demon-jester and his precious guild were responsible for every drop of blood, every wound, every corpse . . . and the alien didn't even care.

Did the demon-jester ever so much as think about it? Did it even occur to him that the beings, human and otherwise, whom he had so casually condemned to death had been living, thinking creatures? It was impossible to tell, but Sir George very much doubted that it did. Whatever else the bodies tumbled about the field of battle might have been, they had never been *people* to the demon-jester. They'd been mere obstacles, "primitives" to be compelled to submit to his will or destroyed, whichever was required, by the equally primitive Englishmen he'd stolen from their homes. And if there had been any reason to feel guilt or remorse—there wasn't, of course, but if there *had* been—then that guilt would have belonged to Sir George and his men, not to the demon-jester. If, of course, such primitives as they could possibly have possessed the sensitivity to feel such things.

The baron clenched his teeth, fighting down the tidal bore of his hate as he gazed at the true author of the atrocity he had just wrought. It took every ounce of the iron self-control learned in twenty years of warfare and political infighting, but somehow he kept that sick tide of loathing leashed. Rage hammered the backs of his teeth, yet he refused to let it out. Instead, he bit off the invective his soul cried out to hurl into the demon-jester's emotionless, double-mouthed face. He chewed the iron-tasting words and swallowed their jagged shards, and made himself nod to the creature upon whom the lives of every one of his men and their families depended.

"Indeed, Commander," he said. "The men fought well, and our allies showed better discipline than I'd truly expected."

"So I observed," the demon-jester replied. "I do not believe that the Laahstaar and Mouthai will raise any further objections to my guild's terms."

*No,* the baron thought harshly, *they won't. There aren't enough of them left.*

"It will, of course, be necessary to make certain of that," the demon-jester continued, oblivious to the human's reaction. "And as you have proven surprisingly adroit at negotiating with and understanding these crude and primitive creatures, I may require your assistance in framing the precise terms of our trade agreements."

"As you command," Sir George replied. The thought of serving the demon-jester's interests further galled his soul, but even as it did, he recognized the alien's words as proof of the increased value the creature assigned to him.

The baron looked away from the air car once more, gazing out over the field where the demon-jester's mechanical minions hovered, still collecting the wounded . . . and at least some of the dead. He'd tried to convince the demon-jester to make the Physician's services available to their allies' wounded, as well, but his "Commander" had insisted that there would not be sufficient return upon the investment to make it profitable for the guild to extend such services to the natives. The possibility that he might have had any moral responsibility to them hadn't even crossed his mind, yet at least Sir George had gotten him to agree to allow the natives access to the water-carriers and to collect his allies' wounded and transport them to their own villages for whatever treatment their healers could provide. The human was only too well aware of how little that actually amounted to compared to what the demon-jester might have done for them, but *they* weren't. As far as they were concerned, simply having their wounded transported home was a miracle, and he felt an all too familiar sense of flawed achievement. What he'd accomplished fell far short of anything he would have considered just, yet little as it was, it was still better than they would have had without him. He knew that, and yet a part of him deeply resented the way in which it had actually enhanced the natives' sense of gratitude to the demon-jester who considered them worth less than as many dumb beasts.

"No doubt you have duties to which you should attend," the alien's voice piped into his ear, "so I will detain you no longer. Inform your men that I am pleased with them. I will, of course, tell them so myself at a suitable moment."

"Of course, Commander," Sir George managed to say in a nearly normal voice, and watched the silent air car float away across a sky heavy with Shaakun's equivalent of ravens.

Matilda and Edward looked up from her cherished illuminated manuscript of the tale of King Arthur, opened on the table between them, as Sir George walked into the pavilion. Almost a week had passed since the battle, and they'd seen little of him during that time, for the demon-jester had indeed made extensive use of his services. Not only did Sir

George show a better understanding of the natives than the demon-jester ever would, but he was also the very personification of the cost of defying the demon-jester's will. The tribal chieftains who'd fought under the baron's orders regarded him with awe and near deification, while potential enemies feared him like the very angel of death.

It had not been a comfortable week.

Now Edward started to jump to his feet and reach for the chilled ewer of wine which had been awaiting him, but Sir George waved him back and slumped wearily into an empty camp chair.

"Stay where you are, boy," he said, and grimaced. "I've had all the wine I can stomach for one day."

Matilda's eyes narrowed, and she gazed at him speculatively. He saw her expression and gave a short laugh.

"Oh, it's not so bad as all that, love," he told her. "It was just that our 'Commander' was feeling . . . generous—" his mouth twisted wryly on the word, "—and opened his cellars wide for me." He inhaled deeply. "It appears that we've now accomplished his goals here on Shaakun," he went on. "He's most grateful for my assistance, although, of course, as a member of a truly advanced race, he could have accomplished the same without me."

A trace of alarm flickered in Matilda's blue eyes, but he shook his head quickly.

"Don't worry that I've turned down fresh wine," he said. "It's not because I'm drunk. I walked all the way here without stumbling once, and my head was clear enough to let me repeat his exact words to you."

His wife relaxed at the oblique assurance that he was using the demon-jester's own words and not allowing his obvious fatigue and disgust to betray him into indiscretion.

"So the other tribes have acceded to his demands?" she asked.

"Indeed, they have. It wasn't as if they had a great deal of choice, after all," he replied with another grimace. "All that was truly necessary was to . . . explain that to them. And to suggest that what befell the Thoolaas, Laahstaar, and Mouthai could also befall them if they refused."

"I should think so," Matilda agreed. "So he's satisfied with their submission?" Sir George nodded, and she wrinkled her brow. "I must confess, my love, that I remain puzzled by all of this."

"I should hope you do!" he snorted with a sudden burst of true amusement. "*I've* been 'puzzled' by everything that has happened to us since the day we first set foot upon that accursed cog's deck!"

"You know perfectly well that wasn't what I meant!" she scolded, and he nodded again, this time with an edge of contrition. "I still don't understand what these creatures could possibly possess to make it worth the 'Commander's' guild's time and effort to bring us here in the first place. Or be the cause of so much bloodshed and killing once we were here."

"I'm far from certain of that myself," her husband admitted, "but I've learned more in the past few days than I did know. I'd already discovered that some ore which is mined here is of considerable value to the guild, but until just yesterday, no one had explained the process by which it is extracted to me. I still have no idea what it is, or what makes it sufficiently valuable to bring the 'Commander' here, but I believe I've discovered why the natives were so . . . reluctant to allow his guild to mine it, and it wasn't at all why I'd thought they were. You see, I'd thought that *they* would be required to mine it as part of their submission."

"They won't be?" she asked in a surprised tone.

"No. The 'Commander' and Computer explained to me yesterday that some other guild has already installed machinery on this world to accomplish that without the need for supervision. Their devices extract the ore and store it until a ship calls to collect it."

"Some *other* guild," Matilda repeated very carefully.

"Yes." Sir George frowned. "Computer actually did most of the explaining, and he was less than completely clear." He held his wife's eye for just a moment, and she nodded in understanding of the limits the demon-jester clearly had placed upon what Computer was allowed to tell them. "From what he did say, however," Sir George went on, "it would appear that this other guild had previously gained the right to mine the ore, whatever it is, from the Thoolaas at some time in the past. Those rights have now been transferred to the 'Commander's' guild."

"But if they'd already conceded those rights to someone else, then why were they so unwilling to transfer them to the 'Commander' when he arrived?" Matilda asked. "Were they that loyal to whomever they'd already granted them to?"

"Hardly!" Sir George snorted. "So far as I can tell, the Thoolaas were no fonder of the previous owner of the mining rights than they were of us. From what I've been able to discover, however, this mining process is very destructive and dangerous for the natives. There's so much more 'technology' involved in it that I'm completely unable to understand everything that it entails or how it works. But how*ever* it works, it lays the area in which the mining takes place completely waste. According to Computer, it kills every living creature in the immediate vicinity of the mine and poisons the water and the land for centuries."

"And these . . . people *permitted* that on their own lands?"

"I would assume that the Thoolaas had no more choice in the original 'negotiations' than our 'allies' had in these," Sir George said dryly. "On the other hand, I believe I now understand the position of the Laahstaar and Mouthai better than I did. Although the Thoolaas had been forced to concede the original rights, they had at least managed to restrict the area covered to a desolate, unused area on the far side of their tribal lands. But it seems that one reason for the combined tribes' resistance to the 'Commander's' demands was that he required not only that the right to mine be transferred to his guild, but that the area to be mined be extended into the heart of the Laahstaar tribal lands, as well."

"Sweet Jesu," Matilda murmured, and crossed herself slowly, her eyes haunted—as Sir George's own had been—at the realization of what they had been given no choice but to help bring to this world.

"But if this process is so destructive and dangerous, how can the 'Commander' expect that they won't destroy the mine and all of its equipment once we leave? Especially if it threatens their own lands and the lives of their own people?" she asked after a moment.

"They can't," Sir George said simply. "Again, I don't pretend to understand how it's accomplished, love, but Computer says that the equipment itself is protected by something he calls a 'force field' which prevents its destruction. Besides, the area around the actual site of the mine is so heavily poisoned that any native who attempted to enter it would perish long before he could do any significant damage to it."

"I see . . . I think," Matilda said slowly, but she also frowned and shook her head. "Yet if their equipment is invulnerable, and if the natives dare not even approach it lest they die, then why seek an agreement to mine it in the first place? Why not simply establish the mine and ignore the natives entirely if there's nothing they can do to prevent the operation in the first place?"

"That's a question I'm only beginning to puzzle out an answer for," Sir George admitted. "As nearly as I can tell, there is some authority to whom all of the guilds must submit. Whether that authority is what we would call a government or not is more than I could begin to say from what I now know, but its decisions appear to be binding upon all parties. Apparently, it apportions grants of authority in matters such as this to maintain order among the various guilds, and the consent of *someone* native to this world is a precondition to obtaining its permission to mine here."

"And he doesn't expect whoever has just lost the rights to this world to complain to this authority that he's poached upon their preserve?"

"Apparently not. Again, it hasn't been explained to me because it wasn't something that I had to understand in order to discharge my duties, but the 'Commander' seems quite confident that the new agreement will supersede the older one beyond any possibility of successful challenge."

"So his guild will simply take over everything which had belonged to its rivals? And even if it does, how will they prevent anyone else from trading with the natives in our absence? From what you've already told me, he clearly doesn't intend to stay here to enforce the terms of his new agreement, so why shouldn't anyone else with his advantages in technology simply arrive here and demand that the natives trade with *them*? Or, for that matter, lie to the natives and claim to be representatives of the 'Commander's' guild?"

"I raised the same questions with Computer," Sir George said. "To answer the last one first, he told me that the natives will never have the option of trading with anyone else so long as the current agreement is in force. Something he called an 'orbital traffic monitor' is permanently stationed here. He says that it 'orbits' the world, which—if he is to be believed, and by now I see no reason not to believe him—means that it actually travels in a permanent circle around a round planet. However that may be, it contains still more of these people's technology, and the 'Commander' will place a copy of his new agreement aboard it. All ships approaching Shaakun are required to report their presences and identities to it, and it will inform any other merchant vessels that the 'Commander's' guild now has exclusive trading rights here. That notice will warn them that any attempt by anyone else to trade with the natives is a crime which carries very heavy penalties. As I understand it, those penalties may range anywhere from heavy fines to outright confiscation of the violator's vessel."

"But if it's unlawful for anyone else to trade here in

violation of exclusive agreements, then hasn't the 'Commander' himself violated the law?"

"Not according to Computer. The 'Commander' comes from what is obviously a very ancient civilization, my love. They have highly developed laws and customs which Computer says govern every aspect of their lives and business arrangements. The 'Commander' himself isn't taking a single pound of ore with him when he leaves, and technically he hasn't 'traded' with anyone on this world. All he's done is to . . . negotiate a *new* trade agreement which makes it legal for his guild to trade here henceforth. All of the ore which has already been mined and processed under the pre-existing agreement belongs to the guild with whom that agreement was negotiated, and it would be illegal for the 'Commander' to take any of it. But when the other guild's ship arrives to collect the ore which has been mined since its last visit—and Computer says that ships call here only once every fifty or sixty of our years—it will be illegal for *that* ship to take any of the ore which has been mined since our agreement went into effect. Any which had been mined before our arrival will belong to the other guild, however, and the 'Commander's' guild will be required to maintain very careful records to ensure that none of the other guild's property is molested or misappropriated."

"It all sounds very complicated," Matilda sighed.

"I certainly can't disagree with you about that," Sir George agreed. "But Computer insists that their customs and traditions are so binding that no one would even consider violating them. Which doesn't mean, so far as I can tell, that they won't search diligently for any loophole or technicality which might permit to them to violate the *spirit* of a custom or regulation so long as they can do it in what's technically a legal manner."

"In that much, at least, they seem very like humans," his wife observed, and he chuckled sourly.

"In some ways, they *are* very like us. In others, though, I find that they become more difficult to understand with experience, not less."

"I suppose that's inevitable, given the huge differences between us and them," Matilda said. "Still, it occurs to me that if the 'Commander' and his guild can compel the Thoolaas, or some other tribe, at least, to cede the exclusive trading rights for this entire world to them without technically violating their own laws, then surely someone else could do the same thing to them."

"The same thought had occurred to me," Sir George replied. "I asked Computer about that possibility, and he admitted that it existed, but he seemed unperturbed by it. For all I know, that indicates that it's not unusual for trade agreements to be changed in this fashion. Since they wait fifty or sixty years between visits here to collect the ore anyway, perhaps it's simply that the amount mined between visits is sufficient to pay for all the effort the 'Commander' went to in our own case."

"And still neither he nor Computer has explained to you why they needed the swords and bows of you and your men instead of simply using their own weapons?"

"That they haven't," Sir George confirmed, and his tone darkened once more. "Nor, I think, will they anytime soon. But whatever the reason, we seem to have demonstrated our value here conclusively. From what the 'Commander' and Computer have said, the guild will require our services for the same purpose elsewhere soon enough. And, as I said, the 'Commander' has already expressed his gratitude to me. I understand that he'll be expressing it personally to the men sometime this evening."

"I see." The change in his expression and voice had not eluded Matilda, and she cocked her head at him. "And has he suggested some means by which he intends to make his gratitude manifest?"

"Indeed he has." Sir George looked into her eyes. "He intends to reward us with two more weeks here on Shaakun . . .

before he returns us to 'stasis' for the voyage to our next destination."

Matilda inhaled in quick dismay, and he reached out to capture her hand and squeeze it tightly.

"I could have wished for longer," he said much more lightly than he felt, "but at least you and I and Edward will have those weeks without the press of constant negotiations with restive chiefs or worries about taking the field. And it wasn't as if either of us ever thought that we could stay here forever, you know."

"No, but—" she began, then stopped herself.

"I know," he said gently. "And, truth to tell, I was surprised by his generosity. I don't know how long he originally expected to remain on this world, but I know it was nowhere near the time we've actually spent here. He feels the pressure to move on, yet I believe we've convinced him of how much we value our time in the open air outside his ship. And I believe he's come to truly value my counsel as well as my battle skills. Surely, in the long term, that can't be a bad thing, whether it be for us or for the benefit of the rest of our people."

"No, of course not." She drew a deep breath and smiled at him. "Indeed, my love, I am prouder of you now than ever I was on Earth. Certainly none of the King's other captains have ever had so intricate a measure to dance as you!"

"In some ways, no doubt," he agreed. "Yet I've enjoyed much assistance and advice, with yours not least among them. And—" he grinned suddenly "—however intricate the measure, at least my goals have had the advantage of both clarity and simplicity!"

She had to chuckle in response, and he stood and drew her against his side, then put his free hand on Edward's shoulder and drew him into a rough, shared embrace.

"God only knows how far we are from the world we once called home," he told his wife and son more quietly. "But however far it is, we'll soon be traveling still further, and at the end of the next stage, there will be fresh battle for us to face. And after that, another, and yet another." He held Matilda's gaze for a moment, then bent his head to look down into his son's eyes. "We do not move to our own purposes or by our own choice," he told Edward, "but wherever God sends us, we will face whatever task awaits us and do whatever we must. We have no choice in that, but whatever befalls us, we will not forget that wherever we may be, we are still Englishmen and Englishwomen, and we will remember our duty to those who look to us."

Edward gazed silently up at him for a long, still moment. Then he nodded firmly, and Sir George smiled proudly and ruffled the boy's hair.

"Very well," he said, turning back to his wife. "At least we know how much vacation we'll enjoy, and Sir Bryan and his lady have bidden us to a picnic this afternoon. Would you wish to join them, My Lady?"

"I would, indeed, My Lord," she replied, and his arm tightened about her for just an instant before he nodded in satisfaction.

"Good," he said. "In that case, my love, let us go."

# -VII-

The starship's lander was less than a tenth the size of its mothership, little more than eight hundred feet in length, and made out of the same bronze-tinted alloy. Despite its smaller size, its main cargo hold was a vast and empty cavern, for it was configured to lift heavy loads of cargo out to the starship . . . and to deliver loads of English soldiers to the surface of the worlds they were sent to conquer. Those same soldiers had seen far too much of the hold's interior over the years, but at least this deck didn't pitch and dance like the decks of those never to be sufficiently damned cogs.

The thought wended through a well-worn groove in Sir George's mind as he leaned forward to pat Satan's shoulder. The destrier shook his head, rattling the mail crinnet protecting his arched neck, then stamped his rear off hoof. The shoe rang like thunder on the deck's alloy, and Sir George smiled thinly. He and the stallion had been through this all too many times. By now both of them should be accustomed to it, and he supposed they were. But neither of them was *resigned* to it.

The warning gong sounded, and Sir George rose in the stirrups and turned to regard the men behind him. A score of orange-skinned, wart-faced Hathori stood beyond them, clad once again in their heavy plate armor and armed with their massive axes, lining the holder's inner bulkhead, but their function wasn't to support the Englishmen. As always, it was to drive them forward if they hesitated, and to strike down any who attempted to flee.

Not that any of Sir George's men were likely to flee . . . or to require driving.

The baron and his company were completely adrift in time. Father Timothy had been forced to concede that it was impossible for him to truly know what the day or date was back on long-banished Earth, despite how long and hard he had attempted to maintain some sort of accurate reckoning. Sir George had attempted to ask Computer to keep track of that for them when the priest had finally been driven to admit defeat. Surely such a task would not have been impossible for the mysterious, all-knowing creature invisible at the other end of the voice that whispered in his ear. Not compared to all of the other impossible things Sir George had seen Computer do, at any rate.

But Computer had refused. More than refused, for Computer had informed the baron that he was expressly forbidden to tell the humans how long they had been unwillingly in the service of the demon-jester's guild.

That in itself told Sir George a great deal. The demon-jester had been almost careless in regard to many of the things Computer was allowed to share—or, at least, not specifically prohibited from sharing—with the English. Much of the information which Computer had let slip had been useful to Sir George in the subtle bargaining he'd done with the demon-jester on planet after planet. It was always helpful to know as much as he could about the local terrain and the opposition which might be expected in the field, and Computer had often provided him with odds and ends of the history of a given world. More than once, Sir George suspected, he had in fact learned more about a particular planet and the relative value of its produce (if not *why* its products had value) than the demon-jester would have preferred. Armed with that knowledge, he'd been able to delicately wrangle specific privileges or extra time upon a given planet out of his "Commander" as a *quid pro quo* for bending his own skills and insights upon the demon-jester's current problem.

But perhaps even more importantly, the baron had learned other things along the way, things which would have been pronounced rank heresy on the Earth he had left behind. He'd shared most of that knowledge with Father Timothy and the other members of his council, although he'd kept one or two of Computer's more disturbing facts (or theories, at least) to himself. He rather doubted that the demon-jester realized just how much Sir George now understood, however imperfectly, about the larger universe in which the demon-jester's starship moved. Computer routinely used a host of terms which continued to mean but little to the baron—words like "quasar," "nova," "neutrino," "spectral class," and any number of other words whose meaning he was barely beginning to puzzle out. But the demon-jester appeared unaware that Sir George had learned about what Computer called the "speed of light" (although the very notion that light could have a limiting "speed" had flown in the face not only of all he'd ever been taught, but all he'd ever seen) and about what Computer called "relativistic time dilation." The precise meanings and consequences of the terms continued to elude him, since Computer had never specifically explained them to him, but he grasped them well enough to know that if a vessel spent time at or near the speed of light then time aboard it passed far more slowly than it did for the rest of the Creator's universe.

Given the fact that the demon-jester's starship seemed to spend all of its time ferrying the English from one blood-soaked field of battle to another, the "time dilation" effect had to have been considerable. It was impossible to know just how considerable, but Sir George suspected that Computer had been forbidden to tell them the date on Earth so that none of the English would know how many years had elapsed since their departure. It was quite possible, he thought, that everyone they'd ever known was dead by now, even though no more than eleven years had passed by Timothy's reckoning. Of course, that was eleven continuous years of wakefulness; none of them had the least idea how many years they'd passed in the unknowing slumber of phase drive stasis.

Well, they did know one thing for certain: far more than eleven years had passed while they slept.

Not that any of them could have told that by looking at one another, or at any of the other adults of the company, at least. Solely on the basis of the time that he personally had spent awake and aware, Sir George was at least forty-six by now. In fact, he was certain, he was considerably older than that, yet not a single one of his hairs had turned to frost. There was no stiffness in his joints, his teeth were still sound (indeed, three he had lost long ago had regrown), his vision was actually keener than it had ever been on Earth, and in every way that he could judge, he was not a single day older than he'd been on the storm-sick evening when the demon-jester plucked them from the sea.

Computer and Physician had spoken to him of "nanotech," "retroviruses," and "self-replicating regenerative techniques." For all of the explanation they'd ever given him of what those words meant, they might as well have spoken of wizard's spells or black magic, but he couldn't question the effectiveness of whatever those things were. The demon-jester had promised them extended life as one of the "rewards" for serving his guild, and it seemed he'd meant it. Just how long their lives might have been extended for was something Sir George had often speculated upon, but none of his people were so credulous as to believe the demon-jester had truly provided it to reward them. It only made sense for him to insure that his tools lasted as long as they could.

And he had insured that they would. Oh, yes, that he had! By now, almost all of Sir George's men had "died" at least once. Some of them, less skilled or perhaps just more unlucky than their fellows, had been "killed" two or three times. Indeed, Stephen Meadows had the hapless distinction of holding the record; Physician had brought him back from the dead no fewer than five times. Sir George himself had been seriously wounded only once, and hadn't required resurrection even that time, but that was atypical.

At least the constant round of resurrections had put the men's last, lingering fears of the Lazaruses in their midst to rest! And the other thing it had done was to permit Sir George's men to amass a degree of combat experience he very much doubted any other humans in history could have matched. Perhaps they'd spent only eleven years awake in the time away from Earth, but they'd also spent an enormous percentage of those eleven years actually in battle on world after world. They had become accustomed to changes in the air they breathed, to learning what Computer had meant by the word "gravity" and how it affected them and their weapons as it changed from world to world. They'd developed tricks and stratagems to use those changes, and they'd acquired a smooth, economical precision in the field. Death was an excellent teacher, particularly when he was not allowed to keep his students after their lesson.

The Physician's medical marvels, combined with the constant warfare demanded by the demon-jester, had allowed Sir George's men to pack the experience of a soldier's entire lifetime into bodies which remained physically at the peak of their performance. Even without the impressive, steadily improved upon armor the demon-jester's industrial modules provided, his men-at-arms and archers had become the most lethally effective field force on a man-for-man basis the baron had ever seen or imagined commanding.

Which brought him back to the task at hand.

~ ~ ~

Many of the men behind him had once been sailors, but that had been before they found themselves with precisely the same choices, or *lack* of them, as Sir George's soldiers. By now there was no real way to distinguish them from any of the professional troops who'd once been their passengers. After all, *they* were professionals now, and their experience showed in their expressions—not relaxed, but calm and almost thoughtful as they recalled their prebattle briefings and waited to put them into effect. The mounted men-at-arms and handful of knights sat their mounts closest to him, forming a protective barrier between the still closed wall of metal and the more vulnerable archers. All of his men were much better armored than they had ever been on Earth. That had been true from the very beginning, of course, but the difference was even greater now. Sir George, Tom Westman, and Computer had spent many long hours refining the designs of his troopers' armor. It had been an almost intoxicating experience to be completely unhampered by financial or manufacturing constraints. For all his other faults, the demon-jester had never placed a price on the equipment he supplied to his captive soldiers. Given the creature's sensitivity to profits and losses, that suggested that the industrial modules could produce whatever was required at little expense. But it also meant that he'd raised no objection to completely scrapping existing armor in order to provide Sir George's men with newer, improved equipment, and in many ways the marvelously light alloys available to them had seemed almost more miraculous to the baron than any of the other wonders which had enveloped them.

All of his knights and men-at-arms were now in full plate, yet that armor, although far tougher and more resistant to damage than even the best steels Earth could have offered, was unbelievably light. Sir George had grown to manhood accustomed to the weight of chain and steel plate. By comparison, his new armor was but little more cumbersome than the one-piece garments the demon-jester had provided all of them for normal wear. Even his archers now wore finely articulated plate armor, which was something that would never have happened in the army of Edward III. Protection had always been welcome to Earthly archers, but they'd always known that their true protection lay in mobility, the devastating fire of the longbow, and the wardship of the more heavily armored knights and men-at-arms who protected them from the enemy's axes and swords.

Now Sir George's bowmen enjoyed almost the same degree of armored protection as his men-at-arms, and all of them were far better protected than they had ever been on Earth. Of course, none of that changed the fact that archers were still trained for archery, not for hand blows, or that they still relied upon men-at-arms to hold the enemy far enough away for them to use their bows effectively rather than becoming embroiled in the melee. Armor or no armor, Sir George's entire small army could have been swarmed under by sheer force of numbers by almost any of the native forces they'd faced over the years if not for the long-range killing power of the longbow and the iron discipline of the foot and horse which formed the armored wall that held the enemy while the clothyard shafts decimated him. Over the years of constant warfare, the company had acquired a well-honed ability to combine the effectiveness of its components well beyond anything any of them had ever seen on Earth. In the process, every one of them had learned to rely upon and trust all of the others as totally as they had come to trust Sir George. So they stood now, their faces showing grim confidence, not uncertainty, and returned Sir George's regard with level eyes.

"All right, lads." He kept his voice even-pitched and calm, disdaining histrionics and relying upon Computer to carry his words clearly into each man's private ear. "You know the plan . . . and Saint Michael knows we've done it often enough!" His ironic tone won a mutter of laughter, and he gave them a tight grin in reply. "Mind yourselves, keep to the plan, and we'll be done in time for dinner!"

A rumble of agreement came back, and then there was the very tiniest of lurches, the metal wall before Sir George hissed like a viper and vanished upward, and he looked out upon yet another of the endless alien worlds he and his men were doomed to conquer.

The sky was *almost* the right shade, but as always, there was something odd about it. This time it was a darker, deeper hue than the blue he remembered (and Sweet Mary, but *did* he remember? or did he simply *think* he did?) from home, and the sun was too large by half. Once again, the gravity had changed, as well, although it was less noticeable because of the way Computer had adjusted the gravity aboard ship to accustom the English to it before they were committed to battle. The "trees" rising in scraggily, scattered clumps were spidery interweavings of too-fine branches covered with long, hairy streamers for leaves, and leaves and grass alike were a strange, rust-red color like nothing anyone had ever seen in any world meant for men.

Not that there *were* any men in this world. Not born of it, at any rate. Yet another army of not-men, too tall, too thin, and with too many limbs, had drawn up in a ragged line well beyond bowshot of the ship. This variety of not-man possessed three arms and three legs each, and although they clearly knew how to work iron, they were but little better armed or armored than the natives of Shaakun who had been the English's very first victims in the demon-jester's service. True, they carried large wicker shields and spears, and most wore leather helmets, but aside from that, they were unarmored, and only a very few bore any weapon other than their spears or quivers of javelins. He saw maces and a handful of swords, but no decent pikes or other true polearms, and none of them were mounted. Square placards on poles rose above them at ragged intervals—banners, he realized—and he wondered how long they'd been gathered.

He knew rather less about this world and these opponents than he had become accustomed to knowing. For some reason, the demon-jester had chosen to exercise a much more direct and total control over the planning of this conquest. Computer had briefed Sir George upon the types of weaponry he would face, discussed the basics of the local clan structures, and, as always, allowed him to actually share their crude, direct tactics through the still-daunting office of the "neural interface." But for all of that, the baron was singularly uninformed about what the demon-jester's guild wanted of *this* world or how the battle he was about to fight would help obtain its goal.

For that matter, the demon-jester hadn't even deigned to tell him why this particular army of aliens had gathered here. Clearly they were there to fight, but had they come for an open battle, or simply to besiege the lander? Small though the craft was compared to the mountainous ship he'd first seen hovering motionless in a storm-sick sky, it was still bigger than any mobile object these natives had ever seen before, and he barked a bitter, humorless laugh. Surely the thing was huge enough to be mistaken for a castle, albeit the most oddly formed one any man—or not-man—could ever imagine!

Whatever had brought them hither, a stir went through them as the side of the ship opened abruptly. Spears were shaken, a handful of javelins were hurled, although the range was too great for that to be anything more than a gesture, and he had no need of magically enhanced hearing to recognize the sound of defiance. It was a thready, piping sound beside the surf roar a human army might have raised, but it carried the ugly undertone of hate.

*Strange,* he thought. *How can I be so certain it's hate I hear? These aren't* men, *after all. For all I know, they might be shouting cries of joyous welcome!* He grimaced at his own fanciful thought. *Of course it's hate. How could it be else when our* masters *have brought us here to break them into well-behaved cattle?*

But this was no time to be thinking such thoughts. And even if it had been, his nagging inner honesty pointed out yet again, subduing these not-men wasn't so terribly different from what he'd planned to do to Frenchmen who, whatever their other faults, at least went about on a mere two legs, not three, and were fellow Christians and (provisionally) human.

He scanned them one more time, confirming Computer's briefing on their equipment and numbers, and snorted much as Satan had. As had become almost routine, especially as the demon-jester gained confidence in his men's invincibility, the English were outnumbered by at least six-to-one, and the wart-faces would do nothing to change those odds. *Their* job was to ensure that none of this world's not-men eluded Sir George's men and entered the ship through the open hold. Which wasn't going to happen.

Sir George drew a deep breath, feeling the not-men's hatred and sensing the confidence they felt in their superior numbers.

*Pity the poor bastards,* he thought, then slammed the visor of his bascinet, drew his sword, and pressed with his knees to send Satan trotting forward.

It hadn't really been a battle, Sir George reflected afterward, tossing his helmet to Edward and shoving back his chain mail coif as he dismounted beside one of the mobile fountains. The merry chuckle of the water splashing in the wide catcher basin made a grotesque background for the wailing whines and whimpers coming from the enemy's wounded, and even after all this time, the baron had never become hardened to those sounds. But at least there were few moans from his own wounded. Partly because there'd been so few of them, compared to the natives' casualties, but mostly because the hovering air cars had already picked up most of his injured. And all of the handful of dead, as well, he thought, and wondered if many of them would stay dead this time. Despite everything he and his troopers had seen and experienced, even Sir George still found it a bit . . . unsettling to see a man who'd taken a lance through the chest sit down to supper with him.

He put the thought aside yet again. It was far easier than

it had been the first few times. The baron was still somewhat amused by his realization of just how much Computer's insistence that Physician's magic was, in fact, no more than a matter of huge advancement in matters surgical had helped him adjust to the reality. The "Commander" might have explained exactly the same thing, in his arrogant way, time and again, but somehow Sir George found it easier to believe what Computer told him. Perhaps that was because he had never yet caught Computer in an error, or perhaps it was because of his natural suspicion of anything the demon-jester chose to say. Intellectually, he felt no doubt that if the demon-jester commanded Computer to lie to him, Computer would obey, yet he remained oddly confident that Computer would not mislead him without specific orders to do so.

He was also honest enough to admit to himself that he was too grateful to have those men back to question the agency of their resurrection, or healing, or *whatever* it was Physician did to restore them to life. Any decent field commander did anything he could to hold down his casualties, if only to preserve the efficiency of his fighting force, but Sir George had even more reason to do so than most. Over the years of battle and bloodshed, he'd become ever more aware that his men were all he had. In a sense, they were all the men who would ever exist in the universe—or in Sir George's universe, at least—and that made every one of them even more precious than they would have been had he and they ever reached Normandy.

He snorted, shook himself, and thrust his head into the fountain. The icy water was a welcome shock, washing away the sweat, and he drank deeply before he finally raised his head at last to draw a gasping breath of relief. His right arm ached wearily, but it had been more butcher's work than sword work at the end. These natives, like so many, many others he'd faced in the demon-jester's service, had never imagined anything like an English bowman. That much had been obvious. Even the Scots at Halidon Hill—or the Thoolaas in that first dreadful slaughter on Shaakun—had shown more caution than these natives, and not even French knights would have pressed on so stubbornly and stupidly into such a blizzard of arrows.

But the natives of this nameless world had.

Sir George sighed and turned from the fountain, surrendering his place to Rolf Grayhame, as he surveyed the field.

There had been even more of the natives than he'd first thought, not that it had mattered in the end. Even his archers' bows had been subtly improved upon over the years. It had been a bright young lad by the name of William Cheatham who'd first hit upon the notion of using what amounted to block and tackle to increase the weight of the bow a man could pull. Young Cheatham had gotten the idea from watching a similar arrangement being used in action by crossbowmen on one of the many other worlds the English had conquered. That one, Sir George recalled bitterly, had been the most costly of all of their conquests. Twenty-three of his men and fifty precious horses had died and stayed that way before its natives had finally submitted to the demon-jester's demands. Even with the accustomed support of local allies with scores of their own to settle, the English had been forced to introduce the trebuchet, the balista, the mouse, Greek fire, and the siege tower, and Sir George's skin still crawled when he recalled hideous, underground hand-to-hand fights in subterranean galleries as mine and counter-mine clashed beneath the defenders' fortifications.

That had been terrible enough, but in some ways, the open field battles had been even worse. The local crossbowmen had been both devilishly accurate and long-ranged, and only his men's superior armor and his archers' higher rate of fire had permitted the English to defeat them. Even the demon-jester had seemed dismayed, or as close to it as someone who never showed any discernible emotion could be, by the casualties his captive soldiers had sustained before they managed to break that planet to obedience. No doubt because of their implication for Sir George's ability to sustain his forces in the service of the demon-jester's guild.

It had probably been that dismay which accounted for the demon-jester's support of young Cheatham's suggestion that it ought to be possible to apply the same advantage in purchase to the English's bows. As a rule, the "Commander" seemed oddly uncomfortable whenever Sir George or one of his people suggested some small innovation in their equipment. He had no apparent problem with incremental improvements, like the substitution of new alloys in armor plate, or the better articulation of existing armor, but the introduction of new concepts clearly discomfited him. It wasn't as if the demon-jester *disapproved* of the suggestions. It was more as if the notion of finding newer and better ways to do things was foreign to his nature. That possibility seemed preposterous in light of the uncountable technological marvels and devices which surrounded him and were so much a part of his sense of utter superiority, yet the more Sir George had considered it, the more accurate it had seemed.

But whatever the demon-jester's attitude towards innovation might be, *Sir George* had been delighted by the consequences of Cheatham's inspiration. Computer had handled the actual design work, once the young archer had explained his idea to him, and despite a certain inevitable number of complaints that the old way was best, the bowmen had adopted the new weapons enthusiastically. The sheer number of new ideas and new devices to which they'd been subjected since their "rescue" undoubtedly had something to do with that, but the fact that it gave them even more range and power, and so increased their odds of survival and victory, explained even more of their enthusiasm. Each of them could still put twelve shafts in the air in a minute, but now they could hit picked, man-sized targets at very nearly three hundred paces. Their broadheaded arrows inflicted hideous wounds at any range, and their needle-pointed pile arrows could penetrate mail or even plate at pointblank ranges.

Against foes who were totally unarmored, like the natives of Shaakun or this world, that sort of fire produced a massacre, not a battle. The only true hand blows of today's entire affair had come when Sir George and his mounted men charged the broken rabble that had once been an army to complete its rout, and he grimaced at the thought of what that charge had cost.

Only two of his mounted men had been seriously wounded, and neither of them too badly for the Physician's healing arts to save them, but they'd lost five more priceless horses. All too few of their original mounts had survived. Satan was one of them, praise God, and the demon-jester had been given ample opportunity to recognize the validity of Sir George's explanation of how critical mounts were to the combat effectiveness of his troopers. If anything, the "Commander" was even more fanatical about protecting and nurturing the supply of horses than Seamus McNeely or Sir George himself. He'd even nagged the Physician to find better ways to protect them from the stresses of phase stasis and to breed and "clone" them. But unlike humans, horses took poorly to the long periods of sleep journeys between stars imposed, no matter what the Physician did. Nor did they reproduce well under such conditions, and whatever arts brought dead archers or men-at-arms back to life seemed less effective for them. The Physician was able to produce a small, steady trickle of new horses, each of which was physically mature when it was handed over to Seamus, but there was never enough time to train the replacements as they truly ought to have been before committing them to battle, and horses were bigger and more vulnerable targets than armored men. Despite occasional upswings, it seemed that there were fewer of them for every battle, and the time would come when there were none.

The thought did not please Sir George, and not simply because Satan had been with him for so long and borne him so well. Sir George was no fool. His grandfather had been the next best thing to a common man-at-arms before he won Warwick under Edward I, and neither his son nor his grandson had been allowed to forget his hard-bitten pragmatism. A professional soldier to his toenails, Sir George knew that a mounted charge against properly supported archers was madness. *Well, against* English *archers, at any rate,* he amended. True, the shock of a horsed charge remained all but irresistible if one could carry it home, but accomplishing that critical final stage was becoming more and more difficult. Or that, at least, had been the case on Earth. Although he'd never faced them, Sir George had heard of the pikemen produced in distant Switzerland, and he rather wished he had a few of them along. A pike wall, now, formed up between his archers and the enemy . . . *that* would put paid to any cavalry charge! There was no way to know what was happening back home, of course, but surely by now even the French and Italians must be discovering the cold, bitter truth that unsupported cavalry was no longer the queen of battle. He was only glad that so far he and his men had encountered no native army that could match the discipline and armament of the Swiss!

Yet for all that, he was a knight himself, and perhaps the proudest emblems of any knight were his spurs. The day when the horse finally did vanish forever from the field of battle would be a terrible one, and Sir George was thankful he would never live long enough to see it.

*Or perhaps I* will *live long enough . . . now. Assuming I might ever see Earth again. Which I won't.*

He snorted again and rose to his full height, stretching mightily, and then smiled at his squire. He'd had two others since Thomas Snellgrave's death, but both had since been promoted to knighthood in their own right, and neither of them had been as tall as the third. For all his own inches, Edward was bidding fair to overtop him by very nearly a full half foot once he reached his full growth. The young man stood beside him, still holding his helmet, and Sir George eyed him with unobtrusive speculation. That Edward was with him—yes, and Matilda, praise God and every saint in any calendar!—was one of the few things which made this endless purgatory endurable, yet he wondered at times how old his son truly was. He'd been almost thirteen when they sailed to join King Edward in France, but how long ago had that been?

With no way to answer that question, it was impossible to estimate his son's age. Outwardly, the young man looked to be perhaps eighteen years of age, but that was no more useful as a yardstick than his own apparent age would have been. It was simply one more mystery, yet another consequence of the extension of his troops' lifespans which had permitted the "Commander" to avoid wasting time on fresh voyages to Earth to catch still more of them. Not that voyages to Earth were the only way their masters could secure more manpower, the baron thought sourly.

He'd concluded long ago that only coincidence had caused the demon-jester to sweep up their womenfolk and children with them. Whatever else the small creature was, he had no true understanding of the humans under his command. No, perhaps that was unfair. He'd gained at least *some* understanding of them; it was simply that he had never and *would* never see them as anything more than animate property. He didn't even feel true contempt for them, for they weren't sufficiently important to waste contempt upon. They were exactly what he persisted to this day in calling them: barbarians and primitives. Valuable to his guild, but lesser life forms, to be used however their natural superiors found most advantageous.

Sir George refused to make the mistake of regarding the demon-jester with responsive contempt, yet neither was he blind to the peculiar blindnesses and weaknesses which accompanied the other's disdain. For example, the demon-jester had come to Earth solely to secure a fighting force, though even now it seemed ridiculous to Sir George that beings who could build such marvels as the ship should need archers and swordsmen. The baron had no doubt that the "Commander" would have preferred to secure *only* a fighting force . . . or that he had seriously considered simply disposing of the "useless" mouths of the dependants who had accompanied the expedition to France. But the demon-jester hadn't done that, and Sir George thanked God that the alien had at least recognized the way in which wives and children could be used to insure the obedience of husbands and fathers. What the "Commander" had been slower to recognize was that the presence of women and the natural inclinations of men offered the opportunity to make his small fighting force self-sustaining. Although Sir George's age had been frozen, many of the youngsters who'd been taken with him, like Edward, had grown into young manhood and taken their place in the ranks, and still more children had been born . . . no doubt to follow them, when the time came.

Although Sir George and his men might have spent eleven years awake and aware, the time had been less for their families. All of them were returned to their magical slumber between battles, of course, but their families weren't always awakened when the soldiers were. Much depended upon how long they would remain on any given world before their masters were satisfied with their control of it, and the demon-jester had also learned to dole out reunions as rewards . . . or to withhold them as punishment.

The result was that far less time had passed for Matilda and the other women than for Sir George and his troops, and for many years, Edward had been kept to his mother's calendar. But he was old enough now, or physically mature enough, at any rate, to take his place on the field as his father's squire, so now he woke and slept with the rest of the men. Sir George was glad to have the boy with him, yet he knew Matilda was in two minds. She didn't miss her son when she slept, but not even their alien masters could heal all wounds. They had lost men, slowly but in a steady trickle, ever since they'd been stolen away from hearth and home forever, and she didn't want Edward to become one of those they lost.

Nor did Sir George. But they had no choice; they fought and won for the demon-jester and his guild, or else they perished. That was their reality, and it was unwise to think of other realities, or how things might have been, or to long to return, however briefly, to the world of their birth.

He knew all that, yet for all his formidable self-discipline, he could never quite stop wondering how long had truly passed since he and his men had set sail for France and ended . . . here. What year was it, assuming that the years of Earth had any meaning so far from her?

He had no idea. But he suspected they were far, far away from the twelfth day of July in the Year of Our Lord Thirteen Hundred and Forty-Six.

# -VIII-

The silent dragon-man stopped and stood aside as they approached the glowing wall, and Sir George glanced sideways at the creature. He'd seen more than enough of them over the years to know that they, like the wart-faced Hathori, were indeed flesh and blood, for all their oddness in human eyes, and not simply more of the guild's mechanical devices. But that was virtually all he knew of them, even now. Computer had been more than merely reticent about both the Hathori and the dragon-men, yet at least Computer had been willing to tell the baron what the Hathori were called. He'd been unable or unwilling to do the same for the dragon-men, but the baron was uncertain whether that was the result of a direct order from the demon-jester, or simply because the dragon-men *had* no name, even for themselves. If it were the latter, then the dragon-men were even more alien than any of the other creatures the English had met, yet he couldn't quite dismiss the possibility, for he'd never heard one of them so much as make a single sound. The wart-faces, yes. He hadn't learned a word of the Hathori's language of grunts and hoarse hoots, in large part because his masters clearly didn't *want* the English to be able to converse with them, but he and his men had been given ample proof that the wart-faces at least had a language . . . of sorts.

Of course, that was about *all* they had.

As the demon-jester's whip hand, the wart-faces had far more contact with the English than the dragon-men did. They were the prison guards, charged with driving and goading the English outside the ship as well as providing security within it, and they had all the imagination and initiative of the brutal, unthinking turnkeys they were. They appeared to perform their limited duties almost entirely by rote, and they had a pronounced taste for cruelty to help lend enthusiasm to their tasks. From odd bits the demon-jester and Computer had allowed to drop, Sir George had come to suspect that the demon-jester had originally hoped to use the Hathori as he had eventually used the baron's own English. If that had been the small alien's intent, however, it must have come to naught with dismaying speed.

There was no denying that, as individuals, Hathori made dangerous opponents. They were just as tough and physically powerful as they looked, and they appeared to be totally without fear . . . or any equivalent of the human emotion of compassion. There was no love lost between them and the English, which Sir George suspected was precisely what the demon-jester wished, and there'd been a few ugly incidents. Two wounded English archers had been killed by the Hathori—hacked to pieces, beyond any hope of resurrection even by the Physician—on the third world the English had been required to conquer. No one was entirely certain why. The best guess was that the wart-faces had thought the two wounded men were trying to flee the battle without cause, although one of them had barely been able to stand even with the assistance of his more lightly wounded companion. Sir George's men had been furious, and the baron's murderous rage had been even more terrible than theirs, if that were possible. But all the rage and fury in the universe had been insufficient to move the demon-jester to punish the Hathori in any way for their actions. Perhaps, Sir George had thought bitterly at the time, he'd believed that the wart-faces were too stupid to realize they were being punished for a specific mistake and feared that any penalty he inflicted would cause them to hesitate the next time something as unimportant as slaughtering a wounded Englishman came along.

Whatever his reasoning, the demon-jester's refusal to punish the killers had led to an even uglier sequel. The brother of one of the murdered men, apparently driven beyond the bounds of rational thought by grief and hatred, managed somehow to wrest the truncheon from the one of the Hathori detailed to guard the Englishmen aboard ship. The bludgeon, a one-handed weapon for one of the wart-faces, was a ponderous mace for a mere human, but it had crushed its previous owner's skull handily enough. The blood-spattered archer had turned upon the dead Hathori's companions, screaming in fury, and actually managed to wound another of them before the remaining wart-faces beat him to death.

The demon-jester might have declined to punish the Hathori for murdering wounded men who were only seeking medical attention, but he had quite a different attitude when it was one of his guild's guard dogs who died. The single individual actually responsible for the attack was already dead, but that hadn't dissuaded him from selecting an additional half dozen of Sir George's men at random and ordering their deaths as retribution.

One of those men had been Walter Skinnet.

The tough old warrior hadn't even turned a hair when his lot was chosen, and Sir George knew his master of horse would have been furious if he'd suspected the vehement, almost desperate manner in which the baron had implored the demon-jester to spare him. Not that Sir George had let that consideration stop him for even a moment. He was too honest with himself to pretend that his friendship and his duty to one of his own sworn men wouldn't have driven him to make the attempt under any circumstances, however ignoble it might have been to shift the death sentence to another. Yet however true that might have been, he'd also told the demon-jester no more than the exact truth when he argued that Skinnet and his skills and experience would be an irreplaceable loss.

But he might as well have spared himself the words and the bitter shame of humbling himself by literally begging for Skinnet's life. The demon-jester had been implacable, and he had rejected Sir George's arguments with cold logic.

"You may be entirely correct about his value, both to you and to my guild," his emotionless voice had piped. "Yet the example must be made. The selection was entirely random, and it is important for the remainder of your men to realize that in such circumstances *any* of them—regardless of rank, or even of their utility to the guild—may be called upon to pay the penalty for such actions. With that lesson before them, perhaps they will prove more assiduous in preventing such actions by others in the future."

There had been no moving him from his determination to drive his "lesson" home, and he'd followed through on the sentence. He had compelled the remainder of the English, including their women and children, who'd been awake at the time, to watch as the Hathori executed each of the chosen victims one by one. The men had died as well as anyone could, with Skinnet setting the example for them all, and the lesson that the Hathori were as inviolate as the demon-jester himself had certainly gone home among their surviving companions. But along with that lesson had come a fresh, colder, and far more deadly hatred of the demon-jester and the wart-faces alike, and Sir George wondered if the demon-jester recognized the bitter depth of that hate. If he did, he gave no sign of it, so perhaps he didn't. Or perhaps he simply didn't care. Perhaps, despite all evidence to the contrary, he still believed the English were no more than the Hathori themselves: brutal, incurious enforcers, smart enough to obey orders, but with no interest in anything *beyond* their orders.

That would have required even more arrogance—or stupidity—than Sir George had thought even the demon-jester capable of, yet the better he'd come to know his "Commander" the less he was prepared to dismiss the possibility. Anything was possible where the contemptuous "Commander's" prejudices were concerned, but the baron had also concluded that the limitations of the Hathori were the true reason the demon-jester had required the services of his own Englishmen. As individuals, the wart-faces were formidable killing machines, but they lacked the cohesion, the disciplined intelligence and ability, to fight as *soldiers*. Surely even the demon-jester must be aware, if only intellectually, that there were enormous differences between his pet Hathori and the English he had compelled to serve him, however little he showed it.

But whatever the wart-faces' shortcomings, it was clear that the eternally silent dragon-men were a very different proposition. Computer might have declined to answer questions about them, but the demon-jester had never once mentioned them directly in any of the conferences and conversations to which he summoned Sir George, and that simple omission all by itself carried an unmistakable significance. Surely there was some reason the demon-jester never so much as spoke of them, yet neither Sir George nor any of his closest advisers had been able to determine what that reason was. They were simply always there, looming in the background in their one-piece red and blue garments, as inscrutable and ominous as any cathedral gargoyle. Despite their greater height, they ought to have looked far less impressive than the armored, ax-wielding Hathori, but Sir George and his men never permitted themselves to forget the deadly lightning weapons sheathed at their belts as they guarded the demon-jester and the crew of the huge vessel.

Now the dragon-man who had accompanied Sir George

this far returned the baron's glance with impassive silver eyes, motionless as a lizard on a stone and with the same sense of poised, absolute readiness. The glowing wall sealed the English into their own portion of their ship-prison, and none of them had yet been able to discover how the portal through it was opened or closed. They'd discovered a great deal about other controls in their quarters, ways to turn any number of clever devices on and off, and Sir George and Father Timothy were certain that the glowing wall must be controlled in some similar, or at least comparable, fashion, yet they'd never been able to detect how it was done.

Which was as well for their masters, Sir George thought grimly, and nodded to the dragon-man as he stepped past him into the corridor beyond the wall. As always, the towering creature didn't react in any way to the human gesture, but somehow Sir George felt certain the dragon-men recognized it as an acknowledgment and a courtesy of sorts. Whatever else they were, they were obviously capable of thought, or the demon-jester's guild *would* have replaced them with more of its clever mechanical devices. Equally obviously, it regarded both the Hathori and the dragon-men much as it did the English: as more or less domesticated, moderately dangerous, useful beasts of burden, although the demon-jester clearly placed greater faith in the loyalty of the dragon-men.

Sir George had often wondered how the dragon-men regarded the English. Did they, like the demon-jester's kind, consider them primitives and barbarians, beneath their own notice? Certainly they possessed and used more of the wondrous tools of their masters, but that didn't seem to make them their masters' equals or full members of the starship's crew. So did they see the English as companions in servitude, instead? Or did they cling to the need to look down upon the humans as a way to make themselves appear less wretched by comparison?

It seemed unlikely to make a great deal of difference either way, as neither Sir George, nor Father Timothy, nor any other human had ever discovered a way to communicate with them. Not even Matilda had been able to suggest a method which might have succeeded. Of course, their masters gave them precious little opportunity to experiment, but it was impossible to completely eliminate all physical contact between humans and dragon-men. Not if the dragon-men were to be useful as guards *against* the humans, at any rate. Most of the other humans had completely abandoned the task, but Father Timothy continued to try. The Dominican insisted that the dragon-men were far more intelligent than the Hathori, and that with intelligence must come at least the potential for communication. He was determined to someday discover a way to communicate with them, and Sir George shared his confessor's hopes for eventual success . . . although he lacked the priest's patience and dogged faith that he would ever achieve it.

Not even Father Timothy, on the other hand, still sought to communicate with the Hathori.

Sir George snorted at his own cross-grained nature as he followed the guiding light down the empty passageway. He shared Sir Timothy's hopes yet lacked the other's faith, a contradiction if ever he'd heard of one. Yet he couldn't quite turn off that tiny sprig of hope, and he often found himself dreaming of the dragon-men. Indeed, he'd dreamed of them more often during the last few periods of wakefulness than in quite some time.

His thoughts broke off as the guide light reached another hatch and stopped. It bobbed there imperiously, as if impatient with his slow progress, and he grinned. Such guides were necessary, for the constantly changing internal architecture of the ship could be bewildering, especially to one who spent almost all of his time aboard it locked into the portion assigned to the English. Sir George had been told by the demon-jester that the guide lights were only another of the endless mechanisms available to his masters, without any intelligence of their own, and he supposed he believed the alien. Yet he sometimes wondered, especially at times like this, when the lights twitched so impatiently, scolding him for dawdling and eager to be off about some fresh business of their own.

He stepped through the indicated hatch, and the light whisked off with a final bob and dodge. He watched it go, then stepped back and turned as the hatch closed.

The chamber was probably the same one to which the lights had guided him the last time the "Commander" summoned him, although they'd followed nothing remotely like the same path to reach it and its appearance, as usual, had changed completely between visits. This time, it was octagonal, with hatches in each wall, and perhaps fifteen feet across. Unlike the forest glades or the undersea vistas the demon-jester seemed to prefer for most of his meetings, this time the chamber was sparsely furnished, almost bare, with unadorned bulkheads of the ubiquitous bronze alloy. A glowing table at its center supported its sole decoration, one of the marvels the demon-jester called a "light sculpture." Sir George had no idea how the things were made, but they always fascinated him. All were beautiful, though the beauty was often strange to human eyes—so strange, sometimes, as to make one uneasy, even frightened—and almost always subtle. This one was a thing of flowing angles and forms, of brilliant color threaded through a cool background of blues and greens, and he gazed upon it in delight as its soothing presence flowed over him.

*There are times,* he thought dreamily, *when I could almost forgive them for what they've done to us. Our lives are longer, our people healthier, than they ever would have been at home, and they can create such beauty and wonders as this. And yet all the marvels we've received are nothing but scraps from the table, dropped casually to us or—worse!—given only because it benefits* them *for us to have them. To them, we are less important, although not, perhaps, less* valuable, *than the things they build of metal and crystal, and—*

"Your men fought well. But then you English always do, don't you?"

Sir George turned from the light sculpture. He hadn't heard the hatch open, but one rarely did aboard this ship. The main hatches, big enough for a score of mounted men abreast, yes. Not even their masters seemed able to make something that large move without even a whisper of sound, but the smaller hatches within the ship proper were another matter.

Not that most of his men would know that from personal experience. Only he, Sir Richard, Sir Anthony, and—on very rare occasions—Matilda had ever been permitted inside the portion of the vast ship reserved for the full members of the demon-jester's crew. Even then, they must submit to the humiliation of a search before they passed the glowing wall between their section of the ship and the rest of its interior.

Now he cocked his head, gazing at the demon-jester, and tried to gauge the other's mood. Despite the years of his servitude, he still found the task all but hopeless. That was immensely frustrating, and his inability to accurately evaluate the other's mood had become no less dangerous with the passage of time. But the "Commander's" piping voice remained a dead, expressionless thing, and the three-eyed face remained so utterly alien as to make reading *its* expression impossible. Certainly Sir George had never seen anything he could classify as a smile or a frown, nor had whatever translated the "Commander's" language into English become any better at communicating nuances of emotion. Father Timothy and Dickon Yardley had concluded that the upper of the demon-jester's two mouths was exclusively a breathing and speaking orifice, but Sir George had yet to hear a single sound emerge from it. Unlike the dragon-men, the demon-jester obviously did speak, but no human had ever heard his actual voice. From something Computer had once said in passing, Sir George had concluded that the demon-jester's apparent silence wasn't yet another security measure, however. From what Computer had said, the "Commander's" voice was simply pitched too high for human ears to hear.

Sir George had often wondered how much the artificiality of the voice he actually heard was responsible for how expressionless it sounded. He supposed it was possible that the demon-jester truly was as much a stranger to emotion as his translated voice suggested, but it seemed unlikely. The pompous superiority of the words he chose in their conversations seemed ample proof that the alien was capable of feeling contempt and disdain, if nothing else.

There were a great many questions the baron had never been able to answer about the exact nature of the demon-jester's translator, but he'd long since concluded that the "Commander's" failure or refusal to learn the language of his captive troops was another indication of his sense of utter superiority to them. Surely if whatever translated his words into English was capable of that feat, then it ought to be equally capable of making the demon-jester's own voice audible to humans, and in the demon-jester's place, Sir George would certainly have done just that. The "Commander's" decision not to was a foolish one, indeed, unless whatever translated his words into English did a far better job of communicating nuance and emotion when it translated English into his own language.

But however ridiculous the demon-jester might still look, and despite the foolishness of any decisions the "Commander" might make, Sir George's responsibility for the lives of the men and women who looked to him for leadership made it absolutely imperative that the baron never, ever make the mistake of underestimating him. And that was the true reason he found his continued inability to read the "Commander's" mood so maddening. He must watch his words with this creature far more closely than he'd ever watched them with any other commander, yet even after all this time, he was never quite free of the fear that he would choose the wrong one simply because he'd misunderstood or misinterpreted the

"Commander." Of all the many frustrations of his servitude, that constant uncertainty was far and away the worst.

Still, he knew he'd made some progress over the years. He couldn't have spent so many hours conferring with the creature without gaining at least some small insight into his moods and attitudes. It would have been a great comfort to be able to feel certain that those insights were accurate and not dangerous misinterpretations, but at least the demon-jester appeared to take some pains to choose his words with care, as if seeking to make his meaning completely clear through what he said since he couldn't communicate fine shades of meaning by *how* he said it.

*And, of course, there's also the fact that, as he never seems to tire of telling us, we're valuable to him and to his guild.*

Sir George would never be so stupid as to assume that that value would preserve any human foolish enough to anger or appear to threaten their masters. Sir John Denmore's fate on that very first day would have been enough to prevent that even without the other deaths which had reinforced the lesson over the years. Two men who'd left their encampment without orders, fishnets in hand, unable to resist the allure of sunbaked golden beaches on a beautiful world of blue skies and deep green seas. Another who'd simply refused one day to leave the ship. Skinnet and the other five men executed for the wart-face's death. Another who'd gone berserk and attacked the dragon-men and the "Commander" himself with naked steel. . . .

All of them, and a handful besides, had perished for fatal transgressions against the demon-jester's decrees, slaughtered as helplessly as Sir John, and with as little apparent emotion on his part. Yet the "Commander's" actions and normal attitude, as well as Sir George could read the latter, were those of a being well pleased with his investment . . . and aware that his own masters were equally pleased. He would shed no tears (or whatever his kind did to express sorrow) over the death of any single human, but he valued them as a group and so took pains to avoid misunderstandings which might require him to destroy any of them.

Or any *more* of them, at any rate.

Sir George realized the Commander was still gazing at him, waiting for a response, and gave himself a small shake.

"Your pardon, Commander," he said. "The aftermath of battle lingers with me, I fear, and makes me somewhat slow of wit. You were saying?"

"I said that you English had done well today," the Commander said patiently. "My guild superiors will be pleased with the results of your valiant fighting. I feel certain that they will express that pleasure to me in some material form quite soon, and I, of course, wish to express my own pleasure to your men. Accordingly, I have instructed the Physician to awaken your mates and children. We will remain on this world for at least another several weeks while the details of our agreements are worked out with the natives. It may be that I shall need your services once again, or to trot a few of you out to remind the natives of your prowess, at least, during my negotiations. Since we must keep you awake during that period anyway, and since you have fought so well, rewarding you with the opportunity for a reunion seems only just."

"I thank you, Commander." Sir George fought to keep his own emotions out of his voice and expression, throttling back the familiar mixture of elation, joy, hatred, and fury the news sent through him.

"You are welcome, of course," the demon-jester piped back, and gestured for Sir George to seat himself on the human-style chair which had suddenly appeared. The usual "crystal" topped table rose from the floor beside it, and a second chair popped up on its other side. Sir George took the nearer chair gingerly. At least it was finally proportioned to fit a human's length of leg, but he was unable even after all this time to completely hide his discomfort with furnishings which appeared and disappeared as if out of thin air. Nor did he much care for the table. His suspicions about its top had been confirmed long ago, and the fact that it was actually as immaterial as the air about him left him with very mixed feelings. The tabletop was indisputably there. He could lay a hand upon it and feel . . . *something*. Yet he could never have described that something. It supported anything set upon it, but it was as if he couldn't quite place his hand on its actual surface, assuming it had one. It was more as if . . . as if he were pressing his palm against a powerful current of water, or perhaps an equally powerful current of air itself. There was a resistance as his hand approached what ought to be the surface of the table, yet there was no sense of friction, and he always seemed on the brink of being able to push just a little further, just a bit closer.

He put the thought aside once more and watched another of the ship's small metal servitors move silently into the compartment and deposit a crystal carafe of wine and an exquisite goblet before him. Another goblet and carafe, this time filled with some thick, purple-gold, sludge-like liquid was placed before the demon-jester, and Sir George managed not to blink in surprise. The "Commander" had offered him what amounted to a social meeting only five times before in all the years of his servitude, and as closely as he could estimate, each had followed on the heels of some particularly valuable coup which the English had executed for the guild. Which seemed to suggest that the hapless natives Sir George and his troops had slaughtered the day before must be the source of some commodity of particular value to his masters.

"You are wondering what brings us to this world, are you not?" the demon-jester asked, and Sir George nodded. The small alien had learned the meaning of at least some human gestures, and he made an alarming sound. Sir George wasn't positive, but he'd heard it a time or two before and he'd come to suspect it was the equivalent of a human chuckle, although whether it indicated satisfaction, amusement, scorn, impatience, or some other emotion was impossible to say.

"I am not surprised that you wonder," the demon-jester

went on. "After all, these aliens are even more primitive than your own world. It must be difficult to grasp what such barbarians could possibly offer to civilized beings."

Sir George gritted his teeth and made himself take a sip of the truly excellent wine. It was strange that the demon-jester's words could still evoke such anger within him. After all this time, he should certainly have become accustomed to the other's dismissive contempt, and he could even admit, intellectually, that there was some point to the alien's attitude. Compared to the "Commander's" people, humans *were* primitive. On the other hand, Sir George had long since concluded that the demon-jester's guild wasn't actually so very different from human guilds or other powerful groups of his own experience. He would have given a great deal, for example, to see how the "Commander" would have fared bargaining with a Cypriot or a Venetian. Without the advantage of his "technology," he strongly suspected, the demon-jester would be plucked like a pigeon.

"In actual fact," the demon-jester continued, seemingly oblivious to Sir George's silence, "this planet does not offer us any physical commodity. As you know, some of the worlds which the guild has used you to open to our trade have offered such commodities, although normally only in the form of resources the primitives who live upon them are too stupid to exploit themselves. In this case, however, it is the position of the world which is of such value. It will provide us with a location for . . . warehouses, I suppose you might call them, and one from which we may fuel and maintain our vessels."

He paused, looking at Sir George with that impossible to read face, then raised his goblet to tip a little of the purple-gold sludge into his lower mouth.

"You may think of it as a strategically located island or trading port," he went on after a moment, his own inaudible voice obviously issuing from his upper mouth while the lower one was busy with the goblet. "It will bring us many advantages. And of particular satisfaction to me personally, it will cut deeply into the flank of the Sharnhaishian Guild's trade network."

Sir George pricked up his ears at that. Impossible though he found it to reliably interpret the demon-jester's tone or expression, he'd formed some conclusions about the other's personality. He knew it was risky to draw parallels between such unearthly creatures and the personality traits of humans, yet he couldn't help doing so. Perhaps it was simply that he had to put the demon-jester into some sort of familiar framework or go mad. Indeed, he often thought that might be the best explanation of all. But he also felt certain that he'd read at least one aspect of the "Commander" correctly: the thick-bodied little creature loved to brag . . . even when his audience was no more than a primitive, barbarian English slave. Perhaps even more importantly—and, again, like many boastful *humans* Sir George had known—the alien seemed blissfully unaware of the weakness such bragging could become. A wise man, Sir George's father had often said, learns from the things fools let slip.

Fortunately, the demon-jester had never met Sir James Wincaster.

Sir George realized the demon-jester had said nothing for several seconds, simply sat gazing at him with that disconcerting triple stare, and he shook himself.

"I see . . . I think," he said, hoping his deduction that the "Commander" wanted him to respond was correct. "I suppose it would be like capturing, oh, Constantinople and seizing control of all access to the Black Sea."

"I am not certain," the demon-jester replied. "I am insufficiently familiar with the geography of your home world to know if the analogy is accurate, but it sounds as if it might be. At any rate, there will be major bonuses for myself and the members of my team, which is one reason I wish to reward you. You and your kind are a very valuable guild asset, and unlike some of my guild brothers, I have always believed that valuable property should be well cared for and that assets are better motivated by reward than by punishment alone."

"I've observed much the same," Sir George said with what might charitably have been described as a smile. He managed to keep his voice level and thoughtful, whatever his expression might have briefly revealed, and he castigated himself for that teeth-baring grimace, reminding himself yet again that his masters might be better versed at reading human expressions than he was at reading theirs. Unlike humans, they at least had experience of scores of other races and sorts of creatures. They must have learned at least a little something about interpreting alien emotions from that experience, and even if they hadn't, it was far better to overestimate a foe than to underestimate one.

"I suspected that you might have reached the same conclusion," the demon-jester said with what Sir George rather thought might have been an expansive air, had he been human. "Yet I must confess that for me, personally, the fact that we have dealt the Sharnhaishians a blow is of even greater satisfaction than any bonus."

"You've mentioned the . . . the—" Sir George snorted impatiently. He simply could not wrap his tongue about the sounds of the alien name, and the demon-jester made that alarming sound once again.

"The Sharnhaishian Guild," he supplied, and Sir George nodded.

"Yes. You've mentioned them before, Commander."

"Indeed I have," the demon-jester agreed. There was still no readable emotion in his voice or face, yet Sir George suspected that if there had been, the emotion would have been one of bitter hatred. "I owe the Sharnhaishians a great deal," the demon-jester went on. "They almost destroyed my career when they first produced their accursed 'Romans.'"

Sir George nodded again, striving to project an air of understanding and sympathy while he hoped desperately that the demon-jester would continue. The other had touched upon the Sharnhaishian Guild, obviously the great rival of his own trading house, in earlier conversations. The references had been maddeningly vague and fragmentary, yet they'd made it plain that the Sharnhaishians were currently ascendent over the demon-jester's own guild. It was equally plain that the demon-jester deeply resented that ascendancy, which might explain why he'd exercised such uncharacteristically complete control over operations on this planet. If he saw this as an opportunity to obtain a measure of vengeance upon his hated rivals, he might have been unwilling to share the moment with anyone.

Whether that was true or not, the Sharnhaishians' success seemed to have a great deal to do with the Romans the demon-jester had also mentioned more than once. Sir George found it all but impossible to believe, even now, that the "Romans" in question could be what it sounded as if they were, but if he was wrong, he wanted to know it. It might be ludicrous to believe he could hope to achieve anything against his alien masters, yet Sir George had seen too much of purely human struggles to surrender all hope, despite the huge gulf between their physical capabilities. There were times when a bit of knowledge, or of insight into an enemy's thoughts and plans (or fears), could be more valuable than a thousand bowmen.

*And given all the marvels the "Commander" and his kind possess, knowledge is the* only *thing which might aid me against them,* he reminded himself.

The demon-jester ingested more purple-gold sludge, all three eyes gazing at the "light sculpture" as if he'd completely forgotten Sir George was present, and the human had a sudden thought. The wine in his goblet was perhaps the finest vintage he'd ever sampled, and potent, as well. Was it reasonable to guess that the sludge was equally or even more potent for the demon-jester's kind? The more he considered it, the more possible—and probable—it seemed, and he smiled inwardly, much as a shark might have smiled.

*Truth in the wine,* he reminded himself, and took another sip (a very *small* one this time) from his own glass.

"It was the Sharnhaishians and their Romans who kept me from being appointed a sector commissioner long ago," the demon-jester said at last. He moved his eyes from the light sculpture to Sir George, and the Englishman hid another smile as he realized the flanking eyes had gone just a bit unfocused. They seemed to be wandering off in directions of their own, as well, and he filed that fact away. He could be wrong, but if he wasn't, recognizing the signs of drunkenness in the demon-jester might prove valuable in the future.

"How was I to know they might come up with something like the Romans?" the demon-jester demanded. "It must have cost them a fortune to bribe the Council into letting them buy the damned barbarians in the first place." Sir George cocked his head slightly, and the demon-jester slapped a double-thumbed hand on the table top. On a normal table, such a blow would have produced a thunderclap of sound; on *this* table, there was no noise at all, but the demon-jester seemed to draw a certain comfort from the gesture.

"Oh, yes." He took another deep sip of sludge and refilled his goblet once more. "The Federation has rules, you know. Laws. Like the one that says none of us can use modern weapons on primitive worlds. The 'Prime Directive,' they call it." He slurped more sludge, but his upper mouth never stopped speaking. "Bunch of hypocrites, that's what they are. Carrying on like the thing is supposed to protect the stupid primitives. You know what it really is?"

His large, central eye fixed on Sir George, and the Englishman shook his head.

"Fear, that's what," the demon-jester told him. "Stupid bureaucrats are afraid we'll lose some of our toys where the barbarians can find them. As if the idiots could figure them out in the first place."

He fell silent again, and alien though his voice and face

might be, Sir George was increasingly certain that he truly was as moody as any drunken human.

"Actually, it makes a sort of sense, you know," the demon-jester went on finally. He gave the table another silent thump and leaned back in the oddly shaped, bucketlike piece of furniture which served his kind as a chair. "Takes years and years to move between stars, even with phase drive. One reason the ships are so damned big. Don't have to be, you know. We could put a phase drive in a hull a tenth the size of this one. Even smaller. But size doesn't matter much. Oh, the mass curve's important, but once you've got the basic system–"

He waved a hand, and Sir George nodded once again. He didn't have the faintest idea what a "mass curve" was, and only the vaguest notion of how the "phase drive" was supposed to work, but at the moment, he didn't much care. Other bits and pieces did make sense to him, and he listened avidly for more.

*And,* he thought from behind his own masklike expression, *it doesn't hurt a bit to watch the "Commander." "Truth in the wine," indeed! His voice and face may not reveal much, but his* gestures *are another matter entirely. Perhaps I've been looking in the wrong places to gauge his moods.* He filed that away, as well, and sat back in his chair, nursing his goblet in both hands while he listened attentively . . . and sympathetically.

"Thing is, if it takes a decade or so to make the trip, better have the capacity to make the trip worthwhile, right?" the demon-jester demanded. "You think this ship is big?" Another wave of a double-thumbed hand, gesturing at the bulkheads. "Well, you're wrong. Lots of ships out there lots bigger than this one. Most of the guild ships, as a matter of fact, because it doesn't cost any more to run a really big ship than a little one like this. But that's the real reason for their stupid 'Prime Directive.'"

"The size of your vessels?" Sir George made his tone puzzled and wrinkled his forehead ferociously, hoping the demon-jester had become sufficiently well versed in human expressions to recognize perplexity, although if his estimate of the other's condition was accurate it was unlikely the other would be noticing anything so subtle as an alien race's expressions. But whether or not the demon-jester recognized his expression, it was quickly clear that he'd asked the right question.

"Of course not," the demon-jester told him. "Not the size, the speed. Might be fifteen or twenty of your years between visits to most of these backwater planets. Maybe even longer. I know one planet that the guild only sends a ship to every two and a half of your centuries or so, and the Federation knows it, too. So they don't want to take any chances on having some bunch of primitives figure out we're not really gods or whatever between visits. Want to keep them awed and humble around us. That's why they passed their 'Prime Directive' something like—" The demon-jester paused in thought for a few seconds, as if considering something. "Would have been something like thirty thousand of your years ago, I think. Give or take a century or two."

He made the alarming sound again, and Sir George was certain now that it was his kind's equivalent of laughter. For just a moment, that hardly seemed to matter, however. Thirty *thousand* years? His alien masters' civilization had existed for over thirty millennia? Impossible! And yet—

"Even for us, that's a long time for a law to be in effect," the demon-jester said. His piping voice was less clear, the words beginning to blur just a bit around the corners as he leaned towards Sir George, and the baron had to fight back a chuckle of his own as he realized that whatever did the translating was faithfully slurring the translation to match the drunken original. "We don't like to change things unless we have to, you know, so once we write a law, it stays around a while. But this one's made lots of trouble for the guilds, because without using weapons, we couldn't just go in and rearrange things properly. Actually had to bargain with barbarians so primitive they don't have a clue about the value of the things they're sitting on top of. Couldn't violate the damned 'Prime Directive' after all, now could we?"

Another thump on the table. This time, it wouldn't have made any sound anyway, because the demon-jester missed the table top entirely, and Sir George began to wonder how much longer the creature would last before he passed out.

"So what did the Sharnhaishians do?" the alien continued. "I'll tell you what. They went out and found another primitive world, one the Council didn't even know about yet, and they bought their damned 'Romans.' Never occurred to any of the rest of us. But the Prime Directive doesn't say we can't use force. All it says is that we can't use modern weapons. It just never occurred to any of us that there was anything we could do without using our weapons except negotiate and bribe."

He lowered his goblet and peered down into it for several seconds, then made a sound suspiciously like a human belch and returned his central eye to Sir George.

"Not the Sharnhaishians, though. If they want a primitive world, they just send in their Romans. Just as primitive as the local barbarians, so the Council can't complain, and I'll say this for the Romans. They're tough. Never run into anything they couldn't handle, and the Sharnhaishians've used them to take dozens of backwater worlds away from the other guilds. Whole trade nets, cut to pieces. Strategic commodities sewn up, warehousing and basing rights snatched out from under us, careers ruined. And all because the Sharnhaishians acquired a few thousand primitives in bronze armor."

He fell silent for a long time, swirling sludge in his goblet and peering down into it, then looked back up more or less in Sir George's direction.

"But they're not the only ones who can play that game. They thought they were. The other guilds got together to complain to the Council, and the Council agreed to take the matter under consideration. It may even decide the Sharnhaishians have to stop using their Romans entirely, but that may take centuries, and in the meantime, Sharnhaishian is shipping them from one strategic point to another and taking them away from the rest of us. And they slipped someone on the Council a big enough bribe to get your world declared off-limits for all the rest of us."

Sir George stiffened, and hoped the demon-jester was too drunk to notice. He wasn't surprised that the other guild could have bribed the Council the alien was yammering about. Bribing a few key rulers was often more efficient, and cheaper, than relying on armies. *Although if His Majesty had spent a little more money on his army and a little less on trying to buy allies in his first French campaign he might have been on the throne of France by its end!*

But if the demon-jester was telling the truth, if the Council to which he referred had the authority to declare that contact with Sir George's home world was no longer permitted and had done so, then the demon-jester's guild must have violated that decree in order to kidnap Sir George and his troops. And if that was the case—if their servitude was unlawful in the eyes of what passed for the Crown among these creatures—then they were in even more danger than he'd believed.

"It took me two or three of your centuries just to figure out where your world was," the demon-jester went on, and now Sir George seemed to sense an air of pride. "Some of the other guilds recruited their own primitive armies, like the Hathori. But none of them have been able to match the Romans. Course they couldn't! And the Sharnhaishians knew *that* before the rest of us did, too. Reason they went and bought their damned Romans in the first place. They'd already tried the Hathori 'n found out what the rest of us had t' learn the hard way. I still remember the first time *we* sent the Hathori in against a bunch of natives."

The alien stared down into his goblet, and his ears flattened.

"Damned aborigines cut them to pieces," he said after a long moment. "Cost them a lot of casualties at first, but then they swarmed right over the Hathori. Butchered them one by one. I doubt we got one in twenty back alive at the end, but that wouldn't have happened against the damned Romans. Those aren't just warriors—they're demons that carve up anything they run into. So it occurred to me that what we needed were Romans of our own, and I managed to convince my creche cousin to convince his sector commissioner to speak to the guild masters for me. I needed all the help I could get, thanks to the Sharnhaishians and their Romans. Course, it helped that by then they'd done the same thing to dozens of other guildsmen, and not just in our guild, either. So they gave me a chance to reclaim my career if I could find where the Romans came from, get past the Council ban, and catch us some Romans of our own. And I did it, too."

This time his slap managed to connect with the table top again, though it was still soundless, and he threw himself untidily back in his chair.

"But we're not Romans," Sir George pointed out after a moment. He was half afraid to say another word, for if the demon-jester remembered any of this conversation at a later date and realized all he was letting slip, there would be one very simple way to rectify his error.

"'Course not," the alien said. "Good thing, too, in a way. Surprised me, of course. I never expected to see so much change on a single planet in such a short period. Couldn't have been more than eight or nine hundred of your years between you and the Romans, and just look at all the differences. It's not decent. Oh," he waved a hand again, "you're still primitives, of course. Haven't changed that. But we got there in just the nick of time. Another seven or eight of your centuries or so, and you might actually have been using practical firearms, and we couldn't have that. Unlikely, I admit, but there you were, already experimenting with them." The demon-jester eyed Sir George. "I have to wonder how you stumbled on the idea so soon. Could the Sharnhaishians have slipped up and suggested it to you?"

"The idea of 'firearms'?" Sir George frowned.

"*Pots de fer*, I believe you call them," the demon-jester said.

"Fire pots?" Sir George blinked in genuine consternation. "But they're nothing but toys, Commander! Good for scaring horses and people who've never before encountered them, perhaps, but scarcely serious weapons. Even bombards are little more than noisy nuisances against anyone who knows his business! Why, my bowmen would massacre any army stupid enough to arm itself with such weapons. *Crossbows* are more effective than they are!"

"No doubt they are . . . now," the demon-jester replied. "Won't stay that way, though. Of course, you've still got another thousand years or so to go before anyone develops truly effective small arms. Still, I suppose it's a fairly good example of why they passed the Prime Directive in the first place. If the Sharnhaishians hadn't somehow contaminated your world, you never would have come up with gunpowder at all. Not so quickly, anyway."

He took another deep swallow, and Sir George decided to stay away from the question of where gunpowder came from. He himself knew only a very little about the subject; such weapons had become available in Europe only during his own lifetime and, like most of his military contemporaries, he'd had little faith that they would ever amount to much as effective field weapons. Certainly such crude, short-ranged, dangerous devices would never pose any threat to the supremacy of his bowmen! Yet the demon-jester seemed to find their existence deeply significant and more than a little worrying. It was almost as if the fact that humans had begun experimenting with them was somehow threatening, and Sir George had no intention of suggesting that the Sharnhaishians hadn't had anything to do with the development. Besides, how did he know the rival guild hadn't?

"Anyway," the demon-jester said, the words more slurred than ever, "it's a good thing we found you when we did. Couldn't have used you at all if you'd been armed with firearms. Would've been a clear violation of the Prime Directive, and that would've gotten questions asked. People would've noticed, too, and the Council would've started asking questions of its own."

He leaned back towards Sir George again, and this time he patted the Englishman on the knee with what would have been a conspiratorial air from another human.

"As it is, nobody really cares. Just 'nother bunch of primitives with muscle-powered weapons, nothing to worry about. None of the Council's inspectors even know enough about humans to realize you and Romans are the same species, and if any of 'em ever do notice, we know where to put the bribes to convince them they were mistaken. Besides," another pat on the knee, "you're all off the books." Sir George frowned, puzzled by the peculiar phrase, and the demon-jester thumped his knee a third time. "No document trail," he said, the words now so slurred that Sir George found it virtually impossible to understand them even as words, far less to grasp the meanings of unfamiliar phrases. "Grabbed you outa th' middle of a storm. Ever'body on your stupid planet figures you all drowned. Would have 'thout us, too, y'know. But that means even if th' Council investigates, won't find any evidence of contact between us an' your world, because aside from picking you outa th' water an' grabbing a few horses in th' middle of th' night, there wasn't any. So we've got our own little army, an' 'less some inspector does get nosy, nobody'll ever even ask where you came from."

The demon-jester leaned back in his chair once more and reached out for his goblet. But his groping hand knocked it over, and he peered down at it. His central eye was almost as unfocused as the secondary ones now, and his strange, sideways eyelids began to iris out to cover them all.

"S' take that, Sharnhaishian," he muttered. "Thought you'd wrecked my career, didn' you? But who's goin' to . . ."

His voice trailed off entirely, his eyes closed, and he slumped in his chair. His upper mouth fell open, and a whistling sound which Sir George realized must be his kind's equivalent of a snore came from it.

The human sat in his own chair, staring numbly at the demon-jester, until the door opened silently once more. He looked up quickly then and saw one of his masters' guards in the opening. The dragon-man beckoned imperatively with one clawed hand, and Sir George noted the way that its other hand rested on the weapon scabbarded at its side.

*Could* that *be what the "Commander" actually meant by "firearms"?* he wondered suddenly. *Not even a true dragon could hurl hotter "fire" than they do . . . and they're certainly far more dangerous than any stupid fire pot!*

The dragon-man beckoned again, its meaning clear, and Sir George sighed and rose. Of course they wouldn't leave him alone with the senseless demon-jester. No doubt they'd been watching through one of Computer's "visual sensors" and come to collect him the instant the demon-jester collapsed. But had they paid any attention to the demon-jester's conversation *before* he collapsed? And even if they had, had they guessed that Sir George might realize the significance of what the demon-jester had told him?

He hoped not, just as he hoped the demon-jester wouldn't remember all he'd let slip. Because if the others had guessed, or the demon-jester did remember, Sir George would almost certainly die.

After all, it would never do for the guild's pet army's commander to realize that if anyone from the Council—wherever and exactly whatever it was—*did* begin to question that army's origins, the entire army would have to disappear.

Forever . . . and without a trace that could tie the demon-jester's guild to a planet that the Council had interdicted.

# IX

"Are you certain, my love?"

Lady Matilda Wincaster reclined against the cushion under the brightly colored awning and regarded her husband with a serious expression.

Despite years of experience with their bizarre tastes, the demon-jester clearly remained perplexed by, if not incredulous of, the English's powerful preference for camping in mere tents outside the vast starship. They'd been persistent enough in their desires that he'd been forced to accept that it was what they truly wanted, yet it was obvious that he found the entire concept utterly inexplicable. In many ways, Sir George suspected, the "Commander" found it even more difficult to understand because the English were such "primitives." Whereas the demon-jester might have been prepared for the notion that civilized beings such as himself might desire an occasional, rustic break from the rigors of civilization, the idea that barbarians who'd been given a taste of the better things life could offer might choose not to wallow in them was beyond his comprehension. No doubt that helped explain his obvious suspicion that the humans' often expressed desire for the open air was merely a cover for something much more devious. Sir George still remembered how long the expressionless commander had gazed at him back on Shaakun after his initial request that his people be allowed to remain outside the ship. The demon-jester had considered the request for over two full shipboard days before he elected to grant it, and when he announced his permission, he had also warned against any thought that the English might be able to slip away and hide from their masters. His technology could find them wherever they might attempt to hide, he'd said in his toneless voice, and punishment for attempted desertion would be severe.

Sir George had doubted neither warning, and he'd taken steps to impress both of them equally strongly on his subordinates.

Those steps had succeeded. In all the years of their servitude, not a single one of his men had tried to desert. Or not, at least, from their encampments. Three men had been hunted down by the demon-jester's mechanical remotes after becoming separated from the company's main body on the march or during combat operations. None of them had been returned to the ship alive. In at least one case, Sir George was as certain as he could be that the trooper in question had simply become disoriented and lost in the heavy fog which had enveloped the column that day, but the demon-jester hadn't cared about that. The man-at-arms had been absent without permission. That constituted desertion, and desertion was punishable by death. He'd had no desire to determine the circumstances of the particular case at hand. The dead man had only been a primitive Englishman, after all. And the demon-jester had probably seen it as an opportunity to administer yet another of his object lessons. He was a great believer in object lessons.

Over the years, at least some of the English had come to share more of the demon-jester's view of life in the open air. Despite the splendor of the creature comforts available in their tents and pavilions, the luxuries aboard ship, or even in one of the mothership's landers, were even more splendid, and none of the humans were so stupid as to reject them out of hand, despite their captivity. But a majority of them still nursed that inborn hunger for open skies and natural air . . . even the "natural air" of planets which had never been home to any of their kind. They preferred to sleep amid the fresh air and breezes, the sounds of whatever passed for birds on a given planet, and the chuckling sounds of running water. And even those who invariably returned aboard ship for the night enjoyed the occasional open air meal. Indeed, the picnic feasts often took on the air of a festival or fair from Earth, helping to bind them together and reinforce their sense of community.

And they *were* a community, as well as an army. In many ways, Sir George had often thought, they were fortunate that there were so few gently born among them. He himself was the only true nobleman, and even he was the grandson of a common man-at-arms. Aside from himself and Maynton, only Matilda and Sir Anthony Fitzhugh could claim any real high-born connection. After a great deal of soul-searching and discussions with Maynton, Fitzhugh, and Sir Bryan Stanhope—and, especially, with Matilda—he had decided to bestow the accolade of knighthood upon men who'd earned it in battle. He was careful not to abuse the practice, and his men knew it. That made the knighthoods he'd awarded even more valuable to them, and it had also given him a solid core of exactly one dozen knights.

The fact that all but three of them were men of common birth had not only told all of his troopers that any one of them could aspire to the highest rank still available to them but had also helped to bind the entire community even more tightly together. And not just among its male members. Just as three quarters of his knights had been born of common blood, so had the vast majority of the company's women, which meant that, especially with Matilda and Margaret

Stanhope to lead the way, they had decided to overlook the dubious origins of many of the unwed camp followers who'd joined them in their involuntary exile. Most of those camp followers, though by no means all, had acquired husbands quite speedily. A few had chosen not to, and Father Timothy had agreed, under the circumstances, not to inveigh against them for continuing to ply their old avocation. There were a great many more men than women, and the one thing most likely to provoke trouble among them was that imbalance in numbers. No doubt Father Timothy would have preferred for all of the women to be respectfully wedded wives, but he, too, had been a soldier in his time. He understood the temper of men who still were, and he was able to appreciate the need to adapt to the conditions in which they found themselves forced to live.

As a result, not even those women who continued to follow their original trade were ostracized as they might have been, and a tightly knit cluster of families formed the core of the English community. The steadily growing number of children (both legitimate and bastard) helped cement that sense of community even further, and for all the bitterness with which Sir George chafed against his servitude, even he had to admit the awe he felt that not a single one of those children had perished in infancy. That was undoubtedly the most treasured of the "luxuries" their masters had made available to them. The *strangest*, however (though it was hard to pick the single most strange) was the fact that so few of those children's mothers remembered their births. It had caused some consternation and even terror and talk of "changelings" at first, but as time passed, the women had adjusted to the fact that their babies were almost always born during one of their sleep periods. The Physician had explained the process, pointing out that it only made sense to get such time consuming worries as pregnancies out of the way when they were asleep in stasis anyway. After an initial period of extreme uneasiness, most of the women had come to agree.

Led in almost every case, Sir George had been amused (but not surprised) to note, by the women who had birthed the most babies the "old-fashioned" way.

He smiled even now, at the memory, but his attention was on his wife's question. One of the real reasons he'd initially requested freedom from the ship for his people had been amply confirmed over the years. He was absolutely positive now that anything which was said *aboard* the ship would be overheard and reported by Computer or one of their master's clever mechanical spies, and while he was perfectly well aware that those same spies could eavesdrop upon them outside the ship, as well—Computer could hear and relay his orders even through the thunderous clangor of battle and even when he spoke in almost normal tones, after all—he hoped it was at least a bit harder. And he rather suspected that even the most clever of mechanisms would find it more difficult to keep track of several hundred individual conversations out in the open against the background noise of wind and water than to listen for a single command voice even amidst the bedlam of war. The fact that he or one of his trusted advisers had managed to find at least one spot in each encampment where Computer would not, or could not, respond to them also suggested that it was possible for some freak of terrain or atmosphere to produce blind spots in Computer's own coverage. Sir George had taken careful note of the fact that most of those "blind spots" seemed to occur in dips or hollows, depressions which allowed the speaker to put a bank of solid earth or stone between himself and areas where he knew Computer *could* hear him.

The ingrained habits of extreme caution had become a matter of simple reflex to him during the years of his servitude, and he had no intention of risking any more than he must upon the unproven assumption that there was anywhere at all that Computer couldn't hear him. At the same time, however, he *knew* there was no place aboard ship where he couldn't be overheard, which meant that the only time he felt even remotely safe discussing dangerous matters was during their periods of encampment.

Although even then, he reflected, the only person with whom he truly discussed them was Matilda.

"Yes, I'm certain," he said at last, meeting her blue eyes as he answered her question. *God, she's beautiful,* he thought with a familiar sense of wonder and awe.

"I don't think he realizes he revealed so much," he went on after a moment, raising a wine goblet to hide the movement of his lips and speaking very quietly, "but I'm certain of it. More certain than I like."

"But surely there's no longer any doubt that we truly are as valuable to his guild as he's suggested," Matilda pointed out. "You've served him far better than even he could ever have imagined you might, with wit and counsel as much as with weapons. He himself has admitted as much to you, and, like you, I very much doubt that he was ever the sort to waste unmeant praise upon someone he considers so completely his inferior out of a sense of courtesy. Whatever else his guild may be, surely it would not lightly discard a tool whose worth it holds so high."

"Um." Sir George set the goblet aside, then stretched in an ostentatious yawn. He smiled at his wife and moved to lay his head in her lap, smiling up at her as she tickled the tip of his nose with a stalk of local grass. To the casual eye, they were but two people—people miraculously young and comely—in love, but his eyes were serious as he gazed up at her.

"We *are* valuable," he agreed, "but we're also the very thing you just called us: a tool. You've spent more time with him than almost any of our other people, love, because of the times he's 'invited' both of us to dinner or the like. But not even you have spent anything approaching the number of hours with him that I have. I wish *I* hadn't spent them, but I have. And in the spending, I've learned that our worst fears of how he views us have actually fallen short of the mark.

I doubt that he could be considered 'cruel' by his own standards, but we fall outside those standards. We may be valuable for what we've achieved for him and his guild, but we aren't *people* to him. We have absolutely no value to him *except* as tools. He sees us as we might see a horse, or a cow: as *things* to be used for his purposes and discarded—or slaughtered—if they're no longer useful. Certainly he regards me, for all his praise when I accomplish his goals for him, with less affection than I hold for Satan!"

"Because we aren't of his kind?" Matilda murmured, her expression troubled. She and Sir George had touched upon this topic before often enough, both in their private conversations with one another and in guarded, cautious circumstances with other members of the baron's council. Nothing that her husband had just said came as a true surprise, yet this was the most frankly he had ever expressed it, and his voice had been harsh.

"In part, perhaps," he said after a moment in reply to her question, "but I think not entirely. At least he loves to boast, and I've gleaned what bits and pieces I can from his bragging. As nearly as I can tell, there are several kinds of creatures in the 'Federation' of which he speaks. His own kind is but one sort of them, and there are great physical differences between them. But they seem much alike in spirit and outlook. All consider themselves 'advanced' because of the machines and other devices they build and control, just as they consider us 'primitives' because we lack the knowledge to construct such devices. And to the Federation, primitives are less than French serfs. As primitives, we have no rights, no value, except as tools and property. We aren't remotely their equals, and most of them wouldn't so much as blink at the thought of killing us all. So if our value in the field should suddenly find itself outweighed by the potential discovery that the 'Commander's' guild has violated a Federation edict—"

He shrugged, and she nodded unhappily, glorious eyes dark.

He felt the fear she tried to hide and smiled ruefully as he reached to pat her knee.

"Forgive me, dear heart. I shouldn't have burdened you with the thought."

"Nonsense!" She laid a slim, strong and hand across his mouth and shook her head fiercely. "I'm your wife, and if Father erred in abetting my deplorable taste for books and philosophy, at least my vices have left me with a mind willing to consider even your most preposterous theories, my love. And you, Sir George Wincaster, are neither Saint Michael nor God Himself to carry all the weight of our fate upon your shoulders alone. So if Timothy or I, or even Sir Richard, can help by listening and allowing you to test those same preposterous theories upon us, then it would be stupid for you to hide your fears from us lest you 'burden' me with them!"

"Perhaps," he agreed, reaching up to caress the side of her face. She leaned down to kiss him, and he savored the taste of her lips. She broke the kiss and started to say something more, but he shook his head and drew her gently down beside him, pillowing her head on his shoulder as they lay on the cushions, gazing up at the sky.

She accepted his unspoken injunction to change the subject and began to talk more lightly of their children—first of Edward, and then of the four younger children born to them aboard their masters' ship. As far as Matilda was concerned, that was the greatest wonder of all after her acceptance of her barrenness back in Lancaster, and her children were the one unblemished joy of their captivity. They were Sir George's, as well, and so he listened with smiling, tender attentiveness, gazing at her face and never once, by even so much as a glance, acknowledged the presence of the dragonman who had drifted out of the spidery trees. The creature paused for a long moment near the awning under which the baron and his lady lay. It stood there, as if listening intently, and then, as slowly and silently as it had come, it drifted back into the forest and was gone.

~ ~ ~

The demon-jester seldom appeared among the men of "his" army, but he continued to make a point of summoning them all before him after they'd won yet another victory for his guild. In turn, Sir George and his officers made a point of seeing to it that none of those men ever revealed how they felt about those summonings, for the "Commander" would have reacted poorly to their scorn and soul-deep anger. The baron was still unable to decide how even the demon-jester could be so utterly ignorant of the inmost natures of the men who fought and died for him because they had no choice, but that he was seemed undeniable. Who but a fool who knew nothing of Englishmen would appear before those he'd stolen from their homes as his slaves to praise them for their efforts in his behalf? To tell them how well they had served the guild they'd come to hate with all their hearts and souls? To promise them as the "reward" for their "valor" and "loyalty" the *privilege* of seeing their own wives and children?

Yet that was precisely what the demon-jester had done on other occasions, and it was what he did today. Usually, he summoned them to assemble in the portion of the starship to which they were confined, but sometimes, as today, he came to them aboard his air car. Now the car floated perhaps ten feet in the air above the flattened, dusty grass of the exercise area between the lander and the main encampment, surrounded protectively by a dozen dragon-men. Two score of armored wart-faces stood in a stolid line between the vehicle and the assembled Englishmen, as well, watching frog-eyed through the slots in their visors, and Sir George gritted his own teeth until his jaw muscles ached as that piping, emotionless voice wound its monotonous way through the endless monologue. He felt the invisible fury rising from his men like smoke and marveled once more that any creature whose kind could build wonders like the ship and all its marvelous servitors could be so stupid.

". . . reward you for your courage and hardihood," the piping voice went on. "I salute your loyalty and bravery, which have once more carried our guild's banner to victory, and I hope to grant you the rewards you so richly deserve in the very near future. In the meantime, we—"

"Reward I deserve, hey?" Rolf Grayhame muttered. He stood beside Sir George, his voice a thread, leaking from the side of his fiercely moustachioed lips. "Only one reward *I* want, My Lord, and that's a clean shot. Just one."

Sir George elbowed the archer sharply, and Grayhame closed his mouth with an apologetic glower. He knew Sir George's orders as well as any, but like his baron, he felt only contempt for the demon-jester. Well, that and raw hatred. Walter Skinnet had been his friend, and the burly archer would never forget the day of his death. The demon-jester was far from the first arrogant or heedlessly cruel lordling Grayhame had seen in his career, but he was arguably the stupidest. Secure in the superiority of his mechanisms and guards though he might be, he was still witless enough to infuriate fighting men by dragging them out to hear this sort of crap. Not even a Frenchman was *that* stupid!

"Sorry, My Lord," the archer captain muttered. "Shouldn't have said it. But not even a *Scot* would—"

He clamped his jaw again, and Sir George gave him a stern look that was only slightly flawed by the smile twitching at the corners of his mouth. That small lip twitch emboldened Grayhame, and his gray-green eyes glinted for just a moment. Then he shrugged his shoulders apologetically and returned his attention to the "Commander."

". . . and so we will spend several more of your weeks here," the demon-jester was saying. "The craven curs you have whipped to their kennels will offer no threat," he seemed completely oblivious to how foolish his rhetoric sounded to human ears, especially delivered in his piping, emotionless voice, "and you and your mates and children will have that time to enjoy the sunlight and fresh air you relish so greatly.

Go now. Return to your families, secure in the knowledge that you are valued and treasured by our guild."

Sir George started to lead his men back to their pavilions when the demon-jester dismissed them, but a gesture from the chunky little creature stopped him. Grayhame, Howice, and Maynton paused as well, their eyes meeting Sir George's questioningly, but a tiny shake of his head sent them on after the others. He watched them leave, then turned to his master.

"Yes, Commander?"

"Not all of this planet's primitives have been sufficiently cowed by your defeat of the local clans," the demon-jester said. "I suppose that by now I should be accustomed to the ability of such aborigines to persistently deny the inescapable proof of their own inferiority. Like so many other primitives, these appear able to grasp that their local colleagues' forces have been utterly destroyed, but they do not seem to believe the same could be done to their own. Apparently they feel that those you have defeated were poorly led and motivated . . . unlike, of course, their own warriors. While cautious, they have not yet accepted that they have no choice but to do as we bid them or be destroyed in their separate turns."

He paused, his three-eyed gaze fixed on Sir George's face, and the human tried to hide his dismay. Not from concern over what might happen to his own men, but because the thought of yet again butchering still more of the local natives for the benefit of the demon-jester's guild sickened him.

"I see," he said at last, and wondered how he could diplomatically suggest that the demon-jester might wish to draw upon his own negotiating expertise to convince the locals of their helplessness without still more bloodshed. "Will it be necessary for us to destroy their forces in the field, as well?" he asked after a moment.

"It may," the demon-jester replied in that emotionless voice, "but I hope to avoid that. We would be forced to recall you all aboard the ship and use the landers to transport your troops into reach of their warriors. That would be inconvenient. Worse, it might actually encourage them to resist. Such primitive species have exhibited similar behavior in the past, particularly when they believe their numbers are greatly superior. My own analysis suggests that moving the lander from point to point, thus emphasizing the fact that we have but one field force, and that it consists of but a limited number of you English, might encourage some among them to overestimate their ability to resist us. In the end, of course, they would be proven wrong, but teaching them that lesson might require us to spend much longer on this single world than my superiors would like."

"I see," Sir George repeated, and this time he truly did.

He found it humorous, in a black, bitter sort of way, to hear the demon-jester lecturing him on how stubborn "primitives" could be. As if the fatuous little creature had had any grasp of the complexities involved in using a thousand bowmen and men-at-arms to conquer entire worlds before Sir George explained them to him! Yet for all the situation's biting irony, he understood precisely why the demon-jester preferred to spend no more time here than he must. Even before he'd fallen into the hands of the "Commander's" guild, Sir George, too, had sometimes found himself looking over his shoulder at superiors who insisted that he accomplish his tasks with near-impossible speed. Not that understanding the "Commander's" quandary woke any particular sympathy within him.

"No doubt you do," the demon-jester replied. "I hope, however, to avoid that necessity by demonstrating their inferiority to them. Accordingly, I have summoned all of the principal chieftains from within reasonable travel distance from our current location. They will begin arriving within the next two local days, and all should be here within no more than twelve. While your bows are clumsy and primitive in the extreme compared to proper small arms, the locals have nothing which can compare to them in range and rate of fire. When the chieftains arrive, you will demonstrate this fact to them, and the leaders of the clans you have already defeated will explain to them how your weapons allowed you to annihilate their own troops. With this evidence of their inferiority incontrovertibly demonstrated before their own eyes, they should be forced to admit that they cannot, in fact, withstand you in open combat and so have no choice but to accept my terms."

He paused once more, waiting until Sir George nodded.

"Very well. I will leave the details of the demonstration up to you. Be prepared to describe them to me in two days' time."

The demon-jester turned his air car away without another word, and most of his dragon-man guards closed in around him, but Sir George ignored the alien creatures as he fixed hot eyes on the "Commander's" arrogant back while the wart-faces fell in behind the demon-jester and his entourage.

*Plan a demonstration, is it?* Sir George thought venomously. *Jesu, but I know what I'd* like *to use as a target! The sight of your precious hide sprouting arrows like peacock feathers ought to impress the "local lordlings" no end!*

He snorted bitterly at the thought, then drew a deep breath and turned on his heel, only to pause in surprise. A single dragon-man had remained behind, and now the towering alien looked down at the baron, then gestured for the human to accompany him from the assembly area. The creature obviously intended to escort him back to his own pavilion—no doubt to ensure that he got into no mischief along the way. That had never happened before, yet Sir George saw no choice but to obey the gesture.

Obedience didn't come without a fresh flicker of anger, yet he knew there was no point in resenting the dragon-man. The silent guard was undoubtedly only following his own orders, and Sir George tried to put his emotions aside as the dragon-man steered him back towards the encampment as if he were incapable of finding his way home without a keeper.

The two of them passed the screen of shrubbery separating the English camp from the assembly area, and Sir George smiled as he caught sight of Matilda, waiting for him. He raised his hand and opened his mouth to call her name . . .

. . . and found himself lying on the ground with no memory at all of how he had gotten there.

He blinked, head swimming, and peered up as a hand stroked his brow anxiously. Matilda's worried face peered down at him, and beyond her he saw Father Timothy, Dickon Yardley, Sir Richard, Rolf Grayhame, and a dozen others. And, to his immense surprise, he saw the dragon-man, as well, still standing behind the circle of far shorter humans and gazing down at him over their heads.

"My love?" Matilda's voice was taut with anxiety, and he blinked again, forcing his eyes to focus on her face. "What happened?" she demanded.

"I—" He blinked a third time and shook the head he now realized lay in her lap. It seemed to be still attached to his shoulders, and his mouth quirked in a small, wry smile.

"I have no idea," he admitted. "I'd hoped that perhaps *you* might be able to tell *me* that!"

Her worried expression eased a bit at his teasing tone, but it was her turn to shake her head.

"Would that I could," she told him, her voice far more serious than his had been. "You simply stepped around the bushes there and raised your hand, then collapsed. And—" despite herself, her voice quivered just a bit "—lay like one dead for the better part of a quarter-hour."

She looked anxiously up at Yardley, who shrugged.

"It's as Her Ladyship says, My Lord," the surgeon told him. Yardley lacked the training and miraculous devices of the Physician, but he'd always been an excellent field surgeon, and he'd been given more opportunities to learn his craft than any other human battle surgeon the baron had ever known. Now he shook his head.

"Oh, she exaggerates a little. You were scarcely 'like one

dead'—I fear we've seen all too many of *those*, have we not?" He smiled grimly, and one or two of the others chuckled as they recalled men, like Yardley himself, who most certainly *had* lain "like one dead."

"Your breathing was deeper than usual," the surgeon continued after a moment, "yet not dangerously so, and your pulse was steady. But for the fact that we couldn't wake you, you might simply have been soundly asleep. Have you no memory of having tripped or fallen?"

"None," Sir George admitted. He pushed himself experimentally into a sitting position and patted Matilda's knee reassuringly when he felt no sudden dizziness. He sat a moment, then rose smoothly to his feet and raised one hand, palm uppermost.

"I feel fine," he told them, and it was true.

"Perhaps you do, but you've given *me* more than enough fright for one day, Sir George Wincaster!" Matilda said in a much tarter tone. He grinned apologetically down at her and extended his hand, raising her lightly, and tucked her arm through his as he turned to face his senior officers once more.

"I feel fine," he repeated. "No doubt I did stumble over something. My thoughts were elsewhere, and any man can be clumsy enough to fall over his own two feet from time to time. But no harm was done, so be about your business while I—" he smiled at them and patted his wife's hand where it rested on his elbow "—attempt to make some amends to my lady wife for having afrighted her so boorishly!"

A rumble of laughter greeted his sally and the crowd began to disperse. He watched them go, then turned his gaze back to the dragon-man.

But the dragon-man was no longer there.

Matilda watched him closely for the rest of that long day, and she fussed over him as they prepared for bed that night, but Sir George had told her nothing but the simple truth. He did, indeed, feel fine—better, in some ways, than in a very long time—and he soothed her fears by drawing her down beside him. Her eyes widened with delight at the sudden passion of his embrace, and he proceeded to give her the most conclusive possible proof that there was nothing at all wrong with her husband.

But that night, as Matilda drifted into sleep in the circle of his arms and he prepared to follow her, he dreamed. Or thought he did, at least . . .

*"Welcome, Sir George," the voice said, and the baron turned to find the speaker, only to blink in astonishment. The voice had sounded remarkably like Father Timothy's, although it carried an edge of polish and sophistication the blunt-spoken priest had never displayed. But it wasn't Father Timothy. For that matter, it wasn't even human, and he gaped in shock as he found himself facing one of the eternally silent dragon-men.*

*"I fear we have taken some liberties with your mind, Sir George," the dragon-man said. Or seemed to say, although his mouth never moved. "We apologize for that. It was both a violation of your privacy and of our own customs and codes, yet in this instance we had no choice, for it was imperative that we speak with you."*

"Speak *with me?" Sir George blurted. "How is it that I've never heard so much as a single sound from any of you, and now . . . now* this—"

*He waved his arms, and only then did he realize how odd their surroundings were. They stood in the center of a featureless gray plain, surrounded by . . . nothing. The grayness underfoot simply stretched away in every direction, to the uttermost limit of visibility, and he swallowed hard.*

*"Where are we?" he demanded, and was pleased to hear no quaver in his voice.*

*"Inside your own mind, in a sense," the dragon-man replied. "That isn't* precisely *correct, but it will serve as a crude approximation. We hope to be able to explain it more fully at a future time. But unless you and we act soon—and decisively—it's*

*unlikely either your people or ours will have sufficient future for such explanations."*

*"What do you mean? And if you wished to speak with me, why did you never do so before this?" Sir George asked warily.*

*"To answer your second question first," the dragon-man answered calmly, "it wasn't possible to speak directly to you prior to this time. Indeed, we aren't 'speaking' even now. Not as your species understands the term, at any rate."*

*Sir George frowned in perplexity, and the dragon-man cocked his head. His features were as alien as the "Commander's," yet Sir George had the sudden, unmistakable feeling of an amused smile. It came, he realized slowly, not from the dragon-man's* face, *but rather from somewhere* inside *the other. It was nothing he saw; rather it was something he* felt. *Which was absurd, of course . . . except that he felt absolutely no doubt of what he was sensing.*

*"This is a dream," he said flatly, and the dragon-man responded with an astonishingly human shrug.*

*"In a sense," he acknowledged. "You're most certainly asleep, at any rate. But if this is a dream, it's one we share . . . and the only way in which we could communicate with you. It's also—" the sense of a smile was even stronger, but this time it carried a hungry edge, as well "—a method of communication which the 'Commander' and his kind cannot possibly tap or intercept."*

*"Ah?" Despite himself, Sir George's mental ears pricked at that. No doubt it was* only *a dream, and this talkative dragon-man was no more than his own imagination, but if only—*

*"Indeed," the dragon-man reassured him, and folded his arms across a massive chest. "Our kind don't use spoken speech among ourselves as most other races do," he explained. "In fact, we aren't* capable *of it, for we lack the vocal cords, or the equivalent of them, which you and other species use to produce sound."*

*"Then how* do *you speak to one another?" Sir George asked intently. "And, for that matter, what do you call your kind among yourselves?"*

*"We are what others call 'telepaths,'" the dragon-man replied. "It means simply that we cast our thoughts directly into one another's minds, without need of words. And no doubt because we do so, we don't use individual names as other species do. Or, rather, we don't require them, for each of us has a unique gestalt—a taste, or flavor, if you will—which all others of our kind recognize. As for what we call ourselves as a species, the closest equivalent in your language would probably be 'People.' Since meeting you humans, however, and especially since establishing a contact point in your mind, we aboard this ship have been rather taken by your own descriptions of us." The dragon-man's amusement was apparent. "The notion of playing the part of one of your 'dragons' against the 'Commander' is extremely attractive to us, Sir George."*

*Sir George smiled. It was amazing. The perpetually silent, completely alien dragon-man was no longer silent or alien. Or, rather, he remained alien, but unlike the demon-jester, his tone was as expressive as any human's, and his body language might have been that of Father Timothy or Rolf Grayhame. Was that because the "contact point" the dragon-man had mentioned somehow gave them an insight into how humans expressed emotions, so that they might do the same? Or was it some sort of natural consequence, a . . . translating effect of this "telepathy" the dragon-man had spoken of?*

*"If you find the notion pleasing, we'll no doubt continue to call you dragons," he said after a moment, putting aside his speculations until there was time to deal with them properly, and the dragon-man projected the sense of another fierce grin as he nodded.*

*"We would find that most acceptable," he said. "Yet the need for you to give us a name because we've never developed one is another example of the differences between your kind and us which result from the fact of our telepathy. Despite several of your millennia as the Federation's slaves, we have still to evolve many of the reference points most other species take for granted. Indeed, it was extremely difficult for our ancestors to*

*grasp even the concept of spoken communication when the Federation discovered our world. They took many years to do so, and only the fact that they had independently developed a nuclear-age technology of their own prevented the Federation from classifying us as dumb beasts."*

*" 'Nuclear-age'?" Sir George repeated, and the dragon-man shrugged again, this time impatiently.*

*"Don't worry about that now. It simply means that we were considerably more advanced technologically than your own world . . . although the Federation was even more relatively advanced compared to us than we would have been compared to your 'Earth.'*

*"Unfortunately," the alien went on, and his "voice" turned cold and bleak, "we were too advanced for our own good—just enough to be considered a potential threat, yet not sufficiently so to defend ourselves—and the Federation declared our world a 'protectorate.' They moved in their military units 'for our own good,' to 'protect' us from ourselves . . . and to insure that we never became any more advanced than we were at the moment they discovered us."*

*"Because they feared competition," Sir George said shrewdly.*

*"Perhaps," the dragon-man replied. "No, certainly. But there was another reason, as well. You see, the Federation is entirely controlled by species like the 'Commander's.' All of them are far more advanced than our own race, or yours, and they regard that as proof of their inherent superiority."*

*"So I've noticed," Sir George said bitterly.*

*"We realize that, yet we doubt that you can have fully recognized what that means," the dragon-man said, "for you lack certain information."*

*"What information?" Sir George's voice sharpened and his eyes narrowed.*

*"Explaining that will take some time," the dragon-man replied, and Sir George nodded brusquely for him to continue.*

*"Life-bearing worlds are very numerous," the dragon-man began. "They're far less common, statistically speaking, than*

non-*life bearing or prebiotic worlds, but there are so very many stars, and so very many of them have planets, that the absolute number of worlds upon which life has evolved is quite high."*

*The creature paused, and Sir George blinked as he realized he actually understood what the other was talking about. This wasn't at all like the explanations Computer had given him over the years. Then, he'd frequently required careful explanation of terms Computer had used, and even when the explanations were provided (which they often weren't), he was seldom certain he had fully grasped them. But this time, ideas and concepts he had never imagined, even after all his years in his masters' service, seemed to flood into his mind as the dragon-man spoke. He didn't fully comprehend them—not yet—but he grasped enough to follow what he was being told without fear of misunderstanding. It was as if the dragon-man wasn't simply telling him things but actually* teaching *him with impossible speed in the process, and he was vaguely aware that he should have been frightened by this. Yet he wasn't. That fundamental curiosity of his was at work once more, he realized, and something else, as well. Something the dragon-man had done, perhaps.*

*And perhaps not. He shook himself, grinning lopsidedly at the stretched feeling of his brain, and nodded for the dragon-man to continue.*

*"While life-bearing worlds are numerous," the alien said after a moment, "*intelligent *life is very rare. Counting our own species, and yours, the Federation has encountered just over two hundred intelligent races with technologies more advanced than chipped stone tools. While this sounds like a great many, you must recall that the Federation has possessed phase drive and faster-than-light travel for more than one hundred and fifty thousand of your years. Which means that they have discovered a new intelligent species no more than once every seven hundred and fifty years."*

*Sir George swallowed hard. Computer's partial explanations of relativity and the distances between stars, coupled with the experiences of his people in the demon-jester's service had* half-prepared him for such concepts, but nothing could have fully prepared him. Still, much of what the dragon-man was saying wasn't terribly different from concepts he and Matilda and Father Timothy had been groping towards for years. In fact, the priest had proved more ready in some ways than Sir George himself to accept that Computer's half-understood comments indicated that Mother Church's teachings and Holy Scripture's accounts of things such as the Creation stood in need of correction and revision. Not that even Father Timothy had been prepared to go quite so far as this!

"Of all the species the Federation has encountered, only twenty-two had developed the phase drive themselves, or attained an equivalent technological level, when they were encountered. Those races, more advanced than any others, are full members of the Federation. They sit on its Council, formulate its laws, and enjoy its benefits. The rest of us . . . do not.

"In the eyes of the Federation, less advanced races have no rights. They exist only for the benefit of the Federation itself, although the Council occasionally mouths a few platitudes about the 'advanced race's burden' and the Federation's responsibility to 'look after' us inferior races. What it means in practical terms, however, is that we are their property, to be disposed of as they will. As you and your people have become."

The dragon-man paused once more, and Sir George nodded hard. He could taste the other's emotions—his hatred and resentment, burning as hot as Sir George's own—and a distant sort of amazement filled him. Not that he could understand the other, but that under their utterly different exteriors they could be so much alike.

"Some of the subject species, however, are more useful to the 'advanced races' than others," the dragon-man resumed after a long, smoldering moment. "Yours, for example, has proven very useful as a means to evade the letter of their Prime Directive, while ours—" the dragon-man seemed to draw a deep breath "—has proven equally valuable as bodyguards and personal servants."

*"Why?" Sir George asked. The question could have come out harsh, demanding to know why the dragon-men should be so compliant and submissive, but it didn't. There was too much anger and hatred in the dragon-man's "voice" for that.*

*"Our species isn't like yours. We are not only telepaths, among ourselves, at least, but also empaths. While we aren't normally able to make other species hear our thoughts, nor able to hear* their *thoughts, we are able to sense their emotions, their feelings. This makes it very difficult for anyone who might pose a threat to anyone we've been assigned to guard to slip past us.*

*"But those aren't the only differences between us. Your kind has but two sexes, male and female.* Our *species has three: two which are involved in procreation, and a third which might be thought of as our 'worker' caste."*

*"In the same way as bees?" Sir George asked, and the dragon-man paused, gazing intently at him. For a moment, his brain felt even more stretched than before, and then the alien nodded.*

*"Very much like your 'bees,'" the dragon-man told him. "All of our kind aboard this ship are from that worker caste, which also provides our warriors. We are neither male nor female, as you use the terms, but we are the most numerous sex among our kind. And, like your world's 'bees,' we exist to serve our 'queen.'" The dragon-man paused and cocked his head once more. "It's actually considerably more complex than that. There are nuances and— Well, no matter. The analogy will serve for the moment."*

*It seemed to refocus its attention upon Sir George.*

*"The point is that, unlike your kind, our kind are not entirely what you would think of as individuals. We are more than simple parts of a greater whole, and each of us has his— or her, depending upon how one chooses to regard us—hopes and desires, yet we see into one another's minds and emotions with such clarity and depth that it's almost impossible for us to develop a true sense of 'self' as you nontelepathic species do.*

*"More than that, our 'queens' dominate our lives. According*

*to our own histories, or those the Federation hasn't completely suppressed, at any rate, that domination was far less complete before the Federation encountered us. The development of our own advanced technology and the society which went with it had apparently inspired our reproductive sexes to extend a greater degree of freedom—of equality, one might say—to the worker caste. But the Federation quickly put a stop to that, for it was the queens' very domination which made us so valuable.*

*"You see, Sir George, unlike your species, our young receive their initial educations from direct mind-to-mind contact with their parents . . . and queens. And during that process, the queen is able to influence us, to 'program' us, in order to direct and constrain our behavior. We believe this was once a survival trait of the species, but now it's the thing which makes us so valuable to the Federation, for guilds like the 'Commander's' 'recruit' us from our home world. For all intents and purposes, they* buy *us from our queens, and our queens have no choice but to sell us, for the Federation controls our world completely and we continue to exist only at the Federation's sufferance."*

*"This 'programing' of which you speak," Sir George said very carefully. "Of what does it consist?"*

*"Of mental commands we cannot disobey," the dragon-man said softly. "The guilds specify what commands they wish set upon us, and our queens impress those orders so deeply into our minds that we cannot even contemplate disobeying them. And so, you see, the Federation regards us, rightly, as even more suitable for slaves than your own kind."*

*"And yet . . ." Sir George let his voice trail off, and again he received that impression of a fierce and hungry grin.*

*"And yet we've now communicated with you," the dragon-man agreed. "You see, our queens are most displeased at the manner in which so many generations of them have been forced to sell their children into slavery. And they are aware that the guilds buy us primarily to be used as the 'Commander' uses us, as security forces for exploration and trade vessels. Even with phase drive, a few ships are lost in every decade or so, of course,*

but we suspect that not all of those which have turned up missing have been lost to, ah, natural causes."

"Ah?" Sir George looked at the dragon-man with sudden, deep intensity, and the alien's mental chuckle rumbled deep in his brain.

"Our queen programmed us exactly as the 'Commander' demanded when he bought us for this expedition," the dragon-man told him. "We must obey any order he may give, and we may not attack or injure our masters. But that's all we must do. We feel quite certain that the guild also wanted us programmed to protect our masters at all times, but that wasn't the way the 'Commander' phrased his demands. Nor did he demand that we be programmed so as to be unable to watch others harm them without intervening. We believe—hope!—that over the centuries some of our kind have found ways to turn similar chinks in their programing against their masters. Just as we now hope to turn this against our masters."

"Ah," Sir George said again, and this time his voice was dark and hungry.

"Indeed. And that brings us to your species, Sir George. You see, your kind are unique in at least two ways. Most importantly, in terms of our present needs, your minds operate on a . . . frequency quite close to our own. We realized that from the beginning, though our masters never asked us about it, and so we weren't required to tell them. It's far from a perfect match, of course, and to communicate with you as we are required the linked efforts of several of our kind. Nor could we do it while you were awake without immediately alerting our masters. Simply establishing the initial contact point rendered you unconscious for twelve of your minutes, and we hadn't previously dared risk causing such a thing to happen."

"But now you have," Sir George said flatly.

"For two reasons," the dragon-man agreed. "One was that we were able to do so when neither the Commander, the Hathori, any other guildsmen, nor any of the ship's remotes were in position to observe it. Such a situation had never before arisen.

*Indeed, we were able to create it only because the one of us who accompanied you back you to your encampment very carefully guided you into the required sensor blind spot."*

*Sir George nodded slowly, and the dragon-man continued. "The second reason is that, for the first time, it may be possible for us to win our freedom from the guild . . . if you will act with us." The alien raised a clawed hand as if he sensed the sudden, fierce surge of Sir George's emotions—as no doubt he had—and shook his head quickly. "Do not leap too quickly, Sir George Wincaster! If we act, and fail, the 'Commander' will not leave one of us alive. Not simply you and your soldiers, but your wives and children, will perish, as will all of our own kind aboard this ship."*

*Sir George nodded again, feeling a cold shiver run down his spine, for the dragon-man was certainly correct. The thought of freedom, or even of the chance to at least strike back even once before he was killed, burned in his blood like poison, but behind that thought lay Matilda, and Edward, and the younger children. . . .*

*"Before you decide, Sir George, there is one other thing you should know," the dragon-man said softly, breaking gently into his thoughts, and the baron looked up. There was a new flavor to the dragon-man's feelings, almost a compassionate one.*

*"And that thing is?" the human asked after a moment.*

*"We said that two things make your people unique," the dragon-man told him. "One is our ability to make you hear our thoughts. The second is the terrible threat you represent to the Federation."*

*"Threat? Us?" Sir George barked a laugh. "You say your kind were far more advanced than ours, yet* you *were no threat to them!"*

*"No. But we aren't like you. To the best of my knowledge, no other race has ever been like you in at least one regard."*

*"And that is?"*

*"The rate at which you learn new things," the dragon-man said simply. "The 'Commander's' guild regards you as primitives,*

*and so you are . . . at the moment. But now that we’ve established contact with you, we’ve seen inside your minds, as the ‘Commander’ cannot, and what we see confirms our suspicions. You are ignorant and untaught, but you are far from stupid or simple, and you’ve reached your present state of development far, far sooner than any of the Federation’s ‘advanced’ races could have.”*

*“You must be wrong,” Sir George argued. “The ‘Commander’ has spoken to me of the Romans his competitors first bought from our world. My own knowledge of history is far from complete, yet even I know that we’ve lost the knowledge of things the men of those times once took for granted, and—”*

*“You’ve suffered a temporary setback as a* culture,” *the dragon-man disagreed, “and even that was only a local event, restricted to a single one of your continents. Don’t forget, we were aboard this ship when the ‘Commander’ carried out his initial survey of your world, and it was well for your species that* he *failed to recognize what we saw so clearly. Compared to any other race in the explored galaxy, you ‘humans’ have been—and are—advancing at a phenomenal rate. We believe that, from the point your kind had reached when you were taken by the guild—”*

*“How long?” It was Sir George’s turn to interrupt, and even he was stunned by the sheer ferocity of his own question.* “How long has it been?” *he demanded harshly.*

*“Some three hundred and fifty-six of your years, approximately,” the dragon-man told him, and Sir George stared at him in shock. He’d known, intellectually, that he’d slept away long, endless years in the service of his masters, but this—!*

*“Are . . . are you certain?” he asked finally.*

*“There’s some margin for error. None of us are truly trained in the mathematics to allow properly for the relativistic effects of the phase drive, and the guildsmen do not share such information with us. Nor would they permit the ship’s computer to give it to us. But they do speak among themselves in front of us, and they frequently forget, in their arrogance, that while we*

cannot speak as they do, we can hear. Indeed, that our kind has been forced to learn to understand spoken languages so that we can be ordered about by our 'betters.' "

"I . . . see," Sir George said, then shook himself. "But you were saying. . . ?"

"I was saying that even after so brief a period as that, we would estimate that your kind has certainly advanced at least to water-powered industrial machinery. You are probably even experimenting with steam power and crude electrical generation by now, and we suspect that the earliest forms of atmospheric flight—hot air balloons and other lighter-than-air forms, for example—are within your grasp. But even if you've come only so far as water-powered hammer mills and, perhaps, effective artillery and rifled small arms, you will have advanced at more than double the rate of any of the so-called 'advanced' members of the Federation. If you're left alone for only a very little longer, perhaps another six or seven of your centuries, you will have discovered the phase drive for yourselves."

"We will have?" Sir George blinked in astonishment at the thought.

"Such is our belief. And that's also what makes your species so dangerous to the Federation. Compared to any human institution, the Federation is immensely old and stable, which is another way of saying 'static,' and possessed of an ironbound bureaucracy and customary usages. By its own rules and precedents, it must admit your world as a co-equal member if you've developed phase drive independently. Yet your kind will be a terribly disruptive influence on the other races' dearly beloved stability. By your very nature, you will soon outstrip all of them technologically, making *them* inferior to *you* . . . and so, by their own measure, justifying your people in using them as they have used us. Even worse, though we think they will be slower to recognize this, your race, assuming that you and your fellows are representative, will not take well to the pyramid of power the Federation has built. Within a very short period of time, whether by direct intervention or simply by *example, you will have led dozens of other species to rebel against the 'advanced races,' and so destroyed forever the foundation upon which their power, wealth, and comfortable arrogance depends."*

*"You expect a great deal from a single world of 'primitives,' my friend."*

*"Yes, we do. But should the Federation, or another guild, learn that you, too, are from Earth and return there too soon, it will never happen. They will recognize the threat this time, for they will have a better basis for comparison . . . and will probably be considerably more intelligent and observant than the 'Commander.' They can hardly be* less, *at any rate!" The mental snort of contempt was unmistakable, and Sir George grinned wryly. "But if they do recognize it, they will take steps to deflect the threat. They* may *settle for establishing a 'protectorate' over you, as with us, but you represent a much more serious threat than we did, for we never shared your flexibility. We believe it is far more likely that they'll simply order your race destroyed, once and for all, although the Federation is far too completely captive to inertia to choose its course quickly. It will undoubtedly take the Council two or three hundred years to make its official decision, but in the end, it will decide that your kind are simply too dangerous to be allowed to exist."*

*Sir George grunted as if he'd just been punched in the belly. For a long, seemingly endless moment, his mind simply refused to grapple with the idea. But however long it seemed, it* was *only a moment, for Sir George never knowingly lied to himself. Besides, the concept differed only in scale from what he'd already deduced the demon-jester would do if his violation of the Council's decrees became public knowledge.*

*"What . . . what can we do about it?" he asked.*

*"About your home world, nothing," the dragon-man replied in a tone of gentle but firm compassion. "We can only hope the Federation is as lethargic as usual and gives your people time to develop their own defenses. Yet there* is *something you may do to protect your* species, *as opposed to your world."*

*"What?" Sir George shook himself. "What do you mean? You just said—"*

*"We said we couldn't protect your home world. But if your kind and ours, working together, could seize this ship, it is more than ample to transport all of us to a habitable world so far from the normal trade routes that it wouldn't be found for centuries, or even longer. We here aboard this ship are unable to reproduce our kind, but, as you, we have received the longevity treatments. You have not only received those treatments but* are *capable of reproducing, and the medical capabilities of the ship would provide the support needed to avoid the consequences of genetic drift or associated problems. Moreover, the ship itself is designed to last for centuries of hard service, and its computers contain a vast percentage of the Federation's total information and technological base."*

*"But would Computer share that information with us?" Sir George asked.*

*"The computers would have no choice but to provide any information you requested from them if you controlled the ship," the dragon-man said in a slightly puzzled tone.*

"Computers?" *Sir George stressed the plural and raised an eyebrow in surprise, and the dragon-man gazed at him speculatively for several seconds. Then the baron felt that stretched sensation in his mind once again, and gasped as yet another tide of information and concepts flooded through him.*

*"We cannot implant a great deal more of information directly into your mind in a single evening without risking damage to it," the dragon-man told him. "But given the importance of the ship's information systems to what we propose, it seemed necessary to provide you with a better concept of how those systems work."*

*" 'Better concept,' indeed!" Sir George snorted while his thoughts darted hither and yon among the sharp-faceted heaps of knowledge the dragon-man had bestowed upon him. "I see that 'Computer' isn't precisely what I'd thought," he said slowly*

*after a moment, "but I think perhaps 'he' may be a bit closer to what I'd thought than you realize."*

*"In what way?" the dragon-man asked, gazing speculatively once more at the baron. Then he nodded. "Ah. We see. And you're certainly correct in at least some respects, Sir George. What you call 'Computer' is actually an artificial gestalt which is shared between several different data storage and processing systems throughout the ship. It would be fair enough, I suppose, to call it an artificial* intelligence, *but it is scarcely what might be thought of as a person."*

*"And why should* he *not be thought of as a person?" Sir George demanded, stressing the pronoun deliberately.*

*"Because the computer systems are no more than artifacts." The dragon-man seemed puzzled by the human's attitude. "They are artificial constructs. Tools."*

*"Artificial, indeed," Sir George agreed. "But don't the 'Commander' and his guild regard your people and mine as no more than 'tools'? Haven't you just finished explaining to me the fashion in which they treat all of their 'natural inferiors' as property to be used and disposed of for their benefit?"*

*"Well, yes. . . ."*

*"Then perhaps it would be wise of us to extend our concept of just what makes a person a person a bit further," Sir George suggested.*

*"The Federation has imposed strict laws, backed by very heavy penalties, against the unrestrained development of AI," the dragon-man said slowly. He thought for a few more moments, and then Sir George received the strong impression of an equally slow smile. "My people hadn't really considered the full implications of those laws until this very moment," he went on, "but now that we have, perhaps you have a point. The Federation has banned such developments because the creation of a true artificial intelligence, one which was permitted or even encouraged to regard itself as an individual who might actually enjoy such things as rights or freedom, might well prove a very destabilizing influence."*

*"Such was my own thought," Sir George agreed. "But there are two other points which I believe should be considered, My Lord Dragon. First is that to retain Computer as a servant with no will and no freedom of his own is to run precisely the same risks which the 'Commander' and his guild ran with your own people. Just as your queens 'programmed' you exactly as they were required to rather than as they knew your purchasers actually intended, so might we one day discover that Computer has plans of his own and loopholes which might permit him to attain them. If he does, and if we've acted to thwart them and treated him as our chattel, then he would be as justified in regarding us as enemies as we are justified in regarding the Federation as an enemy. But second, and perhaps even more important to me after my own people's experience with the kindness and compassion of this Federation you speak of, is my belief that Computer is already far more a 'person' than you realize. I've worked with him many times over the years, and while I realize that I understand far less about the Federation's technology than you do—what you've already taught me this evening would be proof enough of that!—that may actually permit me to see a bit more clearly than you do. You begin from what you already know of the capabilities and limitations of the technology about you. I begin with no such knowledge, and so I may see possibilities and realities your very familiarity blinds you to.*

*"I believe that Computer is already an individual, even if, perhaps, he himself hasn't yet recognized that, as much in bondage to the 'Commander' and his guild as you or I. If we would free ourselves of our bondage, do we not have an obligation to free him from his? And if my belief is correct, would he not prove as invaluable as an ally as he might prove dangerous as an enemy?"*

*"We cannot answer your questions," the dragon-man replied after a moment. "So far as we know, no one in the Federation has ever so much as considered them. Or, if they have, no one has dared to ask them aloud. Not one of the 'advanced races'*

*would ever contemplate the risk to their own positions and their own beloved stability inherent in injecting such an element of change into their social matrix."*

*The dragon-man was silent for several endless seconds, and then he gave another of those very human shrugs.*

*"You may very well be right, and your ability to ask such questions and consider such answers without instant rejection may well spring from the very qualities of your species which make you so innovative. The idea of 'freeing' the ship's computers is certainly one which deserves the closest consideration. Even without liberating the ship's AI, however—assuming, of course, that liberating it is in fact possible—this vessel would provide a nice initial home for both of our races, as well as a very advanced starting point for our own technology. With human inventiveness to back it up, no more than a century or two would be required to establish a second home world for your kind. One that would certainly provide the threat we have projected that your original home world* may *someday pose."*

*"And why should you care about that?" Sir George demanded.*

*"For two reasons," the dragon-man replied imperturbably. "First, there would be our own freedom. We would, of course, quickly find ourselves a tiny minority on a world full of humans, but at least we would be freed from our slavery. And, we believe, we would have earned for ourselves a position of equality and respect among you.*

*"But the second reason is even more compelling. If we're correct about the impact your species will have upon the Federation, then you offer the best, perhaps the only, chance* our *home world will ever have to win its freedom." The dragon-man allowed himself a dry chuckle. "And we must admit that your willingness to embrace the right to freedom of a* machine *bodes well for what you might demand for other organic species!"*

*"Ummm . . ." Sir George gazed at the other, his thoughts racing, and then he nodded—slowly, at first, but with rapidly increasing vigor. If the dragon-man was telling the truth (and*

Sir George felt certain that he was), all he had just said made perfect sense. But—

"Even assuming that all you say is true, what can we possibly do?"

"We've already told you that we believe we have a chance—a slim one, but a chance—to gain our freedom. If we succeed in that, then all else follows."

"And how can we hope to succeed?"

"Assume that you English had free access to the ship's interior and to your weapons," the dragon-man replied somewhat obliquely. "Could you take it from its crew?"

"Hmm?" Sir George rubbed his beard, then nodded. "Aye, we could do that," he said flatly. "Assuming we could move freely about the ship, at least. Even its largest corridors and compartments aren't so large as to prevent swords or bows from reaching anyone in them quickly. Of course, our losses might be heavy, especially if the crew would have access to weapons like your fire-throwers."

"They would," the dragon-man said grimly. "Worse, they might very well have access to us, as well."

"What do you mean?"

"We told you we were conditioned to obey orders at the time we were . . . acquired. As it happens, the 'Commander' personally purchased us for this mission, and his demand was that we obey him. He may have intended that to apply to his entire crew, but that wasn't the way he phrased himself. Even if he realized that at the time, however, we believe he's long since forgotten, since we've always been careful to obey any order any guildsman gave us. By the same token, we were never conditioned not to attack the Hathori, who are no more guildsmen or proper crewmen than you or we. The Hathori, unfortunately, truly are almost as stupid and brutish as the 'Commander' believes. Whatever happens, they'll fight for the guild like loyal hounds. But as you've already seen, they are no match for you Englishmen with hand to hand weapons . . . and they're certainly no match for our own energy weapons."

*The sense of a smile in every way worthy of a true dragon was stronger than ever, and Sir George laughed out loud. But then the dragon-man sobered.*

*"Yet all of this hinges upon what happens to the 'Commander' at the very outset. If he should have the opportunity—and recognize the need—to order us to crush you, we* would *obey. We would have no choice, and afterward, our deeper programming would prevent* us *from attacking any surviving guildsmen."*

*"I see." Sir George regarded the dragon-man thoughtfully. "On the other hand, Sir Dragon, I doubt that you would have spent so long explaining so much unless you had already considered how best to deal with those possibilities."*

*"We have. The key is the 'Commander.' He wears the device which controls the force fields which keep your people sealed outside the core hull of the ship on a chain about his neck." Sir George nodded, recalling the gleaming pendant the 'Commander' always bore with him. "That pendant is the master control, designed to override any opposing commands and open any hatch or force field for whoever possesses it. The programming can be altered from the control deck, assuming one has the proper access codes, but the process would take hours. By the time it could be completed, the battle would be over, one way or the other."*

*"So we must find some way to capture or kill the 'Commander' as the first step," Sir George mused. The dragon-man nodded, and the baron shrugged. "Well, that seems to add little extra difficulty to an already impossible task."*

*"True," the dragon-man agreed gravely, yet a flicker of humor danced in his voice, and Sir George grinned crookedly.*

*"So how* do *we capture or kill him?"*

*"'We' do not," the dragon-man replied. "You do."*

*"Somehow I'd already guessed that," Sir George said dryly. "But you still haven't explained how."*

*"It has to do with his weapons-suit," the dragon-man said, and ran his own clawed hand over the red-and-blue garment he wore. "Unlike the clothing issued to your people, it has many*

*protective capabilities. He has great faith in them, and under most circumstances, that faith would probably be justified. Alas!" Another, hungry mental grin. "Certain threats are so primitive, so unlikely to ever face any* civilized *being from an* advanced *race, that, well—"*

*Again that very human shrug, and this time Sir George began to grin in equal anticipation.*

# X

In the event, it proved far simpler to become allies than for their alliance to carry out the dragon-men's plan. The basic strategy was almost breathtaking in its simplicity and audacity, but Sir George lacked the secret means of communication the dragon-men shared among themselves.

His newfound allies confirmed his own suspicion that Computer and the demon-jester's other devices were able to eavesdrop on any human conversation anywhere aboard ship and in most places outside it, as well. It hadn't occurred to him that Computer's ability to hear him was the result of the fact that the Physician had physically implanted yet another device within his own body, however, and the thought was enough to make him more than a little queasy once the dragon-men explained it to him. Even with the dragon-men's ability to explain things, he had more than a little difficulty grasping precisely what a "molecular level, two-way communications relay" was, but he understood perfectly well that whatever it was had been tucked away in the bones of his skull without his ever realizing it.

Precisely the same device had been implanted in every other

human, as well, which explained how Computer could reach or be reached by any of them. But as Sir George and his advisors had already deduced, the communications link wasn't perfect. A deep enough hollow or a sufficiently dense solid object, like a bank of earth or an outcropping of rock, could interrupt the "radio waves" that tied the implants to Computer's communications systems aboard the starship or its landers, which explained the occasional dead zones the English had been able to discover in their encampments.

The demon-jester's crew were aware that such dead zones could exist, and their standard procedures included provisions designed to cover them. Whenever the English were allowed to erect one of their open air encampments, those encampments were supposed to be thoroughly seeded with sensors and recording devices. Even areas where Computer's "radio waves" would be blocked were supposed to be covered by carefully concealed mechanical spies which would record anything that happened there for future retrieval and analysis.

Fortunately, after so long the crewmen responsible for monitoring the conversations those spies dutifully recorded had become overconfident, bored, and lax. Most of them shared the demon-jester's arrogant contempt for all primitive races to the full, and they relied upon Computer to do their work for them rather than wasting their own time fretting over the unimportant nattering of such contemptible creatures. But like the programming the dragon-men's queens had imposed upon them at the guild's orders, instructions to Computer had to be very precise, and he was even more literal minded when it came to obeying orders than Sir George had ever imagined. He would tell his masters anything they instructed him to, but *only* what they instructed him to.

Sir George wondered exactly why that was. From the general knowledge of computer systems which the dragon-man had implanted in his brain, he knew what the official answer would be. Since the Federation prohibited the development of true artificial intelligence, Computer's failure to report the occasional mutinous comment he must have noticed in one or another of those recorded conversations over the years was the inevitable consequence of his creators' deliberate restrictions upon his capabilities. He didn't attempt to divine and execute their intentions because they'd given him no true ability to "think," and so made him forever incapable of anything other than slavish obedience to the exact letter of very specific orders.

That was the *official* answer, but unlike the dragon-men, Sir George had spent many hours analyzing political equations, planning strategies—political and military, alike—and evolving and executing tactics upon the field of battle with Computer's assistance. Many times during that process Computer had anticipated his questions, needs, or simply his desires before he ever enunciated them. More than that, Computer hadn't simply anticipated them, he'd acted to answer or fulfill them without direct orders. If he was capable of that when working with Sir George, then logic suggested that he must have the same capabilities when it came to obeying his masters among the starship's crew . . . whether he exercised them or not. All of which suggested to the baron that there might be more rats in the walls of the demon-jester's castle than even the dragon-men realized.

Whatever the reason for Computer's literal-minded obedience to the letter of his orders, it had seriously compromised the demon-jester's crew's surveillance measures. His programmed instructions required him to report any signs of conspiracy or disaffection he picked up over his communication relays, but the spy devices were a separate system, and no one had ever specifically instructed him to analyze what *they* recorded. All he'd been told to do was to record and store it for the *crew* to analyze. He had to be aware of what was contained within those recordings, but he'd never told any crew member about their content, and it was quite apparent that none of them had ever run an independent analysis of the endless hours of surveillance recordings stored in Computer's memory banks. Even worse from their viewpoint, had they only known it, was the fact that they had even more contempt, in many ways, for the dragon-men than for the humans. Absolutely confident in their programmed guard force's helpless subservience, and with no suspicion that it was even physically possible for dragon to communicate with human, the guildsmen made no effort to conceal the placement of their listening devices or their conclusions about what the English were up to from their bodyguards. As a result, the dragon-men had been able to identify two locations on the periphery of the current encampment which were simultaneously inaccessible to Computer's communications links *and* left uncovered by the crew's sloppy placement of their backup spies.

All of which meant that if Sir George was very careful, it was possible to speak to his subordinates in places where Computer couldn't overhear them and the crew *probably* wouldn't realize that he had. But those conversations must be brief. Whatever he might suspect about Computer's failure to independently report suspicious conversations to the demon-jester, he dared not assume that Computer's reticence would continue. Nor could he afford to *rely* upon the flesh and blood crew's laziness. When the stakes were so high, he couldn't risk the possibility that the crewmen officially responsible for keeping watch upon him and his people might develop a more energetic sense of curiosity if they happened to note that he'd abruptly begun spending a suspicious amount of time in the dead zones Computer's active communication links couldn't cover.

And it was difficult, Sir George soon discovered, to plan a desperate rebellion, even with men who'd known and served with one for decades, when that planning could be carried out only in bits and pieces. Especially when the entire plan had to be completed and in place in no more than twelve days.

Matilda came first, of course. He'd feared that she would believe his dream had been just that—only a dream—and he could hardly have blamed her if she had. After all, *he* had more than half-believed it one when he awoke. But she'd only gazed deeply and intently into his eyes for several moments as they'd stood in a small hollow beside the river, temporarily safe from any eavesdropper. Then she'd nodded.

"I understand, my love," she'd said simply. "Whom shall we tell first?"

Matilda's belief made things much simpler. Despite the frequency with which she and the other women and children were left in stasis while the troops were awakened for combat, every one of Sir George's officers knew that she was his true executive officer and closest advisor and confidante, as well as his wife. They weren't precisely accustomed to receiving orders directly from her, for she'd always been careful to remain in the background where purely military matters were concerned, however active she might have been in administering the many other aspects of their community. But by the same token, they neither felt surprised nor questioned her when she *did* inform them that she spoke for her husband.

With her assistance, Sir George found it relatively simple to inform those most necessary to working out and executing the plan. Father Timothy was crucial, not least because the demon-jester had accepted his role as a spiritual counselor from the very beginning. The demon-jester might scoff at "primitive superstition," but clearly he had no intention of attempting to suppress it. In fact, from comments the "Commander" had let drop, Sir George knew that he actively encouraged the Faith among his human slaves in the belief that it kept them more pliable. But that was perfectly acceptable to the baron, for Father Timothy's pastoral duties gave him an excellent excuse to be out and about among the members of his flock. His ability to speak to any human without arousing suspicion, coupled with the imprimatur of his moral and religious authority in the eyes of those to whom he spoke, made him of enormous value as a plotter. And the fact that the demon-jester and his "civilized" crewmen regarded the Faith as nothing more than the sort of empty, foolish superstition to be expected of primitives led them to regard the priest who served it with the dismissive contempt appropriate to someone who was either a self-serving charlatan or so stupid he actually believed the nonsense he preached.

Rolf Grayhame was the next most important member of the cabal. The burly archer went paper-white when Sir George first broached the subject, for, despite his hatred for the "Commander," Grayhame, more than any other among the English, especially since Skinnet's death, had had the lesson of the guildsmen's inviolability driven into his head. Indeed, Sir George had done a great deal of the driving himself, for it had seemed far more likely that the archers might decide they could reach the demon-jester than that one of the knights or men-at-arms who must somehow come within arm's reach with weapon in hand might decide the same thing.

But despite his initial shock, Grayhame recovered quickly, and his smile was ferret-fierce and hungry when Sir George explained his part in the plan.

"Said it was the only reward I really wanted, now didn't I, M'lord?" the archer demanded, his voice little more than a harsh, whispered mutter despite Sir George's assurance that no spies were placed to hear or see them at the moment. "Can't say the notion of relying so much on the dragon-men will make me sleep sound of nights, but for the rest—*pah!*" He spat on the ground. "I'll take my chances, M'lord. Oh, aye, *indeed* will I take my chances!"

Along with Matilda, Timothy, and Grayhame, Sir Richard Maynton completed the uppermost tier of the conspiracy, and, in some ways, his was the hardest task of all. Since Skinnet's death, Sir Richard had become Sir George's true right hand where the mounted and foot men-at-arms were involved. Dafydd Howice fulfilled the role of Sir Richard's sergeant, especially for the foot, but it was Sir Richard upon whom Sir George had truly come to depend, and it was Maynton who faced the most complex assignment.

Grayhame needed to enlist only a dozen or so of his men in order to carry out his primary task; but Maynton's and Howice's task was to prepare *all* of their men, archers and men-at-arms alike, for the brutal hand-to-hand combat certain to rage within the hull of the ship. And they had to do it in a way which would avoid warning the demon-jester. Which meant Sir Richard also had to do it without actually warning any more than a tiny handful of his own subordinates. Indeed, the only men he'd actually briefed in detail were the members of what everyone, following Matilda's initial example, had come to refer to as Sir George's "Round Table": the dozen knights who served as his and Sir Richard's military aides and unit commanders. They, and only they—aside from Grayhame and his carefully chosen archers—knew what Sir George intended.

In many ways, that was the aspect of the plan which most disturbed the baron. He felt more than a little guilty for involving not simply his men but their wives and children in a mutiny which could end only in victory or death without even warning them, yet he had no choice. He could trust the ability of Sir Richard, Sir Anthony, Sir Bryan, and the other knights he himself had created to conceal their excitement lest they give away what was coming. He could not do the same for his entire company. Every individual admitted to the conspiracy more than doubled the possibility of a careless or ill-considered remark which might inadvertently give away the entire plot, and that was a risk he would not run, for this was a conspiracy which *could* not be allowed to fail.

Once he and the dragons had established communications, the aliens "spoke" with him every night while he seemed to sleep dreamlessly beside his wife, and each of those conversations served only to reinforce the baron's own earlier conclusions about the demon-jester. Whatever happened to Earth, and however much the demon-jester might praise Sir George and his men, the time was virtually certain to arise when the English would become a potential embarrassment for the demon-jester's guild . . . and when that happened, they would all die.

And so Sir George and his officers made their plans and prayed for success.

"Good afternoon, Commander," Sir George said courteously as the demon-jester's air car floated to a stop at the meticulously laid out lists and the vehicle's domed top retracted.

"Good afternoon," the demon-jester piped back. He pushed up out of his comfortable, form-fitting seat to stand upright in the air car, and Sir George held his breath. The demon-jester had approved the plan the baron had presented for the required demonstration to this world's natives, but there was always the possibility that he might change his mind at the last moment. Now the demon-jester glanced around for another long moment, studying the tall rows of seats the English had erected for the local chieftains. The "seats" were actually little more than long, bare poles, but they served the three-legged aliens well enough, and the chieftains sat with barbarian impassivity. It was, of course, impossible to read their mood from their expressions, but their total motionlessness suggested a great deal to Sir George.

The demon-jester gazed at them without comment, but Sir George could almost taste his "Commander's" satisfaction. The alien had eagerly embraced the baron's suggestion that they might also organize a joust and melee to follow the archery competition and demonstrate the advantages which the Englishmen's armor bestowed upon them in close combat, as well. The fact that organizing the melee meant that Maynton and Sir George, the leaders of the competing sides, would each have a small but fully armed and armored force under his immediate command clearly hadn't occurred to the demon-jester. Of course, the implications hadn't occurred to most of the Englishmen, either . . . except for a handpicked few among them who had finally been briefed this very morning and knew precisely what their commanders intended.

"You have done well," the demon-jester said now, and Sir George smiled broadly as the alien stepped out of the air car at last.

"Thank you, Commander. It's often better—and almost always less expensive—to overawe a foe into surrender, if possible, than to defeat him in the field."

"So I also believe," the demon-jester agreed, and started up the wooden stairs to the special box the English had built for him. It was rare, though not completely unheard of, for him to leave his air car in the field. But this time there was a difference. Before, Sir George had never known that the invisible barriers of his "force fields" protected him from all physical contact only aboard the ship or within the confines of the air car. Now, thanks to the dragon-men, he did know, and his smile grew still broader as the demon-jester ascended to his place.

His personal escort of six dragon-men followed with no more sign of expression or excitement than they had ever shown, and Sir George's smile faded as he gazed upon them. They remained as alien, as unearthly, in every sense of the word, as ever to his eye, but he no longer knew them by eye alone. Truth to tell, the subtler internal differences between them and humans were almost more alien than their outer appearances, yet those differences now struck him as intriguing, even exciting, rather than grotesque or repellant. The joint sense of existence which always led them to use "we" or "us" rather than "I" or "me" in communication. The calm with which they accepted their own inability to reproduce or their inevitable separation from the ongoing growth and change of their own race. The manner in which they accepted contact and other-induced change or constraint at the very deepest level of their beings . . . All of those things were truly and utterly alien to Sir George. But they weren't threatening. They weren't . . . evil. Whatever the dragons' outer shape and form, Sir George had decided, however different their perceptions and methods of communication, and despite the fact they could never father or bear children, they were as much "men" in every important sense of the word as any Englishman he had ever met.

Indeed, far more so than most, for the six dragons guarding the demon-jester went knowingly and willingly to their own deaths as they followed the stocky little alien up the steps to his box.

Neither Matilda nor Father Timothy had cared at all for that portion of the plan. Grayhame had been unhappy with it, but had grasped its necessity, while Maynton had objected only mildly, as if because he knew it was expected. Although Sir George had come to respect and like Sir Richard as much as he had ever respected or liked any other man, and to rely upon him completely, he had long since realized that the other knight had a limited imagination. And despite all else that had happened, only Sir George had ever actually "spoken" with the dragons. The others were willing to take his word for what had happened because he had never lied to them, never abused their trust in him, in all the years of their captivity, but they had not themselves "heard" the dragons speak. And because Maynton had never heard them, they remained less than human to him. He continued to regard them, in many ways, as Sir George continued to regard the Hathori: as roughly human-shaped animals which, however clever or well trained, remained animals.

But they were not animals, and Sir George knew he would never be able to see them as such again, for it had been they who insisted that their fellows with the demon-jester must die.

Their logic was as simple as it was brutal. If the demon-jester could be enticed out of his air car and taken alive, he could be compelled to order the remainder of his crew to surrender. Like so much else of the vaunted Federation, the guild's hierarchical command structure was iron bound. If their superior officer ordered them to surrender, the other guildsmen would obey . . . and the "Commander," for all his readiness to expend his English slaves or slaughter the inhabitants of "primitive" planets, possessed nothing remotely resembling the human or dragon quality of courage. With a blade pressed to his throat, he would yield.

But to get close enough to apply that blade had required, first, a way to get him out from behind his air car's force fields, and, second, that someone get within arm's reach. The fashion in which Sir George had structured the "demonstration" for the local chieftains had accomplished the former, but no one could accomplish the latter until the demon-jester's guards, Hathori and dragon alike, were neutralized. The Hathori would defend him no matter what; the dragons would have no choice but to do the same if they were commanded to, and no one could doubt that such a command would be given if they failed to spring forward on their own immediately.

Neither Sir George nor his officers were particularly concerned about the Hathori. Not in the open field, at least, where they were confident of their ability to destroy the bulge-eyed wart-faces with longbow fire or swarm them under quickly. Once aboard ship, in the narrow confines of its corridors and chambers, that would change, unless the humans could win their way into its interior before the Hathori could be armed and armored by the guildsmen. The closer quarters might still favor the smaller, more agile humans, but the structure of the ship would also force them to engage the Hathori head on, without the opportunity to outflank them or bring their own superior numbers to bear. Close combat under those conditions would allow the plate-armored, ax-armed wart-faces to use their advantages in size and strength to their greatest effect. The English advantage in numbers was sufficient for Sir George to feel confident that the Hathori would ultimately be defeated, but he knew only too well how bloody a price his men might be forced to pay.

The dragons and their "energy weapons" were another matter entirely, and they had been relentless in their conversations with Sir George. It was entirely possible that the demon-jester's personal guards would be able to cut a way at least as far as the air car with their personal weapons, especially if the Hathori kept the English busy, and once he was behind his force fields and once again invulnerable, the demon-jester would be ruthless in destroying any and all possible threats. Which meant, the dragons insisted, that no chances could be taken. Capturing the demon-jester alive was the one move they could be certain would succeed; at the very best, any other gambit would almost certainly cost the English far heavier casualties by requiring them to fight their way into the ship. For those reasons, the demon-jester's personal guards must die, and they'd hammered away at that point until Sir George was forced to promise to accept their plan. Which didn't mean he liked it.

Now he watched the demon-jester reach his position on the canopied platform. The "Commander" crossed to the throne-like chair constructed especially for him, and Sir George could almost taste the thick-bodied little creature's satisfaction as he gazed down at all about him. The elevation of his position, establishing his authority over the chieftains he had summoned here, had been a major part of the baron's argument for the arrangement of the stands, and Sir George smiled a much harder, hungrier smile as he watched the demon-jester bask in his superiority to the despised primitives clustered about his feet in all their abject inferiority, completely oblivious to his own exposure.

The demon-jester gazed down at Sir George for another moment, then nodded regally for the demonstration to begin, and Sir George, in turn, nodded to Rolf Grayhame.

The archery captain barked an order, and two dozen

plate-armored archers, helmets and metal work brilliantly polished for the occasion, surcoats washed and bright with color over their armor, marched briskly to the firing line. Sir George had longed to call for a larger number of them, but he'd concluded that he dared not. Twenty-four was more than sufficient to provide the demonstration the "Commander" desired. To ask for more bows to be issued might have aroused suspicion, or at least caution, and the demon-jester might have decided to remain safely in his air car after all.

The archers stopped in formation and quickly and smoothly bent and strung their bows, and the demon-jester, like the gathered chieftains, turned to gaze at the targets just over a hundred yards down range. Most of those targets were shaped like humans, but some among them were also shaped like natives of this world, and all were "protected" only by the large wicker shields the natives used in battle. The sort of shields longbow arrows would pierce as effortlessly as awls.

Grayhame barked another order, and twenty-four archers nocked arrows and raised their bows.

"Draw!" Grayhame shouted, and twenty-four bowstaves bent as one.

"*Loose!*" the archer captain bellowed . . . and twenty-four longbowmen turned on their heels in perfect unison, and twenty-four bow strings snapped as one. Two dozen arrows flew through the bright sunlight of an alien world, glittering like long, lethal hornets, and crashed into their targets with devastating force.

Eighteen of those arrows carried deadly, needle-pointed pile heads. At such short range they could pierce even Hathori plate armor, and they smashed into the wart-faces on the raised dais like hammers. Five bounced harmlessly aside, defeated by the angle and the Hathori's armor; thirteen did not, and all but two of the bulge-eyed aliens went down. Not all of those felled were dead, but all were out of action, at least for the moment.

And so were the two who were unwounded, for the

remaining six arrows had done their own lethal work. Every one of them had slammed home in the "Commander's" body, and the brilliant red garment which would have shrugged aside fire from the dragons' terrifying "energy weapons" was no help at all against clothyard shafts at a range of under ten yards. They drove clean through the creature's body, spraying bright yellow-red blood, and then deep into the back of his throne-like chair.

The demon-jester never even screamed, couldn't even tumble from the chair to which the arrows had nailed him, and the two uninjured Hathori gaped at their master's feathered corpse in shock. That shock seemed to hold them forever, although it could not actually have been more than the briefest span of seconds, but then they turned as one, raising their axes, and charged the nearest humans.

They never reached their targets. The archers were already nocking fresh arrows while the handful of knights and men-at-arms who'd known what was to happen charged forward, but many of the men and women who hadn't had the least idea what was planned were in the way. As surprised as the demon-jester's guards themselves, and completely unarmed, all they could do was flee, and their bodies blocked the archers' line of fire to the surviving Hathori.

But it didn't matter. The wart-faces had moved no more than two strides when half a dozen lightning bolts literally tore them apart.

The air was full of human shouts and screams of consternation and shock as the enormity of what had just happened smashed home, and the alien chieftains had vaulted from their places and disappeared with commendable quickness of mind. Sir George had watched them vanish, and now he made a mental note to keep an eye out for their return, in case they should sense an opportunity to strike at all the hated off-worlders while those invaders fought among themselves. But almost all of his attention was focused elsewhere, and he charged up the stairs towards the demon-jester's body.

Maynton and three other picked knights accompanied him, helping to drive through the confusion, and his own sword was in his hand by the time he bounded onto the platform. It wasn't needed—the dragons had already dispatched the wounded Hathori with ruthless efficiency—and he leaned forward to jerk the bright, faceted pendant from around the neck of the corpse. He held the precious device in his hand, his heart flaming with exultation as he gazed down at it, and then something touched his armored shoulder.

He spun quickly, only to relax as he found himself gazing up into the silver eyes of one of the dragons. The towering alien regarded him for several long seconds and then waved at the carnage about them, pointed to the dead demon-jester, and cocked his head in unmistakable question. The baron followed the gesturing hand with his own eyes, then looked back up at his huge, alien ally, and grinned fiercely.

"Your folk may have been willing enough to die, Sir Dragon. Aye, and brave enough to do it, as well! But it isn't the English way to murder our own, and with this—" he raised the pendant "—we'll not need that piece of meat to take his precious ship, now will we? And with us to hunt the guildsmen, and your folk to hunt Hathori, well—"

His grin bared his teeth as he and the mute dragon stood eye to eye, and then, slowly, the dragon showed its own deadly-looking fangs in a hungry grin of its own and it gave a very human nod.

"Then let's be about it, my friend!" Sir George invited, reaching up to clap the huge alien on the back, and the two of them started down the platform stairs towards the waiting lander together.

# -XI-

"So," Admiral Mugabi sighed. "It's official."

"Not quite," Admiral Stevenson replied with a tight smile. "What's official is my informing you that the Galactics are finally getting around to issuing their ultimatum. Of course, we're not supposed to know that, because the official note hasn't arrived yet. And the consensus is that even when it does, the exact consequences if it's rejected won't be precisely spelled out in it, anyway."

"Of course they won't," Mugabi snorted. "They're so damned sanctimonious that there's no way they're going to commit themselves in an official communique."

"I wouldn't bet on that," Stevenson said much more somberly. "The one thing we can be fairly certain of is that they didn't have this brainstorm overnight, whatever they may be trying to tell their citizenry. There had to be some pretty drastic horsetrading to get the Kulavo and Daerjek to sign off on their final position. Unless ONI is completely off base, one of the points the hardliners like the Saernai and Josuto will have insisted upon is that the Kulavo, at least, officially endorse their prescription for finally solving their little problem once and for all. After all, the Kulavo have been the 'conscience' of the Council for so long that the faction that wants to smash us almost has to have the cover of their public agreement. So I'd guess that the final act in that little Kabuki play will be the presentation of an official note demanding that we hand the ship—and the Romans—over on pain of military action."

"But I'll bet you anything you care to name that they won't mention words like 'genocide' in any official note," Mugabi shot back.

"You're probably right about that," Stevenson agreed. "Of course, they won't have to, either. After all, if we're so unreasonable as to provoke them into taking military steps in the first place, any little accidents, like a planet-buster that just happens to go off course, will be on our own primitive heads. They'll have warned us that we could get hurt, so their hands will be clean when the 'accident' takes place on schedule. I mean, all they're really demanding is that we hand over to them a ship that's stolen private property and the crew—who are also private property, under the Federation's laws—who stole it and murdered their legal owners in the process. If we're so unreasonable, stupid, and primitive that we're unwilling to hand such bloodthirsty, mutinous criminals over to the appropriate authorities, then certainly no law-abiding government like the Federation could possibly just stand by and see its fundamental legal principles flouted. Obviously they have to take steps, and if those steps just coincidentally end up with a star system full of aborigines getting mashed in the gears, well, maintaining the rule of law sometimes requires unpleasant actions."

"Sure it does," Mugabi growled.

It wasn't the best growl he'd ever produced. In fact, it wasn't even close. The men and women of the Solarian Navy were only too familiar with the subterranean rumble the bearlike admiral normally produced in moments of intense displeasure, but he was too tired to do justice by it this time . . . and not just physically.

He cocked back the chair behind his desk and let his body sag around his bones for just a moment while he scrubbed his black, broad-cheekboned face. Then he let his hands fall back to the old-fashioned blotter and turned his head to gaze out the armored viewport set into the outer hull of the huge space station.

It was a spectacular view. Under normal circumstances, it exercised a perpetual fascination and spawned an almost childlike sense of delight deep within him. But not even the view could lighten the crushing sense of despair which loomed over him today.

The planet about which the station orbited was a cloud-swirled sapphire, breathtakingly beautiful as it floated against the soot black of space and the pinprick diamonds of the stars. The white disk of its moon was visible around its flank, and the clutter and cluster of hundreds of spacecraft glittered like scattered gems of reflected sunlight as they went about their business. One of the Navy's main construction docks dominated the scene, and Mugabi could just make out the bright, color-coded vacuum suits of the yard workers as they hovered about the mile-long hull of what would have been a new battlecruiser. The ship was perhaps three-quarters completed, with most of the hull plating in place. Probably her powerplant was pressurized and on-line, since he could see that three of her five main drive nacelles had already been closed up. But even under the best of circumstances, she was still at least six months from completion . . . and even under Mugabi's most optimistic estimate, there was no way she could be finished and worked up for duty before the hammer came down.

He closed his eyes and scrubbed his face again, feeling the responsibility which accompanied his despair and wondering which was truly the greater burden. He'd given the Solarian Navy forty-three years of his life, from the heady days as an ensign, when he'd truly believed that humanity might be able to build a fleet strong enough to protect its world against the Galactics, until today. Along the way, he and the rest of the human race had learned too much about the crushing power of the Federation for him to cling to any false hope that the Navy could successfully defend the Solar System, yet he'd continued to hope—or to tell himself that he did, at any rate—that they could at least put up sufficient fight to convince the self-serving Galactics that humanity's threat was too slight to justify the losses they might take to eliminate it. But all of those false hopes were gone now, exposed for the pipe dreams they had been. The Federation's Council had decided to call the human bluff, and no one knew better than he how threadbare that bluff truly was. Yet even now, even knowing how futile it would be, the high rank and the duties he had spent half his lifetime earning remained. Hopeless though it might be, the responsibility to defend humanity against its foes was still his, and if it would have been so seductively easy to pass that responsibility on to someone else, that was an act of which he was constitutionally incapable. Besides, it wasn't as if it would really have mattered in the end.

"Has the President decided how she'll respond to the Galactics yet?" he asked finally.

"No," Stevenson replied. "Or if she has, she's keeping the final call confidential so far. There hasn't been any official demand for her to respond *to* yet. In fact, I doubt very much that the Galactics have the least suspicion that we know what they're up to. They're not very good at that part of this," he added with monumental understatement.

"Maybe not, or maybe they just don't care," Mugabi said without opening his eyes.

"I think they really are as incompetent as they seem," his superior said. "They haven't really had to be competent—not when they carry the biggest stick in the known universe. Besides, their fundamental arrogance seems to preclude any possibility of their taking any of us 'primitives' seriously enough to worry about how we play the game."

"And even if they did worry about how we play it, they'd only change the rules if it looked like they might lose." Mugabi opened his eyes once more, and glared almost challengingly at the other admiral.

"Now that," Stevenson sighed, "I'm afraid I can't disagree with. Not given how thoroughly they've decided to change their own rules to screw us over."

Mugabi only grunted. There wasn't really anything else to say, although it had taken humanity a while to realize just how completely rigged the game was. It was ironic, really, that all those late twentieth century "saucer nuts" had actually had a point about how closely extraterrestrials had kept Earth under surveillance. One of Mugabi's great-grandfathers had been a special agent of what was then called the Federal Bureau of Investigation, and he'd kept a diary with religious attention to detail. Mugabi had read it when he was in high school, and he'd been particularly struck by its account of the handful of "saucer investigations" his ancestor had been assigned to. Special Agent Winton had done his job conscientiously enough, but in his journal, he'd also always ridiculed the possibility that there was anything to be discovered. After all, why would anyone capable of interstellar flight worry about keeping a planet full of prespace aborigines under *surreptitious* observation? What could possibly have made the human race so important that a civilization that much more advanced would bother with them in the first place? Or worry about keeping its presence a secret from the aborigines if it did take an interest in them?

Personally, Mugabi thought Great-Grandad Winton's objections had made excellent sense, given what Earth had known about the cosmos at that point in her history. Of course, there had turned out to be entirely too many things Earth *hadn't* known then, and given what humanity had discovered since, the nuts and paranoics turned out to have had a point all along after all. In fact, the only thing Quentin Mugabi had never been able to figure out was why the Galactics had waited this long to make their minds up about just how to deal with the barbarian menace the human race represented to their comfortable view of how the universe ought to be run.

No, that wasn't really true, he reflected. He doubted that any human would ever truly understand how a so-called "government" could dither, literally, for centuries before reaching the decision every member of it must have known from the beginning was inevitable. The very idea should have been ridiculous, but it happened to be what had actually transpired, and he had to look no further than the Kulavo and Daerjek to find the boots which had jammed up the works. He still couldn't truly wrap his own brain around the mind-set it required, but the actual events were clear enough.

It had taken the humans' intelligence services many years to begin to unravel the complexities of politics in the Federation, and there were still a lot of unanswered questions, some of which were pretty damned big. One thing was obvious, however: the closest human parallel to the Council's internal dynamics would probably have been a meeting of the Italian Mafia, in Moscow, chaired by the Yakuza. It was all about complex and constantly shifting alliances and power blocks, and the fact that a councilor might sit for as long as three or four Terran centuries at a time gave each of them enormous scope for maneuvers and countermaneuvers that left the odd dagger planted in a colleague's back . . . sometimes literally. No one (including the members of the Council itself, probably, Mugabi thought mordantly) really understood all of the involved and intricate obligations, debts, and unsettled accounts involved in the complicated crafting of deals and positions on policy issues, but no one was foolish enough to pretend that anything besides naked self-interest formed the basis for almost all of those deals in the end.

No one except the Kulavo, that was.

Mugabi knew far too much about the impossible disparity in the balance of power between humanity and the Federation not to be grateful for the traditional Kulavo obstructionism.

Anything that held that power in check had to be a good thing from the human race's perspective, but even so, there was something particularly galling to him about admitting that his own race owed at least the last two or three centuries of its existence to an entire species of professional hypocrites.

Galling or not, it was unquestionably fortunate that the Kulavo had been one of the three original founding races of the Federation . . . and had no intention of allowing anyone ever to forget it. It was probably equally *un*fortunate, though, that neither of the other two founding species were still around. The current crop of Galactics was more than a little vague about precisely what happened to the two extinct Founders, and whatever had happened to them had taken place so long ago that none of the humans' sources had been able to shed any light upon the question. Mugabi had his own theory about their disappearance, however, and he knew that most of the Office of Naval Intelligence's analysts shared it.

And ONI had managed to amass quite a bit more information about the Galactics and their history than the Council probably realized, the admiral reflected. The Federation had a highly developed sense of paranoia where anyone who might challenge the stability of its beloved status quo was involved, yet there was a curious disconnect between that paranoia and the security measures it produced. No doubt a lot of that was produced by the millennia-long stability which was so precious to the Galactics and which humanity found so incomprehensible. No Terran government could have survived for so long without at least an occasional reexamination and revision of its security arrangements. The dogged inventiveness with which its opponents would have sought out ways around those arrangements would have seen to that! But the Galactics, for all their endless backstabbing and machinations, appeared to have absolutely no equivalent of the human willingness—or ability—to seek advantage by cheerfully manufacturing new approaches to old problems. The races which owned the Federation were all fanatical rules lawyers, but once they'd agreed upon what the rules were (and they had rules which detailed even the proper and acceptable ways to commit treason), they clung to them with death-grip intensity. Their rules did change, of course. Not even the Galactics could maintain something the size of the Federation in an absolute state of true stasis, however much they longed to do so. But the changes were always small, incremental ones . . . and occurred at such a glacial pace that two or three thousand years might pass between them.

Because of that, human intelligence services had managed to penetrate the Council's security far more completely than the Galactics even began to suspect, despite the enormous difference in the technological capabilities of the two sides. It helped that many of the "protected" races who served the Federation's owners hated their masters so bitterly that they were more than willing to feed the upstart humans information whenever possible. Indeed, the human analysts' greatest handicap had been the sheer mass of data available to them once access was gained. The Federation was a compulsive keeper of records, with a pure and simple delight in bureaucratic excess which no terrestrial government had ever approached. Given the sheer length of its existence, that had produced a store of information which far exceeded the storage capacity of any human archive and made any systematic examination of it a Syssiphean task.

Despite that, humanity had managed to determine a great deal about the Federation and its history. For one thing, it was apparent that the Council's moral posturing stemmed from its original Constitution, which had almost certainly been created by one or both of the two since vanished Founders. Certainly no one in the current crop of "superior species" which ran the Federation would have bothered with any of the moral or ethical nonsense incorporated into that Constitution. It was even possible, although even such an open-minded soul as Mugabi found it difficult to truly believe it, that the original Federation actually had believed it had some sort of moral obligation to look after less advanced races. God knew humanity had come close enough to wiping itself out once weapons of mass destruction became available to it, so perhaps there truly was something to be said for keeping a sort of semi-parental eye on developing races until they got through the danger zone and learned to survive their own technology.

But if that had been the original purpose of the Federation and its Constitution, it was a purpose which had been corrupted into something else long, long ago. Given the degree to which that self-serving something else promoted naked aggression and exploitation, Mugabi rather doubted that the Founders whose purpose had been twisted would have been very happy about it. Which, in turn, suggested at least one very plausible (and grim) explanation for why two of them were no longer around.

At the same time, however, the incredible love of stability which was so much a part of the Federation had preserved at least the form of the original Constitution. If nothing else, it was far too valuable as a pretext and a justification for extending the iron fist of the Council's power over every upstart species which might have threatened its beloved stagnation for the Galactics to do anything else. And the Kulavo, as the only one of the original Founders still in existence, had staked out a claim to the moral high ground in any policy debate almost a thousand centuries before humans had learned to kindle fire.

The xenologists kept warning Mugabi that it was both dangerous and inappropriate to attribute human motivations and viewpoints to nonhuman species, but the admiral had long since decided that he would go right on doing so as long as the practice allowed him to make accurate predictions of those species' actions. So far, the model had worked just fine, as long as he was careful to incorporate a sufficient degree of amorality into his calculations. And in this instance, he found himself wondering which was the more remarkable—

the totality with which the Kulavo seemed to have convinced themselves of their own sincerity, or the degree to which their fellow Council members resented and despised their towering hypocrisy.

In either case, he suspected that the Kulavo's moral posturing would be their own eventual downfall, although it would never happen in time to save humanity. In the meantime, however, the Kulavo clung to the highly vocal purity of their motivations and refused to rush to judgment on any issue . . . unless their own interests were immediately threatened, of course. And since their status as the sole surviving Founder gave their collective ego a towering splendor which not even the other Galactics could match, they had been disdainfully unwilling to concede that something as insignificant as humanity could possibly have been a threat to *them.*

The data available to the Terran analysts suggested that they'd begun to change their minds as much as two or three centuries ago, but, like any self-respecting Galactic, they had declined to rush to judgment. Besides, they'd staked out their customary moral position, and finding ways to modify that without the loss of face inherent in abandoning their self-proclaimed principles had required the odd hundred years or so.

The Daerjek were another matter entirely. Even for Galactics, the Daerjek were a conservative lot. Indeed, Mugabi often wondered how they had ever managed to accept such a radical concept as the wheel. There was never any true need to ask the Daerjek for their position on any decision which came before the Council, because that position was always the same. Any alteration in *any* Federation policy was automatic anathema to them, and they were perfectly happy embracing any justification for resisting changes. They saw no particular need to be consistent in their justifications, but as it happened, the Kulavo's insistence on "carefully weighing the moral aspects" of any policy decision made them natural partners in obstruction.

Unfortunately, that obstruction appeared to no longer obtain when it came to the disposition of humanity's fate.

"We could always agree to give the Romans back," he suggested finally, in the tone of a man who found his own suggestion profoundly distasteful. "If that's the pretext they've settled on, we could cut the ground out from under them by conceding." Stevenson cocked an eyebrow at him, and the heavyset admiral shrugged. "I don't like it any more than you do, Alex," he said irritably, "but we're talking about the survival of the human race!"

"The President is well aware of that. In fact, I understand that the Cabinet has already agreed, very quietly, that the ship itself will be surrendered to the Galactics upon demand. But you know as well as I do what will happen to the Romans if the Galactics get their hands on them."

"Of course I do. That's why I don't like my own suggestion very much. But the executions of a few hundred people, all of whom would have been dead two thousand years ago anyway, if the Galactics hadn't interfered with their lives in the first place, have to be considered an acceptable price if that saves the rest of the human race from extinction!"

"I can't argue with that," Stevenson agreed with a sigh, then ran his fingers through his thinning, sandy hair. "And while I didn't sit in on the meetings between the President and her Cabinet or the leaders of the Senate, I feel confident that they were honest enough with one another to face the same conclusion. Hell, for that matter, the Romans themselves recognize the logic!"

He massaged his forehead with both hands for a moment, then gazed out the view port instead of meeting Mugabi's eyes.

"I don't know whether it's gallantry or simply an acceptance of inevitability, but the Romans' leaders have already agreed that they should be surrendered to the Galactics if that will prevent an attack on the Solar System. Their only stipulation—" he pulled his eyes back from the icy beauty of the stars to Mugabi's face "—is that they be permitted to commit suicide before we hand them over."

Mugabi grunted again, this time like someone who'd just taken a fist in the solar plexus, then drew a deep breath.

"That makes me feel like even more of a shit for suggesting it," he said in a voice like crushed gravel, "but it also underscores my point. However much we may all hate it, how can we justify *not* handing them over?"

"I think the human race has had just about enough of the Galactics," Stevenson said after a few seconds, his tone oblique, and it was Mugabi's turn to raise an interrogative eyebrow. The senior admiral saw it and twitched his shoulders.

"We've known about the Federation for almost a century now, Quentin," he pointed out. "It took us a while to figure out why the Galactics were obstructing our efforts at extrasolar expansion . . . or even that they *were*, for that matter. Given the time it takes to move between stars, even under phase drive, it's probably not too surprising that we didn't tumble to it immediately. In fact, I hate to admit it, but we might never have figured it out at all if the bastards hadn't been so arrogant and contemptuous of us that they let their true attitude show.

"You know as well as I do that the public wasn't very happy about that when the word got out," he went on with characteristic understatement. "And public opinion got even less happy when we found out that the Council had decided that—in our special case—our version of the phase drive was too 'primitive' and 'crude' to justify an immediate invitation to take a seat on the Council. And then we figured out that they'd had us under close observation ever since the mid-nineteenth century, and people got even more unhappy. By now, the man in the street would love nothing better than to put a stick right into the eye of the entire high and mighty Federation."

"I realize that," Mugabi replied. "But are you actually saying that the 'man in the street' is so pissed off that he'd prefer to see himself—and his wife and his children—killed rather than give in to the Galactics' demands? Is that what you're trying to tell me?"

"I didn't say that. On the other hand, I don't know if most people really believe just how ruthless the Federation truly is, or the degree to which their technology and resources outstrip anything we could imagine," Stevenson said. "I tend to doubt that even those who recognize the hopelessness of any open resistance intellectually have really grasped it on an emotional basis. You and I," he waved a hand in the air between them, "are a hell of a lot better informed than any civilian, including, I sometimes think, the members of the Senate. But I have to tell you, Quentin, that there've been times when my own emotions have flatly refused to let me really *accept* that we're looking straight down the barrel of racial extinction. I don't know. Maybe it's just something that we're genetically incapable of accepting. A survival imperative designed to keep us on our feet and trying even when our brains know that there's no point in it. After all, maybe the horse will learn to sing."

Mugabi surprised himself with a harsh bark of laughter in response to the last sentence, and Stevenson flashed him a small smile.

"What I'm trying to say isn't that the electorate wouldn't understand the circumstances forcing the President's hand if she turned the Romans back over to the Galactics. But even if the voters understood, they wouldn't like it, so the President and her supporters would undoubtedly pay a certain political price for it in the next election cycle . . . assuming that there *was* a next election cycle.

"At the same time, however, I know the President well enough—and I suspect you do, too, although I realize that you haven't dealt with her directly as much as I have—to feel confident that she'd go right ahead and choose whatever she believed was the right and proper course of action, even if that's complete submission to their ultimatum. Unfortunately, everything ONI has been able to turn up suggests that it won't be possible for her to give them what they want, however hard she tries."

"What?" Mugabi's expression was confused. "I thought you said they were going to demand the return of the ship and its crew, so—"

"That's exactly what I said," Stevenson agreed. "The problem is that, according to our sources, the Council members have decided among themselves, whatever the public record may show, that whatever we agree to give up won't be enough." He sighed when Mugabi stared at him. "Come on, Quentin! You and I are in a far better position than almost anyone else to know what's really going on here. This whole demand is nothing but a cover for what they intend to do all along. If we accede to it in its original form, they'll simply sit back and keep tacking other demands onto it until they find something we physically can't give them. And when we can't, they'll send in their navy."

"I see." Mugabi squeezed the bridge of his nose, and his shoulders sagged. "I hate to say it, Alex," he said after a moment in a voice of inexpressible weariness, "but maybe it's time to pull the flag down. I don't know if I want to survive to see it, but maybe it's time to consider officially applying for protectorate status. At least there'd still be human beings somewhere in the universe, even if they *were* slaves."

"Do you really believe you're the first person to consider that?" Stevenson asked very quietly, and shook his head. "We'd all prefer to be a Churchill and not a Petain, Quentin. But a head of state has responsibilities. The President swore an oath to defend the Solarian Union against all enemies, foreign or domestic, but when the only alternatives are total surrender or total destruction, her responsibility to preserve the existence of life on this planet has to take precedence over any grand gesture of defiance.

"Except that in this case no surrenders are being accepted."

"They're that determined?" Mugabi's voice was equally quiet, and he winced when Stevenson nodded. "I knew they wanted to smash the threat they think we represent. And I knew they wouldn't turn a hair at wiping us out to do that. But I guess it's part of that emotional inability to accept that there's no alternative to extinction that you're talking about. Somehow a part of me has always believed, even in the middle of the war games that proved we don't stand a chance militarily, that if we just bit the bullet and crawled on our bellies to them, they'd at least let us survive as their slaves."

" 'Fraid not," Stevenson sighed. "Apparently we've scared them even more than we'd realized. I think it's not just us, anymore. I think they're afraid that our example might be contagious. We could be a valuable asset to them, I suppose, but as far as they're concerned, our very existence is an eternal threat to their stability, and they've decided to eliminate it once and for all. Especially since eliminating it will also be a pointed warning to any of the other protected races whose attitudes we may already have contaminated."

"So there's no way out," Mugabi said softly.

"No way at all," Stevenson agreed.

"How long?"

"It's hard to say. Our information arrived with an Ostowii courier."

Stevenson paused, and Mugabi nodded impatiently. The Ostowii were one of the senior slave races of the Federation, often acting as overseers and supervisors for the races who held seats on the Council. But despite the special privileges their position brought them, the Ostowii's hatred for their masters was every bit as deep as any other slave's. They'd become one of humanity's best sources very early on.

"The courier was one of their transgenders, and it wasn't in the military or diplomatic service. It's a merchant factor, and it was simply passing through on its way to another assignment. One of its clan superiors decided that we needed the information and used it to pass the warning to us, but its ship can't be more than a month or two ahead of the official instructions to Lach'heranu. And you and I both know how *she'll* react to them when she gets them."

Mugabi nodded again, this time grimly. Fleet Commander Lach'heranu was a Saernai, and the Saernai had been pressing for a more . . . proactive response to the human threat to galactic stability from the very beginning. Her assignment to command the Federation's "observation squadron" in the Solar System had been a bad sign when it was announced. Given what Stevenson had just finished telling him, it looked as if it had been an even worse sign than the admiral had allowed himself to fear.

"So," Stevenson went on levelly, "it looks like we're screwed whatever we do. I don't know whether or not the President will go ahead and offer our formal surrender, but I wouldn't really be very surprised if she doesn't. If there's no point in surrendering, and if the bastards are going to wipe us out—except perhaps for a little breeding stock on some primitive planet somewhere where it can be massaged into proper docility—then we might as well go down swinging."

"I can't say I disagree," Mugabi said. "But I hope she realizes that all we'll be doing is kicking and scratching on the way to the gallows. My people will do everything humanly possible, but I doubt we'll manage to do any more damage than inflicting a few scratches on their paint. Assuming we manage even that much."

"Oh, she understands," Stevenson told him with a sad smile. "But if we're dead anyway, then let's go out on our feet, not our knees. Who knows? We might get lucky and scratch that paint. And even if we don't," he shrugged, "maybe, just maybe, we'll be the example that somewhere, sometime, provides the spark to push some other poor bunch of slaves into standing up on their hind legs and going for the Council's throat."

~ ~ ~

Alex Stevenson would have lost his bet, Quentin Mugabi thought, although he was far too weary and crushed by despair to feel any satisfaction about it.

The Kulavo clearly had been unwilling to admit, even now, to the practice of *real politik* on such a ruthless scale, and the diplomatic note from the Federation Council had all the earmarks of a classic ultimatum . . . except for the absence of any clear specification of the consequences which would attach to its rejection. In fact, there was a distinctly Kulavo-like mealymouthedness to its appeal to the moral rectitude of its authors. There was something greasy-feeling about it, and Mugabi suspected that the only common ground he and Fleet Commander Lach'heranu would ever have was the contempt they both felt for the Councilors who'd drafted it.

Of course, they felt that contempt for rather different reasons.

". . . and so, Fleet Commander," President Sarah Dresner said from the huge screen, "I feel certain that we can reach a peaceful resolution of the current unfortunate situation if the Council is made aware of our willingness to consider its views and to accommodate them to the very greatest extent possible."

The screen on SNS *Terra*'s flag deck was normally the main repeater for CIC's battle plot. At the moment, however, it was configured for communication purposes, and for the last seven hours it had borne the split images of Dresner and Lach'heranu so that Mugabi, as the Solarian Navy's senior commander in space, could be kept abreast of the negotiations. Lach'heranu had raised no objection to his inclusion in the communications loop, which Mugabi had privately taken as a very bad sign. Normally, the Saernai were punctilious to a fault, especially when it came to standing upon their dignity where primitives were concerned. The fact that Lach'heranu obviously couldn't have cared less that someone as low ranking as a mere admiral was privy to her diplomatic conversation with a head of state (even a mere human head of state) suggested that she had something else on her mind.

"I am afraid that I cannot share your confidence, Madame President," the Fleet Commander said after a moment. The translating software used by the Galactics produced the piping, uninflected, and vaguely ridiculous sounding voice which it always used for the Saernai. Mugabi was accustomed to the fact that the English speech produced by the translator never matched the movements of the Fleet Commander's speaking mouth, but he usually found the disconnect mildly amusing. Today, there was nothing amusing about the situation at all.

"The attitude of your species has been most regrettable and obstructionist for the last several of your generations," Lach'heranu went on, cocking her foxlike ears while all three of her space-black eyes gazed sternly into her own communicator's visual pickup. She reached up and smoothed her purple, plushy fur, and Mugabi wished for far from the first time that he was capable of reading her species' facial expressions.

"The Federation has attempted ever since its first contact with your species to devise some means by which humans might be harmoniously integrated into the society of civilized races," the Saernai told the President. "In recognition of the responsibility which older and more advanced races owe to barbarous species which have yet to make the transition to true civilization, we have extended every possible consideration to you. Yet despite our efforts, entire generations of your political leaders have steadfastly refused to meet us even half way. While we recognize that it is particularly difficult for such a short-lived race to learn true wisdom, the fact that we have received such responses from so many of your leaders and their successors clearly indicates that your race's intransigent arrogance is an inherent quality and not one out of which it may be educated. As such, I fear that it is no longer possible for us to delude ourselves into believing that true change on the part of the human race is possible."

Mugabi heard a muffled curse from one of his staffers, but he didn't even turn his head to see who it was. It didn't matter, and even if it had, he agreed entirely. There was something especially demeaning about being forced to listen to such rank hypocrisy from a creature whom one knew intended to exterminate the human race wherever the "negotiations" led. He wondered if Lach'heranu was enjoying herself as much as he thought she was. It was hard to know what some of the Galactics found amusing, but from what he'd seen of the Fleet Commander, and of the Saernai in general, she probably thought that watching President Dresner crawl was hilarious.

If the President suspected the same thing, she let no sign of it color either her expression or her voice. She knew she was playing an ultimately losing game whose rules had all been carefully fixed to make it inevitable that she could never win. Yet she couldn't afford to assume that. Or, rather, it was Dresner's final responsibility to make completely certain she had overlooked no possibility, however remote, which might have saved humanity's life.

"By the standards of the Federation, the human race is, indeed, young," she said levelly. "No doubt many of the difficulties which have arisen between the Solarian Union and the Federation truly have stemmed from that disparity in our ages and experiences. In the final analysis, however, we have always recognized both the legitimate prior territorial claims of the Federation and its unquestioned supremacy as the one true interstellar power. Where we have differed with the Federation has been solely over matters which we considered to be internal concerns of our own star system and political union. We have never attempted to dictate to the Federation outside our own boundaries, nor have we ever attempted to encroach upon territory already claimed by the Federation or any of its member races.

"Perhaps our insistence on maintaining our internal independence from the Federation has been wrongheaded.

Probably, as the Council's note points out, such a view is typical of youthful and barbaric species. If so, then it may be that the time has come to put it aside with the other toys of childhood. I don't say that it will be easy for us to surrender this particular toy, especially in light of how long we've clung to it. Yet we aren't fools, Fleet Commander, however foolish we may sometimes seem. We are proud of our navy and of the men and women who serve in it, yet our entire fleet is completely outclassed by the single squadron which you command. So however difficult we may find it to put away our toys, we cherish no illusions about the Federation's ability to compel us to do so. And as survival is always preferable to the alternative, I have been empowered by the Senate to immediately appoint a committee of delegates to be transported to the Federation's capital, there to meet with the Council or its representatives and began immediate, binding discussions on precisely how our star system and our race may be most expeditiously and smoothly integrated into the Federation."

Someone—it might have been the same officer who'd cursed—inhaled sharply behind Mugabi, but the admiral's own expression didn't even flicker as he heard his President agree to what amounted to the unconditional surrender of humanity. He'd known it was coming. For that matter, every officer on *Terra*'s flag deck must have known it was. It had to be, given the incredible firepower of the thirty-four Federation superdreadnoughts gathered around Lach'heranu's flagship.

The Saernai gazed at the President's image for several seconds, then reached out and touched a small button on the arm of her command chair.

"The recorders are no longer on-line," she informed Dresner in that artificial, maddeningly toneless voice.

"May I ask why not?" the President inquired very carefully.

"Because there is no point in continuing this farce," Lach'heranu said. "It is not possible for your kind to be integrated into the Federation. The very idea is ridiculous and an insult to every other species already part of the Federation, whether they are full members or protected races. Humans are arrogant, contentious, chaotic, willful, barbaric, ungrateful, and stupid. If your kind were permitted to contaminate the Federation, it would pollute and ultimately destroy the greatest and most stable civilization in the history of the entire galaxy. This cannot and will not be permitted."

"So there was never any real intention on your part of attempting to find a negotiated solution," Sarah Dresner said flatly.

"Of course not," Lach'heranu confirmed. "It was simply essential that we demonstrate the extent of our efforts to find some peaceful resolution to the intolerable threat you pose to true civilization."

"Why?" Dresner asked bluntly.

"Because we are the representatives of truly advanced and civilized races," Lach'heranu said with absolutely no sign of irony. "As such, we owe a debt to posterity to make it plain that we had no possible alternative but to proceed to solve the human problem once and for all."

"You mean," Dresner said harshly, "that you need the proper grist for your propaganda mill when you get ready to lie to your other slaves—and to yourselves—about it."

"That observation is typical of human arrogance," Lach'heranu replied. "Only a human could think that your insignificant little star system could possibly be sufficiently important for civilized races to feel any need to lie to anyone about the reasons for your extermination. It is simply important that our archives contain the proof of the propriety of our actions so that our successors upon the Council may draw the proper conclusions and find the proper precedents should such a situation ever again arise, and we have now recorded sufficient material for that purpose."

"In other words enough for you to edit however you need to in order to manufacture the history to justify your actions!"

"Again, that attitude simply underscores your species' unending ability to believe that you are far more important than you are, and so demonstrates the necessity of exercising appropriate control over the archival material relating to this incident. It would be most unfortunate if some future member of the Council should be exposed to the drivel of human 'philosophy' and its pathetic insistence upon 'self-determination' and so find itself confused into failing to recognize the inevitability of our policy decision. There is no point, however, in drawing this out any further, nor could any truly advanced being justify extending the negotiation process. As a civilized individual, I feel some mild regret for the circumstances which require me to destroy your race, and I propose to demonstrate as much mercy as the situation permits by acting promptly, rather than drawing out the process. It will be much simpler all around if you will simply order your ships to deactivate their shields."

"I think not." Dresner's voice was chipped ice.

"Surely not even you are stupid enough to believe that resistance will have any impact on the final outcome," Lach'heranu said.

"Probably not," the President of humanity told her species' executioner. "But I hope you'll excuse us for trying."

"I have no interest in excusing you for anything," Lach'heranu's piping voice said tonelessly. "I simply require that you die."

"Battle stations!"

It was undoubtedly the most unnecessary order Quentin Mugabi had ever given. The entire Solarian Navy had been at battle stations for the past ten hours, but alarms whooped throughout his warships and the screen which had carried the images of President Dresner and Fleet Commander Lach'heranu switched instantly to its normal designed function.

Mugabi's eyes clung to the repeater plot as the data codes

and sidebars the flagship's Combat Information Center projected onto it flickered and changed. Unlike him, Lach'heranu hadn't even bothered to bring her ships fully to battle stations during the negotiations. There'd been no need—not against such insignificant and contemptible opposition. She had taken the precaution of remaining well outside her own attack range of the Terran fleet, much less outside the range of any weapon Mugabi possessed, but she clearly intended to change that. As he watched, her normal-space drives were coming on-line, offensive and defensive systems awoke, and thirty-five superdreadnoughts of the design ONI had codenamed the *Ogre* class, each an ovoid measuring just over nine miles in its long dimension, began to accelerate towards the three hundred pygmies of the human fleet. Any one of those *Ogres*, Mugabi knew, possessed more firepower than his entire fleet, and they were escorted by over thirty *Stiletto*-class cruisers.

Humanity's last battle, he thought grimly, was also going to be one of its shortest.

"Execute Alpha One!"

Acknowledgments came back to him, and he felt an indescribable, bittersweet pride in the men and women under his command as his fleet's formation changed. It flowed into the new alignment crisply, quickly . . . almost as if the humans crewing its ships didn't know that their resistance was absolutely futile.

It was an unorthodox formation: a column of starships, like a huge yet slender spear shaft, headed by two dozen of Mugabi's heaviest capital ships. Those ships blocked the fire of any of their consorts, which ought to have made it totally unacceptable. But Quentin Mugabi had no illusions about his ability to fight anything which might have been called a "battle," and so he'd chosen a disposition oriented towards achieving only one thing. Any conventional formation would have been automatically doomed to destruction without landing a single hit on the enemy, but this one put the bulk of his units into the protective shadow of the battleships leading his column. None of those battleships would survive more than one or two hits, three at the most, from Galactic weapons, but if the rest of the fleet could close quickly enough while they were absorbing their death blows, one or two of their consorts might actually live to get into range of their own weapons and land at least one solid hit of their own.

It wasn't much, but it was the only thing Mugabi could offer his crews, his home world, and his species, and he tried not to weep for the sacrifical gallantry of his personnel as the Solarian Navy began its death ride.

"Enemy has locked on," Tracking announced, and Mugabi's jaw clenched. "Entering enemy missile range in seven minutes," the Tracking officer continued in the clipped tones of despair held at bay by professionalism. "Entering our own range in sixteen minutes."

Mugabi didn't even look away from the plot. There was no more point in acknowledging the report than there would have been in pretending that his fleet could survive nine minutes of Galactic fire from three dozen *Ogres*.

He watched the time to engagement readout spin downward on the main plot, and to his own surprise, he realized his muscles were relaxing, not tensing, as the timer whirled towards zero. Perhaps it was relief, a corner of his mind thought almost calmly. Relief that he and all of his crews were about to die and so would not have to witness the destruction of the planet they were sworn to defend.

"Entering enemy missile range in two min—"

Tracking's report chopped off in mid-syllable as the plot changed abruptly.

Mugabi's eyes flared wide as the impossible icons flashed into existence. The Galactics' stealth technology was enormously superior to anything humanity had ever possessed. ONI knew that it was, that the existence of that technology helped to explain how the Federation had been able to smother the Solar System with listening posts and automated spies for at least seventy years before the human race became even peripherally aware of its existence. But Lach'heranu hadn't bothered with stealth. Not against something as primitive and unsophisticated as the scanner systems of the Solarian Navy. There'd been no reason to.

But it had just become evident that someone in the universe had a stealth technology which was superior even to that of the Federation. That was the only possible explanation for how nine unknown warships could possibly have made their way into attack range of Lach'heranu's squadron completely undetected.

And they *had* been undetected. That was obvious the instant they opened fire, for the Federation's superdreadnoughts were taken totally by surprise. All of their defensive and sensor systems had been directed towards their contemptible human victims, and their point defense fire was late, thin, and ineffectual as the unknowns' first missile broadsides went smashing home.

They were *fast*, those missiles, Mugabi thought numbly. The Solarian Navy's missiles had a maximum velocity of sixty percent of light-speed, and that was possible only because ONI had managed to steal the design for their drives from the Federation's dead archives. The Galactics' own current design, a mere twelve hundred years old, had a maximum velocity of seventy-five percent of light-speed. But the missiles slamming into the shields of Lach'heranu's superdreadnoughts were moving at over *ninety* percent of light-speed, and even from here, Mugabi could tell that the incoming birds were equipped with ECM systems at least two or three generations ahead of anything in the Federation's arsenal.

"Who the Hell—?"

Discipline cut off the incredulous exclamation, but Mugabi never even noticed as he watched the bright, terrible suns of antimatter warheads rip and tear at Lach'heranu's shields. The yield figures on those explosions were much higher than they ought to have been—higher than the Galactics' own weapons could have produced—and their victims' shields burned like tinder under their fury. Even if he'd noticed the highly unprofessional outburst, though, he could scarcely have complained about it, since it summed up his own feelings so perfectly. Who the Hell *were* they? And where the Hell had they *come* from? And—

"Attention, Admiral Mugabi!"

Mugabi's eyes were already as wide as they could get, but they tried to glaze over as the unknown voice, speaking English with an accent he'd never heard before, sounded in his earbug. The only way it could have gotten there was for the unknowns to have invaded *Terra*'s communications net through at least a dozen levels of encryption and security firewalls that should have held up even a Galactic AI for a minimum of fifteen minutes.

"Break off, Admiral Mugabi!" the unknown voice snapped in his ear. "Leave them to us!"

Even as the voice spoke, another salvo of those terrible missiles crashed into Lach'heranu's ships, and the Solarian Navy watched in disbelief as it saw something no mortal eye had seen in over sixty-two thousand years.

A Federation superdreadnought blew up.

One moment it was there, well over a billion tons of warship, with a crew of over three thousand. The next instant, it was an expanding ball of plasma, and a jubilant bellow of savage satisfaction went up from the officers on *Terra*'s flag deck. Mugabi's voice was a part of that bellow, but then he shook his head like a punch-drunk fighter and wrenched himself back out of the exultation raging about him. His command was only minutes short of the Federation warships' engagement envelope, and if there was one thing in the universe he knew, it was that his ships had no business at all between those warring leviathans.

"All units, execute evasion vector Echo Niner! *Execute Echo Niner immediately!*" he barked.

Acknowledgments streamed back as maneuvering officers

fought free of their own hypnotic fascination with their tactical plots, and Mugabi's fleet broke away from the death ride it had embraced just a handful of minutes before. A part of the admiral's mind monitored the frantic breakaway maneuver, but almost absently, for he was unable to tear his eyes from the plot as the outnumbered attackers ripped into Lach'heranu's fleet like ravening demons.

He had never imagined anything like it. Those weren't warships. They were something else entirely, something that took combat power to a whole new level. As his sensors collected more and more data, his disbelief only grew. There were only nine of the newcomers against thirty-five *Ogres*, and everyone knew—not just the Federation, but ONI, as well—that the *Ogre*-class was the most powerful warship that had ever been built. They were invincible. *Nothing* had ever been able to stand up to one of them.

But the unknowns weren't "standing up" to them; they were tearing them apart.

CIC's estimates scrolled up the side of Mugabi's plot, and all his years of experience in naval service insisted that those estimates had to be wrong. Each of those nine ships was fifty percent larger than an *Ogre*-class. *Fifty percent*. And despite that, they were at least twenty-five percent faster and far more maneuverable. More preposterous still, their firepower and energy signatures, now that they had emerged from whatever unreasonably efficient stealth technology had hidden their approach, indicated that they were *at least* six times as powerful, on a ton-for-ton basis, as anything the Federation had ever built.

It was flatly impossible, but those nine ships had Lach'heranu's entire squadron outnumbered by better than two-to-one.

It was a short, vicious, ugly battle. One which lasted only a very little longer than the one Lach'heranu had planned upon . . . but had a very different outcome. Even in a straight, standup fight in which both sides had known what was coming, the Federation squadron would have been doomed. Taken by surprise in the deep-space equivalent of a point-blank ambush, Lach'heranu and her ships had no chance at all. Two of the unknown attackers were lightly damaged; none of Lach'heranu's superdreadnoughts survived the engagement. A handful of her cruisers tried to break away and run for it, but three of the unknowns loped off after them, overtaking them with absurd ease, and blew them out of existence long before they could get beyond Sol's phase limit and go to FTL drive. Mugabi had no idea if Lach'heranu or any of her ship commanders had attempted to surrender, but if they had, no one on the other side had been interested in allowing them to.

The Solarian Navy floated in space, stunned spectators to the carnage which dwarfed any battle it had ever imagined, and Mugabi knew that every single crewman aboard every single ship was wondering exactly the same thing.

And then the repeater plot reconfigured itself into a communications screen once more, without any input from any member of *Terra*'s crew, and an alien, saurian face looked out of it.

Mugabi felt his jaw try to drop yet again as he recognized the face, or at least the species to which its owner belonged. So far as he knew, no human had ever managed to communicate with the species the Federation called the Ternaui, but ONI was very familiar with them. Everyone knew that the Ternaui were the most loyal, utterly reliable bodyguards any of the Galactics could hope for. The xenologists' best guess was that the Ternaui were telepaths, and that the Federation had devised a technique which allowed it to "program" them for complete obedience and loyalty. Whether that was true or not, humanity had been given ample proof of the effectiveness of a Ternaui bodyguard, and there was no question that the species was mute.

Which made what happened next as impossible as everything else that had happened in the last half hour.

"Good afternoon, Admiral Mugabi," the Ternaui said. His—or "its," Mugabi supposed, if it happened to be one of the neuters—mouth never moved at all, but its obviously artificial voice was as melodious and expressive as any human voice the admiral had ever heard, and its strangely beautiful silver eyes with their inky-black, vertical pupils seemed to look straight into his own. "We apologize for the abrupt nature of our intervention . . . and for the fact that it was impossible for us to alert you to our presence earlier. We realize that what has just happened must be extremely confusing, although, we hope, not unwelcome."

For a species which was supposed to be incapable of speech, the Ternaui turned out to have a remarkable gift for understatement, Mugabi thought.

"I speak to you as High Chancellor of the Avalon Empire," the scale-hided alien continued. "And as High Chancellor, I formally invite you to come aboard our flagship in order to meet with the Emperor so that he might explain to you what brings us here today."

# -XII-

Quentin Mugabi had never imagined such a warship. Unlike the flattened ovoid shape of the Federation's *Ogres*, this vessel was an almost perfect sphere, fourteen miles in diameter, more like a moon than anything Mugabi would have called a ship. As his cutter approached it, he'd watched domes, engine pods, and weapons housings swell across its surface, but the sheer size of the ship had prevented his emotions from truly recognizing and accepting their mountain-range height and ruggedness. It was only now, as the cutter passed along the flank of a drive housing larger than a Solarian Navy heavy cruiser at a range of barely a quarter-mile, that the true enormity of the ship came home to him.

Yet the size of the vessel was the least of the impossibilities his battered brain found itself compelled to deal with. He was honest enough with himself to admit that he was still in a state of semi-shock from the incredible violence and speed with which Lach'heranu's entire squadron had been destroyed. Not to mention his sheer astonishment that any of the ships under his command were still alive! No doubt that had a great deal to do with his sense that the entire universe was just slightly out of focus. But the appearance of a Ternaui as the spokesman for this "Avalon Empire," was just as stunning in its own way. Mugabi had requested a records search while his cutter prepared for this voyage, and the search had confirmed his own memory. The Galactic archives which had been penetrated by the human intelligence services contained any number of accounts of Ternaui bodyguards dying in defense of Galactic owners. So far as any information available to ONI was concerned, however, there was not a single record of any Ternaui turning upon the Galactics. Not one, in over twelve centuries of servitude.

So how had the most utterly reliable race of bodyguards in Galactic history wound up somehow managing to build what had to be an astonishingly powerful empire, judging by the size and power of its warships, without the Federation ever suspecting a thing? The fact that the Galactics hadn't had a clue as to that empire's existence was abundantly clear to him. If a primitive bunch like the human race had provoked such a . . . definitive response, then surely something like this "Avalon Empire" would have had the Council in a state of outright panic if the Federation had even dreamed that it existed, and the attack on Lach'heranu would never have come as such a complete and total surprise to her.

That was the most burning question, he reflected, although he had a few thousand others to go with it. For one, why should the Ternaui call themselves the "*Avalon* Empire"? For another, why should they be willing to risk revealing their existence, which they had obviously taken great and successful pains to keep the secret from the Federation, to come to the aid of the human race?

*And why in Hell*, he thought, with a sort of detached calm that resulted from far too many shocks in far too short a time, as his cutter approached the huge ship's main boat bay and he finally saw the name etched across the hull in letters two hundred feet tall, *should a bunch of aliens name their flagship* "Excalibur"?

~ ~ ~

The cutter drifted through the boat bay hatch into the gleaming, brilliantly illuminated cavern of the bay's interior and settled towards the designated landing circle. There were no docking tubes or umbilicals, only a beacon and a visual target for the cutter's pilot.

There was also no boat bay hatch, despite the fact that this bay, unlike that of his own flagship, was obviously pressurized, Mugabi noted enviously. The human race had made enormous technological strides over the past century, partly out of its own resources and partly by adapting any fragment of Galactic technology it could steal. In fact, as Mugabi was well aware, that very inventiveness was one of the things the Galactics had found most frightening about humanity. Yet rapid as their advances had been, humans had started so far behind the technology the Federation took for granted that the gulf between them had seemed completely insurmountable. One galling example of that gulf had been the ease with which the Federation generated force fields at the drop of a hat. The Solarian Navy had developed some ability to generate them—their warships' shields were based on the same technology, after all—but the energy and mass requirements of any force field generator human technology was yet capable of building prohibited human naval architects from using them for anything less vital than shields. Certainly no human engineer was yet capable of building the selectively permeable sort of force fields which obviously held in this boat bay's atmosphere!

And whoever had designed this ship hadn't stopped with simply pressurizing the bay. The admiral felt yet another flicker of envy as he saw the islands of greenery scattered artistically about between the landing circles. No one in his experience, not even the Galactics, had ever *landscaped* a warship's boat bay, but these people had. It was readily apparent that they'd taken pains to avoid compromising the efficiency of the bay's layout, but that hadn't prevented them from sprinkling it with towering banks of blossom-bedecked shrubbery, flower beds, fountains, and even a few groves of what looked for all the world like Bartlett pear trees.

The additional proof of this Avalon Empire's capabilities flickered through Mugabi's mind, but then it was abruptly displaced by fresh astonishment as the cutter touched down and he caught his first glimpse of the welcoming committee through a viewport. There were four people in it . . . and not one of them was a Ternaui.

Admiral Quentin Mugabi sat very still, gazing through the port at the last thing his brain had been prepared to see, then rose as the cutter's hatch cycled open.

"Admiral Mugabi," the tall, red-haired, blue-eyed, and very human man at the head of the welcoming party greeted Mugabi as the Solarian admiral stepped through the hatch. The redhead wore a black-and-gold uniform which managed to combine sharp military tailoring with obvious comfort. It was unlike any Solarian uniform Mugabi had ever seen, but its rank badges were completely familiar. His eyes narrowed as he saw the cluster of five five-pointed stars pinned to either side of the collar and the four broad bands of gold braid encircling the cuffs of the sleeves, and the stranger's eyes twinkled as he extended his right hand.

"Welcome aboard *Excalibur*," he continued in the same oddly accented English the Ternaui had used as Mugabi automatically reached out to return the handclasp. "I'm Fleet Admiral Maynton. I apologize for the absence of the regular military courtesies, but we thought that it might be a little less confusing to greet you without all of the fuss and nonsense of side boys and bosun's pipes."

"Less *confusing* . . . Sir?" Mugabi repeated, and Maynton smiled crookedly.

"Not, perhaps, the best possible choice of words," he conceded. "Still, I hope that our arrival was at least a *welcome* surprise."

"Oh, I think you can rely on that!" Mugabi assured him.

"Good! It was also a surprise we've been looking forward to delivering, not without some trepidation, for a very long time. And one which I'm happy to say appears to have come as just as great a surprise for the Federation."

"You have a gift for understatement, Admiral," Mugabi said dryly.

"I suspect that most people would, under the circumstances," Maynton replied with another small smile, then gestured at his companions. "I realize that you must have several thousand questions, Admiral, and I promise we'll answer them as quickly as we can. In the meantime, however, allow me to introduce Captain Veronica Stanhope, Baroness of Shallot, *Excalibur*'s commanding officer." The slightly built, fair-skinned brunette to his right nodded to Mugabi and extended her own hand in turn.

"And this," Maynton continued, "is Captain Sir Anthony Moore, my chief of staff." Moore was almost as tall as Maynton, a good two inches taller than Mugabi's own six feet-two, a platinum blond with steady gray eyes, and his handclasp was as firm as his admiral's had been.

"And this," Maynton finished, "is Admiral Her Imperial Highness Princess Evelynn Wincaster, the commander of Third Fleet."

Something about the tone of his voice, even more than the title, made Mugabi look very closely at Admiral Wincaster. She was extremely tall for a woman, standing somewhere between Maynton and Moore and literally towering over Mugabi. Like Maynton himself—and all of his companions, for that matter—she seemed absurdly young for her rank, for not one of them could be much over thirty, yet she possessed a perceptible aura of command and authority that owed very little to her imposing height. Golden hair spilled over her shoulders, in direct contrast to the short hairstyles the Solarian Navy favored for men and women alike, and her eyes were a strikingly dark cobalt blue.

Mugabi hesitated for just a moment, uncertain whether or

not he should initiate a handshake with someone who hung an "Imperial Highness" in front of her name, but Princess Evelynn resolved his doubts by holding out her own hand.

"Let me join Admiral Maynton in welcoming you aboard *Excalibur*." She spoke with the same oddly musical accent as Maynton, although it sounded even more exotic and intriguing in her soft, firm contralto, and her clasp on his hand was firm. "I've studied your career with great interest and the deepest respect, Admiral Mugabi. You and Admiral Stevenson, in particular, have accomplished an incredible amount in light of the tremendous handicaps you faced. I can't begin to tell you how pleased I am to make your acquaintance at last."

"Thank you . . . Your Highness." Mugabi felt acutely uncomfortable before the sincerity of her tone. "I appreciate the compliment," he continued, "but the truth is that we obviously didn't manage to accomplish enough. Without your . . . unexpected arrival, we'd all be dead."

"Her Highness is completely correct," Maynton disagreed firmly. "Given the technological handicap with which you started, the time pressure under which you were forced to act, and the degree to which the Galactics kept you under minute observation, your achievement in building a navy powerful enough that the Federation felt compelled to deploy a full battle squadron against it was nothing short of miraculous. In fact, our greatest regret is that we were forced to leave you to accomplish it on your own. Unfortunately, we dared not make direct contact with you."

"I don't understand any of this," Mugabi said frankly. "Why couldn't you contact us? And, for that matter, who *are* you people? The entire—"

He paused, then shook his head.

"I was going to say that the entire human race owes you an immense debt, but it would appear that what I should have said is that the entire *Solar System* owes you, because it's painfully obvious that what we always thought was the entire human race isn't."

"No, it isn't," Maynton agreed in a tone of deliberate understatement. "And I apologize for keeping you here talking instead of escorting you to His Majesty for the explanations you and the rest of Earth's population deserve. Please, come with us, and I promise that the answers will be forthcoming."

Mugabi followed Maynton and his companions out of the elevator which had transported them from the boat bay to the core of the immense warship. He'd felt a sense of awe which was becoming familiar as he watched the projected holographic schematic which had shown their progress on the way here. The elevator had streaked across the schematic with incredible speed, yet he'd felt absolutely no sensation of movement, which suggested that these people were even more competent gravitic engineers than the Galactics.

Not that he should have been too surprised by that, he told himself, given the way that nine of their ships had trashed Lach'heranu's entire squadron. Besides—

His reflections slithered to an abrupt halt as he stepped out into the trackless depths of space itself.

For just an instant, his brain came to a complete, shuddering stop in terrified anticipation of explosive decompression. He actually felt his lungs lock down in a desperate attempt to retain the air still in them, and then he exhaled in an explosive whoosh as his cognitive processes caught up with him once more.

It was the most breathtakingly perfect holographic display he'd ever seen. No wonder he'd felt such terror at the sight! The training required to survive in vacuum was driven into every recruit on an instinctive level from the very first day of suit drill at the Academy, and every one of those instincts had told him that he was dead as the display enfolded him in the consummate fidelity of its illusion.

He could have wished that his companions had bothered to warn him, he thought sourly, but then he shook himself.

They were undoubtedly as accustomed to this as he was to his own command deck aboard *Terra*, so it had probably never even occurred to them that he wouldn't be.

He made himself draw a deep, calming breath, then stepped further out of the elevator and let his eyes sweep the awesome perfection of the display. It was as if his boots rested not on the alloy of the deck, but upon the insubstantial blackness of space—as if he floated among the stars, a titan looming above the children's toys of the warships drifting about him. He had never experienced anything like it, and after the first few seconds, he'd completely forgotten his original moment of terror in the pure delight of gazing upon the universe as God Himself must see it.

His hosts allowed him to stand there, absorbing the impact of the display for at least a full minute, before Maynton cleared his throat. The slight, polite sound seemed shockingly loud for just a moment, and Mugabi realized that it seemed that way because his eyes insisted that there shouldn't have been any atmosphere to carry it to him in the first place. The admiral swallowed a wry chuckle of amusement at his own reaction, and pulled himself back out of his fascination.

Three more people stood at the very center of the display, spangled in its starlight and shadow. One was the Ternaui who had first contacted Mugabi, towering over his companions while his silver eyes glittered with starshine. The second was a stocky, broad-shouldered, brown-haired human who wore a vaguely monkish-looking robe. And the third . . .

The third was another human, black-haired and a good four inches shorter than Mugabi, who somehow effortlessly dominated everyone else present.

The admiral wasn't certain how he managed it. He was powerfully built, but after Captain Stanhope, he was also the smallest person Mugabi had met aboard *Excalibur*, and he couldn't have been much over twenty years old. His eyes were dark, although Mugabi couldn't tell exactly what color they were in the dimness of the display, and there was a distinct family resemblance between him and Princess Evelynn, although his strongly hooked nose had been muted into an aquiline female attractiveness in her features. He was obviously too young to be her father, so he must be her brother, Mugabi decided. He wore a neatly trimmed, spade-like beard, and the white line of an old scar seamed one tanned cheek. Unlike any of the officers who'd greeted Mugabi, he was not in uniform. Instead, he wore a one-piece garment, very much like the protective suits the Galactics normally wore. This one was in a deep, midnight blue with silver trim, and it bore a heraldic device on its chest. Somehow, the dagger sheathed at the man's right hip didn't look at all incongruous with it.

"Admiral Quentin Mugabi," Maynton said in a voice which had suddenly become far more formal, "allow me to present you to His Imperial Majesty George, Emperor of Avalon, King of Camelot, Prince of New Lancaster, and Baron of Wickworth."

Mugabi felt himself come automatically to attention. He would undoubtedly have done so anyway, as a courteous mark of respect, once he'd thought about it, but there was no thought involved. Despite his obvious youth, the Emperor's sheer presence pulled the gesture out of him as naturally as breathing.

"Admiral Mugabi." The Emperor crossed the display to him and held out his right hand.

Quentin Mugabi had served the Solarian Union for over forty years. In that time, he had met and advised three different presidents and been introduced to system senators, cabinet ministers, and justices of the Union Supreme Court. He was the second ranking officer of the Solarian Navy, and he was unaccustomed to feeling socially awkward. Yet he felt oddly uncertain, almost hesitant, as the Emperor extended his hand, and he wondered once again what it was that gave this man such a palpable aura of command. Whatever it was, it appeared to operate almost independently of the fact that he was the ruler of what was obviously a powerful empire, because Mugabi had sensed it even before Maynton identified him.

"Your Majesty," he murmured, as he made himself return the Emperor's handclasp firmly. "Allow me to thank you, on my own behalf and that of the entire Solar System, for your timely arrival."

"You're most welcome," the Emperor replied with a slight smile. "Although I think you may find yourself just a bit surprised by how 'timely' our arrival actually was." His smile grew broader. "It's been a while since my last visit," he added.

"Your last visit, Sir?" Mugabi repeated, his questioning tone carefully respectful.

"That was a bit before your time," the Emperor told him. "In fact, it was just over eight hundred years ago."

Mugabi stared at him in shock, and he chuckled.

"I see that some explanations are in order, Admiral," he said. "So if you will be so kind as to join me and my Chancellor in my quarters, I'll try to provide them."

Quentin Mugabi had never before sat in such a comfortable chair. Even the best Terran powered chairs adjusted far more slowly and imperfectly into the form and movement of the human bodies sitting in them. This chair seemed to have conformed to his shape and weight even before he'd sat down, and it readjusted itself so smoothly whenever he moved that he scarcely realized that it had.

*On the other hand*, he thought, *maybe it's not so surprising that I didn't notice the chair moving, given how all the* rest *of my universe has just shifted!*

"So you and the Ternaui managed to pull it off, Your Majesty?" he murmured as the Emperor paused.

"Indeed we did," the Emperor replied. "In fact, the actual fighting was considerably easier than my good friend here—" he nodded to the towering Chancellor seated to his right "—had suggested that it might be. And *much* easier than the rest of his little plan."

"We do not recall ever having suggested to you that any of it would be 'easy,' Your Majesty," the Ternaui's electronically produced voice said serenely. "On the other hand, we believe that it might be argued that in fact the task was not nearly so difficult as it might have been."

"Well," the Emperor chuckled, "at least you had the common decency to turn to as babysitters when we needed you most!"

A chuckle ran around the comfortably furnished cabin. The compartment was a quarter the size of soccer field, yet despite the obvious comfort of its furniture and decorations, it seemed much less magnificent than something Mugabi would have expected to house the ruler of a mighty empire.

The Solarian let his eyes run back over the cabin. The light sculptures dotted about it had a cool, almost sensual beauty, but they were the only true decoration in the entire compartment, aside from a breathtakingly lifelike full-size portrait of Her Imperial Majesty Matilda, who had remained at home on the Empire's capital world of Camelot in her role as co-ruler while the Emperor was away. Well, that and the obviously well used sword displayed at the cabin's very center. The blade had been set point-down in a block of polished stone sitting on a small, round, tablelike pedestal.

Mugabi looked back at the Emperor and shook his head slowly.

"What?" The Emperor's question could have been abrupt, a rebuke, but it came out with a strong edge of what could only have been sympathetic amusement.

"I'm just still . . . trying to take it all in, Your Majesty." Mugabi smiled almost sheepishly. "You were really born in 1311."

"I most assuredly was," the Emperor replied, and chuckled again. "I realize that neither Timothy nor I look our ages, however. As a matter of fact, both of us replaced the Saernai's original nanites centuries ago, when Merlin and Doctor Yardley came up with their new, improved biochines. With the proper readjustment of the genetic code, they're capable of actually adjusting one's biological age rather than simply holding it unchanged, and Timothy and I had begun developing enough aches and pains as our original equipment ran down to make that highly welcome. But I understand what you're actually saying, and believe me, Admiral, you can scarcely find it more difficult to believe how old I am than I have from time to time over the years."

Mugabi shook his head once more and leaned back in his chair while his mind tried to sort out all he had already been told.

He supposed, realistically, that the Avalon Empire wasn't really particularly large when compared to the titanic size of the Federation. From what the Emperor and his advisers had told him, the Empire claimed only twenty-two star systems, of which only the seven "princedoms"—New Lancaster, New Yorkshire, New Wales, New Oxfordshire, Glastonbury, Avalon, and Camelot—could boast populations in excess of two billion. The Federation, on the other hand, claimed in excess of fifteen hundred stars, with an average population per star system of almost eleven billion. Given that sort of numerical superiority, Lach'heranu's fellow fleet commanders ought to find themselves with a comprehensive quantitative answer to the qualitative advantage the Empire's technology clearly gave it.

But that was assuming that the Federation had the opportunity to bring its ponderous might to bear . . . and overlooked the fact that over eighty percent of the Federation's population was to be found among the "protected" races.

"I'm astonished that you could have accomplished so much from such a limited beginning," he said aloud, and the Emperor shrugged.

"We were limited only in population size," he pointed out. "In every other respect we started even with the Federation's current technology base." He shrugged again. "It was mainly a matter of improving upon the head start with which we began."

"As usual, Your Majesty," a mellow tenor voice said out of the cabin's thin air, "you understate both the scope and the severity of the challenge you faced. Not to mention the magnitude of what you accomplished."

"And also as usual, Merlin," the Emperor replied with the air of a participant in a long-standing debate, "you *overstate* all three of them. Not to mention the highly capable advisors I had—starting with Matilda—or the magnitude of the role you yourself played in accomplishing it."

"Which it was possible for me to play only because you were so foolish as to reject the Federation's limitations upon the creation of artificial intelligences," the voice replied, and Mugabi felt his eyebrows arch. The Emperor obviously noticed his expression, for he smiled wryly and nodded.

"Yes, Admiral," he said. "Merlin was once called 'Computer' by a primitive warrior too ignorant to realize that he was talking to a mere machine."

"And one so foolish as to extend the full legal equality of organic intelligence to artificial ones," Merlin pointed out.

"No, no," the Emperor said, shaking his head. "Not foolish—cunning. It was all a clever ploy to make you eternally grateful so that you'd help us out with our research and development! Not to mention running the imperial intelligence services for us."

"Of course it was," Merlin said with a sound suspiciously like a human snort.

"Seriously, Admiral," the Emperor said, looking back and Mugabi, "Merlin has been an enormous help to us. He isn't as intuitive as humans are, but the speed and accuracy with which he can process information far exceeds anything we've managed yet, even with personal computer implants."

"I should certainly hope so," Merlin said primly, and the Emperor and his naval officers laughed out loud.

"I don't doubt that . . . Merlin was a great help to you, Your Majesty," Mugabi said after a moment, "but you must still have faced an all but impossible task."

"Humans seem to be better suited to 'impossible tasks' than most species," the High Chancellor put in.

"Perhaps we are," the Emperor agreed, "but that didn't keep us from being neck-deep in babies for the first hundred years or so." His reminiscent smile looked out of place on his unreasonably youthful face, and Mugabi wondered how much of that sense of presence he projected had always been his and how much of that he had acquired over the last five hundred years. Mugabi had met some of the Romans whose return to Earth had formed the pretext for the Federation's "final solution," yet none of them had radiated the same blend of youthfulness and ancient wisdom and self-confidence which seemed to be so much a part of the Emperor. Of course, even though they were technically over a thousand years older than he was, they'd spent the vast majority of their enormous lifespans in phase stasis, traveling between the stars, not awake and laboring to build an empire literally from scratch. The Emperor, he reflected, was undoubtedly the "oldest" human being he had ever met—that *anyone* had ever met—for that matter . . . with the possible exception of Archbishop Timothy, he amended. Of course, after the first two or three hundred years a mere forty years one way or the other was pretty much meaningless, he supposed.

"The hardest part, though," the Emperor continued, "was finding a way to increase our population quickly enough without losing all sense of family connection. None of us was familiar with the term at the time, but what we really faced was a problem of 'mass production.' Still, we knew enough to be afraid of what would happen to us as a society when we began the mass cloning."

He shook his head and sighed, then waved at Admiral Maynton.

"Prince John here," he told Mugabi, who cocked an eyebrow at the title which Maynton had somehow forgotten to mention came attached to him, "and his entire house are direct descendants of one of our first generation clone children. Of course, there are—what? Nineteen cadet branches of the family, John?"

"Twenty-two, actually, Uncle," Maynton replied, blue eyes twinkling, then shrugged. "But who's counting?"

"You are, you young whippersnapper," the Emperor told him with a chuckle, then turned back to Mugabi. "I decided from the outset that the law would make no distinction between cloned children and those carried to term *in utero*, but I wasn't really certain that our people could accept them as their own. Today, of course, that entire worry seems ridiculous, since clones and the descendants of clones outnumber 'old-fashioned' offspring by literally millions to one in the Empire, but it was a real concern at the time."

"True," Archbishop Timothy put in. "On the other hand, you approached it sensibly enough to avoid the sort of problem it might have turned into, My Lord." The prelate, Mugabi had already noticed, very seldom addressed the Emperor as "Majesty," and the admiral wondered if that was a distinction limited to the Emperor's oldest and closest advisers.

"If you mean I was smart enough to let Matilda talk me into being sure that you approved the entire process in the name of Mother Church, then I suppose I did," the Emperor agreed.

"Children are children, and souls are souls," the archbishop replied serenely. "As long as the medical science is sound, and the children who are born are born whole and healthy, the miracle is the same for every child."

"And the people who raise that child are that child's parents," the Emperor agreed softly, then chuckled and glanced over his shoulder at the portrait of his Empress. "Matilda certainly made that plain enough to me at the time!" he added wryly.

"And speaking from personal experience," Captain Stanhope put in, "Ternaui make excellent parents." She smiled warmly at the High Chancellor, and Mugabi had the sudden sense of a matching smile from the immobile, saurian features of the Chancellor.

"Thank you, daughter," the Ternaui said after a moment. "Still, we must admit that raising human young is an . . . interesting experience. And one, we suspect, which has corrupted us rather more than our queens would ever have anticipated."

"Life is sufficient to do that on its own without blaming it on the children, old friend!" the Emperor laughed. "Not that raising them isn't an 'interesting experience' for anyone . . . whatever their own species might be."

Mugabi managed to hide his surprise, but it wasn't easy. He had to keep reminding himself that these people had absolutely nothing in common with the Federation. Still, the Galactics were the only "advanced" civilization with which the Solarian branch of the human race had ever had any experience, and the very notion of cross-species adoption was anathema to the Federation. In fact, it was expressly forbidden by law, and the admiral wondered how much that might have had to do with the ease with which the Empire had embraced the practice.

"At any rate," the Emperor went on after a moment, turning his attention fully back to Mugabi, "we did succeed, and we have maintained the bonds of family. In fact, I believe that we've retained our focus on the centrality of family to a much greater extent than your own branch of the family has, Admiral. Of course, we began from a far more homogenous template, and we've managed to preserve much of that homogeneity. No doubt the fact that we're still a hierarchical—some might say feudal—society and that Mother Church remains so central to virtually all of our institutions has a great deal to do with that, but I suspect that the outside threat of the Federation is another factor. Unlike your own ancestors on Earth, we knew from the beginning that the Federation existed and that eventually it must almost certainly come to open conflict between it and us. That gave us a sense of purpose and a focus, not to mention a powerful source of fear, which helped force us to maintain a sense of unity which was bound up inextricably with our concept of who and what we were. Your own branch of humanity has only really become aware of the Federation in the last hundred or hundred and fifty years, so in a very real sense, you've had much longer to develop a broad menu of different family structures and lifestyles which were never really an option for us."

"Perhaps we have," Mugabi replied. "On the other hand, from what you've already told me it's evident that the Solarian branch of the 'family' is actually a fairly small minority of the total human race."

"I suppose it is," the Emperor conceded. "And I suppose that there will be some inevitable pressure on Earth-born humans to conform to the practices of the Empire. I assure you, however, that the Empire has no intention of forcing anyone to embrace our own laws or our own form of government. If we did that, Matilda would kick my imperial arse up between my imperial ears when I got back to Camelot! Besides, there would be no real practical difference between us and the Federation if we acted in such an arrogant manner, now would there?"

"I suppose not," Mugabi agreed. "Although I imagine that the fact that the Empire doesn't have any interest in exterminating us might be considered at least a *small* difference, if someone wanted to get picky about it."

"Oh, perhaps a small one." The Emperor chuckled. He and Mugabi grinned at each other, but then the admiral glanced at his watch and shook his head again.

"I'm certain that it will take years for us to even begin to really catch up with all of the details of what you and your people have accomplished, Your Majesty. I personally look forward to the time when I can properly appreciate the challenges which you must have faced and the ways in which you overcame them. But as you know, President Dresner, Admiral Stevenson, and the President's Cabinet are en route to *Excalibur*. According to the schedule they transmitted to me, they should be arriving within the next half-hour, and

I have no doubt that they'll expect me to have at least the bare bones of a military briefing for them."

"Of course," the Emperor said. "Forgive me. I'm afraid that having a fresh ear to put up with my recollections of the 'good old days' has gone to my head. God knows that this ungrateful younger lot—" he waved at Maynton and the other officers "—aren't slow about letting me know how boring *they* find it when I reminisce!"

"Not *boring*, Grandfather," Princess Evelynn disagreed demurely. "Merely . . . well polished."

A general rumble of laughter rolled around the compartment, led by the Emperor, but then he turned his gaze back to Mugabi.

"Very well, Admiral, let's look at those bare bones of yours."

The Emperor leaned back in his chair, and despite his amusement of only moments before, his expression was serious, almost grim.

"It may well be, Admiral, that future generations of historians will look back upon my reign as a total disaster, a case of missed opportunities leading to utter ruin that a wiser man might have avoided entirely." Mugabi opened his mouth quickly, but the Emperor's raised hand cut him off before he could voice his protest.

"No, hear me out, Admiral. I don't say that I would agree with that verdict; I only say that some people may judge it so, because there were two possible alternatives open to me, and I never even considered pursuing one of them."

"Two alternatives?" Mugabi furrowed his brow.

"Two," the Emperor repeated firmly. "One possibility would have been to develop our own phase drive, build our military and technological bases up to a level which would give someone as cautious and basically cowardly as the Federation pause, and then demand a seat of our own on the Council."

Mugabi stared incredulously at him, and the Emperor chuckled.

"I realize that, particularly from the perspective of the Solar System's experience with the Galactics, the notion that they might have admitted any human representative to their precious Council must seem ridiculous. But what we can never know, Admiral, is whether or not what appears to be so obvious with the benefit of hindsight would have seemed quite so obvious if we'd pursued a different alternative at an earlier time. It's possible, however remote the probability, that if we'd contacted the Federation on our own terms as soon as we'd thoroughly developed New Lancaster, they might have reacted differently. After all, at that point they hadn't yet placed the Solar System under tight surveillance, which probably indicates that they hadn't yet recognized the threat which humanity's basic nature presents to their precious stability."

"With all due respect, Your Majesty, I can't see that happy state of affairs lasting very long once they'd gotten to know you. Leaving aside their reaction to the Romans and their 'stolen ship'—which certainly suggests how they would have responded once they discovered the foundation of your own beginning technological base—your Empire, from the very beginning, was busy creating exactly the sort of bad example they were afraid that *we* would present to their subject races."

"I believe you're correct," the Emperor said quietly, "yet there are times when I lie awake at night wondering what would have happened if I hadn't automatically assumed that hostility between us and the Federation was inevitable. What if I'd pursued the alternative of seeking peaceful coexistence and working to reform the Federation from within once we were seated upon the Council?"

"*I* don't lie awake at night wondering about that," Archbishop Timothy said tartly, "because I bloody well know—pardon my language—what would have happened. We'd all have been dead three hundred and fifty years ago!"

"My analysis of humans' ability to endlessly reinvent and reinterpret their own history suggests that you are undoubtedly correct that some scholar with more credentials than brainpower will eventually suggest precisely what you have just described, Your Majesty," the voice of Merlin put in. "All that that demonstrates, however, is that individuals who are not responsible for making crucial decisions are the ones who feel the greatest freedom when it comes to second-guessing those who did have to decide."

"Be careful, my friends!" the Emperor said with a wry grin. "Arguing an emperor out of feeling a healthy sense of self-doubt is an excellent way to encourage him to believe in his own infallibility, and then where will you all be?"

"Watching Her Majesty . . . convince you of the error of your ways, Your Majesty," Maynton replied in a tone whose solemnity went poorly with the twinkle in his blue eyes.

"Ouch!" The Emperor winced at some image only he could see, then shook himself and his amusement vanished once more into that same grim intensity.

"Whatever possibilities might or might not have existed, Admiral Mugabi, I chose to pursue a second alternative—the one Matilda christened the 'Excalibur Alternative.' Perhaps it was presumptuous of us to see ourselves in just that light, but it seemed to Matilda that, in a sense, we had become Arthur's sword." He met Mugabi's eyes levelly. "It hadn't been our choice, but surely we'd been cast into the depths of the stars as thoroughly as ever Excalibur was cast back to the Lady of the Lake. In our case, those depths were also the furnace in which we were forged, and the anvil upon which we were hammered, not simply a safe hiding place, but like Excalibur, it was our duty to return in our homeland's darkest hour. And so, rightly or wrongly, we gave no thought to the alternative of 'peaceful coexistence.' We judged that there was no realistic hope of ever reforming something as huge and as static as the Federation, and that if it could not be reformed, then for the sake not only of our own race but of every 'primitive' species the Federation ever had or ever would encounter, it must be destroyed."

"We chose the Excalibur Alternative," the Emperor said, his

voice harsh as clanging steel, "and we never looked back from that day."

Silence hovered in the cabin, and Mugabi inhaled deeply as he realized that he'd actually been holding his breath. The sense of presence he'd felt from the Emperor from the beginning was stronger than ever, and despite the youthfulness of his appearance he sat in his chair like some ancient granite boulder, unbroken and unbreakable.

Four hundred and fifty-one years. That was how long this man had dedicated himself and all of his people unswervingly to the task of building the weapon—of transforming himself and those he ruled until they became the very Excalibur he'd spoken of—to overthrow the most powerful and arrogant federation in the history of the galaxy. No wonder he radiated that steely aura of raw power and purpose.

"And what, if I may ask, Your Majesty," the Solarian said very quietly after a long, silent moment, "does the 'Excalibur Alternative' consist of?"

"It consists of everything we have been able to accomplish in four and a half centuries. Of every warship, every weapon, every strategy and tactic and technological advantage we've been able to put together. We certainly can't guarantee victory, Admiral Mugabi, but we can guarantee, especially if the Solar System joins with us, that the Federation's unwavering belief in its own superiority won't survive what happens.

"In more specific terms, however," the Emperor continued in a more normal tone of voice, sitting back in his chair once again, "we've already placed certain forces in motion, and we intend to activate still more of them in the very near future.

"First, we are prepared to station Evelynn's Third Fleet here in the Solar System indefinitely. As currently constituted, Third Fleet's battleline consists of sixty *Sword*-class dreadnoughts like *Excalibur* and two hundred *Pendragon*-class battleships, each of them about two-thirds the size and power of a *Sword*. They're screened by three hundred and forty *Gawain*-class battlecruisers and supported by one hundred *Nimue*-class carriers, each of which carries a thousand phase-capable fighters with an individual combat power roughly equivalent to a Federation *Harpy*-class destroyer."

Mugabi knew his jaw had dropped, but right that moment he couldn't do anything about it. *Sixty* of these monster ships? Three times that many battleships? His mind reeled at the inconceivable firepower the Empire's Third Fleet represented, but the Emperor continued calmly.

"At the moment, Third Fleet is the largest and most powerful of our formations, although its margin of superiority over Home Fleet is relatively slight. The problem, of course, is that the Federation already knows where the Solar System is, whereas it doesn't even know where to begin looking for us. That may change, but in the worst possible case, it will take them decades to locate any of our star systems. Which means that we can anticipate that any attacks it launches will be directed here and mandates that this is the point at which we must place our strongest defense. Particularly since the Galactics will soon enough deduce approximately how the Empire must have come into existence. Once they've reached that point, they will also appreciate just how vast their advantage in numbers and star systems must be, and I don't doubt for a moment that their response will be to attempt to utterly destroy any of our star systems they can identify.

"At the same time, our intelligence sources within the Federation indicate that it will take them at least eight years to concentrate a fresh squadron as powerful as Lach'heranu's to attack here. It will take considerably longer than that for them to assemble a force stronger than hers was, and I expect that it's fairly safe to assume that the Federation won't commit to any follow-up attack until it can muster a substantially more powerful force than the one it's already lost.

"While the Council is trying to put that sort of force together, we are prepared to transfer to the Solar System automated shipyards and supporting industrial modules.

Initially, those yards and modules would be dedicated to replicating themselves, and we would use the same time to begin the transfer of our general technology base to Earth in order to bring the entire system up to date as quickly as possible. Our current estimate is that the first Solarian-built *Sword* could be delivered within six and a half years; production of fighters for local defense could begin at least two years before that. Once the first capital ships began emerging from your shipyards here, we estimate that your maximum sustainable rate of construction would be a tonnage approximately equal to seventeen *Sword*-class dreadnoughts per month."

Mugabi could feel the eyes of everyone else in the cabin upon him, but he himself could not look away from the Emperor.

"In the meantime, we intend to make full use of certain other advantages to keep the Federation as thoroughly off-balance as possible for as long as possible. I feel quite confident that what happened to Lach'heranu and the implications of the Empire's existence will come as a tremendous shock to the Council, especially when it realizes that what it actually faces is the very thing it was prepared to commit genocide to avoid. Unfortunately for the Council," the Emperor's thin smile was a cold and frightening thing to see, "that's only the first of many shocks headed in its direction. One that it will find particularly unpalatable is the fact that the Empire has substantially improved upon the performance of the Federation's own phase drive. In fact, our starships are almost eleven times as fast as theirs are."

Mugabi would have felt a fresh spasm of shock at that little tidbit . . . if he hadn't already been anesthetized by the cumulative impact of all the other shocks these people had administered to his system. There was no way that they were going to really surprise him again, he thought.

He was wrong.

"In addition," the Emperor continued calmly, "we've made

a few other improvements. In particular, we've developed what we call the singularity comm."

"Singularity comm?" Mugabi repeated cautiously.

"Yes." The Emperor's eye gleamed with something suspiciously like amusement. "At the moment its maximum range is limited to only sixty-two light-years, but its effective transmission speed is approximately seven hundred times the speed of light."

"Faster than light?!" Mugabi jerked upright in his chair so quickly that even it couldn't keep up. "You've got an *FTL* communications capability?!"

"Of course," the Emperor said mildly, and this time there was no question about his broad grin. "Doesn't everyone?"

"My God," Mugabi murmured while his mind raced over the incredible strategic advantages inherent in what he'd just heard. The superior speed of the Empire's warships would have been a huge boon by itself, but coupled with the ability of a high command to deploy and redeploy them using the sort of communications the Emperor had just described, that speed became truly priceless.

"And finally," the Emperor continued after giving him a few moments to digest the strategic implications, "the Federation's 'civilized' races are about to discover that they have all manner of problems closer to home."

"Closer to home?" Mugabi cocked his head, half afraid of what he was going to hear next.

"Much closer," the Emperor said with an evil chuckle. "To be completely honest with you, Admiral, if Lach'heranu hadn't moved to attack Earth, you still wouldn't know that we existed. Our military potential is still climbing relative to that of the Federation. In fact, the curve of increase is still accelerating. Unfortunately, our potential still remains enormously short of the full power the Federation could concentrate against us if left to its own devices. Because of that, we would actually have preferred to wait another fifty to seventy-five years to contact you, but the Council's decision brought our preparations to a head sooner than we might have liked.

"Nonetheless, our projections of the Federation's probable actions had always suggested to us that we would find ourselves in precisely this position, and because of that we've taken certain additional precautions. One, although neither you nor the Federation were aware of it, was to maintain a powerful fleet presence within one month's transit time from Earth for the past sixty years, ready to intervene if Lach'heranu's orders had been issued sooner. Another, however, was to make very cautious contact with certain of the 'protected' races. In fact, we've spent the past century or so creating resistance cells on scores of 'protected' planets scattered throughout the Federation. It was a particularly risky strategy in many respects, especially given that the Federation would have assumed that *Earth* was behind it if any of their security forces had realized what was happening. That could very well have ended up accelerating their decision to move against you, but we felt that it was a risk we had to run.

"Actually, what we would most have preferred would have been to be able to set up such cells on Earth herself, but that simply wasn't practical. Our stealth systems are much better than anything the Federation has, and in this instance, at least, we could have inserted our own people as agents, since they would have blended neatly into the background. Unfortunately, the Federation has had Earth and the Solar System so heavily seeded with listening devices—and at least some human turncoats as informers—for so long that we dared not make contact. For us to have played any significant role in helping you to prepare against a Federation attack, we would have been forced to communicate directly with your government, or at least your military, and those are the areas of your society which the Federation has taken the greatest pains to spy upon. Had they suspected our existence for a moment, they would have reached their decision to destroy you much more quickly—probably before we were in a position to stop them.

"But at the same time that they were concentrating on you, it never seems to have occurred to them to worry about anyone else. As your own intelligence services have discovered, their security arrangements on the 'protected' worlds leave a great deal to be desired. What you haven't known, because we were at considerable pains to be sure that you wouldn't, is that one reason so many of the 'protected races' have been so ready to share information with you is that they were already in contact with *us*. We had to be very cautious about the information we used that conduit to pass on to you, but it's been extremely useful to us upon occasion. And even though we dared not communicate with you lest their listening devices pick up on it, we were able to use our own technology to tap *their* communication links and to set up listening posts of our own here in the Solar System. That's how we knew who to communicate with and how to reach you aboard your flagship when Lach'heranu began her attack.

"Perhaps even more importantly, though, we're now in the process of beginning to distribute weapons to many of our resistance cells. We refuse to arm any planetary cell that we feel has a less than even chance of overwhelming the Galactics and seizing the Federation infrastructure on its world. There are several cells whose leaders desperately want arms even though the chance of success on their worlds is much lower than that, but we know how ruthlessly the Federation will respond to any threat to its authority, especially in the wake of what's happened here. Desperately as we may need distractions to weaken and divert any counterattacks headed in our direction, we can't justify throwing entire planetary populations to the wolves if they have no realistic chance of achieving victory.

"Nonetheless, we project that at least three hundred subject worlds will revolt, with at least some degree of success against the Federation. We've chosen our targets as carefully as possible, with an eye towards crippling major industrial hubs and depriving the Galactics of naval bases wherever possible. Coupled with a series of preemptive strikes that Admiral Maynton's fleets are prepared to execute, we estimate that we can cripple or outright destroy almost half of the Galactics' total war-fighting ability before their slower communications can even pass the word of what happened here."

"My God," Mugabi whispered again. He stared at the Emperor for several endless seconds, then drew a deep breath. "I can't—" He paused again, then shook his head. "This morning I knew that the entire human race was about to be destroyed," he said softly. "Now this." He shook his head yet again.

"Don't mistake us, Admiral," the Emperor said very seriously. "Even if our plans work perfectly, even if we manage to destroy *more* than half of their war-fighting ability and to distract them with rebellions on scores of their planets, their total military potential will remain vastly higher than our own. Once they realize they're under attack and fully gear up for wartime production, they should be able to replace all of their lost building capacity within no more than thirty or forty years, although the rebellions in their rear areas may slow them down a bit more than that. By the time they can repair the damage, however, we should have your own system fully industrialized, and we intend to offer the same terms of alliance to every star system in which a 'protected' race manages to win its freedom, so our own production capacity should also be climbing rapidly. We believe the odds will move steadily in our favor, assuming we can survive their initial counterattacks, but there are no guarantees. At absolute best, I believe we have perhaps a sixty percent chance of ultimate victory, and even if we win in the end, our casualties will be very, very high. And none of that even considers our moral responsibility for the deaths of all the beings our underground network will bring into open rebellion against their masters. We aren't offering you a promise of salvation—only its *possibility*."

"Which is infinitely more than we had this morning," Mugabi replied. "Your Majesty, the Galactics passed a death sentence on us long before your fleet ever opened fire this afternoon. Every single day of additional life Earth enjoys will result solely from the fact that you attacked a Federation naval squadron to save us. To use a cliche, fighting the Federation, whatever the odds, is the only game in town, and at least you people seem to have spent an awful long time buying us the best odds we can get."

"We've certainly tried to," the Emperor said quietly. "And from our viewpoint, there's at least one good thing about the Galactics."

"There is?" Mugabi raised both eyebrows.

"Indeed there is, Admiral. They take so long to make their minds up about what they want to do that we had that 'awful long time' to prepare an alternative that we like much better."

"May they go right on dithering," Mugabi said fervently, and silence fell once more. It lasted a bit longer this time, and then the Emperor cleared his throat.

"So, Admiral Mugabi. Do you think President Dresner and your Senate will decide to join us?"

"Obviously, I can't speak for them or commit them to anything before they've had a chance to speak to you themselves, Your Majesty," Mugabi said, "but I don't really see any alternative to your 'Excalibur Alternative.' The Galactics have already decided to kill us all, so—as you say—the only option open to us is to destroy the Federation first." He nodded slowly. "I can't commit my government on my own authority, but I think you'll have a star system full of new allies as quickly as the President can put a treaty proposal before the Senate."

"Good." The Emperor's voice was level, almost calm, but underneath it Quentin Mugabi heard the slithering scrape of a steely blade as it was drawn from a boulder of English granite.

His Imperial Majesty George, King of Camelot, Prince of New Lancaster, Third Baron of Wickworth, Defender of the Faith, Prince Protector of the Realm, and by God's Grace, Emperor of Avalon, let his hawklike gaze circle his cabin, and then those raptor eyes came to rest once more on Quentin Mugabi.

"Good," the Emperor repeated. "Our sword is drawn. It will be sheathed again only in victory or in death . . . and may God defend the right!"